Hot Tropics
& Cold Feet

Other Books by Diann Hunt

Hot Flashes & Cold Cream
RV There Yet?

Hot Tropics & Cold Feet

DIANN HUNT

WestBow
PRESS
A Division of Thomas Nelson Publishers
Since 1798
www.thomasnelson.com

Published in Nashville, Tennessee, by WestBow Press, a Division of Thomas Nelson, Inc.

NIV HOLY BIBLE, NEW INTERNATIONAL VERSION.® Copyright © 1973, 1978, 1984 by International Bible Society. Used by permission of Zondervan. All rights reserved.

WestBow Press books may be purchased in bulk for educational, business, fund-raising, or sales promotional use. For information, please e-mail SpecialMarkets@ThomasNelson.com.

Publisher's Note: This novel is a work of fiction. Names, characters, places, and incidents are either products of the author's imagination or used fictitiously. All characters are fictional, and any similarity to people living or dead is purely coincidental.

Library of Congress Cataloging-in-Publication Data

Hunt, Diann.
  Hot tropics and cold feet / Diann Hunt.
    p. cm.
  ISBN-13: 978-1-59554-193-2 (pbk.)
  ISBN-10: 1-59554-193-4 (pbk.)
  1. Middle-aged women--Fiction. 2. Marriage--Fiction. 3. Florida--Fiction. I. Title.
  PS3608.U573H686 2007
  813'.6--dc22

                                                                2006032092

Printed in the United States of America
06 07 08 09 RRD 5 4 3 2 1

Just like Maggie and Lily, our friendship started in grade school and has weathered the changing seasons of our lives up to midlife. We've shared tears, laughter, and now wrinkles (well, okay, I keep trying to share mine with you, but you're just not very gracious in that receiving thing).

I thank God for bringing you into my life, and in the true spirit of sisterhood, I dedicate Maggie and Lily's friendship—and this book—to you, Diana Kennedy, my friend for a lifetime.

1

"Maggie, you've got to help me. Lily is acting weird," Ron Albert, Lily's soon-to-be-husband, says in a higher-than-normal baritone voice.

"Lily *is* weird, Captain." Once he and Lily started dating on a regular basis, I began calling him Captain. Everyone thinks I call him that because he loves boats. The reality is he reminds me of Captain Kangaroo. "She was born that way, and there's not a thing I can do about it. I'm her best friend. I've earned the right to say that." With coffee mug in one hand and my cordless phone in the other, I walk into the living room and sit down on my sofa, causing the dappled sunlight to splay across my black pant legs as the recliner stool flips out.

"Come on, Maggie," he says, followed by a heavy sigh.

Okay, he's serious and I'm, well, not. "Sorry. What's up?" Lifting the warm cup to my lips, I take a quick sip. The smell of coffee mingles with the cinnamon scent coming from a nearby wall plug-in. The aroma relaxes me while Captain tries to undo my contented moment.

He lets out another exasperated sigh that gets my attention. I can almost see him raking his fingers through his white hair, a habit to which

I've become accustomed. And let me just say here that Captain has a mustache as thick as his hair. But who am I to talk? I did, too, until I discovered that waxing thing. My husband hates it when I talk that way. Gordon says I'm perfect. Peacemaker that I am, I'm not about to argue.

"I don't know. She's acting as though she's having second thoughts about the wedding," Captain says, pulling my thoughts away from Gordon.

That comment makes me smile. How cute. He's getting jitters that she'll back out. Placing my coffee cup in a coaster on the stand, I mentally put on my counselor's hat. "What makes you think that?" Fingernail clippers on the stand catch my attention, and I reach for them. There's a hangnail on my right pinkie that has been driving me wild.

"Last night when I told her everything was set for the honeymoon on Bermuda Island, she said she wasn't sure she wanted to go."

I stop midclip. This *is* serious. If there's one thing I know about Lily Newgent, it's that she would not miss a chance to go to Bermuda Island. She's wanted to go there ever since she heard about that whole Triangle thing. Twisted, I know, but there it is.

"Maybe she was just tired. She had to do two perms yesterday." Okay, that excuse sounds lame even to my ears, but it's the best I can do on short notice. Back to clipping.

"I can't help thinking it's more than that." There's no mistaking the concern in his voice. It's probably that going from baritone to high tenor deal.

"Maybe she just needs some time to relax. She's been busy planning the wedding and all. She's probably worn out." With the determination of a lion going in for the kill, I snip off that troublesome hangnail and set the clippers aside, feeling rather victorious.

"That's why I'm calling you," he says. "I know this is asking a lot, and maybe you can't arrange it, but well, I was wondering if you could gather your coffee group—the Late Girls, or whatever you call yourselves—and take her somewhere to talk things out. You know, sort of a weekend getaway or something."

"Um, that would be *Latte* Girls." *Get it right, will ya? Why is it men always put the words* late *and* women *together in the same sentence?* "You really think it's that serious?" *And I'm questioning this, why? A weekend getaway sounds heavenly.*

"I wouldn't be calling you if I didn't. Every time I try to talk to her about the wedding, she changes the subject to that dollhouse she's decorating," he says.

She'd rather decorate a dollhouse than plan a wedding? Frightening moment here. This is our call to arms. Lily's in trouble, and we have to do something about it.

Doggone her, anyway. My nerves cannot handle any more. First Lily's Internet dating, then our son Nick comes home—laundry and all—and insists that he is not going back to college in the fall. Now this? She has to marry Captain so I can get my life back to normal. Well, as normal as my life tends to be anyway. Besides, I know Lily, and there is no doubt in my mind she loves him. If I can see it, why can't she?

"Let me call the girls and see what I can do. By the way, what *exactly* is it that you want me to do?"

"Convince her that marrying me is the right thing."

Someone has the jitters, and I don't think it's Lily. But if there is any truth to his way of thinking, as stubborn as Lily is, I'd put that challenge right up there with obtaining world peace.

"Maggie, the wedding is about six weeks away. We need to settle this now." Okay, now his voice could pass for a soloist in the Vienna Boys' Choir. I'm picturing him in a navy robe with a sailor-type sash. Somehow the white hair isn't working for me—to say nothing of his bushy eyebrows. The Fuller Brush Man could market those babies.

Vacation spells freedom, and with freedom right around the corner, my adrenaline kicks into gear. "Okay, Captain. Don't worry. I'll see what's going on." I plump the decorative pillows on my sofa, already attempting to formulate a plan. Some of my best ideas come while I plump pillows.

"It's going to take more than a little talk. She needs some girl time or something."

Plumping stops. "You know, most men would be clueless. That alone should get her to the altar."

He lets out a nervous laugh. Think chicken before the slaughter. "Hopefully, you're right."

"I'll call the girls."

"Maggie, dive into bushes if need be. Do whatever it takes."

"I dive into a bush one time to protect my best friend and people just can't let that die."

"Well, you have to admit that was a bit extreme, Maggie. Even for you."

My back straightens. "If you want me to help you, you're going about this all wrong."

"Okay, I'm sorry. Thanks for your help."

"No problem," I say, softening a tad when I hear the concern in his voice.

As soon as we click off, I dial another number. "Hello, Jill? We have an emergency. My house, tomorrow morning at ten. Tell Louise when you see her."

☞

"Now, Maggie Lynn, you know how I feel about you interfering in other people's affairs," my husband says after brushing his teeth, rinsing off his toothbrush, tapping it against the sink for good measure, and putting it away.

Though I'm in our bedroom and Gordon is in the adjoining bathroom, I hear him pour mouthwash into a cup. His gargling resembles the caw of an exotic bird choking to death, and I'm suddenly transported to an isolated jungle, surrounded by monstrous plants and gnarled trees. The chance of him hearing me over his tribal ritual is remote, so I wait a moment before I respond.

He rinses out his cup then steps back into the bedroom. I half expect him to beat his chest and feel a twinge of disappointment when he doesn't. Instead he does another manly thing and picks up his socks with his talented viselike toes.

Too bad his colleagues at the law firm will never see this talented side of my husband.

"Lily is my best friend, Gordon. If she's having second thoughts, I need to help her." I spritz on some perfume and rub in the last of the cold cream on my neck, which, by the way, is so slick, it's a wonder my head can stay on my pillow at night.

"She and Captain will be better off without people interfering." It's cute how Gordon's picked up my nickname for Ron. "This is a decision only she can make, Maggie. Other people should not push their feelings upon her." After checking the alarm clock, he takes off his slippers and glasses, then crawls in between the bedcovers.

"Yeah, right, like that's gonna happen. Lily won't let us push her. You know as well as I do that if she thinks we're pushing, she'll back out of the wedding for sure." I remember well how my concerns for her Internet dating didn't deter her in the least. In fact, it ignited her passion for adventure. I crawl between clean, icy sheets. After my recent bouts with hot flashes, this is sheer bliss.

Gordon grins and rubs his jaw. "I guess you're right about that. Still, you always have fussed too much over her. She's your best friend, not your daughter." He turns to me. "By the way, Heather called tonight while you were at the grocery."

"You mean our married daughter whose husband took her five hours away from our Charming, Indiana, home to live in Illinois, *that* daughter?"

"Well, since she's the only one we have, I'd say she's the one."

I fluff the blanket around me. "I'm still bitter about that."

"I can see that."

"Is everything okay?"

"Yeah, she just called to talk." Gordon nuzzles next to me, and his goatee tickles my forehead. What Gordon lacks in sandy-brown hair on top of his head, he makes up for in his bushy, peppered-with-gray goatee. What a man. His cold feet press against the tops of my feet, soothing me. My skin hasn't been cold since 1998.

"So how's my favorite brunette?" Gordon gives me a squeeze.

"Okay, we both know that's using the term loosely, since I have a little help from my hairdresser."

"Hey, whatever works," he says, reminding me of all the reasons I married him.

"Oh, I meant to ask you, what time is Nick coming home?"

"He said something about midnight."

"Boomerang kids."

"What?"

"They call his generation the boomerang kids. They leave home and come back."

"How about we throw him one more time and see what happens?" Gordon says in a teasing voice.

Visions of Nick's messy room flood my mind. "Might not be a bad idea."

"After all you went through with the empty nest, I figured you'd be happy that he's back home."

I straighten around and look at Gordon. "See, that's just it. I've finally settled into this new life. You're working less hours—well, you keep promising to anyway—and we're getting to the point where we can travel and do some fun things together. With Nick home, I feel torn."

"Well, he's not staying home and doing nothing, I'll tell you that right now," Gordon says, his body stiffening with every word. "That boy is going back to school in the fall, or he's getting a job. He can stay here if he chooses to go to school, but if he opts for a job, he can save and move out. I'm not trying to be harsh, but he has to develop his 'responsibility' muscles."

"Stay here?" My voice squeaks. I settle in to the fact we have an empty nest, and now this? I love my boy, I really do, but thoughts of pizza boxes, potato chip bags, and video game boxes strewn about the living room floor make me, well, nervous.

Here we go again, Lord. Things just get comfortable and—wham— another change. Will I never get these lessons learned?

"Well, hopefully, Nick will come to his senses and go back to school," Gordon says.

"So you don't think I should round up the girls? After all, Captain asked me to," I say, changing the subject before we work ourselves up into a parental fit.

Gordon sinks back into the covers and pulls me closer to him, resting his chin on the top of my head. "I don't care if you take Lily somewhere and you girls have a nice little getaway, just behave yourself." When I look up, his finger taps the tip of my nose.

"Hey, did I tell you that Jill said Donny Osmond is giving a benefit concert in Sarasota next week? Sources say he may be vacationing in Siesta Key beforehand."

Gordon's left eyebrow shoots up. "Something tells me you're headed for Siesta Key." He frowns. "Maybe I should go along."

"Why? You know you can trust me."

"I was thinking more about protecting Donny."

"Ha, ha."

"Besides, I can belt out a pretty good rendition of 'Puppy Love' myself, you know."

"Yes, you can. It just doesn't sound anything like Donny Osmond." I laugh.

"Oh, that's cute. What does he have that I don't have?" Gordon flexes his muscles here.

"I'm clueless." It tickles me to no end when Gordon acts jealous. "He's got his voice, but I have, um, well, um—"

"Me?"

He squeezes me into the circle of his arms. "Exactly." Without another word he kisses me with his usual tenderness, causing all thoughts of Donny Osmond and Lily to momentarily leave my brain. I've got better things to occupy my thoughts.

⑥ ⟋ ⑥

"Okay, girls, grab your mugs, and we'll get down to business." While they look the other way, I stuff cold, half-eaten pepperoni pizza down my garbage disposal, empty a glass filled with watered-down pop, then shove the dirty plates and glass into the dishwasher. Obviously once Nick got home last night, he had a pizza attack. Our garbage can is vomiting pizza boxes and chip bags. The reality of fast food and video games are quickly replacing my dream of taking a cruise with Gordon.

I place the coffee tray with the pot and all the fixings in the middle of the oak kitchen table. Jill Graham trots, literally, from the living room into the kitchen. She has been a fitness guru for as long as I've known her. If there's an opportunity to exercise, she'll snatch it. She's forty-five years old and could pass for twenty-five. I've seen pictures of her younger days. Her trim figure hasn't increased since she was twelve, doggone her. In fact, she looks as though she's lost a couple of pounds since I saw her last week. Oh well, she has her skinny waist, I have my sweets. We're good.

Makeup perfectly in place, Chico jewelry dangling from her neck and ears, and Ann Taylor fashions complimenting her size ten body, forty-eight-year-old Louise Montgomery waltzes into the kitchen with all the glamour of Miss America. Golden-brown hair sways on her shoulders with every elegant step. There's no denying Louise is as pretty as she is sweet. The one thing that drives me to distraction about her is that no matter if she's happy, sad, or indifferent, her expression never changes. She says she doesn't want to accentuate unbecoming lines, a.k.a. wrinkles. Truth be known, I secretly suspect she's getting Botox injections—though I've never dared to ask her. She might pop a stitch or something and then her face would sag all over the place. I just couldn't live with that.

On the other hand, my face shows every rut in my journey. I don't mind, really. Ditches would upset me, but ruts I can handle.

Louise pours herself a cup of coffee in a mug that says "Today is the first day of the rest of your life." It's my mug, but it fits her perfectly.

They both settle into their seats.

"Don't you want anything, Jill?" I ask.

"No, I haven't been drinking much coffee lately," she says. This coming from Mrs. Chihuahua in Heels. A little espresso in her veins, and she could outrun Superman. It's better for everyone involved if she cuts back awhile. Say what you will about Jill, her face is as animated as her body. She's a chipper little thing, with all the bounce of Flubber.

I haven't bounced since I was five.

"If you keep this up, you'll live to be a hundred and twenty-five." I pour myself a cup. "Though I'm thinking all the cold cream in the world can't help a century-old face."

"Well, I don't know," Louise says with pure sweetness. "The cosmetic industry is making great strides in wrinkle creams and youthful skin products."

The thing that scares me? I think she's serious.

"Good grief, Maggie, I stayed up half the night worrying about what you were going to tell us," Jill says. "Is it Nick? You could have told me ahead of time so I wouldn't have these dark shadows today."

Now that she mentions it, she does look tired. Serves her right for doing all that exercise.

"I've got the very thing for that," Louise, ever the Mary Kay consultant, says. She cups her hand near her mouth and whispers, "See me after this. I think I have something in the car."

Louise is the resident domestic diva and fashion queen and the fourth person in our coffee group, which we've now dubbed the "Latte Girls." We all go to church together. Jill and Louise started attending around the same time close to five years ago. We have been good friends since. For the past six months we've been meeting on a weekly basis for coffee and chats.

They both look to me. My fingers curl around the warmth of my coffee cup that has bold black letters that read, "Touch my coffee, and I'll break your fingers."

I hide it when the pastor comes over.

"Though you should probably throw in a few prayers for Nick that Gordon and I won't hurt him, he is not the reason I've called you here." After taking a sip of coffee, I explain my conversation with Captain to the girls.

"Do you think there's really a problem, or is Ron just getting paranoid?" Jill asks.

"I'm not sure. But I know we can make Lily talk. If there's a problem, we'll find out," I say, shoving away the gnawing reminder of Lily's stubborn ways.

Louise's perfectly arched brow lifts slightly. Not too much, mind you, because that could leave a crease. "From what I remember, Lily doesn't appreciate being told what to do."

"It's all in the *how* she's being told." I wiggle my eyebrows.

"What's in this for you, Maggie?" Jill's voice is thick with suspicion.

"Peace. I just want to get Lily safely married to a good man."

Jill's eyebrow arches. "Shouldn't Lily's happiness be in the mix there somewhere?"

"Happiness, schmappiness. That happiness thing is way overrated."

Louise gasps. Jill's eyebrows shoot straight up, and her expression freezes there. Reminds me of a figurine in a wax museum.

"Kidding. I'm kidding. Come on, you guys, you know Lily. She always gets nervous when she's making a major decision. Remember her potato binge before she bought her new refrigerator? Baked potatoes, chips, potato salad, you name it, she ate it. She gained five pounds over that whole ordeal. For what, I ask you?"

"A Maytag?" Jill offers.

"Exactly. She loves Captain. You've seen the way she lights up when you mention his name. You've heard her drone on ad nauseam about him. 'Ron this and Ron that.' It's actually quite sickening."

"That's true, she does do that." Louise's breathing has finally returned to its normal rhythm.

"Yeah. I can't tell you how many times I've heard about his contest and trivia addiction and 'Isn't that so cute?' business," Jill says with a slight case of the nasties.

"Lily hasn't been this happy in a long time. She deserves it," Louise says.

"Right," Jill agrees.

"Lily has cold feet, that's all. She just needs a little nudge from her friends to push her in the right direction." I kick off my shoes, scratch the arch of my left foot with my big right toe, then slip my shoes back on. I'm thinking Gordon's toe talent is rubbing off on me.

"Well, you know what I do when I get cold feet," Louise says matter-of-factly before taking a drink of her coffee.

"What?" I ask.

"I put on socks."

This is Louise's attempt at humor, which is why she will never be a comedian.

Another sip of coffee. "Do you know she did the same thing prior to her first marriage? The day before her wedding, Lily disappeared. I drove over to Rosetown and found her at our favorite ice cream place, downing a hot fudge sundae the size of Texas."

In wide-eyed wonder Louise asks, "What did you do?"

"I sat down with her and matched her sundae for sundae." The memory makes me laugh. "We waddled out of there, but we had a great talk and, well, she got married."

"She could be dubbed the Runaway Bride," Jill says with a nod, her pixie cut strawberry blonde hair never moving an inch. She's petite, right down to her elfin nose—which is smaller than my belly button. How wrong is that? "Lily has a reputation."

I brighten. "Don't we all?" My eyebrows wiggle deviously.

"Well, you do anyway," Jill points out.

"Where will we go?" Louise jumps in, trapping my sarcastic response behind my teeth. "For how long?"

The schedule queen has to have all the details. I drum my freshly manicured fingernails on the table.

"By the way, that red polish looks good on you, Maggie," Louise says, looking proud that she talked me into buying it.

"Thanks. I don't know where we'll go, but I'm open to suggestions."

The hall clock ticks as we sit in troubled silence, each of us trying to come up with an idea.

"Hey, is your condo in Siesta Key available?"

Jill smacks her forehead with the palm of her hand. "Duh, why didn't I think of that? We don't have any guests coming until the end of August."

"Siesta Key, Florida?" Louise asks.

"Yes." Jill's getting into the idea. Her eyes are flashing so bright, an accompanying siren would not surprise me. Then she hesitates and turns to me. "Does this have anything to do with Donny Osmond being there?"

"Donny Osmond will be there?" Louise claps her hands. "Oh, what fun!"

"Maggie?" Jill just won't let it go.

Bringing my hand to my chest, I do my best to look innocent. "I don't know what you mean."

They're not buying it.

"Now, Maggie, you have to promise to behave yourself," Jill says.

"I just want a picture, is that too much to ask?"

"Picture or two. Period. None of that getting us into trouble stuff."

With my index finger I cross my heart. "Scouts honor."

"Were you ever a scout?" Louise, the nosy one, wants to know.

"What does that have to do with anything?" Good grief, these guys are so paranoid. "Besides, I could use a little break from the kid," I say, pointing to Nick's socks that I've just spotted beside the recliner in the living room.

Louise and Jill look over and laugh.

"What's the deal with Donny Osmond? I thought you said *Lily* had the crush on him," Louise says.

"True. My real heartthrob was more Kurt Russell. But Donny was my *singing* heartthrob." I laugh. "I have all of his records."

"How do you know he's going to be in Siesta Key?" Louise asks.

"My neighbor there zipped me an e-mail and told me that Donny is doing a benefit concert in Sarasota, and the word on the street is that he and his family are vacationing in Siesta Key before the show," Jill says.

"Well, a Florida getaway sounds pretty good to me," Louise says.

My mind kicks into gear. "I'll get tickets online for the concert."

Jill tosses me a worried look then turns to the matter at hand. "We can go down, stay for a couple of weeks, and by the time we return, Lily will be longing for her wedding day the way a hormonal woman longs for chocolate."

"What would *you* know about that?" I ask Jill.

"Oh, I have my chocolate binges, believe me. I just don't give them a chance to linger on my hips."

If she glances at my hips, I *will* hurt her.

Skipping over the chocolate discussion, Louise turns to Jill and cuts right to the point. "You may have saved Lily's entire future."

Louise looks at life far too seriously—but then it could just be that whole her-face-doesn't-move thing.

Jill shrugs as though it's all in a day's work.

"It's settled then," I say. "Of course, tomorrow when we meet for coffee at The New Brew, you can come in and suggest it as a girl-friend's getaway before the big day so Lily won't get suspicious. We'll all act surprised." It's a little devious, I know, but when your friend is in trouble, you do what you've got to do. Besides, we get a Florida vacation out of the deal. Who am I to complain?

Lifting my mug in the air, I reach to the middle of the table and say, "To the happy couple!"

Louise and Jill join me in the spirit of the moment, each clinking their mugs—Jill's is invisible—against mine. "To Lily, Ron, and wedded bliss!"

And just maybe a glimpse of Donny Osmond on the streets of Siesta Key . . .

2

Lily is already waiting at a table, coffee in hand, when I step into The New Brew. She looks up and we share a wave. Her bobbed blonde hair stops near her shoulders, and she is decked out in a bright yellow top with green pinstripes. A pair of matching green and yellow capris completes her outfit.

Lily has found herself. She's totally lost that worrying-about-what-other-people-think thing. When her first husband, Bob—or Bobby, as we sometimes called him—died over six years ago, she went through a metamorphosis and has emerged a colorful butterfly. She told me life was too short to spend it worrying about inconsequential things, such as people's opinion of her. She's bolder these days. Hence the Internet dating that led her to Ron Albert whom she will marry in a few weeks, if the Latte Girls have their say in the matter.

"Hi, Tyler, how are you?" I ask the manager behind the counter. Her springy blonde curls bounce as her hands get to work.

"Great. Skinny mocha with whipped cream today?" she asks.

I nod.

"You're sure you are happy working the few hours I've given you lately?" Tyler asks, referring to my fill-in-as-needed position at the coffee shop.

"Yes, it's been great. In fact, I need to talk to you about something, but I'll call you about it later, okay?"

"You're not leaving us, are you?" she asks with a frown while working the cappuccino machine.

"No, no." I lean into the counter and whisper, "Just maybe taking a little vacation."

Tyler brightens. "Oh, I can handle that." She finishes putting together my drink and squirts an abundance of whipped cream through the hole in the lid. I'd probably be down five pounds by now if I'd leave off the whipped cream, but as Lily says, "Life's too short."

"Hey, Maggie." Just then Jade Black steps into view, walking up beside Tyler at the counter. Jade's dark hair is a little longer than last time I saw her. Though she and her dad attend our church, she's been away at college and working a part-time job, so she hasn't been able to get home much on the weekends.

"Jade!" I reach my arms across the counter and give her an awkward hug. "Are you helping out here?"

She nods. "I decided to come home for summer break and spend some time with Dad. Tyler was sweet enough to work me into the schedule," she says, smiling at Tyler.

"I'm so glad. You look good, Jade." She's been through a lot with her parents' divorce and then her struggle with anorexia. I'm pleased to see that she's put on a few pounds. Not much, but every pound is a celebration.

"Thanks. I'm feeling lots better."

For a few minutes Jade fills me in on what's been going on with her life this semester. I tell her I look forward to working with her this summer, then I say good-bye and walk over to join Lily.

"So how are you doing this morning?" I ask Lily as I slide into my seat.

Before she can answer, the bell on the door jangles again, and Jill and Louise enter together. As Jill comes over, she drops her keys, does a couple of knee bends, grabs her keys, and springs back up. She dropped them on purpose, I'm almost sure of it. Jill will use any reason to exercise. The woman needs some serious counseling.

The thing that surprises me, though—and I admit to a little private glee here—Jill doesn't bounce back up with her usual gusto. Seems to me somebody's joints are getting a little rusty, but far be it for me to point that out.

"I'm doing fine," Lily says, but her eyes are hiding a secret. Lily and I are practically joined at the hip. Being best friends since first grade does that to people. I know her well, and let me just say I'm downright offended that she hasn't shared her concerns with me. In her defense, Lily has been very busy snipping, cutting, and coloring the hair of half the population in our small town.

I look at Lily and smile. She's probably wondering why I'm not digging for answers. But I don't want to ruin the chances of her going on this trip. "Listen, could we go to my house when we leave here? I've put on a couple of pounds since my thirtieth anniversary ceremony, and I'm afraid my dress is getting a little tight. I need your opinion since it's the dress I'm wearing to your wedding."

A moment of hesitation.

"Is something wrong?"

She blinks. "Oh, just preoccupied. Sure, I'll come."

Uh-oh, Captain may be onto something.

Jill and Louise join us. "So how's your dollhouse coming along, Lily?" Jill asks, referring to Lily's hobby that she started after her first husband's death.

"No new furniture since I bought the British tea set," she says.

I tease her about how long it's taking for her to finish decorating

17

the dollhouse, but she says it takes time to get your house in order. It must be some type of therapy for her.

"I'm almost finished, though. Just have to find the perfect bedroom suite."

Never mind that she said that very thing four months ago. "Well, if the bedroom has to be as perfect as the other furniture, you should finish by the time we're in a nursing home," I say.

"No one has a perfect home, you know," Jill adds with a wink.

"Hello? Anyone besides me realize that dollhouses are for pretend? As in, real people don't live in them?" I'm wondering just how well I know these girls.

"Spoilsport," Lily says.

I give Jill the go-ahead with a nod.

"Say, girls, I've been thinking—" A moment of pause to make sure she has Lily's attention. "We could use a little 'girl time' before Lily's big day. Jeff and I have a wonderful condo in Siesta Key, Florida, that we rarely get a chance to enjoy, due to his work schedule. Though we rent it out to vacationers, it's open for the next few weeks. How about we take a little time off for a Latte Girls' getaway?" Jill's eyes sparkle and her smile is contagious.

Louise and I don't skip a beat. "That's a great idea," Louise says with as much enthusiasm as she would give a facial.

"Oh, that would be fun," I try to match their enthusiasm, but with a bit of caution. Don't want to overdo it. Lily's suspicion is automatic where I'm concerned.

Lily stares at us a moment. I'm afraid she knows we're up to something. "Go to Florida?"

We hold a collective breath. She could go either way here.

"But the wedding isn't that far off," she says, letting us know all is not lost—yet.

"Precisely why you need to get away," Jill says.

All that exercise, jumping around, and bending knee joints must bring on Jill's chipper, high voice. Which would explain why mine could rival Tennessee Ernie Ford.

"Come on, Lily, we would have such fun," Louise pleads, all smiles and twinkles.

Lily blinks. She knows Louise's idea of fun is a makeup party. We just can't relate to that.

"What would we do? How long would we stay? I have my salon to think about," Lily says.

"Oh come on, Lily, you could get away for two weeks," I say before taking a drink. "Lori Bell could cover for you. You've been slowly surrendering your customers to her anyway."

"I suppose." As we watch Lily process the idea, I can almost see a think bubble over her head.

"I'm not sure how Ron would feel about it." Lily turns her engagement ring back and forth nervously on her finger.

Oh, trust me, he's okay with this idea.

"He's so nervous right now."

"How do you know? Did he admit that to you? That's a rare thing for a guy to admit," Louise says.

"He didn't have to." Lily's fingers stop fiddling with her ring. "His car is so clean, I practically slide out of the leather seats." She looks up, and we all laugh.

"That's hilarious. He's just like Bob—" Louise's hand flies to her mouth. A muffled "I'm sorry, Lily," escapes between her fingers.

Lily stares at her a moment. "It's all right, Louise. Ron and Bob are a lot alike." She stares down at the table, and I shoot Louise a way-to-go look.

"It's a man thing," I say. "Gordon is a clean freak about his cars, too. So what do you think about the trip, Lil?" Not the best transition, but I have to do something to cover up Louise's blooper.

"I guess I could go. When?" she asks.

"As soon as we can get airline tickets," Jill says. "The condo is ready and waiting."

"Woo-hoo, the Latte Girls are Florida-bound!" Louise says, cheerleader voice still in place.

Lily smiles, and I can almost hear her mind clicking. She's probably wondering how all this came about and what I have to do with it.

We soon part ways and Lily comes to my house. She settles onto the sofa while I shrug on my yellow chiffon dress and wrap. Heather picked it out for me to wear to Gordon's and my thirtieth anniversary celebration. She insists that it's not yellow, but rather a "butter" color. But it's yellow. Too yellow for my tastes, if the truth be known. Still, it's very special because of the memory attached to it.

"Well, what do you think?" I twirl as enthusiastically as I dare without tipping over.

"It looks just fine, Maggie. What are you worried about?"

"Chocolate chip cookies."

"Huh?"

"That's what I'm worried about. I think about them day and night. Your wedding is still a few weeks away and, well, I don't mean to sound all squirrelly or anything, but I can pack away a lot of cookies by then."

"You're pathetic."

"I know. You don't think it looks too tight in, um, the delicate places?" My hand runs over my hips and stomach.

She rolls her eyes and shakes her head. "You worry far too much. I absolutely love that dress."

"Okay, I feel better. If I have your approval, I'm good." I head back to the bedroom, dress into my original clothes, hang up my dress, then rejoin Lily in the living room.

"Now that we've got that settled, let's go to the kitchen and eat some cookies."

3

We drop our luggage on the ceramic tile entryway of the Florida condo. The room is warm from nonuse. The entryway that spills into the kitchen and living room is spotlessly clean.

"Okay, group shot," I say, pulling the digital camera from my handbag. Jill, Louise, and Lily huddle together. "On the count of three. One, two, three." Smiles, a flash, and we've snapped a memory of the starting moments of our Siesta Key vacation.

Afterwards, Lily gropes for the kitchen counter.

"Oh come on, the flash wasn't that bad," I say.

"Yeah? Then why is there a light where your head should be?"

"I'm angelic, that's why."

Everyone groans.

"Oh, this is very nice," I say, running my fingers along the round glass-top table in the small but functional white kitchen, nearly tripping over a wicker chair with a flowered cushion. The others agree. With the tip of her blouse, Louise wipes the smudge I left behind on the table.

We turn toward the living room to see white leather furniture, glass-covered stands holding fat white lamps, and colorful seaside portraits in white wicker frames against mauve-painted walls. Kicking off my shoes, I let the thick carpet squish between my toes. I snap a picture of the living room, then turn to the bedrooms. Both are roomy and have two beds. Two bathrooms make it perfect for a group of women. For a moment I wonder about the two-bed thing in the master bedroom, but most likely the extra beds are to accommodate more people when Jeff and Jill rent out their condo.

"Oh my, look out there," I say, slipping my sandals back on and sliding open the patio doors that open to a screened-in back porch—or *lanai* as they call it here—and then the screen door that opens to a grassy lawn and small pond—well, back home we'd call it a pond. Jill tells me here they call it a lake.

A whiff of warm, summer air greets us as we step into the after-noon breeze to admire the palm trees and big leafy bushes circling the lake. A manicured lawn and sidewalk separates the back side of each condo from the lake.

A movement on a nearby rock snags my attention. A small lizard lies down to make himself comfortable in the warmth of the sun. Easing the camera to my face, I snap another picture. The sound causes him to dart into a pile of rocks for cover.

Three seagulls fly overhead, and a couple of pelicans swoop toward the lake in search of an early dinner. Those suckers are big enough to carry one of us off. Okay, so Lily and I aren't in danger. But they could carry Jill or Louise off.

"This is really nice," Lily says, taking in a deep breath.

We comment on how wonderful it is to be here, then step back inside the lanai and through the patio doors to the living room.

I'm nervous about room assignments because I want to make sure I get in the same room with Lily. She will tell me what's going on if we get some time alone. Things have been too hectic back home.

Between her job fixing hair and planning for the wedding, she's hardly had time for anything.

On the other hand, I don't want Louise and Jill to think I don't want to be with them. But the idea of waiting on Ms. Beauty Queen to get out of the bathroom and Ms. Buns of Steel to run through her exercise routine each day could quite possibly send me into a hormonal hissy fit, and that just couldn't be good for anyone.

"Where do you want us?" Lily asks, holding onto the leash of her luggage as though she's preparing to walk a dog.

Louise is standing near the guest bedroom door. I'm standing near Louise, while Jill and Lily are closer to the master bedroom. Now I don't care which bedroom I'm in, as long as I'm Lily's roommate. I have to be Lily's roommate!

With no time to lose, I lift my luggage and wedge myself in between Lily and Jill. Once I'm there, I drop my suitcase and look up at Jill with a smile.

"Just wanted to make sure I could hear you," I say.

She gives me a funny look and takes one step backward. I'm okay with that. Her gaze goes from Louise to Lily to me. "How about you and Maggie take the master bedroom, while Louise and I take the guest room?"

Mission accomplished. I should be ashamed of myself, and I probably would be were my friend's future not at stake here. My menopausal attitude comes in handy every now and then.

"Oh, we couldn't do that," Lily protests. "You should have the master bedroom."

"Yes, we can," I say.

Everybody looks at me. I hate it when I do that. Think words that somehow find their way out of my mouth. I laugh as though I'm kidding. Which of course, I'm not. What is Lily thinking? We'd have our own bathroom.

"Nonsense. It's the least I can do for the bride-to-be." Jill scoots up next to the wall and puts the palm of her hand against it. I don't know if she's going to pray for the condo or if she's feeling for studs—as in boards behind the drywall.

"I know what you're thinking," Jill says, "but there's a bathroom right next to the guest room, so it's no big deal." With her leg extended to the side of her body, it's up-two-three, down-two-three. I figure I use up enough calories just standing here watching her. My eyeballs move, after all. "Besides, Lily is the bride-to-be, and you two have been friends the longest."

"Who are we to argue?" I ask Lily.

"Exactly," Lily says. Grabbing the leash for her luggage, she starts rolling it toward the bedroom. "I still can't believe we're here," she calls over her shoulder. "Maggie had to put you up to this."

Louise, Jill, and I exchange glances, and I'm pretty sure I see Jill swallow her gum.

"She's the only one who would think of going away a month before a wedding."

I force a laugh. Louise and Jill look relieved then head for their bedroom to unpack.

"What's the big deal?" I say, following Lily. My luggage lacks a handle, so I drag it into the bedroom much the same as I haul my hefty self out of a swimming pool. Gordon is so gonna get me a new set when I get home. "You said yourself everything was in place. It's just a matter of waiting now, right?"

We discuss which bed we want, and Lily lifts her luggage on top of the mattress, unzips her suitcase, then starts to unpack. I do the same.

"You're right. Everything is ready, and I really need this time away to thin—"

My gaze jerks up to her.

"I mean, uh, girl time and all," she fumbles.

Her face flushes, and since I know Lily has never struggled with hot flashes, I can only assume one thing. There is definitely something up with her, and the look on her face tells me she knows that I know. Everything in me wants to dig for information, but she'll clamp her mouth shut with the determination of a snapping turtle if she thinks I'm prying. Patience is a virtue.

Wish I had some.

◎ ✍ ◎

"Wait! Is that Donny Osmond?" I point excitedly while Jill slows the car, and I fumble for my camera.

Lily's head jerks to where I'm pointing. "Oh, for goodness sake, Maggie, that's not him. Donny's much more handsome."

I lower my camera and take another look. "Yeah, I guess you're right." With a sigh, I stuff my camera back in my bag.

We continue on through this tropical paradise where quaint shops decked with enticing window displays crowd side-by-side along the roadways, decorative pink flamingos are as abundant as palm trees and oranges, and colorful condos with wrought iron balconies overlook beach fronts.

We giggle like school girls, talk excitedly about our teen years, browse through a couple of clothing shops, and finally settle into a booth at a local restaurant.

"I can't believe you bought that housedress, Maggie," Louise says with a dainty chuckle.

"It's for our neighbor, Elvira Pepple. She wears them all the time, and I thought this one would give her that tropical look, what with the flowers and all."

"Elvira is like a grandma to Maggie's kids. She's lived next door to you forever, right, Maggie?" Lily asks before taking a bite of her sandwich.

"Right. She's a little eccentric, but a greater prayer warrior, you'll never find. She's a gem."

When we're ready to leave, I notice Jill's only eaten half of her salad.

"You're not anorexic, are you?" I ask her, straight up. After going through this with Jade, I'm not going to mess around this time.

Jill looks up with a start. "Absolutely not," she says, sounding a bit irritated. "You know I go to great measures to take care of myself."

It seems I have a knack for offending people.

"Aren't you hungry?" Louise asks. "You didn't eat much lunch either."

Jill wrinkles her nose—something you would never see Louise do. "Traveling does that to me. You'll be asking me where I put it all when I eat like a horse tomorrow."

"Speaking of horses," I say with a chuckle, looking at Lily, "remember that guy you dated—what was his name—Dilbert somebody?"

Lily gasps. "Maggie Lynn! Don't you start!"

"I haven't said anything yet."

Lily turns to Jill and Louise. "She said Dilbert resembled Mr. Ed, can you imagine?"

They both try not to laugh, but it's happening anyway, much to Lily's dismay.

Her nose hikes up a notch. "Dilbert was nice."

"Oh come on, Lil. You have to admit he had very large teeth. It was all I could do not to whinny when I saw him."

"Maggie!" Louise tosses this dainty little chuckle while her fingers flutter against her mouth to maintain decorum.

Jill—and to my surprise, Lily—laugh right out loud.

Once Lily regains control of herself, with chin jutting forward she says, "Well, I don't care what you say, he was nice."

"Yes, he was a nice guy. With big teeth." Before I can get into trouble I add, "Wonder whatever happened to him?"

Lily shrugs.

"You suppose he's out graz—"

"*Maggie Lynn!*" Lily cuts me off.

"I remember you going through that Internet dating," Louise says. "I was so surprised that you were doing that."

Before Lily can comment, Jill jumps in. "And it's a good thing. She wouldn't be getting married if she hadn't been adventurous." A broad smile breaks out on Jill's face until she looks at Lily—the only one who isn't smiling.

"By the way, Maggie, since you brought up the subject of eating disorders, I wanted to mention that Jade looked pretty good at the coffee shop. She doing all right?" Louise asks.

"She's doing great." We discuss how wonderful it is that she has turned her life around despite what she's been through in the last year. "It's a long haul, but she'll get there. I'm so proud of her."

"She's a sweet kid," Louise says. "Her dad is nice, too. Too bad we don't know any eligible women for him."

"Don't give Maggie any ideas," Lily says.

I shrug. "I have a reputation. So sue me."

The girls laugh.

"We'd better get some groceries tonight," Lily says.

"Yeah, we need to do that. How about we get enough for breakfast and lunch tomorrow, then we'll go back later to get enough for the next two weeks? I'm too pooped to do it all tonight," Jill says.

"I'm feeling young and sprightly since I have more energy than Miss Fitness here," I tease.

"Must be those *senior* vitamins you're taking," Lily says, trying to annoy me, no doubt because of my Dilbert comments.

"Well, they come with a discount and all."

"You should try some Siberian ginseng," Lily says.

"Oh, here we go." My eyes roll back in my head, and my mouth sags open.

"You can make fun all you want, but it helps with fatigue and fading memories. But then you wouldn't remember that, would you, Maggie, because you don't take it?" There's a bit of a snit in her voice.

"Oh come on, Lily. I can't take those horse pills. That would be Dilbert's department." I duck.

"You're terrible."

"Blame my mother. She gave birth to me."

"Someone should shoot her."

We all gasp at Lily.

"I'm kidding," she says. "Sheesh. Maggie says that kind of stuff all the time."

"Yeah, but we expect it from her."

"Thanks, Jill," I say dryly. "I'm serious. I could choke to death on those pills, Lily."

"Don't blame me when you can't remember Gordon's name."

"Gordon who?"

Louise and Jill laugh. Lily doesn't. I'm enjoying myself just the same.

"I might check it out," Jill says.

Lily brightens then throws me a ha-ha look.

Being the mature woman that I am, I make a face. The fact that Louise is writing on a napkin captures my attention. "What are you doing, Louise?"

"Making a grocery list."

"Remember, we're not getting a lot tonight," Jill says, looking worried.

"I know, but I don't want to forget the essentials." She writes a couple more words.

"Come on," Jill says before she stops to yawn, "We'd better get to the store."

Now I know we're not twenty anymore, but as I watch Jill drag herself out of the booth, I can't help but wonder how much fun we're going to have on this trip.

Did I mention that it's only eight o'clock?

4

"Good morning, sleepyhead," Lily says, placing a bookmark in her Bible and putting it back on the stand. "Do you smell that?" She plumps the pillow behind her head and sinks into it.

Squinting my eyes, I struggle to adjust to the morning light that has squeezed through the blinds. The scent of fried sausage, eggs, rich coffee, and buttermilk biscuits reaches me. "Yeah. Did somebody send out for breakfast?" I yawn.

"I don't know, but I'm hungry. Let's go check it out." Lily yanks off the covers, puts on her slippers and robe, then heads out to the kitchen. I'm right on her heels.

Jill enters the kitchen about the same time we do. There we find Louise fluttering about—actually, it's more of a graceful dance—as she puts the finishing touches on the table decorated in linens, nice dishware, and a vase of silk flowers she must have found stashed away in a cupboard.

"Oh my, you shouldn't start us out this way, Louise, we'll come to expect it," I say, letting her know right here and now there is no way I'll settle for generic cereal from now on.

She turns to me and smiles. "I'm glad to do it. Now, you take your seats, and I'll pour your coffee and pass the food." A slight pink fans her cheeks, and she looks positively breathless. The Food Network's Paula Deen would be proud.

"There ought to be a law against anyone looking as good as you do first thing in the morning," I say, scooting my chair into the table.

"It's because I'm doing what I love to do. We always look our best when we follow our passions."

"You know, Maggie. That's the way you look when Gordon takes you to a restaurant," Lily says, smirking.

My fuzzy brain searches for a comeback, but it's all I can do to remember the first names of the people in this room.

We no sooner say our prayers than we get down to some serious eating. And let me just point out here that the locusts in that plague on Egypt thing have nothing on the four of us.

"The breakfast was fabulous, Louise," I say while helping to clear the table and stack the dishwasher. "Feel free to follow your passions every morning."

Louise tosses me a glowing smile. She's totally in her element.

Before we know it, the kitchen is clean and the red convertible we convinced the rental car company to let us have carries the Latte Girls to our true destination: the beach.

We pull the car into the picnic area of Siesta Key Beach, gather our sunscreen, towels, books, and water bottles then head for the beach. We walk through a nice building with a gift shop and the bath area. I've never been to Siesta Key before, and I'm in awe of the white sandy beach.

"Yeah, it's awesome, isn't it?" Jill says. "I never get used to it."

"I can see why. It's incredible," Lily says. We stand with a sort of reverence, viewing the ocean as only landlocked Hoosiers can do.

"I read somewhere the sand is made from 99 percent pure quartz. It's soft and cool to the touch," Louise says.

"Well, we won't know if we don't dig our toes into it," Lily says with a sudden outburst, kicking off her flip-flops. "Last one in is a rotten egg," she shouts while running for all she's worth straight toward the water.

Now, I love Lily, I really do, but the truth of the matter is Lily and I just don't have the bodies that we did twenty-five years ago. Okay, we don't even have the bodies we had five years ago. In fact, mine's probably changed in the last five days. If only I hadn't spotted that bag of chocolate chips.

But there Lily is, in all her glory, plump legs scurrying toward the water, wispy little bathing suit skirt blowing in the breeze, and a grand finale splash that nearly brings on a tsunami.

I'm sure I look just as crazy as I follow her, but I'm okay with that.

"Look out! Fabulous Fifty coming through!" I scream as I take a flying leap and plunge into the Gulf, causing water to explode in all directions and people to scatter a full city block.

The two babes with the bodies, Louise and Jill, are much more refined in their approach. They barely kick up the sand as they take one graceful step after another in their slow-motion, swan-dance-kind-of-trot toward the water. Once they leap in, the water hardly musters a ripple. It makes me so aggravated I jump up and down a few times to get things stirred up again.

"Isn't this great, Maggie?" Lily says, her hands cupped, dipping water, then pouring it out.

We edge in deeper. "It's awesome. And it's good to see you relax." With my arms stretched out to the sides, I kick my feet to keep afloat.

"I am having a great time. I really am. I didn't realize how much I needed this," Lily says, leaning onto her back in a full body float.

"Things get pretty overwhelming when you're planning a wedding," I say, trying to pull information from her. The water feels as warm as a bath.

Faceup, Lily gently fans the water with her hands, her feet moving in rhythm as she floats lazily nearby. "It's more than that, really—"

"This water is cold," Louise says, within earshot as she heads our way.

I turn back to Lily. "You were saying?"

"Oh, nothing really." She pulls herself into an upright position, wipes the water from her face, blinks, and looks at Louise. "You're too skinny, that's why. Maggie and I are just fine."

"Hey, speak for yourself," I say, acting all offended.

"What, you don't want to be lumped in with me?" Lily acts surprised.

"Do you have to use that word? My body is so lumpy—well, my first attempt at mashed potatoes comes to mind."

Jill drifts our way. "You know, girls, a few exercises on a regular basis could make all the difference."

I cup my hand in bullhorn fashion around my mouth. "This is a Denise Austin alert. Go into your homes, grab your chips, bolt the doors, and bar the windows."

Lily and Louise laugh, but for some reason Jill doesn't get the humor. "Thank you, but I exercise daily."

"Oh, what sort of exercise?" Jill asks.

A snicker escapes Lily because she knows what's coming.

"It takes me a good fifteen minutes every day to twist, tug, bend, and work my panty hose all the way up to my waist. Trust me, once those babies are on, I've surpassed my target heart rate."

Jill stops bobbing in the water and stares at me.

Ignoring her, I continue. "Besides, I feel light as a feather. How about you, Lily?" I say, bobbing with the waves, the sand squishing between my toes.

She grins. "Sure do. Bring on the M&Ms."

"Now that's the Lily we know and love," I say with a giggle.

"Still, it wouldn't hurt to build those muscles a little—beyond the panty hose workout."

She's getting on my nerves. "My muscles are atrophied, Jill. It's time we both gave it up."

"There's always hope," Jill says with the authority of a fitness guru. "You should try water ballet."

"Been there, done that," I say, remembering some sweet ladies I met at a class and the things they taught me when I was going through a rough time. Though fitness wasn't one of them. Of course, if I had gone back after one class, I might have benefited more—or drowned. I'm not sure which.

Jill talks more about exercise, but I don't hear a word she's saying. My mind just shuts off things like that. It's a type of filtering process for which I'm thankful. Leaning my body backward, my legs lift in response, and I stretch out on my back into a full float, my face warmed by the sun as water fills my ears and laps against my cheeks. My thoughts turn to Lily and Captain. I've got to figure out a way to get her alone so we can talk.

"You know, for something different, I think we should rent a surrey to drive around the beach and to the shops," Louise says.

"What's that?" Lily wants to know.

"It's sort of a bicycle for four people. It reminds me of a golf cart, only bigger, and powered by foot pedals," Louise explains.

Her comment causes my hands to flip me upright. I brush the water from my face. "Why would we want to do that when we've got a perfectly good red convertible?" I ask.

"It's called *exercise*, Maggie," Jill says.

"You know, I've heard of it. I had a hamster that was into it. He spent endless hours on a wheel that took him nowhere. I decided then and there that was not the life for me."

Jill takes on the look of a first grade teacher and lowers her voice as though I'm a child. "Now, Maggie, though we may not want to do something, that doesn't change the fact that it's good for us."

"The hamster died, Jill, does that mean nothing to you?"

Her argument is just not working for me.

"Is she always like this?" Jill asks Lily as though I'm not even here.

"Oh come on, Maggie, let's do it!" Lily says.

"Traitor," I whisper to Lily as we make our way out of the water.

Before we know it, we're whooping and hollering from the surrey as women and children dodge to get out of our way on the beach. As much as I hate to admit it, I'm getting a workout and having fun all at the same time. How is that possible? The wind and the surrey's red canopy with dangling white fringe around the edges keep the heat at bay. Good thing, too. In this sizzling Florida sun we could resemble slabs of beef jerky by day's end.

ⓖ ✍ ⓖ

"Girls, this has been a great day," Louise says, adjusting the bowl of popcorn on her lap.

"Yeah, and I got some good pictures." I take a sip of soda, then grab a handful of popcorn from my bowl.

"I managed not to hurt anyone." Jill takes a swig from her bottled water.

"Well, if you don't count that old lady who teetered a moment when we whizzed past her," I say.

Lily laughs. "I needed today."

We look at her.

"I've been really worn out planning for the wedding and all. Getting cranky, not quite myself."

"I've noticed." Everyone turns to me. "What? I'm kidding."

We wait for Lily to say more, but she doesn't. Just then my cell phone rings. It's Nick.

"Where do you keep the chocolate cupcakes?"

"What? No 'Hi, Mom, are you having a good time?'"

"Oh yeah. How's it going? Ya havin' fun?"

"Yes, thanks for asking."

"No problem. Now about those cupcakes?"

"Where's your dad?"

"He's working."

"This late?"

"I guess. A kid could starve around here, ya know?"

I can hear him clawing through the cupboards in search of food. Nick would have never made it in the pioneer days. If the food isn't delivered to him in a bag, a box, or cellophane, he'll starve. "That's the whole point of a college education. So you can eat."

"Yeah, whatever. The cupcakes?"

There's no question my blood pressure is steadily rising, but I figure now is not the time to get into a discussion about college with Nick. "Third shelf down on the right."

"Thanks, Mom." Cellophane ripping here. "Oh, and have a good time." Click.

His concern for me is touching. "He'll put me in a smelly nursing home, no doubt about it."

"Who?" Lily asks.

"Nick. Calls me in Florida to see where I keep the chocolate cupcakes."

Lily laughs. But then that's because she doesn't have a college man-child in her house.

We talk a little while longer then go to bed. In the darkness of the room I decide to give Lily one last chance to tell me if she's going to back out of the wedding.

"You know, Lily, I'm surprised you haven't gotten nervous at all about this wedding. I mean, most people would, the second time around and all. Plus, I remember you went through that when you and Bobby got married. Remember?"

Silence.

"Lily?"

A slight snore sounds from her side of the room. With a sigh, I punch my pillow a couple of times, turn over, and settle in for the night.

I'm beginning to think Captain was just being paranoid.

⑥ ⚶ ⑥

The bedroom is still shrouded in darkness when the familiar night sweats wake me in the wee hours of the morning. If I don't get over this soon, I'll have to start sleeping with ice packs. That could be a good thing. Could stop wrinkles right in their tracks. Still, do I want to be known as the Ice Queen? I think not.

Throwing off the covers, I stare through the shadows. It's obviously too early to get up, but I know I can't go back to sleep. Quietly, I shrug on my thin housecoat and warm socks, then tiptoe into the kitchen. Although I have occasional hot flashes, I can't stand for my feet to get cold. Hence, the socks.

In the hushed morning light, I prepare a cup of instant coffee then take my mug out to the screened-in porch.

There's something about getting alone, enveloped by nature sounds, that does wonders for my spirit. Course, not too many birds are up this time of day.

By the time I finish my reading, Lily opens the patio door. "Is it okay if I join you?"

"Sure." I place my Bible on a stand.

"So what are we doing today?" Lily asks as she takes her seat, careful not to spill coffee from the mug she's holding.

"Someone mentioned going to a movie, though I don't know which one."

"Yeah, that was tonight. But didn't Jill say something about parasailing?"

My gaze shoots to Lily. "She did? I don't know if I want to try that."

"Are you kidding me? Ms. Indiana Jones herself?"

"You know I'm not crazy about heights. Nosebleeds and all that."

"Oh, that's right. When you threw your wedding bouquet off the balcony, you got dizzy and almost fell over the railing. Gordon had to catch you."

"Exactly."

"But you know you really wouldn't have fallen over. The railing was too high. You would have had to climb over it to fall."

I sniff defensively. "Still, I could have."

Rather than comment, Lily wisely opts to take a drink of coffee. "You've really gotten over all that paranoia with getting older, haven't you?"

I nod. "I'm doing pretty well. It hits every now and then—when some oily-faced teenager behind a fast-food counter offers me a senior discount."

"He's lucky to still be alive."

"You know it."

"Well, I think you look great, and I'm proud of you for coming to terms with it."

Her comment causes me to sit up a little taller in my seat.

"I haven't told you this, Maggie. Um, I've tried to a couple of times, but we keep getting interrupted."

My friend radar is up and bleeping.

Lily fingers her coffee cup while she seems to search for words. "The truth is, I've been struggling with the marriage idea." She looks up at me.

"Why, Lil? You love Captain, don't you?"

"Yes, I think I do."

Her words squeeze my heart, causing a dull ache.

"The thing is, I was lying in bed one night thinking about something he did, and I realized he has many of the same qualities as Bobby. That made me worry. Am I marrying him because he reminds me of Bobby? If that's true, Ron deserves better." Tears fill her eyes.

"I guess only you can answer that, but I don't think that's true, Lily. If you're worried about that car thing, I told you, Gordon is the same way."

"It's more than that."

"They're different in a lot of ways."

"Such as?"

"Well, Bob never enjoyed the computer. Captain loves it. Bob could throw away a hundred dollars after five minutes in Target, but Captain is a little more, well, frugal. Bob never entered contests—"

"And Ron has won enough mugs to throw a party for the entire state of Indiana," Lily says with a laugh. "And as far as T-shirts go, he could mow the lawn every day from spring through fall and never wear the same shirt twice."

"As long as he provides you with plenty of cabinets and dresser space for his T-shirts, you'll be good. You thought that whole contest thing was cute when you first met him. Remember? You told me you could see the little boy inside him because of that."

"I remember." She stares into her coffee cup. "He says it gives him something to look forward to in the mail. Otherwise, he only gets a handful of bills." Her mouth lifts in a smile.

The morning air stirs with birdsong while we think about Lily's situation.

"There's that thing with Tara, too," she says, referring to Captain's only child.

"Lily, his wife died almost five years ago. Besides that, Captain dated other women before you."

"True, but they were never serious. Tara and I got along fine until Ron asked me to marry him."

"How many times have you seen her?"

"Well, when she and her husband came to visit Ron and when Ron and I went to Fort Myers to see his dad. She lives just down the road from Ron's dad."

I nod.

"We hit it off okay, and we've even e-mailed a couple of times, talking about her pregnancy. But after Ron announced our engagement, she called me and made it perfectly clear I was to back off. In her mind, Ron doesn't need a wife, and she doesn't need a replacement mother. She told me if I didn't comply, she would make her father choose between her and me." Lily stares at her hands. "There is no way I can come between Ron and Tara like that."

"Does Captain know she said that to you?"

Lily shakes her head.

"You need to tell him, Lily."

"I don't want to cause problems between him and Tara. They've been through enough."

"So have you." The hair on my neck bristles. "This is totally ridiculous. She can't make him choose between you."

Lily shrugs.

"You can't let her run your lives, Lily. If you love him, fight for him."

"Dive into bushes?" she asks with an ornery grin.

"You got it. Besides, you know how pregnant women are. Maybe Tara is just hormonal."

"No, I don't know. I've never been pregnant, remember?" Before I can answer, she goes on. "Maybe it's a good thing. Obviously, I'm not starting out all that great as a stepmother."

"You'll be wonderful, Lily. Tara just has to get used to the idea."

She doesn't say anything.

"What are you going to do, Lil?"

"I don't know." She looks back to me. "That's why this trip is a godsend. It gives me some time to think, away from Ron, away from the busyness of my shop, the wedding, and all that."

I nod. It's better that she not know that we know. She might feel Captain betrayed her by telling me. She just needs time to think it through. It will all work out in the end.

"Don't tell the others, okay? When I'm ready for advice, I'll let them know."

"We'll figure things out, Lil. We always do." I make the comment with as much confidence as I can muster, but I have to admit, even I'm not sure about this one.

5

"Still no coffee?" I ask when Jill and Louise join us on the back porch.

Dressed in a peach-colored tee, khaki shorts, and comfortable slip-ons, Jill shakes her head. "You know, the last time we went out for coffee, I ordered an Americano. That was the first time I'd had one, and the barista made it really strong. I could hardly drink it, but I did because I didn't want to waste it. It made me sick, and now I don't want coffee. Haven't even enjoyed the smell of it since then."

"And to think you were the one who got me drinking coffee. In fact, I have you to thank for these brown teeth," I say.

Jill cringes. "Sorry about that, but I don't think I would have talked you into it if they hadn't started adding chocolate to the bitter brew."

"I know that's true for me," Lily says.

"Not me. Just give me my plain old coffee with a little cream," Louise says.

"You're so practical, Louise. How do you live like that?" I ask.

"Just lucky, I guess."

"Well, I hope you get over your no coffee phase soon, Jill. It's not good for business," I say, thinking of The New Brew.

"I'm sure it will pass, but for a while anyway, I'm sticking with decaf tea or water. It's better for me anyway."

One glance at Jill, and I'm thinking she could use a little perk from the caffeine. Though she's still the fitness queen, her crown is a little whopper-jawed. "Oh sure, point out that we're poisoning our bodies with the artificial creamers and sugars, saying nothing of the caffeine," I say.

Jill shrugs. "To each her own." She stands up and looks out the screened windows. "I think I'm going to take a walk around the lake. Since you two aren't dressed yet, I have time, right?"

"Go ahead. We have no agenda. Enjoy the walk," I say.

"Great. See you later." Jill pushes through the door.

Louise sits quietly on her chair, sipping coffee. She's dressed in a navy blue and white boatneck sweater, navy blue capris, and matching sandals that lace up the ankles. Her flawless skin is made up to perfection. My skin resembles crackled paint.

"You know, if you could just muster up one wrinkle, Louise, all would be right with my world."

Surprise covers her face. "What?"

"Never mind."

"Say, would you girls like a big breakfast this morning?" She looks as though she'll dart out of her chair if we say yes.

"No, I'm fine," Lily says, making me want to inflict pain upon her person. I'm seeing that sugared cereal coming up in our future.

Louise turns to me.

"I'm fine, too. But you were sweet to fix all that for us yesterday." *Doggone it, I hate it when I'm forced to be nice.*

"I love to do it," she insists. *So why are we spoiling all her fun?*

"Well, you need to relax while we're here," Lily says in her Dr. Phil voice. If I were close enough, I'd pinch her toe.

"If you girls don't mind, I'm going to check out the cooking channel," Louise says, already making her way inside.

"I suppose I should take my shower," Lily says, though I notice she doesn't move. "She's not quite doing the power walking she usually does." Lily points toward Jill who is about three-quarters of the way around the lake.

"Her 'normal' walking makes me want to take a nap."

Lily laughs and shakes her head. "Well, I really am going to get dressed. Hey, thanks for listening this morning. I have no idea which way this is going to go."

"What do you mean?"

"The wedding. I'm not sure if it's going to happen." She turns and goes back into the house.

This being friends thing can work havoc on the nerves.

⑥ ⟁ ⑥

"Boy, that felt great," Jill says when she steps back inside.

"A full body massage feels great, Jill. A walk around the lake? Doesn't work for me."

"All this sitting around makes me feel sluggish."

"Excuse me? Sitting around, did you say? Maybe my memory deceives me, but it seems to me we rode a surrey only yesterday." I don't bother to tell her my leg muscles are still bitter about it and are letting me know.

"Oh, that was nothing. There were four of us doing the work, you know. Not only one person pedaling a bike."

"Tell that to my legs."

She looks at me as though I'm a wimp. "Just for the record, I work my heart muscles every time I climb into the car with Gordon."

Right then my cell phone rings. While I answer it, Jill steps inside the condo to give me some privacy.

"Hi, Mom!" Heather squeals.

"Well, hello. Aren't you the chipper one today," I say.

I catch Heather up on the details of our trip, and she tells me what's going on with her and Josh.

"I can't wait to see you when we come to Aunt Lily's wedding," Heather says. Though Lily is not related to our kids, they think of her as family.

"It's been too long. Can't wait to see you, either," I say, not filling her in on the details of Lily's cold feet. It's better to wait and see how it all turns out before worrying Heather.

We talk a few minutes longer and Heather finally says, "Well, I'd better get going. I just wanted to check in and see how your trip is going. Love you, Mom."

A smile springs to my lips. Heather's phone call reminds me how blessed we are to have such great kids. Okay, so Nick's going through a phase, but we love him and know that God has a plan for his life. The question is, will Nick follow it? I'm wondering how rewarding life can be when one is a professional video game player . . .

⑥ ⚮ ⑥

"You're awfully quiet today, Maggie. You okay?" Jill asks when we're seated at the Village Café for lunch.

Let me just say here they've placed us in a corner table. I'm so close to a mirror on the wall that my pores look the size of the Grand Canyon. As if I don't have enough pressure.

"I'm fine," I say, doing my best to sound perky, but since I haven't perked in years, well, it's just not happening. Gordon says my mood changes as often as gasoline prices. He's comparing me to gas. How wrong is that?

Still, there's some truth in it. Though I'm taking hormone medication, I continue to have bouts with mood swings from time to time.

The server returns with our meals. "You girls on vacation?" she asks while plopping the plates down.

"Yeah," we say simultaneously.

"Sisters?"

"Friends," I say.

"That's so cute. I hope me and my friends do that when we're older, too," she says before turning on her skinny little heels and walking away.

She's in the kitchen by the time her comment sinks in, which is probably a good thing given my hormonal mood and all.

"I do believe we've been insulted," Lily says.

Jill shrugs. "What does she know? She's a kid."

"Right," Louise says.

"Doesn't bother me," I say, taking a sip from my iced tea. When I look up, my eyes lock with Lily's, who's not buying it.

"Okay, it bothers me."

She smiles and nods, like a know-it-all.

While the others concentrate on their meals, I dare a quick glance of myself in the mirror. If I just weren't so doggone happy all the time—well, except for the mood swings—I could get rid of these laugh lines.

"I'm looking forward to going to Turtle Beach," Lily says, interrupting my slight bout of paranoia. "They say you can find some nice shells there." She stabs a piece of lettuce salad with her fork.

"Are you collecting shells, Lily?" I ask, forcing myself to be congenial even though the idea that I could get a call from the crypt keeper does cross my mind.

"I thought it might be fun to collect some and put them in a glass jar with a little sand."

"Oh, collecting shells is a good idea, Lily. I'm planning to scrapbook some of our pictures for a small album of our trip," Louise says.

"And here I was just planning to enjoy myself," I say.

Jill laughs. "Me, too. I'm not especially gifted when it comes to that kind of stuff. My mementos are up here," she says, tapping her temple.

"Uh-oh. With all the diet pop I'm drinking, that part of me is going fast, so maybe I should gather some tangible mementos," I say.

"I thought you were trying to drink less diet pop," Lily says.

"Yeah, I'm drinking more water—when I remember to switch."

"We can make extra copies of the pictures we take so we'll each have a set," Louise interrupts, her mind obviously still on the scrapbook. "If you wouldn't mind, Maggie."

"No problem. That's a great idea," I say.

Soon we finish our meal with small talk, and we decide to visit Turtle Beach today, which is located on the south side of Siesta Key.

Once we get out of the car, Jill steps over to me and pulls me slightly away from the others. "Has Lily said anything about the wedding yet?"

I nod. "I'll tell you later, but we need to encourage her."

Jill's eyes grow wide. "That's what I was afraid of. Okay, we'll get to work."

We quicken our steps to catch up with Lily and Louise who are discussing the beach.

We pause to take pictures from different angles. A passerby snaps our picture with Louise's camera.

"If anyone posts that picture on the Internet, I'll sue," I say.

"Oh come on, Maggie. We're not worrying about our bodies. We're on vacation," Lily says.

"That's the best news I've heard all day," I say. "You know, I'm surprised there are so few people here."

"Believe me, it's much less crowded than Siesta Key Beach, as you will remember," Jill says.

"That's a beautiful beach," Lily says.

"Yes, the white sand is unique. But if it's shells you want, Turtle Beach is covered with shells. Is this okay?" she asks, pointing to the area.

We nod, each of us spreading our towels and placing our belongings nearby. "I'm so slicked up with suntan lotion, I could pass for Flipper."

Lily laughs.

"Better to be slick than burned. Healthy skin makes for a beautiful body," Louise says, spreading her towel.

"Come on, Louise, no matter how you look at it, an old body is still, well, old."

"Yes, but you can choose to look your age or not."

"Yeah, whatever." I know she's right, but I'm feeling rebellious enough right now to take off my lotion.

"Want to look for shells?" Lily asks, eyes sparkling.

We all agree and pull ourselves up from our towels. My legs don't want to follow me here. I'm afraid if I get up, they will stay behind and suffer from separation anxiety. That can't be good.

"Come on, Maggie, you can do it," Miss I-can-run-the-Boston-Marathon-without-breaking-into-a-sweat encourages. She and Lily reach out their hands and pull me up. Though I may get tired of their bits of "wisdom" on health and skin care and whatever else inspires them on a given day, this is why we are all good friends. We look out for one another.

"Look at this." Jill shows us a cracked shell of unusual color then tosses it out to sea.

"That's us. Cracked and tossed aside," Lily says with a laugh.

"Speak for yourself." The tide forms a sudsy wash upon the tops of my feet then races back out to sea, leaving more shells behind.

Lily stoops to pick through the shells that are gritty with sand. Finally, she plunks several into the soda cup she had at the restaurant. An egret patters by us, enjoying a sunny stroll on the beach. There's something to be said for that kind of life. Where all you do is sleep, search for food, eat, sleep, search for food . . . Hey, wait. That's *my* life.

"Don't you love that smell?" Jill says, taking a deep breath.

"The smell of fish?" I ask.

All three women stare at me as though I've swallowed a crab whole. Guess I ruined their sensory moment.

"Okay, okay, salty sea smell, right?"

"Right," they say in unison.

After a leisurely walk, we return to our towels and settle upon the soft sand. I hope Lily is around when I need to get up, or I may fossilize right here on this beach. My joints could use a little oil.

"So, Lily, how's Captain making it with you out of town and all?" Jill asks, straightening her towel.

"I suppose he's doing all right," she says.

"You don't know? He hasn't called every ten minutes to declare his undying devotion and beg you to come back?" Louise asks with a laugh.

"No. We've decided it best to have little contact while I'm gone, to give us both time to think." Lily keeps her eyes down while the three of us exchange a glance.

"Time to think about what?" Jill presses.

Lily glances up and blows out a sigh. "I might as well tell you. I'm struggling a little about the wedding."

Louise and Jill gasp appropriately. She has our full attention.

"What's wrong, Lily?" Louise asks as though she's never heard this before, making me wonder if she's ever fibbed to me.

Lily stares out to sea. "I have no idea. Just can't get past this feeling that I'm making a mistake."

"That's it? Just a feeling?" Jill asks, stretching her toes forward and backward, forward, backward. If I tried that, my toes would be saying, "You're kidding, right?"

Lily turns to Jill. "I hadn't realized until recently how much he reminds me of Bobby—not in appearance, but in the things he does. When that hit me, I started worrying that maybe I'm marrying him for the wrong reasons. That's not fair to Ron."

"Though I don't know him as well as you, I don't really see the similarities—except for cleaning the car," Louise says. "Can you give examples?"

"He's the gentle giant type. You know, the macho man who loves

48

animals. He's practically gotten us killed on more than one occasion while dodging animals in the road. He has a dog. Did I tell you that? A brown wiener dog. Lulu. A hot dog with a head and a tail."

"Oh, dachshunds are so cute," Louise says.

"Cute, yes. Macho, no. Forget the Doberman pinscher, he has a wiener dog."

Everyone laughs.

"But I've never had a house pet."

"You don't know what you're missing, Lil. You know how much you love Crusher," I say, referring to our thirteen-year-old Chihuahua with three teeth.

Lily chuckles. "Crusher and I have grown up together."

"That's true enough," I say with a chuckle.

"Lulu is just, well, long."

We laugh again.

"I wouldn't let Lulu stop you from getting married, Lily," Louise says.

"Did I tell you Captain eats oatmeal every morning for breakfast, without fail? Bobby did the same thing."

I stare at her. "Lily, the entire population over fifty eats oatmeal for breakfast. It helps with cholesterol and all that, remember? Besides, just how do you know what he eats for breakfast?" My eyes narrow to slits as I stare at her with suspicion. Louise scoots to the edge of her seat, her eyes sparking with eagerness. It throws off my concentration for a millisecond.

Lily throws me a pointed glare. "He told me." She stares at her fingers. "Another thing is I always loved the way Bobby protected me. But I was a kid when we got married. I've lived on my own for years now. I'm so different now. What if I feel smothered by Ron's protection? Can I be the kind of wife I used to be?"

Silence hovers while we wait on Lily to empty her heart.

"Then there's that thing with his daughter. I've told you all about

49

my visits with her when we came to Florida and when she came to visit her dad. She's friendly, but the warmth is missing. She and her mother were close. How can I compete with that?"

"You can't. You just be yourself, Lil. Tara will come around," I say. "Besides, other than family gatherings, it's not as though you'll be around her all that much with her living in Florida and you in Indiana."

"Hey, are you going to visit her while we're here?" Louise asks.

"I told her I was coming, and we thought we might do lunch one day. We'll see."

"Do you love Ron?" Jill asks, surprising us all. "Because if you do, don't let his daughter or anyone else stop you from marrying him."

Lily hesitates. "I know, but there's something to be said about family unity."

Reaching for my beach bag, I pull out my spray bottle of water and spray like the dickens. Is sunning something a woman with hot flashes should be doing? I'm thinking no.

"There are no guarantees. I mean, even once you get married and the match seems perfect, things can go wrong," Jill says.

What does she think she's doing? With that kind of counseling, Lily will never marry again.

"True, things can go wrong, but when you love someone, you work hard to get through it," I say.

"Easier said than done," Louise says, and I'm thinking these two would never qualify as marriage counselors.

"No one said it would be easy, Louise," I say with a bit of a growl to my voice. While Lily glances out to sea, I shoot Louise and Jill a look of warning. "But a marriage worth saving is worth the trouble."

The ocean tide fills in the silence while I think of how to ditch Louise and Jill so I can talk some sense into Lily.

6

"This is such a blast from the past, it wouldn't surprise me to see Richie, Potsie, and the Fonz in here," I say the next day at lunch as we push through the doors at Johnny Rockets, diner extraordinaire.

Everyone scoots into the red booth and table bordered with chrome, and I snap some pictures.

"Oh, cool. Look at this," Jill says, pointing to the tabletop jukebox.

"Scrape up your nickels, girls, we're gonna have some fun."

Lily groans. "If you dance on the table, Maggie, I'm out of here."

Louise gasps. "You wouldn't do that, would you?"

Lily giggles. "She would. You'd better watch her at the Donny Osmond concert. She's been known to dance in the aisles and sneak backstage." She grins at me.

"I'm so excited we were able to get tickets," I say.

"Well, I'm not sneaking backstage for anyone," Louise says.

"I'll have to side with Louise on that. I'll go to the concert, but no sneaking backstage for me," Jill says.

I bite my lip. "You in, Lil?"

"Well, let's wait and see how it turns out. I don't want to end up in jail."

"Good point. But if we do, I know a good lawyer."

With my party mood back in place, I consider the whole dancing on the table thing for just a moment then think better of it. Gordon would probably not approve.

"No dancing, Maggie." Lily knows me well.

"I won't. I'm wearing the wrong shoes."

"Besides, you'd throw out your back at your age," Jill says, teasing.

Party mood waning here. Lily's gaze collides with my own. She knows I'm about to breathe fire. Most likely the smoke coming from my nostrils is a dead giveaway.

"Excuse me, Miss Preschool—"

"Maggie's the youngest fifty-year-old I know," Lily interrupts, reducing my fire to a sizzle.

"Oh, Maggie knows I'm kidding," Jill says, thereby salvaging her Christmas present.

We order our burgers, fries, and chocolate malts—hey, we're on vacation—and flip through the jukebox selections. Dropping our nickels into the machine, we select a couple of Beach Boys, Carpenters, and Chicago numbers and settle in for a fun time. Jill picks at her food, barely eating anything. I suppose she's trying to make a statement about it not being good for us, but I ignore her. If she had her way, we'd be eating brussel sprouts on vacation. That is just wrong.

The smell of frying burgers fills the air as the music overhead goes into the Bee Gees's tune of "Night Fever." We're engrossed in chatter, having a great time, when suddenly five servers gather at the front of the room. Dressed in white shirts and aprons, black pants and bow ties, and white hats that pretty much resemble the paper boats we used to make as kids, the Johnny Rockets crew starts dancing a rendition of "Night Fever" that could quite possibly make it to Broadway.

Lily and I whoop and holler while Jill laughs and Louise sinks further under the table. We're clapping in rhythm and totally get into the spirit of the moment. Apparently, a couple of other ladies feel the same way. Amid giggling and clapping, the two older ladies—well, they *could* be older—make their way up to join the dancers.

The women, clothed in purple tops, black pants, and red hats, clap their hands, turn on cue, throw out catcalls, and even throw in a hip swivel where appropriate.

"They'll never believe this back home," I say, snapping a couple of pictures of the Ginger Rogers wannabes.

The whole room comes alive with the show. Everyone claps and whistles louder with every measure. One of the ladies gets so inspired that by the time they reach the end of the song, she does a can-can kick for a grand finale and knocks over a pitcher of water on the table in front of her. A woman happens by just as the pitcher falls, and ice water douses her feet. Luckily for everyone, she says she was having a hot flash at the time. She actually thanks the old woman for the cool respite, and we all enjoy a good laugh.

As the two red hat ladies make their way back to the table, I find myself wishing that I could be that free. Maybe by the time I'm their age, I will be that free. Wait. I *am* their age. Or at least pretty close. Something tells me I've got my work cut out for me.

ⓖ ✎ ⓖ

"What am I going to do, Maggie?" Lily's words squeeze through the despair in her voice.

The ground near the lake is bumpy, so I take careful steps.

"Captain's a good man, Lily. He wears weird T-shirts, but he's a good man."

She giggles. "I admit his Elvis sighting shirt is a bit much."

"And my personal favorite: 'I'm a Trivia Geek.'"

Dusk falls over us as we laugh and turn around the far tip of the lake to head back for the condo. The sweet scent of nearby jasmine and orange blossoms perfumes the air.

"It's probably not my place to say, but I think you are right for each other," I say.

"This from the woman who I distinctly recall dove into bushes to keep me from dating?"

"I had my reasons. This is the first normal one you've dated. Though he does have two first names."

"Which would explain why you call him Captain." She laughs then pauses a moment. "You're a good friend, Maggie Hayden."

"I just want you to be happy, Lil."

"I know."

"Isn't Tara's due date coming up?" I ask.

"Yeah, she probably won't make the wedding. The baby is due the week before. Who knows, maybe she wouldn't come anyway."

"She'll come around, Lil. Give her time."

"Her mom's been gone a long time. You'd think she could open a little space in her heart for me. I'm not trying to take her mother's place."

"I know, but didn't you say she took on the job of watching over her dad after her mother's death? She's having to let go, in a sense, just the way I had to let go of Heather and Nick—course, I didn't know Nick would come back."

Lily chuckles. "Yeah, I guess."

Just then I glance over at our condo and see Jill standing outside with her arms waving. She's shouting something, but her words are carried away with the evening breeze. The look on her face doesn't register panic, but there's something about it that makes me think whatever she's trying to tell us is important.

"What's up with her?" I ask.

"I don't know. I can't hear her."

"She's pointing at something." I turn to my right to see what's there. "I don't see anything."

Lily follows my gaze. "I don't either."

By now Louise has joined her.

"The look on Louise's face scares me," I say, picking up my step. "Wonder if something is wrong."

Louise's arms wave frantically.

"What in the world—" Lily's words are replaced by a piercing scream.

Turning to her, I see an alligator not too far behind us. My feet and heart kick into gear and start pumping at a speed that would win me a spot on a Nike commercial. There's no aerobic program known to mankind that could set my heart to thumping this way. Yet Lightning Lily passes me as though I'm standing still.

We're both screaming so loud, we sound like a tornado alarm back home. Neighbors step out of their condos. I nearly blow out a lung screaming for them to go back inside. By the time I step inside the back door, I have little breath left in me. When I turn around, I see that the alligator is gone, but what shocks me to the core is that the neighbors are laughing.

This is a sick world.

"You all right?" Lily asks.

"An oxygen tank would be nice right about now, but I think I'll live." The amusement on Jill's lips irritates me. "There is a wild alligator in our lake, and you're okay with this?" I ask. "And what's with your psycho neighbors?"

"I'm sorry, Maggie. While you can't tame gators, we consider Gator George fairly harmless. He's very old, and I haven't seen him run in years. He's snaggletoothed. I've watched him through binoculars. He only has enough teeth to snag some food now and then, but that's the extent of it. In fact, you probably scared him back into the lake. If you look at him next time, you'll see that he's not even five feet long," she says laughing. "He's pretty much an old runt as far as alligators go."

My mouth drops. "Gator George? You've named him Gator George?"

Jill shrugs. "Like I said, he's been around awhile. For some reason he's taken a liking to our lake. When he can catch them, he feeds on turtles, fish, that kind of thing, so he's sort of become a novelty here. Course, with recent alligator attacks, George's days may be numbered. Still, I don't believe he would ever bother anyone."

"I could have had a heart attack, Jill. I would call that bothersome. Besides, I think people should be warned." I'm ready to make posters for telephone poles. Though my efforts obviously would be useless around here.

"Florida folks are used to wild alligators. They show up in people's pools, lakes, roadsides, everywhere. If they pose any kind of threat—and we know that some do—we call the Nuisance Alligator Program." Jill doesn't appear ruffled at all. I'm not sure whether to give her my respect or a reality pill. "Believe me, you would know if it was an aggressive gator. They can run pretty fast for a short distance," Jill says.

"And this is supposed to make us feel better? Say what you will about Indiana, at least we don't have alligators. Snakes, yes. Gators, no."

Jill laughs again. "As I said, as long as people don't feed him, George will leave us all alone. On the other hand, if you spot a big gator, you'd better run. They won't hesitate to eat you, shoes and all."

"For crying out loud, Jill, you could have at least warned us before we went out—especially in the evening."

"If I had known you were going for a walk, I would have told you. Though I think the worst that George could do to you is scare you half to death. Still, it pays to be careful. I took a bath and just came out to join Louise. We watched the cooking channel for a few minutes when I asked her where you were. That's when I came outside."

That softens me a little. "Well, if Gator George is any indication of what the Florida sun does to skin, I'm glad I live in Indiana."

"Maggie, Mary Kay skin products can keep your face as soft as a baby's bottom," Louise recites like a memory piece.

"I'm not sure I want my face compared to a baby's bottom, but whatever."

"By the way, I got some good snapshots of you and Lily running for your lives," Louise says with a laugh.

"Hey, if we had it on video, we could probably win big money on *America's Funniest Home Videos*," Jill chimes in. "Do they still have that program?"

"Oh, goody. We risk our lives, and you're trying to make money from it." I don't bother to hide my irritation.

"I think you're safe with George. I told you before—"

"Okay, okay, I get it," I say. "If he's not dangerous, I might try to get a picture of him before we leave here."

"Well, just be careful," Jill says. "You don't want to tempt fate. Especially where you're concerned, Maggie."

As I said, she's getting on my nerves.

ⓖ ⬿ ⓖ

"That was a good movie," Lily says later that evening, getting up to take the DVD from the player and putting it back into its case. "I hope I have that much fun when I retire. Hey, Louise, aren't you and Donald retiring this year?"

"Well, that's the plan."

"That's so cool," Jill says. "Are you going to do anything special?"

A dreamy look comes over Louise. "We've talked about taking another cruise. We might even buy a condo, move to Florida, who knows?" She stretches her arms as though the sky is the limit.

"Wow, you would leave Charming?" I ask.

Louise shrugs. "I don't know. I'm just throwing out some possibilities. I love the water, so it would be cool to live near the ocean. But I definitely want to take a cruise."

"Any idea where you want to go?" Lily asks.

"We want to take the Alaskan cruise. I hear it's beautiful beyond words. We've already been to the Bahamas and the Caribbean."

"Gordon and I want to do that sometime. We've never been on a cruise, and we're making plans for it now—well, we were. That discussion was pre-Nick. With Nick back in the house, well, it changes things, that's all."

"I don't see how. He's big enough to stay by himself while you go on a cruise," Jill says.

"Yes, but there's the little matter of money. It costs us an arm and a leg to feed him."

"So make him get a job," Jill continues as though she knows something about parenting, which of course, she doesn't.

"Working at the Gap just doesn't cover the food bill," I say. Not really wanting to get into further discussion about Nick, I change the subject. "Besides, I'd probably get seasick if I went on a cruise."

"Oh, you get used to it. They have medicine for that, too, you know. On those big ships, you don't notice it the way you would in a small boat," Louise insists. "And, oh my, they have so much food!"

"Desserts?" I ask.

"By the boatload—pardon the pun," Louise says in another miserable attempt to be funny. I want to tell her to hang on to her day job, but since she doesn't have one, I let it go.

"Okay, I'm in," I say.

"Desserts will not change the world, Maggie," Lily says as though she knows what she's talking about.

"Excuse me, but I believe chocolate éclairs are making a statement."

"I'd have to agree with you there," Jill says. But before I can get satisfied with my winning comment she adds, "They say, 'Start an exercise program.'" The others laugh.

I don't.

"You know, Rodney's goal is to run in every state in the United States. He only has two to go, Washington and Iowa."

"Who's Rodney?" Lily asks.

"What's he running for, Congress?" I ask.

"Exercise, Maggie. Maybe you've heard of it?" Jill says.

"Excuse me, are we close enough for you to talk to me this way?" Jill laughs. "Yes, we are."

"Of course I've heard of it. I exercise my right to vote every chance I get."

"Who's Rodney?" Lily asks again.

"I might try that one day. Hey, maybe I should start while we're here!" Jill says with as much excitement as I would give an ice cream sundae.

"Vote? You can't vote. You're not from around here," I protest.

Jill ignores me. "I've already been running in Indiana, so Florida can be my second state."

Now I'm curious. "Who's Rodney?" Jill blinks as though she didn't hear Lily the first two times.

"Oh, Rodney is a friend of mine. He's a trainer at the fitness center where I work out."

Lily and I share a glance.

"It's nothing like that," Jill says after seeing our exchange. "We're just friends. I would never lead a guy on that way. You know me better than that. We talk about our families. He has a wife and two kids."

Knowing the problems Jill and Jeff have had in their marriage, I try not to worry.

"Well, just so he knows. You know how some men are. You toss them a polite smile, and they think you're coming on to them.

Wouldn't matter if you had a house full of kids. They still think they're the hope for all women," Louise says, surprising us all.

Lily and I start laughing.

"Well, it's true," Louise says, emphatically. "I've seen women swoon over my Donald, can you imagine?"

Frankly, no.

"Gordon wouldn't go along with that. He's not really the jealous type; he just wouldn't feel comfortable with me having a guy friend at a fitness center." Jill can be a little gullible. I hope she's careful. "Jeff doesn't mind?"

She blinks. "You know, to tell you the truth, I've never told him. Just never thought about it, really. I was going to tell him after I met Rodney at the coffeehouse, just in case Jeff heard about it, but—"

"You had coffee with him?" Lily looks worried.

"Well, not on purpose. We sort of bumped into each other there and just started talking. That's all."

"You don't see any danger in it?" I ask.

"Why, no. It wasn't a planned thing." There's a slightly defensive edge to her voice.

"He's aware there's nothing to your friendship?" I know it's really none of my business, but Jill and Jeff both are my friends. I'd hate to see anything happen to them.

"Of course. As I told you, we talk about our families." Jill tucks her hair behind her ear and shifts in her seat.

"Anybody want more popcorn?" I ask, taking the empty bowl toward the kitchen.

"No way, I'm stuffed," Louise says.

"No, thanks, Maggie. I'm tired. I think I'll go on to bed." Without another word, Jill gets up, goes to her bedroom, and shuts the door.

We thought we came down here for Lily but with everything else going on, it looks like more than one Latte Girl needs help . . .

7

"It's so nice out. Why don't we go rollerblading?" Jill asks the next day after we go to church and eat lunch.

My heart halts midbeat. "You mean, skates?" I think about adding "at my age?" but I do not want to hear the comments that are sure to follow. I don't need that kind of grief.

Jill laughs. "Yes, skates."

"If we weren't staying at your condo, I'd make you go home."

Jill laughs. "Oh come on, Maggie, you can do this."

Lily looks as doubtful as I feel. "Well—"

"I've never done it, but it sounds fun," Louise says, raring to go.

Miss Beauty Queen on skates? I'm having trouble visualizing it. She could scrape up her knees, then where would she be? I'm wondering if I should point out the bruises, the broken bones, the gashes, the concussions, the ER? Surely she would reconsider.

Lily and I look at each other. "You up for it, Old Lady?" Lily asks with a wink.

Okay, with that comment alone, wild horses couldn't stop me

from rollerblading. Most likely I'm pretty safe with the added cushion on my backside. There's no doubt in my mind that I'm going to need it. "I am if you are, *Granny*," I say. With the I'm-not-sure-it's-happening-for-me look Lily throws my way, I wish I hadn't brought it up.

In no time we go to a nearby shop that rents rollerblades, and we're back at an open lot, ready and waiting to hurt ourselves. Remind me again. Why are we doing this?

"You strap them on this way," Jill says, illustrating. "Once you get them on, hang on to the bench here until you get your balance."

"And you thought you had to tell me that?" I ask.

Jill laughs. "Well, just wanted you to be safe."

"No, if that were the case, we wouldn't be in these things," I say.

"Come on, Maggie. You can go home and prove you're the hippest old lady in Charm—" Jill's breath stops midword with one look at my face. "I didn't mean you were old, exactly, just—"

"Save your breath," Lily jumps in. "If there's one thing I've learned over the years, you just can't fix it when you trip over your tongue where Maggie is concerned."

"And they say she can't be taught, ladies and gentlemen!" I say in my county fair sideshow announcing voice.

Jill laughs but her gaze never leaves my face. It's good to keep them guessing.

Pulling myself up, I wobble like a Weeble. Still I'm standing, so that's good, and Weebles wobble, but they don't fall down. Right? I'm a Weeble wobble wonder. Try saying that ten times fast.

Once we're all upright—though Lily and I are clutching the bench as though it's our only means of life support—Jill turns to us.

"I think we're ready. Now we'll get used to the skates in this area here before we go into the public domain. We don't want to hurt anyone," Jill says.

"Hurt anyone, as in ourselves, right?" I say, still clutching the bench.

In fact, the bench and I are so close, I may invite it to our next family gathering.

"That, too." Jill gives us a quick—and I do mean quick—lesson on skating techniques: the staggered stance, heel stop, parallel turn, and stride and glide. Then before I can work up another good wobble, she shoves off and skates across the lot with all the confidence of Dorothy Hamill.

It's at this point in time I have to ask, why am I putting myself through this? Then I remember Jill's comment about being a hip old lady and without another thought, I shove away from the bench. My hands stretch out at my sides as though I'm a woman on a tightrope, only that balancing act deal isn't happening for me here. I teeter from side to side, hopefully taking inches off my waistline, and before I can blink, a scream pierces the air—mine. My backside hits the ground in two seconds flat. My body is sprawled out on the pavement like roadkill, and I'm beginning to see why old women stick to rockers. This Weeble definitely fell down. I want my money back.

When I turn, I see that the bench is only two yards away from me. Lily's still holding on to it for all she's worth—as in, her fingers have permanently left their mark in the wood. I can see it from here.

Something tells me this is going to be a long afternoon.

Louise joins Jill out on the pavement with the greatest of ease, and it takes them a moment to realize I've fallen. Though I would have thought my scream might have given them a clue.

My rump hurts, and I'm tempted to stay here and count the ants on the pavement, but when Jill and Louise skate toward me, I know I'm destined to repeat this performance. Wonder if there's a flight going out to Indiana today?

Jill and Louise reach me, stoop down, and attempt to haul me back up.

"Let's try it again," Jill says, making me want to thwack her at the back of the knees so she'll join me on the pavement. All right, I need to do a study on that "Love thy neighbor as thyself" thing, but right now, I'm not feeling very charitable. Have I mentioned the pain in my backside?

Jill and Louise stand on either side of me and loop their arms through mine. Without so much as a single twitch, Lily continues to keep her death grip on the bench. Paint her white, and they'd attach a historical plaque in her honor. A seagull swoops overhead. If he lands on Lily, I'm guessing she'll be back in Charming by nightfall.

"You need to look forward, Maggie, or you'll get off balance again," Jill says, pulling my gaze from Lily.

"Why aren't you guys going after Lily?" I want to know.

"Oh, she'll get hers in a minute after we get you off and running," Louise says.

I guess that means Lily's good beside the bench for the rest of the day, because that up and running thing with me? Ain't gonna happen.

"Okay, Maggie, just pretend you're on a bicycle, roller skates, whatever, and keep focused." Jill blathers on and on, but the thumping of my heart against my chest drowns out her voice. Before I can yell, "Call 911," they let go of me. My scream rips through the air while the edge of the cement rolls toward me at breakneck speed.

"Stop yourself, Maggie!" Jill shouts as though I hadn't thought of that. It reminds me of those stupid exercise videos where the petite little instructor says in her nasally voice, "Don't forget to breathe."

I try to bend forward at the hip and knees the way Jill told me, but obviously, it's not happening for me here. In a panic, I extend my right foot, lift my toes, and press down on my heel for the heel stop, but instead, my foot slips out from under me. *Traitor.* Landing on my backside once more, the backs of my skates flop down so hard I'm wondering if I cracked the cement.

In a matter of seconds, Louise and Jill race up to my side, stopping themselves with all the grace of Olympic skaters. If I had the energy, I'd trip 'em.

"Do you know where you went wrong? You should have—"

"Jill, I appreciate that you're trying to help me here, but you may as well save your breath," I say, trying but failing to get up. Merciful Louise bends over and helps me. "If you could just walk me to the bench, I will give you dibs on my son," I say.

"That's a nice offer, but I already have one, remember?" Louise says with a laugh.

"It's rude to turn down a gift, just so you know," I say.

Louise chuckles while she and Jill roll me closer to the bench—the one that Lily is still clutching—I'm thinking heaven is just in sight.

"Your turn, Lily," Jill says.

"Oh no. I may be going on a honeymoon soon, and I don't need all those bruises I'm sure Maggie has acquired by now."

With a grimace, I rub my leg. "Thanks for the reminder." Still, I'm encouraged that there's hope for her wedding.

"Well, this isn't quite working out," Jill says, defeat lining her voice.

"You two go ahead and knock yourselves out while we sit and talk here on our nice little bench." My fingers work furiously to yank off my rollerblades before they try to pull me back out to the pavement.

Lily has now moved around to the seat, and she's yanking hers off as well.

"That's what I love about you, Maggie," Lily says once Louise and Jill take off. "You don't buckle under peer pressure." She pulls off the last rollerblade. "You know, Ron is the same way. He might try something to please others, but if he decides it's not the way to go, he'll say so."

"This is definitely not the way to go for me," I say, making a face while I rub my heels. I want to pursue this conversation, but don't want to push Lily too hard. Not to mention the fact it's too painful to talk.

"Well, you're braver than I was. I wouldn't even get out there. But I did manage to snap a few pictures of you."

I turn to glare at her. "I *will* hurt you if you show those to anyone, including Captain's dog." I'm wondering how she pried her fingers loose from the bench to take a picture.

"You're so touchy."

"If you had the bruises I have, you'd be touchy too, Miss I'm-not-leaving-this-bench." Stretching my legs out in front of me, I try to wiggle my toes, but they just stand there looking stiff. "Still haven't talked to Captain?" I ask.

Lily shakes her head and sighs. "If only I had the answer. I need to make a decision soon. There's not much time left, and it's not fair for me to keep Ron hanging. It hurts me that I'm causing him pain."

Louise skates toward us, stops, and answers the phone that's hooked onto the waistband of her shorts. "Donald, hi!" she says, then edges away from us.

"She hasn't talked to him much since we've been here. Probably glad to hear from him," I say.

Lily nods.

I hesitate here, not wanting to gossip, but wondering if I should discuss my concerns about Jill with Lily. "Lily, about Jill—"

"I know, I'm concerned too."

With a smile, I nod. It's so Lily to know exactly what I'm thinking. That's what best friends do. I don't know what I'd do without her. Well, all except for that picture thing.

"Have you talked to Gordon today?" Lily asks, grabbing a bottle of water from her quilted bag and taking a drink.

"Not yet. He's called me every day before I have the chance to call him," I say with a chuckle. "I think he misses me—especially since he's the one picking up after Nick." The sun's heat sizzles down upon the bench, making it hard to sit still. If Lily spills water on me, smoke will rise from my skin like steam on hot pavement.

"Honestly, Maggie, Nick's not usually that sloppy. Are you exaggerating again, or do you think he's sort of depressed?"

"Yeah, I think he is depressed. Poor kid. But, Lil, you know as well as I do he did it to himself. If he had paid as much attention to his studies as he did to having a good time, he wouldn't be in this mess."

"Ah, the lessons of life," Lily says.

"Yeah, but something tells me we're suffering as much as he is."

"You don't think there's a certain amount of humiliation at being back home with the parents?"

"I guess you're right. But if it's all the same to you, I'll sulk a little longer."

"Enjoy your pain," she says with a chuckle when Jill skates up to us.

"What are you laughing about?" She sits down and starts working with her rollerblades.

"Maggie's funny," Lily says.

"Are you stopping?" I ask.

"Yeah, I think we've all had enough. Guess I'm a little more into exercise than the rest of you," she says.

I don't know whether to be offended or apologize. "It's not for everybody."

Jill turns to me, and I brace myself for a lecture on how exercise should be for everybody and all the benefits it offers. Instead, she turns her attention back to her skates.

Louise comes back to join us looking none-too-happy. I'm wondering if everyone is having a hormonal day or what.

"Everything all right, Louise?" I ask upon seeing her expression.

She lifts her chin. "Everything is fine," she quips, thereby letting us know that indeed everything is not fine.

"It's not quite time to eat dinner. What do you want to do now?" Jill says, looking tired.

"How about we go back to the condo awhile and rest before dinner?" Lily offers.

Jill looks relieved. "Sounds great."

Hopefully, we'll all still be friends by the end of this trip.

"How's your leg? And your backside?" Lily asks when we settle into living at the condo.

I grab a snack cake and tear open the cellophane. "I suppose I'll live, but I'm surprised I can still sit." After a slight chuckle I delve into my cake.

"You're braver than I am. When I saw how you struggled, I wasn't about to go out there."

"Gravity has a way of pulling us down. Come to think of it, it's a wonder I can walk."

Lily laughs then covers her mouth so she won't wake up Louise who is taking a nap in her room.

"Besides, you have a wedding to think about." Once I see the look on her face, I add, "Maybe."

She nods but says nothing more.

I glance out the window. "You know, I'm a little worried about Jill."

"Why, because she's walking out by the lake? Gator George and all that?"

"Well, that too. But she's not eating a whole lot."

"I noticed that."

"It could just be me, but I think she overdoes it with that exercise, eating right thing."

Lily nods. "Only time will tell. When she's running circles around us at the old folks home, we might change our minds."

Right then Jill enters, her face all aglow with health—well, sort of. Something is a little off-kilter, but I can't put my finger on it. Maybe bitterness is taking root. I'm pretty sure she's shed a pound since morning. Before she can go into her exercise-is-good-for-you speech, I snatch the last bite of my cake.

"Any sign of our scaly friend out there?" I ask with a lighthearted laugh that could easily turn into a scream.

She chuckles and shakes her head. "I told you, they don't want to see you any more than you want to see them."

"You do realize I'm talking about the alligator, not our neighbor, right?" I ask.

"Ha, ha," she says.

A door squeaks open, and we look up to see Louise coming toward us. Her face is red, as in she maybe should have skipped the nap.

"Is everything all right?" I ask, which is just about as smart as the fitness instructor reminding us to breathe.

She shakes her head.

"No one is hurt, are they?" Lily asks.

"No." She sniffs and dabs at her nose with a hankie.

We all stare at Louise for a full minute before she says anything. She stares at the handkerchief she's twisting in her hands. "You know that Donald has recently made a new commitment in his walk with the Lord."

We smile and nod.

"I'm happy for him, I really am. He's gotten involved in a men's Bible study and prayer group in town, and as you know he's meeting with Gordon for accountability. I think that's great," Louise says, and I hear a "but" in there somewhere.

"Boy, I know I've never seen him so excited," Jill says with a smile.

"Gordon was talking about that just the other day, how great it was to see Donald getting involved." I'm wondering where this is all going. So far it sounds good. So why is she upset?

"There's no denying the huge change in him, that's for sure." Louise looks up at us here. "You'll probably think I'm horrible, but well, he's driving me crazy with all his enthusiasm."

We stare at her, waiting for more.

She blows out a breath. "It's just that I've been a Christian way longer than he has, and he's acting all superior and self-righteous." Her fingers twirl the end of the handkerchief. "I don't know, maybe

I'm just jealous that my passion isn't as fervent as his. I can practically hear him glowing over the phone."

I want to offer her a snack cake, but somehow the timing seems off. "Wish people would say that about me."

"They do, every time you have a hot flash," Lily says.

"Ha, ha."

"He'll come off the mountaintop soon enough, Louise. In the meantime, enjoy it. He's doing better than before," Lily says.

"Yeah, I know you're right. But if he checks one more time to make sure I'm reading my Bible, I'm going to bop him."

This little outburst of violence from Louise just makes my day.

"Guess I just needed to vent."

"I heard somewhere that venting is good for the soul," I say.

"I think that's 'Confession is good for the soul,' Maggie," Lily corrects me.

"Talk about your know-it-alls."

8

"Hey, babe," Gordon says in his chipper morning voice when I answer my cell phone.

"Hi," I answer sleepily. My eyes blink a couple of times, while I try to decide if I really want to open them. Reluctantly, I push myself up in bed.

"How's the trip going?" he asks.

"Hang on a sec. Give me a minute to figure out who I am, who's president, and how I know you."

"Uh-oh, you haven't had your morning coffee. Maybe I should call back."

"Ha, ha. I'm going to the other room where I can talk without waking Lily," I whisper. Slipping out from beneath the covers, I grab my robe and socks, then head to the lanai. "Almost there." Sliding open the patio doors, I close them behind me. Finally, I settle into a chair. "All right, I can talk now." After I pull on my socks, I hug my legs close to me on the chair. Why, I don't know. I won't be able to untangle them until it's time to go home.

"So what's going on with Lily? She still getting married?"

"Who knows? We haven't talked a lot about it yet. She usually changes the subject if we say too much."

"Captain's beside himself with worry. Ouch!"

"What's wrong?"

"Doggone that kid."

"What kid? The funny looking one we brought home from the hospital years ago?"

"That's the one. He leaves junk all over the house."

"Sounds like someone else I know," I say, referring to Gordon's habit of leaving piles of miscellaneous debris around the house. If I believed in reincarnation, which I don't, I'd say he was a squirrel in another life.

"Hey, my piles are orderly, thank you. This living room looks like a scene from *Jumanji*."

My stomach rolls. "This is not what I need to hear first thing in the morning."

"I think I broke the remote."

"It was on the floor?" I hear Gordon fiddling with the remote, turning the TV on and off. "Um, Gordon, I'm still here."

"Oh, right. Sorry. I think the remote is going to be all right."

"Just make sure Nick cleans the house before I get home."

"You'd better believe he'll clean it."

"You were saying, about Captain?"

"Oh yeah. Since he and Lily are hardly talking, he's been calling me almost every day to see if I've heard anything." Gordon pauses. "He's crazy about her."

Knowing he'll take good care of Lily and cherish her—if she gives him the chance—makes me want to do all that I can to help them stay together. "You still feel that way about me?"

"You know it, babe," Gordon says, turning my heart to mush.

"Do you think she loves him, Maggie?"

"I really do. I share some of Lily's concerns."

"Yeah, Captain mentioned that Tara was struggling with it all. I'm sure he doesn't know about Tara's phone call to Lily, though. Still, he also said Tara has her own life, and he wasn't going to let her run his."

"That's good news. But you know Lily, she won't come between him and his daughter."

Gordon sighs. "He says he thinks Tara's feeling replaced. She's pretty much doted on him since her mother died. She doesn't want another woman to move in and take over." He pauses a moment. "You women sure are complicated."

"Keeps you on your tocs."

"True enough." Gordon sighs.

"By the time we get through with Lily, she'll be running back to Captain's waiting arms no matter what Tara says."

Gordon chuckles. "Uh-oh. Anything in particular that you have in mind?"

A frustrated sigh escapes me. "Not really. Watching Jill's constant exercising is totally zapping me of my creativity. How do people live that way?"

"You'd better get out of there. It's not healthy," Gordon says with a chuckle.

"Don't I know it. Hey, what's up with Donald? Louise says he's driving her crazy with all his enthusiasm. Anything that you can tell me without breaking confidence?"

"They don't care if we talk to our wives—within reason. He's just got that new-commitment fire burning in him, you know?"

"Yeah," I say, vaguely remembering when I had the energy to get excited about something. Let's see, fifth birthday. New tricycle.

"Hey, are you keeping your stacks to a minimum?" I ask with a warning edge to my voice.

"It's the kid you need to worry about." Before I can work up an attitude he says, "But we'll try to have all the piles and debris cleaned up before you get home."

"Try?"

"Um, we'll have it cleaned."

"I should start calling you Rocky."

"Rocky?"

"You know, the squirrel, Bullwinkle's friend? Get it, squirrel, piles, hoarding?"

Silence.

"Nesting? Stowing away food for winter? Stacks?"

Silence.

"Never mind."

"Oh, I get it. Stacks, yeah," he says with a forced chuckle.

Gordon and I are from different worlds. That whole "Men are from Mars, Women are from Venus" thing.

"Listen, I'd better get to work. I'll call you later," he says.

"I love you."

"I love you, too. Try not to have too much fun without me. And stay out of trouble, what with Donny Osmond being there and all."

"Yeah, whatever," I say.

"Take care, Maggie girl," he says, making my heart flip the way he did in high school.

After we hang up, my mind lingers on the man who stole my heart so many years ago. It's beyond my comprehension how Lily has survived without Bob these past few years. At least now she has a second chance at happiness—if I can make her come to her senses.

Warm air seeps through the screened porch, and I watch our resident lizard crawl upon the rocks near the lake. He glances at me. I think we're bonding.

This place is a tropical paradise, rich with palm trees, lush foliage, and flowering shrubs. A couple of herons strut across the lawn as though to check out the tourists. I see no sign of Gator George, so

I'm comfortable for now. But if I start hearing the *Jaws* theme song, I'm outta here.

"Good morning."

I turn to see Louise holding two cups of coffee and waiting to get through the patio door. Quickly, I rush over to help her inside.

"This one is for you," she says, placing my coffee on the stand beside my chair.

"You're a doll. Thank you." We settle into our seats and take a sip from our mugs. "Did you sleep well?"

She shrugs and sits down. "Not great, but I'll survive."

"I've been meaning to ask you how Chad is doing," I say, referring to her twenty-five-year-old son.

A mother's pride takes over her expression. "Chad is doing well. Settling into the routine of military life at Fort Bragg and all that."

"Do you think he'll stay in the Army?" I ask.

Louise nods. "He really enjoys it. He's working his way up the ranks." A shadow flickers in her eyes. "Sure wish we could see him more often, though." This seems the perfect time to keep silent. Chad and his dad have never really gotten along.

"How are Heather and Josh doing?" she asks, changing the subject.

"Doing well. She still loves teaching second grade—well, right now she's off for the summer." I'm enjoying the hot coffee, morning nature sounds, conversation with a friend. What could be better?

"That's good. She's great with kids."

"Yeah."

"Is she coming to Lily's wedding"—Louise leans in toward me—"if there is one, I mean?"

"Yeah, they're coming. I can hardly wait to see her."

Beyond Louise, I see Jill stepping into the hallway. Clad in exercise shorts, she does a couple of squats, then jogs the five steps to the kitchen. Hey, even I could do that.

"Boy, Lily sure is sleeping in this morning," Louise says after craning her neck to see the clock on the living room wall.

"Yeah, I think all the mental strain is getting to her."

"Good morning, all," Jill says, joining us. "I'm going for my morning walk. Anybody want to go along?"

"I've already done my morning walk," I say.

Jill's head jerks to me in surprise. "You did?"

"I came out here, didn't I?"

"You're pathetic, Maggie," Jill says with a chuckle, shoving open the screen door.

"Yeah, I know. But I'm happy."

"Whatever. I'll be back in a little while," she says.

"Knock yourself out," I say.

Louise watches after Jill. "We need to fatten her up. You watch how she eats. She's not eating a whole lot at dinnertime especially. No snacking at night."

"That's so wrong. How can she live like that?"

Louise shrugs. "Hey, what's on the agenda today?"

"Somebody mentioned jet skiing. Though I'm not real excited about the idea."

"Oh, it will be fun. Look at it this way, Maggie. This trip is stretching you."

"Yeah. Just call me Gumby."

⑥ ∾ ⑥

"You want to drive the boat, Lily?" What teensy bit of courage I might have mustered on the way here disappears at the first sight of the Jet Ski bobbing around in the endless waters. I ask the question like I'm sacrificing to give her the privilege.

"Well, not if you really want to," she says.

"Oh, no, that's all right. I don't mind either way." I say, which isn't exactly how I feel, but I hate to make Lily do it. Excitement lights Lily's eyes. "Okay, I'll drive," she says with so much enthusiasm, I wonder if I should reconsider.

We settle up with the rental place—let me just point out the man behind the register has to practically pry my money from my hands.

I lean in toward him. "Do you need emergency contact numbers, you know, in the event of death or whatever?" I whisper to him.

He laughs and shakes his head. "You'll be fine." I don't miss the fact he says that while yanking the money from my hand.

"Did I mention my husband is a lawyer? Handles a lot of personal injury cases."

Lily walks up behind me. "Come on, Maggie." She pulls me by the arm.

"Just thought you'd like to know," I call over my shoulder. There's no mistaking the threat in my voice, but I don't care.

We head for our machines. The stench of mildew is strong as I shrug on the yellow and black life jacket. Not exactly Chanel No. 5. We climb aboard our personal watercraft, and Louise takes pictures of everyone before we take off.

Amid the hum of the engines, the tour guide gives us a bit of orientation. Seems harmless enough. Squeeze the handle, you accelerate; let go, you stop. Even I can do that. The man whose name tag says "Doug" tells those who are driving to allow for about three to four hundred feet stopping distance. Good thing Gordon isn't driving. He's still trying to break his old record of stopping within five inches of the car in front of us.

Doug tells us to respect the machine, stay with the group, and we will be fine.

I believe him. It's Lily I'm not too sure about.

Our personal watercrafts bob in the water as fresh waves spill toward the shore. Doug says he will be taking us off the beaten path to places where dolphins and manatees play in quiet waters. Sounds nice and relaxing. I could use that today. My nerves have been a little frazzled lately, what with Lily's indecision about the wedding, Louise's frustration with Donald, and then Jill flirting with danger, well, I just don't have all the answers, that's all.

Doug gives the signal and the other machines pitch forward leaving us behind. Lily fumbles with her key a moment and then grips the handle. With a squeeze, our machine lurches then slows. Lurch, slow, lurch, slow.

Can you say *whiplash*?

"Lily, what's the matter?" I call over her shoulder.

"I'm just trying to get used to this machine," she yells, clearly frustrated.

Jill and Louise are disappearing before our eyes, leaving only a wake behind. Lily steers to the right of the wake and instead of enjoying a nice smooth ride in the center of it, we're jumping waves. "Surfin' USA" is playing in my mind and that normally makes me feel better, but it's not working for me today.

A wave slaps against us, drenching us from head to toe. The rest of the group is barely visible. The water is cool and since I'm having a hot flash, I'm not minding this so much, though the idea of drowning bothers me.

This machine is bucking like a bronco in a rodeo while visions of my life with Gordon and the kids flicker before my eyes. Lily's scream crescendos through the misty air, and we're attacked by another wave.

Just then I hear a sort of laugh. Between heaving gulps of air, I struggle to listen. Another laugh. Actually, more of a guffaw. And it's coming from Lily Newgent!

With the wind in her face, sun on her shoulders, and stringy wet hair flapping in the breeze, Lily seizes the moment. I'm speechless. Of course, I have no choice. The saltwater spray and Lily's daredevil stunts have sucked the air from my lungs.

I'm not certain, but I'm pretty sure I hear a "Yee-haw" shout, and suddenly I'm convinced Lily is going through a midlife crisis. This whole ride seems so surreal, I think I'm having an out-of-body experience.

Just then, without warning, Lily takes a sharp left, trying her best to do a 360-degree turn. My voice shrieks through the air and the next thing I know, I'm sloshing and kicking around in the water, my life jacket the only thing holding me up.

"Lily," I scream, but she doesn't hear me. Panic slashes through me as I consider the fact that she might leave. Tomorrow's headline will read, *Friend Drowns in Menopausal Madness!* Another woman will take my place as Gordon's wife.

Okay, that thought alone sets me to kicking and screaming with a vengeance. No one is taking my place just yet, doggone it.

Finally, Lily turns and sees me, her face resembling the color of the white sand on Crescent Beach.

She turns the machine around and angles over. "Maggie, what are you doing?"

"I was hot and thought I'd take a swim," I say sarcastically. "What do you think I was doing, for crying out loud?"

"I'm so sorry," she says, reaching out her hand. It's then that I notice the change in her expression. It goes from worry to—do my eyes deceive me?—amusement!

"I'm glad you think this is so funny," I grumble, grabbing her hand and trying to pull myself up.

"I'm sorry, Maggie, it's just that—"

Her words are forever lost because right then *she* slips and falls into the water with me. Once I see that she's all right, we both break out into a full fit of laughter.

"Now how are we going to get back on that thing?" We both look over to see our watercraft bobbing nearby.

"I'm just thankful they attach the keys with a string to the driver so that drivers aren't stranded when this happens," Lily says.

We edge over to the machine and try to pull ourselves up. My arm muscles just ain't what they used to be. Lily's in the same boat, so to speak.

"Guess we should have listened to Jill about all that exercise stuff, huh?" she says.

"I'm not gladiator woman, so shoot me."

"Well, you have to admit, Maggie, strong arms might benefit us right now."

"Who knew?"

Fortunately, we don't have long to languish in our misery. Our fearless leader comes back to us.

"Did you have a problem with your machine?" he asks, looking worried.

"No, just the driver," I mumble under my breath.

Lily tries to hit me but splashes the water instead.

Doug edges his machine over to us and tells us how to get back up onto the watercraft. I'm tempted to ask him if I can ride with him, but figure I'd hurt Lily's feelings.

Once we're back in place, we see the other machines bob as a group in the water.

Okay, this is embarrassing.

"If you have any more problems, let me know. I need you to keep up with the rest of the group," he says before speeding off.

"We'll keep up. I've got it figured out now." Lily mimics an obedient child.

I want to call out, *Don't believe her! It's a cover-up. She's wild, I tell you. Wild!*

"Hey, Maggie, let up on my stomach, will ya? You're clutching so hard, I'm gonna get a hernia."

"You're worried about a hernia. I'm worried about drowning. We're even," I say.

"All right, all right. I'll slow down. What happened to Miss Adventure?"

"Forget the adventure. I choose life."

We pull up to the others, and they look a little miffed that we're holding them up. Tucked discretely behind Lily, I point to her, give the crazy sign, and shrug. The others smile and nod.

Doug takes us to some quiet alcoves where he tells us to cut the engines and wait—that we're sure to see some dolphins at play. For a moment I'm wondering if this is anything like waiting for chickens to hatch, but in no time at all, two dolphins appear above the water's surface. They jump and dive, showing off their dorsal fins. I'm almost sure Esther Williams will burst through the water at any moment.

She doesn't, doggone it.

We venture further, spotting a manatee here and there, passing beautiful beach homes and resorts, watching pelicans and osprey that are resting along the shoreline.

Our last stop takes us to an alcove of turquoise water where people sometimes scuba dive, though no one is here now. We pull up to the sandbar and stroll the beach for a few minutes. The sand is a soft blanket beneath my feet. A warm, sudsy tide rushes upon my feet and wipes clean the footprints behind me. Assorted shells catch my attention. I reach for them, dust off the sand, and dip them in water until they shine. My chin lifts to catch the salt-laden breeze, and I'm in heaven.

All too soon we go back to our machines where we started.

The afternoon passes far too soon, and I truly enjoyed myself. Lily handled the watercraft fairly well once she got the hang of it. Still, I'm thankful to have my feet on solid ground.

By the slight tinge of green on Jill's face, I'm thinking she's glad, too.

9

The server from Ophelia's on the Bay ushers us to the back patio that offers a tropical view of Little Sarasota Bay, complete with mangroves, palm trees, and seagulls. Louise and I grab our cameras and take some pictures.

After the server fills our water glasses and takes our drink orders, she snaps a picture of the four of us scrunched together at our table.

The environment begs for propriety, so with my pinkie extended, I lift my water glass toward my lips and take a drink.

"An elegant restaurant and I order water with lemon. How boring is that?" I say.

"Water is good for you," Jill says. "People truly have no idea how important it is to watch what they put into their bodies."

My eyelids flutter as I force my eyes not to roll back in my head. All this talk about healthy food makes me feel transported back to my eighth grade home economics class.

"I'm sorry to go on about this. I just feel so passionate to get the word out to people about the importance of eating right," Jill says.

Shall I mention that Miss Health still looks a little green? Probably from all that talk of spinach, broccoli, and brussel sprouts. My teeth clamp firm, holding my tongue in place.

"You're absolutely right, Jill," Louise encourages. The thought of kicking her under the table occurs to me, but I rebuke it. "After my dad developed diabetes, he totally changed his diet, per his doctor's instructions. Made all the difference in his quality of life. He's doing great to this day."

"Okay, I get the idea. I'll pass up the chocolate cake tonight," I say with bitterness.

Jill laughs. "You don't have to do that. Just make little changes here and there, Maggie. Eventually, you'll get there. If you do that now, it may save you from being forced into an abrupt change in diet later on in life."

There's a lot of wisdom in what she says, but do I want to hear this now just before we order from this fabulous menu? No. I stare at my menu and throw caution to the wind.

"Girls, let me get us an appetizer. They have jumbo lump blue crab cake," Louise says, licking her lips.

I'm not a seafood lover, but since it has the word *cake* in it, I figure it can't be too bad.

We place our orders with the server then I turn to Lily. "When you talked to Tara about coming tonight, did she say she would?"

"She didn't commit one way or the other." Lily cranes her neck to see inside the restaurant. "Who knows?" Sadness flickers in her eyes. I can't imagine anyone not loving Lily.

Before long we eat our way through the appetizer—well, the others do. I've learned something tonight. Just because the word *cake* is in something, doesn't mean that it's sweet.

"Sorry I'm late," a voice calls out, causing us to turn.

"Tara, I'm so glad you could come!" Lily says, pushing her chair out so she can rush over to Tara and give her a hug. Tara's arms barely brush against Lily in the so-called hug. The young woman towers over Lily. A plethora of blonde hair drapes over her shoulders like a warm scarf. That family does not lack for hair, I'll give them that. Tara has a kind face and friendly gray-blue eyes—at least when they're turned toward us. It's hard to imagine her being so mean to Lily. One glance at Tara's stomach, and I'm praying we don't have to deliver a baby tonight. The word ripe comes to mind.

Lily makes the necessary introductions, and Tara places her order with the server.

"I'm so glad you were able to join us," Lily says, eyes sparkling. There's no doubt in my mind she really wants this to work.

"Well, Matt was meeting a friend, so it worked out," Tara says, her nose tipping upward. She settles into her chair. "Besides, Dad would have a fit if I didn't make the effort." Nice of her to point out that she's doing it for her dad and definitely not Lily.

The Latte Girls exchange glances, each of us, no doubt, wanting to bop Captain's daughter. Just wait 'til she has children of her own. She'll find out life isn't always so easy.

The thing is, Captain and Lily are old enough to do what they want, no matter what the "children" think. But since Lily never had children of her own—though she desperately wanted them—I know she would never knowingly cause trouble in a family. Seeing Lily and Tara together makes me think this very well could be enough to keep Lily from getting married.

"So do you have a name picked out for your baby?" Louise asks.

Tara brightens. "Yeah, we're naming her Brenda after my mom." Her pointed gaze turns to Lily, then flits off again.

"That's nice," Louise says.

Lily drops her fork and asks the waiter for a new one. An awkward silence follows.

"So how's the vacation?" Tara asks, keeping her gaze fixed on everyone but Lily.

We talk excitedly about what we've been doing, but I can't get past the hurt on Lily's face. If there's anyone I know who deserves happiness, it's Lily. It takes everything in me not to give Tara a piece of my mind.

Our server removes our soiled appetizer dishes and fills our table with plates of gray sole, wild king salmon, filet mignon (for me), and shrimp scampi.

I lift my nose. "Mmm, take a whiff of that," I say. A tangy scent lifts from our table, and we all linger there a moment.

Jill says the blessing, and we dive into our meals.

"This is absolutely wonderful," Lily says. "The food, the atmosphere, the fellowship, everything."

"Dad loved to bring Mom here. It is one of their favorite places—well, it was," she says, her sad eyes trying to move us to compassion. It's not working for me. The only thing I want to move is my tongue to give her a good lashing for making Lily uncomfortable. "I'm sure it holds lots of memories for him," Tara warns as though Lily should never bring him here. Her lips lift in a smirk and my blood pressure skyrockets.

Who cares if they come here or not? It's not as though they're going to be in Florida all that often—especially if Tara plans to make it rough on them.

"We don't have this in Charming, but we have some pretty glitzy restaurants in Rosetown. In fact, Captain—Ron—has already taken Lily to a couple of those." Okay, I'm acting as childish as Tara, but I'm struggling to stop myself. I take an ambitious bite of the filet mignon and chew forcefully, almost forgetting to enjoy the taste. Almost.

"Oh, look!" Lily says, pointing, "There's a dolphin!" She's squealing like a kid who's never seen a dolphin before. The others gaze at the dolphin while I study Lily. That dolphin offered a quick change of subject. Blended families are never easy.

I sure hope Lily is up to the challenge.

"Hey, he looks like—" The man who I thought was Donny Osmond turns around and he's, well, not him. Lily and Louise look at me. "Never mind."

◯ ∞ ◯

We push our cart through the grocery store, where we've decided to stop on our way back to the condo. Bananas, apples, grapes, and oranges line the cart. That's how you know when you're old. Instead of grabbing cartfuls of junk food, you come home with fruit.

"I'm sorry, but your future soon-to-be stepdaughter is a piece of work, Lily," Jill says, placing some yogurt in the cart.

"This isn't easy on her," Lily says.

"Oh come on. She's not ten. She's a grown woman and should know better." I slip a half gallon of chocolate chip ice cream into the cart. Jill's eyebrows raise, and I shove the ice cream under the fruit.

"I suppose," Lily says.

Louise crooks her arm through Lily's right arm, and I do the same with her left arm, as we stroll through the aisle. "Don't you worry, Lil. No one can know you for very long without loving you."

Jill stops the cart, and they all stare at me.

"This sappy little moment brought to you by Maggie Hayden."

They laugh and we move on. I'm cheap entertainment.

"Thanks, Maggie," she says.

We continue our shopping, saying very little, and finally climb back into the car.

"I'm totally stuffed," Lily says on our way back to the condo.

"Must have been that key lime pie you had," I say. I lean in and whisper to her, "I wanted the chocolate truffle cake but Jill made me feel guilty. I say we ditch her tomorrow and go back for the cake."

"I heard that," Jill says.

86

I shrug.

"You'll thank me one day, Maggie," she says.

"It's just not coming to me yet, but maybe one day. I'd rather put your theory to practice when I can no longer taste or smell. Would that work?"

Spoilsport that she is, Jill shakes her head. "It will be too late by then."

"You know what they say, Jill. If the ladies on the *Titanic* had known what was going to happen, they wouldn't have passed up dessert the night before the disaster." I've got her there.

"Well, it's a gamble, Maggie. If you want to test the odds, go for it."

Doggone it, why did she have to go and put it that way? I don't want to talk about it anymore. Sheesh, can't even enjoy a good hot dog these days.

We pull up to the condo, climb out of the car with the groceries in hand, and step inside the door of our building.

"Oh, that smells good," Lily says, when we are greeted by the smell of cinnamon from a nearby plug-in when we walk into the condo. It's the same kind that I use back home. It makes me miss Gordon.

I pull the fruit from the grocery bag. "Oh, dear, we forgot to buy pea—"

"Don't you dare say it, Maggie Lynn!" Lily stops me midspeech, and I grin. She can't stand the mention of peaches. Why, I don't know, but I love to throw the word around just to creep her out. I'm kind of cruel that way.

After stowing away the groceries, I ask if anyone wants decaf coffee.

Everyone but Miss Healthy Choice wants some. She doesn't even want tea. To make matters worse, I'm in the living room and can see her exercising in her bedroom. I wish she'd close her door.

"I'll bring out my manicure set and if any of you wants to fix your nails, you're welcome to use my product," Louise says.

First they try to make me eat right. Now they want me to have nice nails, too? Thankfully, I've had a recent manicure, so my nails aren't horrible. Still, they could stand a touch up.

Once the coffee is made, we fill our cups and settle in at the kitchen table where Louise sets out her nail colors and assorted accessories for the making of a good manicure.

"Are you all right, Jill?" I ask, noticing she still doesn't look quite right. Could be all that exercise.

She sighs and hesitates. "I didn't really want to mention this. We're here to have fun." She's filing the index finger on her right hand with such a vengeance, I'm afraid she'll whittle it down to a stub.

Lily sorts through the nail colors and finally decides on a flamingo shade of pink. She's probably caught up in the Florida thing and all.

"Well, I don't know if you read about it in the paper, but the school corporation is restructuring. The building where I have taught the last twenty-three years is going to hold third, fourth, and fifth graders next year."

"So you'll have to move to another building?" I ask before carefully sipping from my coffee cup. A bright red polish captures my attention, and I reach for it. It's not all that different from what I have on.

"Right. Since I teach first grade, I'll have to go to the building for kindergarten through second grade." She's buffing the top of her nail with a little more ease than she did the filing.

"Why does that bother you?" Louise asks. She's chosen a coral polish and puts it on with all the skill of an artist.

Jill looks up. "I guess it's the idea of changing. I've been in the same classroom all these years, worked with a lot of the same people. My principal is the best in the system."

It seems none of us enjoys change. Here I thought my struggle with change was an age issue.

"What are you going to do?" I ask, globbing polish past the sides of my nails. "I was never good at coloring within the lines," I say with a chuckle when I look up and see Louise staring at my blotched fingers.

"There's not much I can do. If I want a job, I have to move buildings. Period." Tears fill her eyes.

While I study Jill, it strikes as odd that nerves could make a person's skin tone turn that way. It seems to me that whole health kick thing just isn't working for her—or maybe there's more going on here than she's letting on. I can't figure it out. "Life is full of adjustments, right? I mean, hello? I have a boomerang kid." I know I should be more sensitive and not joke at times like this, but I just can't take the tension.

"Maybe you'll find out that it's better than what you thought it would be," Louise, ever the encourager, says.

We sit in silence for a moment.

"You're not trying to lose weight, are you, Jill?" Lily asks.

"No, why?"

"I just notice you haven't eaten a lot while we've been here, and you look as though you've lost a little weight."

The pale shade of beige leaves Jill's face, turning her skin to a milky white.

Lily and I glance at each other.

"Is it because of your concern over the school situation?" I ask.

"I don't know. I just haven't felt good in a while. Food doesn't appeal to me, especially in the evening. I'm tired all the time." She stops polishing and looks at me. "I think there's something wrong with me."

"Maybe you have a flu bug," I suggest.

She shakes her head. "I've been this way for a little while."

"It's probably nothing," Louise says. "All these airborne viruses floating around these days, it's a wonder all of us aren't sick." She finishes her second coat and screws the cap back on the polish.

"My hormones are crazy, too. It's as though I'm a teenager again."

"Uh-oh, you may be entering the perimenopause phase, Jill," I say, sitting straighter in my chair.

"Oh, talk to Maggie about it. She's the resident expert when it comes to menopause symptoms," Lily says with a chuckle.

"Yeah, I wondered if that might be what it was, too," Jill says.

"Well, if anyone can get you through it, Maggie can," Louise says.

I don't know whether to be proud or hide in a hole. I mean, Menopause Expert? What kind of title is that?

"There are some good supplements out there to help with those symptoms, too," Lily says, and I'm wondering how I can make an escape before she dives into her supplement speech. "But then you know all about that." Lily and Jill share a glance that says they understand each other.

"Well, I'm sorry you're not feeling well, Jill. If we can do anything to help you, let us know," I say, tossing up a quick prayer for her.

"I'm sure it's nothing," Jill says, perk back in place. "You know, a banana sounds good to me right about now." Jill rises from her seat. "Anyone else want one?"

Louise does.

Jill does look a little thinner than usual. But then she reaches for bananas and yogurt while I reach for chocolate chip ice cream. Still, I hope she's all right . . .

10

"It's another beautiful day," Lily says in an irritating sing-song voice.

"I wouldn't know," I grouse, pulling my pillow over my head.

"Oh come on, Maggie, let's go get our coffee and head for the lanai. You can sleep back in Charming."

"Throw in some chocolate, and you're on," I say, pulling the pillow from my face.

"At seven o'clock in the morning?"

I shrug. "Oh, all right. Skip the chocolate."

We make our way to the kitchen, quietly prepare our coffee, fill our mugs, then head for our chairs.

With sunlight barely peeking into the porch, Lily flips on the light. No sooner does she do that than I hear something stir just outside. I turn to look and right next to our screened-in window is Gator George!

My breath catches in my throat.

"Don't move," Lily says, fumbling with the latch on the patio door.

Oh sure. She's backing out of the room and telling me not to move.

The alligator's head lifts. He takes one look at me and saunters away toward the lake. Well, that's a little harsh.

It's only after he's far enough away that we can safely move without fear of him breaking in to swallow us whole that we race through the patio door into the condo and close the door firmly behind us. Lily rushes over, grabs her camera, and takes a shot of his scaly backside.

"What's up with you two?" Jill asks.

Whoa, Jill's got that bed head thing going on. Spiked hair going every which way. Reminds me of those scary things that poke out of old potatoes. If only I could take her picture. She'd get bitter about it, though. I'm sure of it. Then she'd resort to vengeance, and I'd have to hide from her for the rest of our vacation. It's just not worth it.

We tell her of our morning visitor. She laughs. Maybe I will take that picture. "I'm telling you, he's too old to care. Just stay clear of him."

"And you feel the need to tell us that, why?" I ask.

She ignores me and grabs some tea. We follow her into the kitchen for breakfast.

Louise joins us for our morning chat, opting for orange juice. With attitude I pour boring cereal into my bowl, hoping all the while Louise will have mercy on us. She settles into her chair without so much as a twitch of insight.

"So, Maggie, where are your parents these days?" Louise asks.

"Last week they were in Montana. My dad was in the service with a guy who lives there. They visit them every year."

"It's amazing how active they are at their age," Jill says.

"And you're wondering how they ended up with a daughter like me?" Boring cereal and an attack on my person? Things are getting ugly.

Jill laughs. "No reflection on you, Maggie. I just think it's cool that they're enjoying life."

Something is so not right with this picture. Mom and Dad are having the time of their lives traveling the countryside in their RV while Gordon and I spend our life savings on pizza for our offspring.

Our discussion turns to our parents and the high cost of health care. After we solve the world's problems, Louise changes the subject.

"So what are we doing today?"

"I don't know how you all feel about it, but I was really hoping we could go parasailing. Jeff and I went once and it was a blast," Miss Forty-five-year-old says. She must be feeling a lot better this morning. "Course that was before he became a workaholic."

Lily's gaze collides with my own. She looks up for it about as much as I do.

"Sounds fun," Louise says before taking a drink of orange juice from her glass.

"Great. Lily, Maggie?"

Lily looks to me. "That's fine," I say with more enthusiasm than I feel.

Lily nods reluctantly.

I'm not hoping for a hurricane, mind you, but if Florida's got to have one, today might be good.

Jill seems satisfied with that and runs into the kitchen to grab an orange then rejoins us. "I haven't had one of these in forever," she says, rolling the orange on the table and finally peeling it in one piece. That takes real talent. I've never been able to do it.

Jill shoves a slice into her mouth and props her feet up on the chair, hugging her legs next to her.

We talk a little longer when Jill's cell phone rings.

"Hi, Jeff," she says, going into the bedroom for some privacy while the rest of us continue talking about nothing in particular.

When I edge my way to the kitchen for a glass of water, I hear Jill complaining to Jeff about him working too much. I feel her pain.

Soon Jill pokes her head out of her bedroom door. "I'm going to shower now. We need to get signed up for the parasailing if we want to try it today." She sounds chipper, but there seems to be sadness in her eyes. Maybe I'm just imagining it. Hopefully, everything is all right back home.

Louise, Lily, and I gather our mugs, stack them in the dishwasher, and head to our rooms to get ready for parasailing.

Maybe I should call Gordon to update our wills.

⑤ ✍ ⑥

"Is something wrong?" Louise asks Jill while she's driving to Bradenton where we will try our hands at parasailing.

"For some reason, I just can't stop scratching," she says.

"Might be all this hot weather. Dries a person out," Lily says. "Better put some lotion on before you try parasailing."

Louise digs in her purse and pulls out some lotion. "Here. This stuff is great for dry skin."

Louise squeezes a glob into Jill's palm. Jill carefully rubs it in while driving. I'm praying her hands don't slide off the steering wheel.

She's itching, my stomach is churning. Something tells me we should turn around and go back to Siesta Key. Now.

The ride to Bradenton is fairly uneventful, and I must admit my stomach has calmed down a little. With our life vests on, we step up to the back of the boat. The air whips around us. A tangy scent lifts on the warm breeze and a light mist from the Gulf sprays my face. Some big burly guy who reminds me of Brutus on *Popeye* tells us to climb into the harness, then he hooks us into the parasail. It's at that point I hear another lady say, "I'm not getting on there. Didn't you hear about that couple who died in an accident last year on one of these things?"

My eyes lock with Lily's.

"Don't worry, we'll be fine," she says with a smile. But her eyes tell me not to believe a word of it.

Brutus tells us we'll be flying at a maximum altitude of about two hundred twenty-five feet. I could have gone all day without knowing that.

The boat idles out until the towline is taut and extended. The crew holds up the sides of the canopy and someone hollers, "Hit it!"

A ripple of panic—okay, a huge wave of panic—rolls through me. Per instructions, Lily and I resist the pull to keep the line tight and maintain our balance. It takes three steps before we lift off. The crumpled parasail canopy balloons into a vibrant display of reds, whites, and blues as the boat gains speed. My heart zips to my throat and takes up residence. As in, it's not moving back down into my chest anytime soon. Lily laughs with the thrill of it all, and I want to hurl.

As we rise higher and higher, I attempt to get comfortable in the harness—which, by the way, is just not happening.

"I'll probably get a nosebleed," I shout over the wind to Lily, my legs flailing about. If Louise or Jill takes a picture of me just now, I'll hire a hit man to get it back.

"You'll be fine," she says, her face all aglow, eyes sparkling.

"Do we need oxygen?" I practically shriek. "At what point does oxygen cut off?"

"You don't need oxygen. A sack perhaps for hyperventilating, but definitely not oxygen."

When did Lily and I switch places? She's becoming adventurous, and I'm totally not.

"Show my future grandchildren my picture and talk of me often, okay? Oh, and I bequeath my vacuum to Nick."

"Cut it out, Maggie. You'll be fine."

"Tell Gordon I love him and to stay away from Thelma Waters. She's trouble and only wants his money."

"Maggie Lynn Hayden."

"She has no patience with dogs, so Crusher would be dumped at an obedience school in Europe."

"Maggie!"

"With three teeth and a bladder control problem, that's just not right."

"Maggie, stop talking and look around you. Have you ever seen a more breathtaking view?"

"If I wanted to be an astronaut, I would have gone to school for it." I swallow hard and dare to turn my head to take in the sweeping view of the Gulf of Mexico.

The parasail reaches the nosebleed altitude and stays there. Our legs dangle like worms on a fishing pole.

"Over there is Anna Maria Island," Lily says, pointing with gusto.

"Don't wiggle. You'll shake us loose."

She frowns. "Oh my goodness, Maggie, look, there's a sea turtle."

"See any alligators?"

"Look at the dolphins, Maggie!"

Squinting more from fear than sunlight, I dare to look down and see a big old sea turtle slug his way toward the isolated shoreline. His slow pace makes me think of Crusher—and, well, me.

"Do you see the dolphins?" Lily's squealing like a kid and making me a nervous wreck with her squirming around.

"I see." In the distance two dolphins play and splash about the waves.

"And there are some pelicans."

I nod. "Look at that bird." Right then we see an egret snatch a fish from the water. "Yum, an afternoon snack," I say with a nervous chuckle. Okay, I'm getting into this a little.

"Do you notice how the colors are more vibrant from up here?" Lily says. "Look at those palm and banyan trees. Don't they look so green? And the sky, Maggie, I think I could reach out and touch a cloud."

"Please don't." My nerves settle down, or maybe Lily's getting through to me with the way she's viewing all this with wide-eyed wonder. She's in love, no doubt about it. I'm in love too, but I was born with a heavy dose of realism.

Just when I think I could get into this, the boat slows, and we start drifting downward. I can handle that. The boat finally stops completely, and the boat crew reels us in to the back of the boat with their towrope. They playfully dip our feet a couple of times into the warm salty water before pulling us onto the back of the boat. We unhook from the chute, and the boat crew assists us in getting onto the dock at the beach.

"Oh my goodness, Maggie, you were hilarious," Louise says. "Your legs were—"

"Did you take a picture?" I cut her off.

She blinks. "What? Um, no. I should have," she says, with a snap of her fingers.

"No, you shouldn't have."

Before we can argue further, it's Louise and Jill's turn. Lily and I snap a picture of them during their ride—yeah, we're just that kind of friends—and soon we're all talking a mile a minute as we head back to the car.

"That was fabulous," Lily says.

"Wasn't it? I haven't had that much fun in I don't know how long," Louise says. "How about you, Maggie? Did you like it?"

"You know, I did."

"You sound surprised," Louise says.

"I am. I'm not crazy about heights, so I thought I would freak, but Lily helped me to enjoy it." I turn to Lily, and we exchange a smile. "How about you, Jill, did you have a good time?"

She scratches her arm. "My stomach was a little upset, but it was beautiful. I'm glad we went."

"You still itching?" I ask, which is a dumb question, by the way, because she's digging at her arm with the determination of an archaeologist at an excavation site.

"I'm fine," she says, but I'm beginning to wonder if she has fleas.

We climb into the car. "You know, my feet are all yucky, what do you girls think about getting a pedicure? We passed a place in Siesta Key that said no appointment necessary," Louise says.

"I'm up for it," Lily says. I try not to gape at her.

"What?" she asks.

"Where did all this enthusiasm come from?"

"I'm having fun."

I'm beginning to think Lily is Odie and I'm Garfield. The truth is when Lily is dealing with a problem she tends to put the matter on a shelf and throws herself into projects—in this case, having fun. She's doing a good job, I might add.

Louise explains to Jill how to get to the Hand and Foot Spa. We soon arrive and step inside. They have four stations and we've caught them at a good time. The last customer is drying her fingernails, so the pedicure spots are free.

A pretty woman in her early twenties with short dark hair takes us to our chairs, and we climb on board.

"I have the ugliest toes known to mankind, Lily."

"You're not going to start with that ingrown-toenail-surgery-when-you-were-in-eighth-grade story again, are you?"

"You're all compassion, Lily." Forget the Odie thing.

"I've seen your toes, Maggie, and they're fine. A little bumpy, but fine."

"You see there. That's what I mean. They are bumpy. Right where the surgeon cut into my toes. He has no idea the pain and suffering he has caused me."

"Got rid of your ingrown toenails, though."

"Did I ever tell you there was a cute junior high boy that was waiting in the hallway when they wheeled me outside of my room, big bandages wrapped mummy-style around my toes which were, by the way, sticking out from under my covers?"

"A few hundred times."

"It scarred me for life."

"I can see that."

Just then a young man comes over to where I'm sitting, smiles, and lifts my feet into the small tub.

"Lily, I don't want a man to wash my feet," I say, in a strained whisper.

"Maggie, he doesn't care about your toes. He sees a hundred of them a day." One look at my face and she corrects herself. "I forgot. Yours are special."

"They're bumpy. You said so yourself."

"He doesn't care, Maggie. You're old enough to be his mother." Right after Lily says this, her hand flies to her mouth. "I didn't mean—"

"I know exactly what you mean," I say. "You think I'm old."

"Don't start with the old paranoia again, please, Maggie. I can't take it."

"You think you can't take it. I'm old, and I have bumpy toes, Lily. Does that mean nothing to you?"

"I'm sorry, Maggie."

The young man lifts my feet out of the water and starts whacking at the dead skin on my heels.

"You think we ought to offer him an ice pick?" Lily says smothering a laugh behind her hand.

"Oh, that's cute. So I have cracked heels. I can think of worse things."

"Like bumpy toes?" Lily's giggling out loud now.

The man whispers something to the person working on Lily's feet. Then he laughs.

"They're talking about me, I just know it," I say.

"It's the bumpy toes. They've never seen anything like it."

"Now cut that out." I'm getting an attitude.

"What are you laughing about, Lily?" Louise, who is sitting in the other chair beside Lily, wants to know.

"Don't you dare tell her," I growl. It's humiliating enough that Lily and Gordon know about my toes. Now this strange young man knows about my toes. Do we need to point it out to Louise and Jill? I think not.

"You know I'm kidding you," Lily says. She makes a comment that seems to satisfy Louise, then turns back to me.

"I know," I say and grin in spite of myself. "You really are having a good time, aren't you, Lily?" I'll do anything to get the conversation away from my toes.

"The best. I think I really needed to get away."

"Any more insight about the wedding?"

"I'm still not sure, Maggie. I'm just trying to concentrate on having a good time with my friends. Maybe we would be better off just to postpone the wedding for a little while. To be sure, I mean."

"Well, what's that my mother used to always tell us when we were kids?"

"When in doubt, don't," we say in unison then laugh.

"Still, it's not without risk. I mean, Captain is a good-looking man and if you wait too long, well, there are always women ready and waiting." That kind of talk always gets to a woman.

"Speaking of which, how is Celine Loveland?" I hate it when Lily uses my own psychology back on me.

"Gordon's paralegal?"

Lily nods.

"I didn't tell you the news? She gave her notice last week. She found out she's pregnant and plans to work up until a month before the baby is due."

"Oh, that's great. I'm so happy for her and her husband. Do you remember how jealous you were of her?"

"I was not jealous." Just then Pedicure Man burrows into my toenail like Indiana Jones on a dig. I consider thwacking him upside the head, but there's that little matter of him still holding my foot.

"You were too jealous, Maggie Hayden."

"Well, okay, maybe a little." Between Lily's reminder of my shortcomings and Pedicure Man sawing on my toenails like a lumberjack on a redwood, I'm getting a tad irritated.

"I'm just glad your hormones are under control. That's helped a lot. Well, that and the fact that Debra Stiffler got back with her husband. You were worried about her, too, if I remember correctly."

Well, thank you for pointing that out.

"In fact, anyone under a size ten was suspect in your mind."

"Lily, I'm not running for election. You do not have to dig up all my dirt." Besides, Pedicure Man is doing that for you.

She giggles. "Okay, okay."

By the time the young man finishes whacking, filing, scrubbing, and cleaning my feet, I'm surprised I have any nails left. Shoot, I'm lucky to have toes. He tells me to pick out a nail color, and I go with my usual cherry red. After sticking spongy separators between my toes, he quickly and expertly paints my nails then points to another station where I'm to have my manicure done. I waddle to the next place while Lily laughs at me.

The four of us primp and laugh our way through the next hour or so and are soon on our way back to the condo. Jill is driving, but her scratching is getting on my nerves.

"Maybe we should stop and get you some Benadryl," I say. "Are you sure you're all right?"

"I'm fine," she snaps.

Something tells me she just might be in that perimenopause stage of life.

Louise looks over at Jill. "I don't know, Jill. You've got some funny little bumps on your face."

We pull up to a stoplight. Jill looks in the mirror and gasps.

"What is it?" Lily asks. We're in the backseat, and we can't see her.

She turns to us. With one look at her red puffy face, we all gasp. "Pull over in that gas station," I say. "We'll ask for directions to the hospital. You're having some kind of allergic reaction."

"Trust Maggie on this one," Lily says. "She's been through it," referring to the time I had an allergic reaction to wrinkle cream.

Jill pulls over. The station attendant gives us directions, and we're soon at the hospital.

"What do you think it is?" Lily asks once we sit down in the waiting area and Jill is hauled off to see a doctor.

"It could be an allergic reaction to something she ate or maybe even sun poisoning," I say.

"Yeah, I thought of that, too," Louise says, looking worried.

"I'm sure it's no big deal," Lily says. "Just a little skin rash."

We read through magazines and say very little while we wait for Jill. Finally, she comes down the hall to join us. The look on her face tells us it's worse than we thought. When she gets closer, we see the tears making wet tracks down her cheeks.

"Everything all right, Jill?" Louise asks.

"I have an allergy to oranges."

For this she is crying? Chocolate, I can understand. Oranges, no. She wipes her nose on a tissue from her purse.

"Jill, that's not the end of the world. There's always apples, bananas, grapes, grapefruit, papayas. The sky's the limit!" I encourage.

"You don't understand."

Work with me here, I'm doing the best I can. Allergic to oranges? I'm just not moved to tears.

"I'm forty-five years old, and I'm—I'm pregnant."

Excuse me, but I think I'm beginning to understand why God throws us into menopause at middle age.

The only thing worse than me in menopause would be me pregnant when I *should be* in menopause.

11

"Thanks for coming here, girls. I've been craving a Frosty like nobody's business," Jill says, scratching her arm and trying to recover from the shock as we squeak across the plastic seats at our booth at a Wendy's in Sarasota.

"This from Miss Healthy Choice?" I say with a wink.

"I admit it. This isn't exactly the best thing for me to eat, but if I don't get a Frosty, someone will pay," Jill says with a laugh.

"She's pregnant, all right," Louise says. "Just remember, you're allowed three hundred extra calories a day when you're pregnant, but you don't want them all to satisfy the sweet tooth or baby will take your nutrition and leave you with the fat."

We all stare at Louise.

"What?"

"Who made you the pregnancy expert?" I ask.

She shrugs. "I volunteer from time to time at the Crisis Pregnancy Center."

"Well, stop it," I say.

Louise gasps.

"I'm only kidding."

"Actually, that's good to know, because you can help me if I have questions," Jill says.

Louise smiles and sits up taller in her seat.

"Hey, do you mind if I get your picture, Jill? I mean, you're pregnant and covered with a rash. How many times will that happen?"

"Oh, Maggie, you're cruel," Louise says with a chuckle.

"Sick is the word," Lily says.

"Sticks and stones." I grab my camera.

"I'm okay with it." Jill smiles brightly, and I capture the memory.

We soon dig in to our hamburgers, fries, chili, salad—and Frosty. Just for the record, I ordered hamburger and fries, and I'm proud of it. Jill ordered the salad. But she also ordered a Frosty, so that should hold any hoity-toity attitude to a minimum.

"Isn't this what you've always wanted, Jill? I mean, didn't you tell us that you and Jeff tried for a long time to have a child?" Lily dips her spoon into the chili, takes a bite, and practically purrs. Over chili.

Okie-dokie then.

"That's true, but that's been a while. We're older now. Probably shouldn't have put our careers first," she says with a sigh. "After waiting so long to get started on our family, well, when it didn't happen, we settled into life and made the best of it. Now with Jeff's job and my interests"—she pauses here—"we've both changed, that's all."

Lily waves her hand. "You are not too old. Lots of couples wait until they build their nest eggs, enjoy a good career, all that before having children."

"The good news is you won't have to worry about the school changes for too long since you'll get to go on pregnancy leave," I say, hoping to lighten the moment, but it doesn't.

Jill rubs at a spot on the table but says nothing.

"You're still in shock, that's all. Give it time to sink in. You'll be thrilled," I say, smiling.

All eyes turn to her.

"Jeff's never home anymore. Things are different now. We have our jobs, our independence. We'll be paying for college from our retirement funds."

Welcome to my world.

"Jeff's job keeps him away that much?" Louise asks.

She nods. "Seems as though they keep increasing his territory. He loves what he does, and he makes great money, but at what cost?" She sets aside her salad after only two or three bites and starts eating her Frosty.

I don't blame her.

"Have you tried talking to him?" Lily asks.

"He never has time. When he's only home for a short stretch, I hate to bring it up." Jill looks up at us. "To be honest, things are a little strained between us, and I don't think this is going to help matters."

"You're going to have to talk to him, Jill. He may be clueless. You know how men are," Lily says as though she's an expert. *Good advice, but excuse me? Should I bring up the fact that you're due to get married in a few weeks and you're thinking of backing out? Am I the only normal person at this table?*

"Yeah, I know. It's all in the timing."

"Well, you're not going to be able to put it off much longer," Louise says with a chuckle.

Jill puts the spoonful of Frosty near her lips back in the cup and sighs. "You're right."

"So how's it going with you and Donald, Louise? Is he calming down at all?" Lily asks, finishing off the last of her chili.

"Not really. I try not to discourage him. I don't want to squelch his passion. It's just that—well, I hope he sticks to it this time," Louise says.

Just then my cell phone rings. It's Nick.

"Hey, Mom. What are you doing? You having fun?"

He *is* teachable. Let the heavens rejoice! "Eating at Wendy's."

"You go all the way to Florida, and that's the best you can do?"

"Yeah."

"I would think without college bills to pay you could do better than that."

"Don't get me started."

"Good point. Have you seen that jacket I bought at Old Navy last year?"

"Hmm, I don't remember seeing it after you left for school. Did you take it with you to campus?"

"No."

"I can't help you. Sorry. Are you keeping the clutter to a minimum?"

"If I did that, you wouldn't feel needed, and I just couldn't live with myself."

"Trust me on this one. I want you to pick up the clutter. I feel most appreciated when you try to keep me happy." Between Nick and Tara, my voice could easily turn to a growl.

"Well, gotta go, Mom. Nice talking to you."

"Nick—"

"Love you, bye."

If my blood pressure gets any higher, I'm pretty sure I'll pop.

"Well, I don't know about you girls, but I'm ready to go back to the condo. It's been a long day," Jill says. "Besides I need to put on this cream that the hospital gave me before I go out of my mind." She scratches then yawns.

We pile into the car and soon arrive at the condo. There's a note on our door from the neighbor asking us to let her know when we get home.

"I'll go over and see what Connie needs," Jill says while we push through the door. "Be right back."

Louise, Lily, and I go to our rooms to get ready for bed.

"I can hardly believe we've been parasailing, had pedicures and manicures, and took Jill to the hospital all in one day," I say, shrugging on my pajamas. Though it could be the reason that I almost trip over the bags under my eyes. "And still no sign of Donny."

Lily doesn't say anything, so I'm not sure if she heard me. "Lil, you all right?"

"Huh? Oh yeah, I'm fine. Just wondering what Ron's doing tonight."

"You miss him?"

"Yeah, I do."

"That's a good sign," I say.

Jill walks up to our doorway before Lily can respond. She's holding the most beautiful orchid that I have ever seen. Large delicate petals of soft yellow with a creamy white center explode at the tips of long green stems.

Lily turns around and gasps. "I love orchids. And yellow—my favorite color! Did Jeff send that to you?" she asks, smiling.

Jill smiles back. "No. Ron sent it to you."

"He did?" She gulps.

Jill nods and takes the blooming plant over to Lily. "There's a card attached," she says, pointing. She looks my way, and we exchange a smile. I follow Jill out of the room, leaving Lily alone with her thoughts and closing the door behind me.

Louise, Jill, and I gather in the living room. I get a tickle in my throat and cough a couple of times.

"What do you think?" Louise whispers. "Is she going to go through with it?"

"It's anybody's guess," I say between coughs. "One minute I think she will, the next minute, I'm not so sure."

"Yeah, that's what I thought, too," Jill says.

"Excuse me, I'm going to get a drink of water," I say, heading for the kitchen. Louise and Jill carry on a conversation while I get a glass of water and my cough finally dies down. Just as I start to head back to the living room, someone knocks at the front door.

"I'll get it," I call out. Opening the door, I see an attractive older woman with short gray hair, petite build.

"Hello, I'm Connie Meinser, the next door neighbor."

"Oh yes, come on in," I say.

"No, no, I don't need to bother you girls. I just wanted to drop off this packet of plant food for that gal's orchid. It dropped from the packaging, and well, I don't know if you're my age, but I'm a tad forgetful. Anyway, here it is," she says shoving it my way.

"Thank you," I say.

She smiles and walks away.

"Who was that?" Jill asks.

"Your neighbor." I explain why she came and wave the packet.

"She's a sweetheart."

"How old is she?" I ask.

"She celebrated her seventieth birthday last fall."

Shock registers in my stomach.

Jill laughs. "I know. Hopefully, we'll look that good at seventy, too."

"What's wrong, Maggie? You look as though you've swallowed a beach ball," Louise says.

"Nothing," I say. Jill and Louise go on to talk about other sights they want to see while in Florida, but their words are lost to me. Why would Connie say, "I don't know if you're my age." Whatever would make her think I was seventy? I'd better get a different cold cream. I'll check through Louise's stash.

Before I can work up a good hissy fit, Lily's door creaks open. We all look at her red puffy eyes.

"I don't deserve him," she says, embracing the pot with the orchid.

She loves him. There's no doubt in my mind. We have to convince her to go through with it. She'll be miserable if she doesn't.

Lily walks over to the kitchen table and sets the plant in the middle as a centerpiece, then joins us in the living room.

"So what's on the agenda tomorrow?" she asks, letting us know in a not-so-subtle way that she doesn't want to talk about Captain.

"I was thinking we might go to Weeki Wachee Springs," Jill says. "It's a couple of hours from here. They have an underwater theater."

"No, thank you. I can't hold my breath that long," I say.

Lily throws me one of her *oh, brother* looks.

Jill laughs. "You won't be underwater, I promise. The theater is built into a spring and live mermaids perform sixteen feet below the water's surface while visitors watch from inside. You'll see turtles, manatees, fish—even an occasional alligator in the show."

I groan. "I've seen enough alligators on this trip, thank you very much."

"Oh come on, Maggie, don't act like such an old woman," Lily says with a laugh. "It will be fun."

She has no idea how her words pierce me. Especially in light of the fact the neighbor thinks I'm seventy.

"Just call me a clump of wrinkled skin."

"Oh no you don't. You're not going there with that whole age thing again. I won't let you. You need to get your party self back in place."

"I vote for Weeki Wachee and the mermaids," Louise says, sticking her hand in the air—for us to count, I guess.

"If everyone agrees." Jill looks at me.

Louise—with her hand still up—and Lily turn my way. Talk about peer pressure.

"As long as you promise not to put me close to an alligator," I say.

Lily groans.

"It's settled then," Jill says, clapping her hands together as though she's rounding up her first graders. "We'll go there tomorrow."

At my age life is good with a comfortable pair of shoes, but mermaids? What a concept.

12

"I can't believe we've been here a week!" Lily says when we drink our morning coffee together.

Her comment rattles me a little. That means we only have a little over a week left to convince Lily to marry the man of her dreams. So much to do and so little time.

"That sure was sweet of Captain to send you the orchid," I say.

Lily's eyes take on a distant look. "Yeah, it was. I thought I might call him this morning to thank him."

"That's a good idea," I encourage.

"Do you think I'm a total idiot, Maggie? For risking my future with Ron, I mean?"

"Well, there's no harm in wanting to make sure you're doing the right thing. Still, you don't want to wait too long."

"You think he's right for me, don't you?" Her gaze is unwavering as she waits for my answer.

"Yeah, I do."

"And we both know you aren't easily convinced." She sighs.

"True enough. My motive has always been for your well-being, Lil," I say before taking a sip of coffee.

"I know." She pauses. "I don't know what I would do without you, Maggie."

"Well, I know I'm fifty, but as far as I know, the Lord isn't calling me home just yet," I say with a chuckle. It kind of freaks me out when Lily doesn't laugh here. "What? Do you know something I don't? Are you listening to those blabbing fortune cookies again? It's sheer gossip, Lily, and you know it."

She laughs. The fact that it sounds forced bugs me to no end.

"You're a great friend, Maggie, that's all."

"Lily, we were best friends when you were married to Bobby. Nothing changed that. Being married to Captain won't change that, either." Somehow I get the feeling she thinks she has to choose between us. Scooting my Bible further back on the table, I return my coffee cup to the coaster.

She merely nods then looks outside. "I wonder where George is this morning," she says as if he's an old friend.

"That alligator is no friend of mine, thank you very much." With a shiver, I hug my legs, trying to shake the image of the so-called "snaggletoothed" reptile with a bad case of eczema.

Lily giggles. "I can only imagine how we looked running away from him."

I chuckle in spite of myself. "I know. Our guys would pay big money for that picture." Another drink of coffee.

"Speaking of the guys, I think I'll go call Ron before he gets too busy with work." Lily heads for the door. "We'll always be best friends, right, Maggie?"

Her question almost makes me choke on my coffee. "Of course," I say with a wide smile. Lily turns and walks away.

Now why did she ask that? Captain and I get along, so it's not as though he wouldn't want her to be my friend. After all, he's the reason we're all here together in the first place. Jill steps onto the porch, giving me no time to analyze it.

"How are you this morning?" I'm trying not to gape here, but to say that Jill must have had a rough night is an understatement. "Looks as though you had a fight with your mattress and lost," I say with a snicker. Actually, it's more like the mattress pulverized her and is accepting the gold cup as we speak.

Jill runs her right hand through her short hair as if she didn't hear a word I said. Her wispy strawberry blonde locks fall easily into place, but her face is another matter entirely. If Louise gets one look at Jill's face, she'll come out here with her entire inventory of Mary Kay.

"I didn't sleep well," Jill admits.

Now *there's* a news flash. "Were you sick?"

"A little. I'm not sure if it was the baby or anxiety over having to tell Jeff the news."

"I'll bet you'll be pleasantly surprised, Jill. Remember, Jeff wanted a baby, too," I say before draining the last bit of coffee from my cup.

"Yeah, that's true, but as I said, things are different now."

"I don't know what's going on with you and Jeff, but I can tell you that marriage has its up and down moments. We all go through them, and they can make our union stronger, or we can allow them to tear us apart." I should know. It wasn't that long ago I thought Gordon was having an affair with his paralegal, the Paris Hilton wannabe. He wasn't, but it sure caused me a few gray hairs. Come to think of it, I was a youthful brunette before all that happened, doggone him. Well, okay, I had a few gray hairs, but I was nowhere near winning the Granny Clampett look-alike contest.

Jill studies her fingers. "I know you're right, Maggie. I'm just not sure how it will all turn out for us."

"Are you going to call him and tell him, or do you plan to wait until you get home?"

"I don't want to tell him on the phone. It's important that I see his reaction, to know if he's really okay with this."

"Well, there's not much you can do about it even if he isn't. I mean, you *are* pregnant, after all." The look on her face worries me. "You wouldn't—wouldn't—"

"Of course not," she jumps in, understanding my concern. "I could never harm my child."

I totally refuse to point out the Frosty thing. Who am I to cast stones? My kids chowed down chocolate chip cookies daily while in the womb.

"The question is whether I will raise the baby on my own or with Jeff by my side."

Her words shock me. "Are you serious, Jill? Are things that bad between you two?"

"Maybe *bad* isn't the right word. Let's just say our romance no longer sizzles. Maybe we've become too comfortable with one another. I don't know."

"Have you thought about going to the pastor for some counseling?"

She shakes her head. "I doubt that Jeff would go. You've probably noticed he hasn't been to church for quite some time."

"I had noticed, but I figured his job had kept him away."

"Most people think that. Makes it easier for him to slip through the cracks, you know?"

I nod, feeling guilty that we haven't checked on him.

"Besides, Jeff doesn't think we have a problem. He acts as though everything is fine. But it isn't."

When I open my mouth to respond, Louise slides open the patio door and looks at Jill. She's smiling. "You have a visitor."

Louise is looking far too happy for it to be Connie next door. Just then Louise takes a step sideways.

"Jeff! What are you doing here?" Jill fingers her hair again.

He flashes a lopsided grin and whips a bouquet of spring flowers from behind his back. "I had to come here and talk to a couple of doctors, then I have some free time. I thought I'd come and see my best girl," he says with a wink. "I hope you ladies don't mind." Jeff's a little over six feet, lean build—most likely because Jill won't let him eat anything fun—with salt and pepper hair. Why do men look distinguished with gray hair but women look old?

"Of course we don't mind," Louise and I say.

"Jill?"

"Why, no. This is great," she says. By the look on her face, I'd say she's tempted to pinch him to make sure he's real.

"I thought we could go around town this morning, then out for lunch. I'll try not to hog you the whole time. I don't want to horn in on you and your friends." He smiles.

"If you want to go out, I'd better get cleaned up. I'm a mess." She buries her nose in the flowers and takes a whiff. "Oh, these are awesome, Jeff. Thanks."

"You're welcome. By the way, you look great to me," he says, his gaze never flinching.

There's love in his eyes, so I'm not sure what the problem is with these two. Maybe he's oblivious to how Jill's feeling. She's in need of some validation, and he hasn't taken the time to notice there's even a problem. Men can be so clueless.

I've been there, done that, and I've learned it doesn't get any better until the couple talks it out.

She gets up from her chair, steps over the patio opening, and gives him a hug.

"How about you talk to the girls while I get ready," Jill says.

"Sure." Jeff says, tossing a grin my way. He steps inside and sits in an empty chair.

"So are the Latte Girls having a good time?" he asks with a grin.

You mean besides the fact we're trying to get Lily not to back out of her wedding, Louise not to commit domestic violence, keep your own

*wife from putting your only child up for adoption, and me from buying
stock in a nursing home? Oh, sure, we're having a great time.* I won't
even bring up Gator George, the threat of nosebleeds from parasailing, broken tailbones from rollerblading, or sliced feet from walking
on broken shells. Why complain?

"Yes, we're having fun. It's great to get away," I say. And of course
it is, though it might have helped to come when life was a little
calmer. "I miss Gordon, though," I say, meaning it.

"Already? Boy, you guys must not be apart much. Jill and I are
used to being apart," says the clueless one.

"Are you?"

He stretches back in his chair. "Oh yeah. With my job, I'm gone
all the time."

"That must be hard," I say, hoping he'll get my drift.

"Nah. Only the first few months after I started traveling. It's no
big deal now."

"Does Jill feel the same way?"

Looking puzzled, his gaze locks with mine.

"Hi, Jeff. I didn't know you were here," Lily says as she joins us.
"Can I get you something to drink?"

"No, thanks, I'm fine. Good to see you, Lily."

"What's the matter, couldn't stay away from the little wife, huh?"
she teases.

His gaze shoots straight at me for some reason. Maybe he got my
drift. That just improves my faith in mankind.

"What, was it something I said?" Lily asks.

Jeff looks back at her. A smile lifts the corners of his mouth. "I
had to come here and check in with a couple of doctors. I have some
free time, so I thought it might be fun to spend some time with Jill
while I'm here. I hope you girls don't mind."

"Of course we don't mind. We're glad you're here and you two
can spend some time together." Lily smiles.

We talk awhile about things back in Charming, people we know, the price of gas.

"Well, I'm ready," Jill says holding a bottled water and looking positively transformed in her aqua-blue top, white shorts with a cute rattan belt, and blue-and-white sandals.

"Wow, you look great." Jeff stands to meet his wife then turns back to Lily and me. "Nice talking with you two," he says.

We watch the couple walk through the living room, stop and talk a moment to Louise who is putting something in the crock pot, then off they go.

"You think they'll make it?" I ask.

"Well, the lunch traffic is bothersome, but I don't see why it should stop them from eating lunch all together," Lily says, making me realize it's not always just the men who are clueless.

⑥ ✍ ⑥

"Wow, this is great. We get the whole place to ourselves," Lily says as we step into the empty pool area at one of the pools at our resort. "Not exactly Weeki Wachee, but it will have to do."

"Everyone must be down at the beach," I say.

Once we pick out some lawn chairs, we stretch our towels across them and get comfortable. There's something about the clean smell of chlorine. It makes me think I've scrubbed the house all day, and it's time for a break.

Grabbing the sunscreen from my bag, I slather it on all over.

"Whoa, Maggie, you don't need to use the whole bottle at one sitting," Lily says.

"I'm just following Louise's advice."

Louise smiles.

Leaning back in my chair and facing the sun, I try to relax, but I can't.

"Why are you squirming, Maggie? Is something wrong?" Lily wants to know.

Yanking the back of my lawn chair forward, I sit up and face them. "I can't breathe. I smell like a coconut."

Louise and Lily laugh.

"Well, why don't you take a swim?" Louise suggests.

Sounds like a good idea, so I get up.

"Just don't sit at the edge of the pool. You'll slide right into the water," Lily says, laughing.

"Now I know how a seal feels. All sleek and shiny. Hey, this is the first time I've ever had a sleek body, Lil!" I call over my shoulder.

"Do you want me to set up a row of horns for you to toot?" she calls back.

"Ar-ar," I imitate a barking seal and clap my *flippers* together just before slipping into the water. The strong smell of chlorine replaces the coconut scent.

"Oh, I think I'll come join you," Lily says. She races toward the water like an Olympic runner going for the gold and jumps in with purpose.

"Me, too," Louise says, quietly dipping herself into the water, making nary a sound.

Lily and I frown. Then I remember the wrinkle thing, and I go for no expression.

"The water isn't cold at all. This is nice," Louise says, bouncing with the delicacy of a ballerina.

"Wait. Do you hear that?" Lily asks, her body tense, looking every inch the bird dog.

"Hear what?" I ask with tension, hating these kinds of moments. My gaze darts about the water, making sure Gator George is nowhere to be found.

"Come on, Jill, we'll work it out," a man's voice calls out.

"Yeah, right, Jeff. You're never home for us to work anything out." Right then Jill comes storming toward the pool.

"Duck!" I say. All three of us plunk our heads underwater and paddle to the side of the pool, hopefully out of sight. We surface and gasp quietly, water dripping down our faces, hair sleeked back and stringy.

"Jill, don't do this." Jeff's voice sounds tired.

"What, Jeff? Leave? The way you do every other day?"

His voice comes closer. "What do you want from me, Jill? I'm trying to provide a living for us."

"I don't want a living, Jeff. I want a life." Jill stomps off, then we hear her scream.

"Jill!"

We look up in time to see Jeff running for Jill. He grabs her hand and yanks her back into the bushes mere feet from the pool.

Louise gasps. "He's hurting her!"

"Well, he's not going to if I have anything to say about it." I climb out of the pool with every intention of clobbering that young man senseless.

What I see once I surface stops me cold. It's an alligator, and he's headed straight toward us.

"Maggie, get over here!" Jeff shouts.

Lily, Louise, and I are out of that pool and hiding in the bushes before that alligator can blink.

"Shh, don't move," Jeff says, holding Jill close to his side.

The alligator soon saunters by and takes a dip in the pool, opening his mouth just enough for us to see his teeth—or what's left of them.

"Oh, it's just George," Jill says, blowing out a breath of relief.

13

"Let's go some place and talk," Jeff says to Jill once we're out of harm's way and we've gathered our things.

We say good-bye and watch them drive off.

"Whew, that was close," I say as we haul our dripping selves back to the condo.

"Yeah. That was pretty cool how Jeff came to Jill's rescue like that," Lily says. "Sort of a knight in shining armor."

"Smart guy. By the sounds of their conversation, things weren't going so well. His heroic act no doubt bought him some time," I say.

Lily brushes something off her arm. "Maggie, I still can't figure out what you find so fascinating about the bushes."

"Ha, ha. I'm telling you, Lily, you could be another Chonda Pierce, what with your quick wit and all."

She laughs.

"You okay, Louise?" I ask, wondering why she's so quiet.

"Yeah, I'm fine," she says, though I'm not convinced.

Boy, everyone is a mess here. I'm glad Gordon and I are still intact—at least we were when I left. Come to think of it, he hasn't called in a while.

"I'm going to call Gordon," I say, picking up my cell phone. "Hi, Heide. Is Gordon there?" Heide is the day receptionist at Gordon's office.

"No, Maggie, he's at the courthouse. You want me to have him call you?"

"Oh, nothing urgent. Just when he has time, if he wants to call, that would be great. Thanks," I say, before clicking my phone closed.

"I'll be right back. I'm going to the restroom," Louise says once we get inside our home away from home.

"Gordon is not there, huh?" Lily asks.

With a pout, I shake my head. "Did you get to talk to Captain?"

"Yeah," Lily says. "We had a nice talk."

"Feeling any better, Lil?" I drop my handbag on the counter. We settle into our chairs.

"A little. Still, I'm not sure what I'm going to do. There's this uneasy feeling in the pit of my stomach," she says.

"Are you sure it's not something you ate? Green apples? Or perhaps you have a little intestinal bug?"

"That doesn't seem to be it." She applies baby lotion to her arms. "He's such a good man, Maggie. He deserves a woman who loves him, and I want to make sure I love him for himself, not because he reminds me of Bobby." She puts the cap back on the lotion and looks at me. "I'm sure that doesn't make any sense to you."

"Yes, it does. But I don't think that's why you're attracted to Captain."

Just then a cell phone rings. It's coming from Louise's bag.

"Do you think we should answer it?" Lily asks.

Picking it up, I glance at the screen. "It's Donald. We'll just tell her he called. He'll probably leave a message on her voice mail."

Lily nods. "Do you think Bob and Ron look similar—you know, through the eyes?" she asks.

"That's something I've never thought about before," I say. "Besides, you were attracted to him before you ever saw him face-to-face, remember? You corresponded on e-mail."

"I remember," she says, thinking a moment.

"Did you ever consider you're attracted to the same thing in both Bob and Captain?"

"Huh?" She's just not used to pure wisdom pouring out of my mouth.

"The things you're attracted to in Captain are not because they remind you of Bobby, but rather they're because those are the qualities you enjoy in a man. We talked about that before."

"Yeah, I know."

"Well, what do you think about that theory?"

"I'm not sure." She pulls a glass from the cupboard. "A postcard from heaven would be nice right about now."

My eyebrows raise, but I quickly lower them so I won't get a crease in my forehead. "If you get a postcard from heaven, I just hope it's not inviting you to come to a party there any time soon."

She chuckles. "You're gonna get struck talking that way, Maggie Hayden."

"Well, I'm just not ready for you to leave me." I smile.

Lily's smile fades.

"Well, that was an exciting excursion," Louise says when she returns, brushing her hands together.

"That kind of excitement, we can do without," Lily says. "Oh, by the way, Donald called."

"He did?" Louise hesitates, then settles into her chair. "Wonder what he wants."

Ever hopeful, I watch for the teensiest of lines to sprout. Nothing. Maybe there's something to Louise's product. I'd better get some. Tonight.

She punches in a number and waits. "I'll call him later." Forcing a smile, she snaps her cell phone closed.

⑥ ✍ ⑥

"Before you say anything, I haven't told Jeff yet," Jill says when she walks in the door. She grabs a bottled water from the refrigerator. "The timing wasn't right." Kicking off her shoes, she walks over to the sofa and plops down beside Louise. "Every time I tried to give Jeff the news, we were interrupted, or Jeff would start talking about work and I couldn't tell him."

"Don't worry, Jill, you'll know when the time is right," Louise says.

We talk about it awhile then grow silent.

"Hey, let's brave the heat and head for a snack on Siesta Key Beach," Lily says.

"You're on," we say, grabbing our things.

Once at the beach concession stand, we place our orders, then clutch our artery-clogging treasures—all except for Jill who ordered a bottled water and yogurt—and sit down.

Jill rifles through her handbag.

"Lose something?" Louise asks.

"My sunglasses must be in the car," she says, zipping her handbag closed. "Oh well, guess it won't hurt for me to squint for a little while."

It truly amazes me that Louise doesn't pounce on that one. You think you know a person.

After swallowing a bite of my hot dog and french fries, I glance up at Jill. "So is Jeff visiting the doctors right now?"

"Yeah, he's having dinner with a couple of them tonight," she says. I'm almost certain there is disappointment in her eyes. That's a good sign. "Seems we always get only a snippet of time together." She takes a bite of her small fat free, plain—as in boring—yogurt.

No one says anything for a few moments.

"Is he coming back over tonight?" Lily asks.

"Who knows? Depends on how long the doctors keep him. He said if it was too late, he'd go on back to the hotel."

"Tell you what. I'll sleep on the couch. That way if he comes over, you two can have our room," Louise jumps in. "Unless you plan to join him at his hotel."

"Woo-hoo," Lily and I say with upraised brows.

"I don't know," Jill says, but I can tell she likes the idea. "He's not expecting me there, and he won't come here for fear of barging in on our girls' time."

"Well, maybe he'll call, and you can tell him then. We'll plan it that way, and if he does happen to come over, you'll be all set," Louise says with a wink.

"Thanks, girls," Jill says.

We finish our meals and decide to walk around on the beach.

"The sun should dip over the horizon in another half hour or so. You have to experience a sunset on Siesta Key. There is absolutely nothing to compare to it," Jill says with passion.

"That's what Ron says," Lily adds.

"Maybe he'll bring you here for your honeymoon. That is if you, well, get married and all," Louise says.

"The plan was Bermuda, though I'm sure we'll spend plenty of time in Florida if he has his way." Lily gives me a sideways glance.

"Don't you want to visit Florida, Lil?" I ask. "It's a nice place. Especially in this area."

"Oh sure, I enjoy Florida as well as the next person."

Maybe the problem is Tara. It's probably best that I let the matter drop.

"This is one of my favorite places," Jill says. "Jeff and I come here several times a year—or at least we used to. We've had some of our best times here." She stoops to pick up a shell in her path.

"Maybe you can rediscover the magic here," Lily says, eyes twinkling.

Wait. We're supposed to be helping Lily with love, aren't we? I'm so confused.

"Wow, looks as though they're having fun," Louise says as we pass a guy spiking a ball over a volleyball net.

"Oh my goodness," Jill says, gasping for breath, "that's—that's—I have to get out of here." Her legs fumble in the sand as her gaze darts about the beach like a nervous egret. She shoots off ahead of us.

"Jill, what is it?" I call after her, running as fast as my legs will carry me. If I keep up this pace, I'll need life support before sunset. "Jill!"

She turns wild eyes toward us. "That's Rodney. Back there. Playing volleyball." Her arms jerk and her feet move so fast, she puts me to mind of Jim Carrey on a triple shot of espresso. "I can't let him see me."

"Why not?" The sand is nice to walk in, but it's not ideal for running a marathon.

"I don't know. It's just weird that he's here."

Spotting the red lifeguard station nearby, I say, "Let's go over there."

The four of us rush over. Jill leans against the wooden boards, bending over, gasping for breath. "What is he doing here?"

Everything in me wants to say "playing volleyball?" but I figure my sarcasm wouldn't be appreciated right about now. With a quick glance back at the players I ask, "Which one is he?"

Jill dares a look in that direction. "He's—he's—oh my, he's coming this way! What am I going to do?"

"Go up into the lifeguard stand, we'll cover for you," I say.

"What will I say to the lifeguard?" she asks.

"I don't know. Talk about the weather, Red Tide, Jacques Cousteau, whatever. Now go!" We push her toward the stairway of the little building. It would seem a whole lot easier to me if she would just talk to him and get over it.

She takes the steps two at a time while the three of us talk together, bending now and then to reach for a shell or just to run the soft, cool sand between our fingers.

"Excuse me, ladies."

We look up to see a handsome man. He's about six-two, two hundred pounds, I'd say, dark brown eyes, dark hair with a tiny thread of gray running through here and there, and a smile that could tug at the heart of the most guarded of women.

"Was there someone else with you a moment ago?"

"Someone else?" Lily says nary another word but puts on an expression that says he's seeing things.

He rubs his jaw. "Oh, I don't know, I thought I saw someone I knew with you."

"Has that line ever worked for you before?" Lily asks, clearly catching him off guard and surprising the socks off me—if I had any on.

His mouth spreads into a full blown smile. "Can't say that it has."

"Rodney Pierceton from Indiana," he says, extending his hand to Lily then to Louise and me.

Wisely, we avoid the Indiana part. "So are you on vacation?"

What in the world is Lily doing, writing a biography? We need to get rid of this guy.

"Well, sort of. I'm staying nearby for a fitness convention. My boss was going to come and something came up, so he asked me to cover it." His gaze shoots over our heads, scanning the beach. "I have a friend who was coming to this area, but I don't know where she's staying. I thought I lucked out when I saw you. But I must have been imagining it."

Lily laughs and tucks a strand of hair behind her ear. "She must be a special friend."

"I'd like her to be," he says.

Look here, buster, she's a happily married woman. Now buzz off!

"Well, good luck in your search, Rodney Pierceton," Lily says, dismissing him.

"Uh, thanks." He glances around the area once more then jogs back to the volleyball gang.

"Don't tell me he mesmerized you, too," I say to Lily, slightly irritated at the pink color I see fanned across her cheeks.

Lily shrugs. "Hardly. Someone had to keep him from looking up at the lifeguard stand. With all those windows, he was bound to see Jill."

"The coast clear?" Jill whispers when she steps outside.

"It's clear," Lily says. "Now how are we going to get past that guy?"

"Here, put on my sweater." I reach in and pull it out of my bag and hand it to her. "It might plump you up."

"And put on my sombrero," Louise says, shoving the oversized straw hat into Jill's hand.

Every time I look at that thing, I have this overwhelming urge to trill my Rs.

"And put these sunglasses on. They're big enough to cover that part of your face that the sombrero doesn't hide," Lily says.

"Okay, everrrybody rrrready to go?" I ask, leading the way back to the car. They groan and follow.

As we head back to the car, I have to say it does my heart good to see Jill this way. She resembles a skinny version of me, and it practically inspires me to swear off all food. Then again it's probably because I'm still full from the hot dog and french fries.

"Why wouldn't you talk to him, Jill?" Lily asks.

"I don't know. It stunned me to see him, and I didn't have time to think. It scared me a little."

"Well, at least you know why he's here," I say.

"Yeah, I heard him. Still, it bothers me that he knows I'm here and is keeping a lookout for me."

We walk close to our car in the parking lot when a voice stops us in our tracks.

"You're not leaving before we experience a sunset together, are you?"

Jill gulps out loud as Jeff steps out of the shadows and into view.

14

Fitness Boy is on the beach, and now Jill's husband shows up? As my mother used to say, "Be sure your sins will find you out."

"What's with the getup?" Jeff asks Jill with a laugh.

She runs a finger through a curl at the base of her neck. "Oh, the sun was getting to me," she says.

His right eyebrow lifts to his hairline. "So that would explain the sweater."

"Oh, that. Well, the sun was blaring, so Lily gave me the sunglasses and Louise gave me the hat, and then I got cold, so Maggie let me borrow her sweater." Jill takes off the sweater and sunglasses and hands them back. Then she pulls off the hat. "Thanks."

"Where are your sunglasses?" he asks.

"Left them in the car."

An awkward moment follows.

"So what are you doing back so early?" Jill asks.

"I told the doctors my wife was here, and they asked me what I was doing with them when there was a wife and sunset waiting on me." Jeff laughs. "They're good guys."

"So did you eat dinner?" Jill asks.

"Inhaled would be a better word," Jeff says with a wink. That shows me there's hope for these two. Why else would a husband gulp down his food and rush to get to his wife if not for love?

"Listen, why don't we go on back to the condo, and you two can come later—or not," Lily says with an ornery grin.

Jeff grins back. "Sounds good to me." He puts his arm around Jill. "See you later, girls," he says, edging her toward the beach.

By the look on Jill's face, one would think Jaws was spotted beachside.

"Oh, wait. Can't you two go out for a dessert with us?" I say.

Jill's facial muscles relax. All three girls stare at me. I throw them an I-know-what-I'm-doing glance.

"Well—" Jeff doesn't want to go, I can see it in his eyes, but neither does he want to be rude.

"We won't take too much of your time, I promise."

"To be honest, Maggie, I was hoping Jill and I could experience a sunset together. Um, alone," he says, lopsided grin in place.

"Sunset, schmunset. You can do that tomorrow night," I say, acting completely clueless of his need to be alone with her, and enjoying myself immensely. "How often can you go out with four beautiful women such as ourselves?" I suck in my cheeks and give a shot of my profile. Okay, so I resemble one of the Golden Girls rather than one of Charlie's Angels. I can live with that. I'm trying my best to keep Rodney and Jeff apart. You do what you've got to do to help a friend.

Louise's mouth gapes, Lily stifles a giggle. Jill looks as though she'll buy me a present.

Jeff turns to Jill. "Is that okay with you, hon?"

"Sure," she says.

He looks up and shrugs. "Guess we'll go."

Jill mouths "Thank you," and I feel I have saved the day.

"Hey, we could grab an ice cream cone at the concession and still come out in time to see the light display over the horizon," he says.

Gulp.

"Oh, I was thinking more along the lines of pie and gourmet coffee," Lily jumps in.

"I'd really like to see that sunset with Jill." There's a teensy bit of a growl in his voice here.

Jill looks as though she's a crab about to be shelled. "Well, maybe we'll just hang around awhile, too. Do you mind if we join you?" I push for Jill's sake.

Jeff blinks. "Well, I guess. If you don't mind hanging out with an old married couple."

We're totally ruining his evening, and guilt plagues me for the span of a heartbeat.

I get over it.

"Oh no, we don't mind at all." If I were a man, there's no telling what Jeff might do to me right about now. By the look on his face, I'd say he'd stuff me on a boat and set it out to sea in a menopausal minute if given half a chance.

"Fine," he says. "Let's go." That smoke rising from his ears thing could have landed him a spot in *Lord of the Rings*.

Lily throws me a worried glance, but I try to appear confident, as though I know what I'm doing. Which, of course, I don't.

The happy couple walks in front of us. Well, one of them is happy anyway.

"What are we going to do?" Lily whispers to me when she and Louise huddle closer.

"Good question." My mind swims with ideas. "Think of college ball. Rodney is the basketball. Jill and Jeff are the basket. We are the players standing in the way of Rodney, um, scoring—so to speak."

Louise and Lily throw a worried glance.

"Well, I hope we're successful," Louise says. "And I thought I had problems."

"Yeah, I was thinking the same thing about me," Lily says.

"Come on, you two, we have to keep up with them." Our steps quicken.

"Hey, look at that boy," I say, pointing. A teenager saunters past. "Doesn't he look like Donny Osmond? Could be one of his kids. He has a couple of boys, doesn't he? Where's my camera?"

"What's with you and this fascination to see Donny Osmond?" Lily asks.

I ignore her, grab my camera, and walk over to the kid. "Hi." He's cute. Has the same dark eyes and hair as Donny. "So what's your dad's name?"

The kid looks at me like I'm crazy and keeps walking.

"I mean, is his first name Donny?" I'm sort of skipping sideways to keep up with him.

The kid raises an eyebrow and looks like he's going to bolt.

Now I'm running backward, and let me just say, it's not an easy thing to do. "You know, as in last name Osmond?" I ask, ever hopeful.

"You ready to go, Ryan?" a deep voice calls from my left.

I turn and see a blond, middle-aged man.

"This is my dad. And his name isn't Donny." The kid walks on past, shaking his head, and I want to give him a swift kick in the behind, but I simply smile at the man.

"I thought maybe you were, um, what I mean to say is—"

Lily pulls on my arm. "I'm sorry," she says to the man. "She's escaped from the loony bin, and we have to take her back." She drags me away from the man who is staring after us. She whispers, "You're embarrassing us, Maggie. Get over this Donny Osmond fixation, will ya?"

"Hello? Like you didn't embarrass me with that whole loony bin thing? Besides, I don't have a fixation. I just want his picture. What's the big deal?"

"Come on girls, we've got to get to the concession area," Louise says.

If I eat one more thing tonight, I think I'll puke. On the other hand, if it takes a hot fudge sundae to save my friend's marriage, I'll do what I have to do.

"Okay, we need to take our ice cream with us so we can get a good view," Jeff says.

We grab our orders and follow him. He's leading us past the volleyball courts. Too bad Jill didn't keep the sunglasses and sweater. Louise's sombrero would definitely come in handy here too.

Hopefully, Rodney is no longer there, but since we haven't been gone all that long, I have my doubts. It takes talent, but I somehow manage to keep an eye on the volleyball court and keep walking forward at the same time. Rodney is still there.

"Hey, what's your hurry?" I hear Jeff say to Jill. Her face is turned the opposite direction of the volleyball court.

"We want to get a good seat, like you said," Louise jumps in.

We walk through the maze of the crowd, and suddenly, what I see makes my heart plummet. It's Rodney, and he's headed straight for Jill. Even if Rodney doesn't realize that's Jill's husband, what kind of guy would approach a woman who is with another man?

I turn to the girls. "Let's go, we can't let him reach Jill."

Louise, Lily, and I join together like the Mod Squad and march straight toward Rodney. He doesn't see us because his gaze is fixed on Jill, who is, by now, pretty much leaping across the beach with all the grace of a frog.

Lily jumps ahead. "Well, well, look here, girls. It's Rodney from Indiana." We form a wall in front of him. "How good to see you again."

He blinks and looks past us toward Jill who's quickly fading into the sunset. And let me just point out here that the sunset is everything they say it is and more. No picture could ever capture the profusion of reds, oranges, and golds that's exploding from the shimmering sun across the horizon at this very moment.

"Uh, hi," he says, clearly irritated.

His charm is never-ending.

"Listen, I'd love to talk but . . ." His eyes are still searching for Jill, and he tries to break through us, but it's not happening. I guess my morning routine of lifting the chocolate milk jug from the refrigerator is paying off.

"I think I see my friend again, and I need to talk to her." If we had admitted to being with Jill earlier, I would tell Rodney that she is with her husband and to leave them alone. Then again, she might think I was taking this friendship thing a little too far. Still, I never let that stop me where Lily is concerned.

He takes another step forward, and Lily's hand clamps on his arm in a death grip.

"Oh no you don't. You have to settle something between us."

Woo-hoo, Lily Newgent takes charge!

Rodney stops and stares at her with disbelief. "Look, lady, I need to go." The veins in his neck suddenly become very obvious. I'm wondering how much iron he pumps every day. Shoot, from the looks of those babies, he *eats* iron.

"Oh please, won't you settle just this one thing?" Lily jumps up and down and whines here.

Who *is* this person?

We all look toward Jill, and she is nowhere in sight. His gaze returns to Lily, and he looks as though he might chew her up and spit her out. "O-kay," he says through clenched teeth, "what is it?"

"Well, it's easy to see that you keep physically fit," Lily says as though she's having the best time. "We want to know if you guzzle down those healthy-type drinks in the morning. You know, the kind with raw egg and all that?"

My jaw drops right then and there. Lily is morphing into, well, me. This is a little frightening.

He looks at her. Well, actually it's more like his eyes are boring a hole through her skull. "I don't drink raw eggs. Now, if you'll excuse me." He stomps off, but Jill and Jeff are still nowhere in sight.

"How rude," Lily says as Rodney runs away, kicking up sand behind him.

"Why don't we just tell him she's with her husband?" Louise asks.

"For some reason Jill doesn't want him to know she's here. She seems a little unnerved that he's seeking her out. I think she's just stressed out with Jeff, and Rodney complicates things. She doesn't want to deal with him right now," Lily says.

With stylish shades over her eyes Louise glances around the beach. "Where do you think they are?"

"I have no idea. My guess is Jeff took her to an isolated spot as quickly as he could to get her away from us," I say.

"We're not very popular tonight, huh?" Lily laughs.

"You noticed that, too?" Louise joins in.

"Something tells me Rodney doesn't view their friendship quite the way Jill does," I say.

"Yeah, I get that feeling, too," Lily says.

We walk a few paces in silence, stopping a moment to dump our melting ice cream in a nearby bin.

"Oh, well. What say we head out for the nightlife in Siesta Key," I say, locking my arms into theirs.

"You thinking what I'm thinking?" Lily asks.

"Yep, pick up a movie, grab a bag of popcorn, and settle into our chairs at the condo," I say.

"You got it. Let's go."

After watching another romantic comedy, we browse through our magazines.

"Hey, Maggie, I was going to tell you, I was cutting a gal's hair the other day, and she told me a dentist has come out with something called a 'Snap-On Smile.' I guess it fits on the same as a retainer, and it gives you the smile of a celebrity," Lily says.

I look up from my Paula Deen magazine. "And you're telling me this, why?"

"Well, I just know how you always complain that you wish you had a different smile. Here's your chance to do something about it without all the major dental work."

"Probably costs an arm and a leg," I grouse.

"It depends on how badly you want a new look," she says.

The idea does appeal to me. A Cameron Diaz smile would give me a new, young look. Okay, try total makeover.

"Remember, Gordon said he'd pay for whatever you wanted so you would feel better about yourself," Lily presses.

Excitement rushes through me. "He did say that, didn't he?"

Lily sits up, eyes sparkling. "He sure did."

"Wonder how I can find out about it?"

"I can tell you," Louise says, entering the living room in her pajamas. We turn to her. "You're talking about the Snap-On Smile, right?"

"Right," I say.

"My dentist in Rosetown does it," Louise says. "Several people in town already have them." She's chuckling now. "You know Old Man Jacob?"

"That Amish-turned-Baptist guy?"

"He's the one. When is the last time you saw him?"

"Oh, it's been a good six to eight months," I say. "Why?"

"I don't know if you remember his smile, but let's just say Brad Pitt has nothing on him—well, the smile part anyway."

Now I'm sitting up in my chair, laughing. "No way!"

"Yes, way!" Louise says.

"An Amish-turned-Baptist Brad Pitt? It boggles the mind."

We get excited and start chattering about the possibilities.

"I wonder what smiles they offer," I say. "Why couldn't I have known about these back when I thought Gordon was involved with Paris Hilton?"

Louise looks at me. "Who?"

"Don't ask," Lily says. "You'll have to check it out when you get back to Charming. It's an easy fix. A lot easier than plastic surgery or braces."

"I'm all for pain-free makeovers," I say.

"Speaking of makeovers—"

Lily and I groan. We know what's coming next. Louise consistently tries to make us beautiful. And I hate to tell her, but it just ain't happening here.

"I know what you're thinking. I'm not trying to get you to buy my product, and you know it. I'm offering you a service," Louise says, already pulling out a Mary Kay book and slapping it on the coffee table.

"She's right, Maggie. If you're going to flaunt Cameron Diaz's teeth, the least you can do is fix up your face to go with that smile," Lily says with a chuckle.

"Excuse me? Do I know you well enough for you to talk to me this way?"

"Yes, you do. I'll get a makeover if you will," Lily encourages.

"Do you remember the last time we had a facial, Lil? What a fiasco that was!"

"What happened?" Louise wants to know.

"We had this paste on our faces. It hardened and when we laughed, it cracked like the San Andreas fault. On top of all that, when the glamorous Debra Stiffler came to my door, I forgot I had the facial paste on, and I answered the door pretty much resembling a ghoul with leprosy."

Louise starts laughing. "Only you, Maggie."

"Yeah, yeah, I know." I don't need to be reminded of the fixes I get myself into, thank you very much.

"Well, I'm not going to give you the facials. Though it would be fun to put makeup on you," Louise says.

"What's the point?" I ask. "We're going to bed afterwards. Why leave my face on the pillow?"

"That's true enough, but we all know we're waiting to see if Jill will come home, so we might as well do something fun while we're waiting," Louise says.

"Well, I guess—" Before I can agree to another makeover disaster, Jill pushes through the door. Her face is swollen, her skin red and splotchy. I don't know whether she's eaten an orange or if she's been crying.

"Are you all right, Jill?" Lily asks.

"I'm fine. I don't know why I wasted my time this evening, when I could have been having fun with you." She goes into her bedroom and shuts the door. Hard.

We look at each other.

"Something tells me things didn't work out quite the way we had hoped."

"Nothing gets by you, Lily," I say.

Right then it hits me that I haven't heard back from Gordon. How odd. He's really good about calling and checking in on me. Walking over to a nearby stand, I pick up my cell phone. "You're not going to call Gordon this late at night, are you?" Lily says. "It's midnight."

"Oh, that's right. I'll call him tomorrow." I click it closed. "Seems odd he didn't call me back tonight."

"Yeah, Gordon always calls you. But then you haven't been away this long before," Lily says, wiggling her eyebrows.

"Thanks, Lil. That makes me feel better."

"Do you girls want to get that makeover or not?" Louise asks, makeup brush in hand, poised and ready to go. For a moment, I envision Leonardo da Vinci in our midst. Just as quickly, the vision fades.

"I think we'll pass for now. Maybe tomorrow," I say.

Louise shrugs. "It's your face. If you're happy with the way it is, fine."

Something in that comment makes me want to mix up the caps on her lipstick tubes.

15

"Gordon? What are you doing home this time of morning?" I ask.

"I live here," he says, yawning.

"Are you sick?"

"No, just tired. I've been working a lot of overtime."

"Now there's a surprise. When are you going to slow down?"

"Can't be helped," he says, giving me the same old story.

"You've cut your hours, remember?"

"Well, I admit since you've been gone, I've been working more hours."

"How many more?"

He yawns. "Can we talk about it later?"

My insides go soft. Much as I want to get on him for overworking, I don't want to argue with him. "Are you staying home today?"

"No. I just decided to go in late."

Why can't he ever do that when I'm home? I hear him scratch his jaw, something he does every morning when he starts to think about shaving.

"What time is it?"

I tell him.

"I'd better get ready then." Almost as an afterthought—like father, like son—he says, "How you doing, Maggie? Having a good time?"

"Yeah," I say, feeling a sudden melancholy settle over me. The sound of Gordon's voice makes me homesick, but he seems more preoccupied with work than me. Though it's not the first time.

"I miss you," I say in a sappy voice. He's quiet a moment, which gets my attention. "Gordon, did you hear me?"

"What? Oh, I miss you too, babe," he says.

His hesitation makes me feel worse.

"I'm sorry, Maggie. I've got a lot to do today. My gears are already in motion, you know how that is."

"No, I don't. My gears haven't moved in years."

Gordon laughs.

"He lives, ladies and gentlemen!" I say.

"Hey, you're one to talk. Remember when I called you the other morning and you needed a moment to get your bearings?"

"Yeah, whatever. Listen, Gordon—" I start to give him the life-is too-short-to-spend-so-much-time-working speech, but he cuts me off.

"Before you get started, Maggie, just let me say I'm working over-time to keep up with the grocery bill."

"Uh-oh. Nick?"

"Yes. I will never again complain about the high cost of college. His grocery bills are higher than tuition. He's going back."

Only one of us is laughing.

"You won't hurt him, right?"

"I haven't the strength. By the time I get home, the cupboards are bare."

"That bad?"

"That bad."

I'm feeling guilty about the hamburger and french fries I've been eating. "I'll be home soon. Take out a loan and go to Wendy's."

"Already did. The papers on the second mortgage are signed. When are you coming home?" he asks, yawning again.

"We'll be home next Saturday."

"That long?" The surprise in his voice makes me feel a little better.

"Yeah."

"It seems forever."

"That makes me feel better. Keep it coming, Gordy boy."

"You know I miss you, babe."

"I miss you, too."

"Well, you take care of yourself. Stay out of trouble," he says. Romantic moment over. Oh well, a romantic moment that lasted all of two seconds is better than none at all. "And stay away from Donny Osmond."

"Haven't seen him—yet. I love you."

"Love you, too, Maggie."

After hanging up, I stare at the phone. I refuse to allow my paranoia to slip in again. I've grown past that. Still, I could have used a little more romance this morning. After all, I've been gone a week. He should be missing me.

The smell of ham and spices reaches me, making my mouth water. Maybe that's what I should do so Gordon will miss me when I'm away. Cook more. When the kids left home, I stuffed my June Cleaver apron in the back of a drawer and haven't thought about it since. In the mornings I throw Gordon a breakfast bar as he heads out the door, and in the evenings, we usually eat out. Maybe if I cook more, Gordon might be tempted to stay home and work less.

"That smells heavenly, Louise," I say, watching her prance around the kitchen, vaguely remembering the days when I enjoyed doing that. Some things are best left forgotten.

"It's ham and egg quiche," she says with a smile.

"What is that smell?" Lily asks, her nose leading the way to the kitchen.

Louise stretches a little taller at all our gushing over her breakfast and tells Lily what she's preparing. We talk a moment about breakfast while Lily and I place white dishes with flecks of blue around the rim onto the table and Louise finishes the food preparations.

"Have you talked with Jill this morning?" I ask, setting the last fork in place.

Louise shakes her head. "She's in our room working out to her exercise video."

"That's one way to relieve stress, I suppose. Though I'd choose chocolate."

Louise smiles. Lily rolls her eyes.

"I hope Rodney didn't show up and cause a big problem between her and Jeff," I say.

"That's exactly what I was thinking," Lily says, laying a handful of supplements beside her plate.

"You take all those?" I ask with disbelief at the bazillion pills she placed there.

She nods. "You'll see the difference, Maggie, when we're both seventy. I'll be happy and healthy, going this place and that, while you'll be taking a handful of pills for various ailments and slugging around in big, fluffy slippers.

"Way to cheer someone up, Lil. Besides, I don't wear slippers. I prefer socks."

"Whatever. It's still true. You need to take care of yourself."

"Excuse me? I take care of myself. Have you not noticed that I eat oatmeal almost every day? It's supposedly good for your heart and cholesterol, all that," I say feeling quite proud of myself.

"Yes, I've noticed."

My chin lifts here, and I'm feeling a little hoity-toity.

"But I've also noticed how much sugar you dump into the bowl to make it palatable for you."

My chin comes down. "You're never satisfied, Lily."

"Well, there is some truth to that, Maggie," Louise jumps in, making me feel as though they're ganging up on me.

Do I want to hear from Mary Kay? No.

She continues. "I take my calcium, my daily vitamin, vitamin E, and some others. It's just good stewardship of our bodies. And of course, I feel passionate about taking care of our external bodies as well."

"Oh sure, bring in the spiritual element," I say, wishing I hadn't given her my ticket to the Women of Faith Conference last February.

"Louise takes care of the face. I take care of the heart and muscles," Jill joins in as she jogs into the room.

Why do I get the feeling I'm taking part in a health experiment? "Hey, I did Curves for a while. How did it go last night?" I ask Jill, trying to change the subject.

"I don't really want to talk about it right now, if you girls don't mind."

Lily and I look at each other but say nothing. Louise puts the plate of wheat toast on the table, while I put some strawberry jam in a white bowl, plunge a spoon into it, and set it out to serve—right next to my place at the table.

"Tell 'em how long you went to Curves," Lily says, making me mad. She looks up. "Tell 'em."

Doggone it, Lily's like a snapping turtle hanging onto its prey. She just won't let it go.

"For a month or two," I say with this feeble little voice that reminds me of my great-grandmother. God rest her soul.

"More like a couple of weeks," Lily interjects. "If I remember right, you were just too busy at the coffee shop."

"Does it matter to you that you're taking my blood pressure to the next level?" I glare at Lily. "I mean, you're so concerned about my health and all."

"Before we get into further discussion, how about I pray for our breakfast," Louise says, doing so before anyone can say anything further.

Doggone her. It's hard to work up a good fit when someone stops to pray.

"When is the last time you had a checkup?" Lily asks before the prayer barely reaches heaven, once again getting on my nerves.

I shrug and snag a piece of toast, slathering on great dollops of jam just to show them.

"You do go for your annual female checkups, right?" Louise asks, lifting her square of quiche from the glass serving dish and putting it onto her plate. She passes the dish to me. "You know, the normal paps and mammograms."

Concentrating on my piece of quiche, I dig it from the dish and place it on my plate, saying nothing. Too bad I'm not home with Gordon and Crusher. They understand me.

Louise looks at me as though I have a fatal disease. "Maggie, tell me you get checkups," she prods.

Every fork drops, and they all stare at me like I'm an unidentifiable organism coughed up by the sea.

I swallow hard. "I do."

They relax and turn their attention back to their plates.

"Sometimes," I add in a whisper.

"Maggie, you promised me you would get one this year. You didn't do it?" Lily asks. The look in her eyes makes me feel guilty.

"I haven't yet. That doesn't mean I won't."

"But you said you were going to do it in January," Lily pushes.

"Can I help it that Tyler scheduled me to work that day?"

"You could have said no. Besides, you told me you rescheduled for February."

"Had to get the car worked on."

"March," Lily presses.

"Remember how you felt when I got involved with your Internet dates?" I ask.

"You stalked," Lily says matter-of-factly.

"I did not stalk." We can't seem to get past this argument. "Anyway, that's how you're making me feel."

"What keeps you from it, Maggie?" Jill asks before taking a drink of apple juice.

After chewing my toast, I swallow and wait a moment. "I'm not sure. Maybe I'm afraid they'll find something. That sounds lame, I know." Talk about feeling vulnerable. Why can't they just eat their quiche and leave me alone?

"It's not lame," Louise says. "I worry about that every time I go in—especially for my mammogram because my aunt had breast cancer. Still, if they find it, I have a chance for survival. If I don't get regular checkups, it could be too late before they would know."

Excuse me, all this talk is taking away my appetite.

"Same with the annual pap smear. Women don't think it's a big deal, but let me tell you, plenty of women die from uterine cancer, too," Jill says.

Okay, that's it. I put my fork down and stare at them. "Do we have to talk about this right now? You are annoying my happy self and ruining this wonderful quiche."

"Yes, we do," Lily says under no uncertain terms. "We care about you, Maggie."

"Then I might point out that my quiche is growing cold while I starve to death."

They continue to stare.

Blowing out a sigh, I pick up my fork again, refusing to let them get to me. "At the first sign of pain, I promise I'll go in, okay? Good grief, you guys are worse than my parents."

"Speaking of which, do you want me to write to your mom?"

"That's not fair, Lily. Besides, you'll never reach her. Their mail is sent to me, so I'd intercept your mail."

"It's a federal offense, Maggie."

"Let me know when they're taking the mug shot. I'll have a facial ahead of time."

Lily groans.

"Maggie, seriously, you can't wait for pain," Jill says. "With uterine cancer, many times there is no pain at all. If you wait for pain, you're too late. Maggie, this is so serious. Get your exams. If you care about Gordon, if you care about your children and future grandchildren, you'll do it."

"Not only that, but the choices you make today will affect your future, Maggie. How you will look, how you will feel, all that," Louise says.

"Okay, so I will only have five years to live, my body and attitude will resemble a leopard seal, and I'll feel as though I've been run over by a Mack truck," I say with a chuckle.

They don't laugh.

As I look around the table at the concern in their eyes, it frightens me a little, almost making me *want* to go call my doctor and schedule the appointment.

"To say nothing of Thelma Waters," Lily adds.

"Doggone it, Lily, now you've gone too far. I'll call when we get home."

"Promise?"

"If I remember."

"I'll remind you."

"Fine."

"Maggie, don't let Lily know you're talking to me," Captain says when I answer my cell phone in the bedroom. "I need you to get her to Siesta Key Beach this afternoon at three o'clock."

"Okay. Any special reason? Something we should look for?"

"It's a surprise. You'll know when you see it. Gotta go." He clicks off.

Once I'm showered and dressed, I join the others in the living room. Someone knocks on the door and Louise answers it. Lily, Jill, and I engage in small talk while Louise handles the caller. She interrupts our conversation when she steps into the room with a dozen yellow roses, and we all gasp.

Louise is smiling from ear-to-ear. "Lily, these are for you," she says, handing the glass vase of roses, greenery, and babies breath, over to Lily.

"Oh my," she says, her eyes sparkling. She pulls out the card, reads it, then looks at us. "They're from Ron."

"Hold everything," I say, grabbing my camera and taking a shot of Lily holding her flowers.

"That is so sweet," Louise says. "He's such a romantic. I'm glad to get a card on our anniversary. Donald isn't the sentimental, romantic type. Count your blessings," Louise says off-the-cuff, but I can tell it strikes a cord with Lily.

"He really is a neat guy. Didn't I hear that he sent you flowers and chocolates for Valentine's Day?" Jill asks, her voice vibrating as she walks in place.

"Yeah, he did," Lily says with a grin. "I'd forgotten that. I think he learned all that from Gordon. They're friends, and Gordon has always been a romantic."

Jill bends over and touches her toes, then stretches upward, back down, upward. "Trust me, that's something they're born with. You can't teach an old dog new tricks," she says on her way down.

Lily takes a whiff from her roses. "Yeah, I suppose you're right." Love twinkles in her eyes, and I'm beginning to think everything will be all right.

Jill straightens and walks over to a chair. "I guess I owe you girls an explanation about last night."

"You don't owe us anything, Jill. What happens between you and Jeff is your business, not ours," Louise says.

"Hello? I beg to differ. Spill your guts, Jill," I say, flopping my legs on the coffee table and crossing them at the ankles. "You know I'm kidding, Jill, but if you want to share, we're here for you." I cup my hand around my ear and lean toward her.

"Well, first off, we did not run into Rodney, for which I'm thankful." She smiles and we relax a little. "I'm sure Rodney has only the best of intentions, but it just unnerved me that he showed up here. Though as he told you, he's here for a conference, and it has nothing to do with me."

I'm not convinced of Rodney's intentions, and by the expressions on Louise and Lily's faces, I'm thinking they aren't convinced either.

"Still, Jeff and I have enough problems without adding Rodney to the mix. We were having the best night. We watched the sunset together, talking about nothing in particular. Then Jeff brought up goals he had for us, and it was great listening to what he hoped for our future. He actually listened to me and what things I wanted for our future. It seemed the perfect opportunity to tell him about the baby—plus, he was worried about me because I've lost a little weight since being here, and he wondered why I didn't have an appetite."

She stares at her fingers a moment here, and we wait. Tears fall from her eyes and spill onto her hands. She keeps her head down. "I told him I was pregnant, and he told me it was impossible, that there has to be another explanation. He kept saying how old we were, and asked me if I thought the baby would even be normal! Here I'm presenting him with the most wonderful news, the very news for which we had prayed for so long, and all he can think about is how old we are and if the baby will be normal? I know that's a question we need to consider and there is testing, but it would make no difference as to whether we would keep the child. The baby is ours. Period. So why did he bring that up—and in that way—as though he didn't want a broken toy?"

"I'm sure it was just shock talking," Lily says.

"But how could he be so insensitive, Lily? I needed his encouragement and support, his assurance that he loves me, not his fears. Trust me, I have enough doubts and fears of my own." Her hands cover her face as she weeps. A gentle hush falls upon the room as we gather around her and say a prayer.

By the time we've finished, we're all crying and hugging.

"Thank you so much. I don't know what I would do without you girls. Jeff got a call from his boss while we were still together last night. He has to go back to Charming today. That upset me because it cut our time together here short, and of course work always gets first place."

My thoughts flit to Gordon. "Seems a lot of men have that problem."

"Yeah. Anyway, he was going to try to get a flight out this morning. I had hoped to hear from him by now, but I guess he's not going to call. He probably already left."

"The separation now is good. It will give you both time to think," Louise encourages.

"Yeah, I guess."

"Hey, I was thinking we all should go to the Siesta Key Beach today. If I go back to Charming without a tan, I'll never hear the end of it from Gordon," I say.

"Sure, we're up for it," Lily says.

Louise and Jill go to their room, and I follow them while Lily goes to our room. I explain the phone call from Captain, and we're on a mission to have Lily at the beach by three o'clock if it kills us.

And with what I know about stalking fitness boy, it just might . . .

148

16

Seagulls cry and swoop over the waters while great blue herons strut and quick little sandpipers dart on spindly legs in search of food. If I could be assured of skinny legs like theirs, I'd live on the beach, too.

The sound of the surf rushing to the shoreline mingles with the quiet murmurs of the crowd as we stroll along the beach in search of the perfect spot to call our own. Once we find it, we settle in with towels, water bottles, lotion, and magazines. Jill cups her hand over her eyes and looks across the beach toward the volleyball area.

"Looking for Rodney?" I ask.

"Yeah. I decided to stop running and make my intentions clear right here and now. Somehow he may have gotten the wrong impression of our friendship, and I need to set the record straight. Maybe he hasn't, but I just want to make sure." She drops her hand and turns to me. "He's probably at his conference. Maybe we should stick around. I can't live with myself another minute if I've given him the wrong impression. Though I can't imagine how Rodney could have misconstrued my friendship."

She obviously didn't hear him tell us he'd like there to be something between them.

Nearby, a cluster of children chatter happily as they build sandcastles, distracting me for a moment.

"That's a man for you," Lily says. "It's fine with me if we stay here awhile. It will give us time to bake"—Lily shoots a glance at Louise and corrects herself—"I mean this will give us time to put a little color in our cheeks." She smiles at Louise.

Before Louise can give Lily a lecture on the sun's damage to the skin, a cell phone rings, and we all dive for our phones until we recognize the tune. It's Louise's phone.

To my right a chubby-legged toddler scampers across the sand while her frazzled mother chases after her. Maybe that's what I need, a toddler to run after. Might work off some of this weight.

"Well, I left my cell phone back at the condo," Jill says, jarring my attention back to her. "I won't know if Jeff tries to call me or not." She pauses. "Maybe it's better that we don't talk just now. He needs time to adjust to the idea of a baby. We both do."

I'm not sure what to say.

I lift my face toward the sun that's sailing overhead in a perfectly blue sky. A breeze stirs and the sea salt perfumes the air, making me glad I'm here.

"Hey, you know, we might as well stay here until lunch," Lily says. "That's only an hour. Then we can come back and look for Rodney later in the day, if you want."

"Now that's a plan," Jill says. "Hey, look over there." Lily and I glance where Jill is pointing. Louise continues talking on the phone and moves a few feet away to talk in private.

"What is that woman doing?" I ask.

"She's braiding people's hair into cornrows," Jill says. "Want to do it?" Excitement reflects from her eyes.

"Are you kidding?" Lily asks, looking unsure about the idea.

"No. Come on, it will be fun," she says. "Maggie?"

Now my hair isn't all that long, so I'm wondering how that girl can do it, but I decide to get into the tropical feel of things—though I'm sure wearing a lei would be less painful. "Sure, why not—as long as no one takes pictures. And as long as I don't have to wear a grass skirt."

"Well, trust me," Lily says, heaving herself up with a grunt, "I won't take pictures if you won't. The world is just not ready for you and me in grass skirts. And since you're directionally challenged, Maggie, I might point out that we're in Florida not Hawaii."

"I wondered what they did with all the volcanoes. Thanks for clearing that up," I say dryly. Cool, fine sand seeps between my toes and my flip-flops as we make our way to the woman. Seeing the bronze beauties standing in line makes me feel I'm with the in-crowd. Never mind that I stick out like a beached whale among copper swans.

Once we set up an afternoon appointment with the stylist, we return to our towels.

"Where did you guys go?" Louise asks, putting her cell phone away.

We start laughing and Jill explains. "By the way, I put your name on the list, too. Are you game?"

Louise looks totally mortified. "Cornrows? I don't know that the idea appeals to me," she says. Does this surprise me? No. Her hair is perfectly coifed at all times. Seeing Louise in cornrows would be like seeing June Cleaver in ripped jeans and a flannel shirt. It just isn't going to happen.

"Well, you don't have to," Jill says. "Your hair is long, so it's a bigger deal for you." Her hair is shoulder length. If she had her hair done, I'd say we'd be stuck in Siesta Key until retirement. Not that that would be a bad thing, but I'd want Gordon to join me.

"Your hair will take no time at all," Lily says to Jill. "I'm thinking my hair is even too long." Lily's looking for a way out of this, no doubt about it. Her hair does stretch to her neck, so she has a point.

"Will no one do this with me?" Jill asks with a pout.

"I will," I say.

"You will?" Lily asks with disbelief. The others look at me with the same shock on their faces.

"Why not? It's my one chance to resemble Bo Derek."

Lily's eyebrows rise to the top of her head.

"Well, if you really, really, really use your imagination."

Everyone laughs.

"Besides, no one should have to do cornrows alone. But someone else will have to drive home. Friends don't let friends do cornrows and drive."

Jill brightens. "Great." She turns to Louise. "You and Lily can go shopping—search for more doll furniture, scrapbook stuff, or whatever, then we can call you on your cell phone when we're finished."

We pass the next few hours on the beach and picnic area, moving from shady patches to full sun, then take time out for lunch. No sign of Rodney anywhere, so we stop worrying about trying to get to him, and we focus on just enjoying our vacation. Louise and Lily take off for shopping, while Jill and I walk over to our hair appointment.

The woman has a partner who has joined her, so they set to work on both of us at the same time. One look at their petite selves, I'm thinking a good stiff wind could blow them into Italy. Of course their size emphasizes my ample figure all the more. If this girl weren't fixing my hair, I'd offer her some M&Ms. Minus the blue ones.

My gal has black hair that's as skinny as she is. Cropped at her neck, her hair is tucked away from her face, showing off six studs on each ear. Baby fine strands frame her eyes. It bothers me a little that everyone on the beach can see us. We're under a canopy so at least we won't be fried to a crisp, but a few rows into this thing, I'm wondering what came over me. These hair braids are so tiny that by the time this girl finishes with me, I'm thinking my great-grandchildren will have graduated high school.

With a glance over at Jill, I'm definitely rethinking this whole thing. If *she* looks that way as pretty as she is, one glance at me will cause a wave of panic to spread across the beach with the force of a tsunami. And might I point out that this whole thing is no picnic. As in, Jill forgot to mention the pain. This woman is pulling my hair so hard that I have half a mind to file a complaint with the police department.

"You having fun on your vacation?" she asks while popping and snapping her gum.

"All except for this part," I say with honesty.

She laughs. "I know it's a pain to be beautiful and cool, isn't it?"

One look at Jill makes me wonder about the beautiful part. Still, "cool" sounds good to this occasional hot flash queen.

"Since we're in the patriotic month of July, I'm weaving some red, white, and blue ribbon in your cornrows, is that okay?" she asks. "Here, take a peek," she says, handing me a mirror.

"Sure," I say, my stomach plunging with one glance. Though I doubt the ribbon will help hide the fact that I look like Yul Brynner with hair plugs.

We continue to chat, and I find out this girl is paying her way through college one head at a time. As in, creating cornrows for vacationers who land on the beach. That knowledge gives this pain a little more of a martyr feel. A type of suffering-for-my-fellow-man kind of thing.

A few bikini-clad women have gathered around us to watch these hairstylists perform their artistry. I'm not exactly thrilled with an audience—especially an audience that makes me intensely aware that my thighs are sagging over the chair.

This whole ordeal becomes overwhelmingly tedious and tiresome. Not only that, but by the time Gidget has finished my last row, I have such a crowd before me that I'm tempted to break into a rendition of the "The Star Spangled Banner." It must be the ribbon.

My face feels tight. I'm thinking if I keep my hair this way, I need never use another drop of cold cream. Why, I can't feel a single wrinkle on my face. Come to think of it, I can't feel my face.

"If you have a camera with you, I'll take your picture," Gidget says with a perky smile. I try to smile back, but my face doesn't move. This must be how Louise feels. I give Gidget my camera.

Jill and I lean toward one another and smile at the camera. All the while I'm wondering if I want actual evidence of me looking this way.

We pay the hairdressers, say our good-byes, and take three steps when a man's voice calls out Jill's name. We turn to face him.

"Rodney, hi." Jill's face turns an interesting shade of pink, and it has nothing to do with the sun. It could just be that her hair is pulled so tight, it's heightened the circulation in her face, but I'm thinking no.

"I wasn't sure that was you. I had to do a double take," he says with a laugh. He looks at me. "You! So you do know her," he says, looking from me to Jill.

"What are you talking about?" I act dumb.

"Remember, I told you I was looking for a woman—" One glance into my eyes, and he gives up. "Oh, never mind." He turns to Jill. "Aren't you going to ask me why I'm here?"

Jill's eyes grow wide. She isn't supposed to know why he's here, so it's an obvious question. They discuss it for a minute, and I start to feel very much an outsider—an outsider with skinny little braids all over my head and a face so tight I'm sure it will sag to my knees when I take my hair down.

"Hey, how about we go have a soda?" Rodney's all smiles, and I want to bop him one. He knows she's married, not to mention that he has a family of his own.

"No, I don't think so, Rodney, but I want to talk to you a moment." Jill looks around the area.

"Why don't you go over to the concession area, Jill? I can wait out here on the beach for you," I say, figuring she'll have time to tell him to get lost while people are around to rescue her if she gets into trouble.

Rodney frowns. He was definitely hoping for more time with her. With his hand against the small of her back, he starts to usher her away. She moves away from his touch.

"Let's wait here with Maggie until the other girls come," she says, looking a tad uncomfortable.

Her comment seems to surprise him. "Oh. Well, okay."

Lily and Louise arrive back in no time. Lily's eyes grow wide as beach balls when she sees my hair.

"Yul Brynner?" I ask.

She chuckles behind her hand.

"You'd better be nice if you want a wedding gift, and if you decide not to go through with the wedding, I'll skip your birthday."

"That's just harsh, Maggie," Lily says.

"At least I tried something different," I say in defense.

"Internet dating is different. This is—well, okay, different."

My fingers reach up to the braids. "Do I look horrible, Lil?"

Her expression softens. "No, you don't, Maggie. You look very, um, tropical. Festive. You know, Bermuda-ish."

"I get it. As in, paint yourself pink, Maggie, and you could be a flamingo."

"Well, you know, I could use something in the front yard."

"Ha, ha."

"Honestly, it's not bad, Maggie. You're getting a tan, so with the braids you look pretty hip," Lily says.

"I can do hip," I say, "as long as it does not have the word *replacement* attached to it."

"I like the patriotic touch," Louise says.

"Yeah, though I think a tropical flower tucked into a braid would be cute," Lily says.

"I'd better stay with the ribbon. Otherwise, someone will plunk an umbrella in my hand and stick me in their drink."

"Only you, Maggie," Louise says, shaking her head.

The girls comment on Jill's hair, exchange half-hearted pleasantries with Rodney, tell us about their purchases, and then Jill and Rodney turn to walk down the beach.

"Here, take this with you in case you need to get in touch with us," I say to Jill, handing her my cell phone and tossing her a motherly look that I hope tells her to be careful.

Rodney gives me a "get real" stare. "We're going to the concession area, *Mom*," he gloats. Handbag in place, I swing back my arm, and Lily clamps down on it, stopping me midattitude, all the while smiling at Rodney and Jill.

"We'll be waiting for you. Bye." Lily waves. As soon as they turn around, Lily turns on me. "What do you think you're doing, Maggie Hayden?"

"Did you hear him? He called me Mom!"

"When will you learn to ignore people when they make those kinds of comments?"

"When I'm through menopause?"

"You can't use that excuse forever, Maggie," Lily says.

"It's not an excuse," I defend. "You know I used to be able to ignore those things, but well, my fuse is shorter, that's all."

"A short fuse, Maggie?" Lily asks. "You don't have a short fuse, you have a stub."

The tide tugs at my attention. Now would be a good time to separate myself from the masses. "I'm going swimming."

"We'll join you as soon as we put our cameras and things in the car," Louise says.

I nod and run toward the water. The feel of the wind against my face, the race toward the Gulf—okay, maybe not a race exactly but a snappy trot—all help to ease my tension. Wading through, I finally flop into the water. It feels silky and warm around me, helping me to calm down. The waves lap against my shoulders. My feet dance upon the shells and sand beneath my feet.

Soon Louise and Lily come toward me and ease into the waves.

We bob around awhile and talk about our trip. Finally, I bring up the thing we're all most likely worrying about.

"I wonder how it's going with Jill and Rodney," I say.

"Gives me the shivers just thinking about it," Lily says.

"Why?" Louise asks.

"I don't know. It's just that she and Jeff seem a little fragile right now, and then there's the shock of the baby. Rodney being here concerns me. Jill seems a little vulnerable. That's all," Lily says.

"Yeah, I know what you mean," I say. "Well, after this meeting, things should be squared away, and she can put this behind her. Then she can concentrate on setting things right between her and Jeff."

"Ron called me this morning," Lily says to me when Louise strikes up a conversation with a woman nearby.

"Oh?"

"He told me he made reservations for us to eat in Rosetown the night I get home."

Louise rejoins us.

"We're going to Pierre LaRone's."

"Wow, that's a fabulous place! He won't wear one of his weird contest T-shirts, will he?" I ask with a grin.

"Ha, ha."

"Are you going there instead of Bermuda?"

"Why do you ask that?" Lily wants to know.

"Because they both cost the same."

"You'd better think twice before you let him get away, Lily. He's a peach," Louise says.

Lily shivers. "Ooooh . . ."

"Are you okay?" Louise looks at Lily with concern.

"You used the *P* word," I say as though she's committed a heinous crime. Leaning in, I whisper, "Peaches. The mere mention of that word gives Lily the willies. The fuzzy skin and all that."

Lily shivers again and puts her hands over her ears. Louise studies Lily as though she's a rare—as in weird—sea creature.

"Don't try to figure her out. It can't be done," I say.

Lily's chin lifts skyward. "I'm no more complicated than you, Miss I-have-weird-toes."

Sharp intake of breath here. "Now, Lily, don't you make this ugly."

"What's wrong with your—"

"Nothing," I snap at Louise, all the while thankful that my toes are hidden beneath the water. In fact, there are probably little sea creatures making fun of them at this very moment.

"I'm sorry, Maggie. I shouldn't have said that. I know how sensitive you are about your—well, I shouldn't have said it."

"It's all right, but next time, leave my toes out of it, will you?"

"Done."

For the next few minutes, we bob contentedly in the water.

"Ron is a great guy," Lily says. "He told me he's been rethinking some things."

"Don't tell me he's having second thoughts now," I say, wondering why he'd take her to such a nice restaurant to call it quits.

Lily smiles. "Yes, he's having second thoughts, but not about what you think." She pauses. "Um, remember how bored Bobby used to get when he didn't have a lot to do?"

"Yeah."

"Well, Ron is thinking of retiring—"

"Don't worry about that, Lil. He won't be bored. He's got hobbies. Why, you'll probably be going on some great trips when he wins endless contests. Not only that, but think about all the coffee visits we'll get while he plays on the computer."

"Yes, but—"

"Is that who I think it is?" Louise cuts in.

My gaze follows to where Louise is pointing. One look and my breath catches in my throat.

"It's Jeff," Lily says as though she's staring at a plate of catfish when she ordered shrimp. "I thought he was going home."

"Yeah, that's what Jill said," I say.

"What are we going to do?" Louise asks.

"Well, he's headed toward the building, so we'd better stop him in case he goes to the concession area," I say, already standing.

We heave ourselves out of the water, and with all the grace of Ma Kettle, Lily hollers out, "Jeff, woo-hoo, we're over here." She wildly waves her arms.

Jeff spots us—now there's a surprise—and walks toward us while we grab our nearby towels. "Hey, how's it going?"

"We're doing, uh, great, Jeff," I say. "We're surprised to see you."

With his hands in his khakis, he looks down and rubs the soles of his Dockers through the sand. "Yeah, I changed my flight." After a moment, his gaze shoots to me. "Where's Jill?"

"Jill?" I say—actually, it's more of a squeak.

"Yeah, you know, your friend, my wife, teacher extraordinaire." He laughs.

Lily and Louise are wearing that deer-in-the-headlights look.

"Uh, she went to grab a bite to eat," Louise blurts.

"Alone?"

Awkward pause here.

"Without you?" he presses.

"Well, we weren't hungry," I say. He probably thinks we're some kind of friends.

"When is she coming back?" he asks, glancing at his watch.

My brain scrambles for the answer that's just not coming to me when suddenly I spot Rodney and Jill exiting the building.

To make matters worse? They're headed this way.

17

"Hey, Jeff," I blurt, "I want to show you the coolest starfish we found on the beach." Before he has a chance to refuse, I grab one of his arms, Lily takes hold of the other, and Louise gets our cue to stall Jill and Rodney.

"Well, I . . ." He tries to protest, but it gets him nowhere as Lily and I keep pulling him toward the shoreline.

"It was the coolest thing," Lily jumps in. "All starrylike and everything."

All starrylike? Can't she do better than that?

She looks at me and shrugs.

"I don't mean to be rude, girls, but I have seen a starfish before." While we pull him forward, his heels dig into the sand, leaving a trail behind us.

"Oh, not like this one," I say with great drama. Quickly, I glance over my shoulder and see that Louise has intercepted Jill and Rodney.

"Whoa, don't push me in the water," Jeff says as we get to the shoreline and stop just in the nick of time, causing him to wobble.

"Oh, sorry," we say with a chuckle.

"Well?" Jeff says.

"Well, what?" I say.

"Where's the starfish?"

"Oh, yeah. Lily, do you see it?" We scout the area for a starfish we're sure must have come ashore in this area if not in this century, most likely in the last.

"It's not over here," she says, looking all disappointed. "Maybe the tide took it out," she says, taking four or five steps into the water directly in front of us.

"Oh, that's too bad," I say to Jeff with a smile. Stepping behind Jeff, I glance toward Louise just in time to see Jill and Rodney walk past her and head toward us! My mind races for a distraction. A couple of kids dash our way, a tad to my left, but they're close enough that one brushes slightly against me. I stumble then fall against Jeff, who shoves into Lily, and the three of us tumble forward into the water with a splash.

Gasping and sputtering for air, I thrash my arms about, figuring this little display will keep half of Florida distracted.

"Maggie Hayden, what are you doing?" Jeff yells.

"I don't want to drown," I say in a frantic voice between gasps.

"You're in shallow water, Maggie," he says, dragging himself up. "You would sooner drown in your bathtub." The look on his face tells me he thinks that wouldn't be a bad idea.

I stop thrashing. He flips water my way as he edges onto the beach. Talk about your bad attitude.

"Way to go, Maggie," Lily whispers with a wink, rising from the water.

Well, if Jeff has anything to say about it, I won't win a popularity contest, but at least I distracted him for the time being.

"I'm so sorry, Jeff," I blather as I lift heavy legs from the water and shuffle over to him. "I'll be happy to pay for your clothes to be cleaned."

People around us are laughing, but he isn't. I feel awful that I've messed up his nice khaki pants. Not to mention that the green crisp button-down shirt he has on now resembles limp seaweed.

"Jeff, are you all right?" Jill asks, grabbing his arm to help him further onto the beach. Rodney is nowhere in sight. Jill's gaze cuts to me, and I mouth "I'm sorry." She smiles and nods.

"I'm fine. Just a little soaked," he says, throwing a frown my way.

"We're so sorry," Lily says. "All for that stupid starfish," she says with a pouting lower lip.

"It's all right, girls." The look on his face says otherwise. Jill hands him her beach towel, and he dries off. "I can think of worse things. They're not coming to me right now, but I'm sure if I try hard enough, I can." He lifts a slight smile, just enough of one to make us feel better. Lily and I smile back.

"Let us buy you lunch. It's the least we can do," I say, relieved that this whole ordeal is over.

"Well, I'd better find a place to change my clothes first. Thankfully, my suitcase is in my car."

We head back toward the bathhouse to change from our bathing suits when we hear Rodney's voice calling behind us. We all turn.

He's standing there as big as you please, bronze muscles rippling and sparkling in the afternoon sun. "See you back in Charming, Jill," he says, arm waving.

A groan hovers in my throat, but I swallow hard.

"Who was that?" Jeff asks in a demanding voice.

Something tells me we're not going to have that nice little lunch after all.

⑥ ⚬ ⑥

After changing into our clothes, Louise and I go to the car to wait for Jill. Lily stays behind to browse through the gift shop.

"Well, that was a disaster," I say, yanking the car door closed. The leather seat burns my wet legs, so I tuck my towel beneath me.

Louise spreads her towel on the seat, climbs onto the seat, and shuts her door. "I'll say. How are we going to help Lily when we can't even get our own problems worked out? I had no idea Jill was going through this stuff."

"Yeah, me neither," I say, feeling ashamed that I haven't been more involved in my friends' lives. Leaning over, I put the key in the ignition and turn it so we can roll our windows down. The stale, hot air exits and a wave of hot, fresh air rushes inside. If Jill doesn't hurry back, we'll have to turn on the air-conditioning.

"Remember that phone call I got this morning?"

I turn to Louise. "Yeah."

"It was Chad."

"Oh, great! How's he doing?"

She glances at her hands. "He's fine, but I'm afraid Donald is getting on Chad's nerves, too. Their relationship isn't the best, so Donald really isn't in a position to reach Chad, at least not yet."

"Maybe with time, they'll work it out," I say.

"It's never too late to work on a relationship, Louise. You know that," Lily says.

"Yes, but it's something I can't fix. They have to do it themselves."

My heart catches for a moment, thinking how I would feel if it were Gordon and Nick having the problems. Fortunately, they have a wonderful father-son relationship. Of course, that was before Nick came home, devoured the food, and trashed the house.

"Are you sure that Chad is ready for it to be fixed?"

Louise looks up at me. "What do you mean?"

"Just that the timing has to be right. Both parties have to be ready for a reconciliation to take place."

"Yeah, I guess." The slightest ripple rears itself between her brows, and I struggle with everything in me to keep the band from playing in my head. It's only a slight wrinkle, mind you, but still it's there. Bring on the cold cream! Shame on me. She needs my help, and I'm wishing a wrinkle on her.

Louise sighs. "Why does life have to get so complicated?"

"It does seem to sometimes," I say, wondering why I worry about my dinky problems when they're so trivial compared to what some people experience. Still, change—the kind that alters life—is never easy.

Louise pulls down the visor and dabs on a little more blush.

"Boy, that gift shop sure was crowded," Lily says, climbing into the car. "But all is not lost. The cashier gave me the name of another great place that sells doll furniture," Lily says, waving a business card.

"Oh, good. Maybe you can find that bedroom suite you're wanting for the house," I say, getting caught up in the dollhouse hobby, of all things.

Lily nods. "Any news from Jill?"

We shake our heads.

"Poor girl. I hope Jeff gives her a chance to explain things and that he looks at it all with a level head."

"Well, we're about to find out," I say. "Here she comes."

"Can I sit there while you drive, Maggie?" Jill asks when she reaches my window.

"Sure." I climb out of the car, walk to the driver's side, and get inside.

"I'll tell you about it in a little bit," Jill says. "I just need time to digest everything right now." Her words are separated by hiccups as she snaps her seat belt over the tiny bump in her belly. By the way, I have more bump than that when I eat a burrito.

"So where do you want to go now?" I ask.

"I'll go wherever everyone else wants to go," Jill says.

"Want to visit the little boutique down the street?" Lily suggests.

We agree.

No one utters a word all the way to the shop.

⑥ ∞ ⑥

After shopping we head back to the beach with ten minutes to spare before Captain's surprise.

We've barely settled onto our towels when Lily says, "You know, I'm kind of tired of being in the sun. I think I'll go back to the gift shop and get a book I saw earlier. Anybody else want to go?"

She can't do this, she'll ruin everything. "I'll go with you in a minute, Lily. I've been reading this article in my magazine. Would you mind if I finished it before we went inside?"

"Oh, sure, that's fine," she says, sitting down.

Whew. So far so good. I just hope Ron's surprise—whatever it is—is on time.

After about eight minutes, Lily stirs on her seat. "Aren't you finished with that article yet, Maggie?"

"Not quite."

She heaves a definite sigh here. Some people have no patience.

"Listen, why don't I just go in, and you can join me when you're done," she says.

Louise, Jill, and I open our mouths to object, but the sound of an airplane engine overhead and people shouting, "Look," stops us. We all turn our gaze skyward.

There, a cream-colored Cessna with a red stripe on the side flies overhead with a yellow banner waving in the breeze behind it. In large black letters the banner says, "Marry me, Lily. Ron."

Lily gasps and covers her mouth with her hand. Tears trickle down her cheeks.

We cluster around her like junior high girls at a sock hop. "He really does love you, Lily," I say.

She nods and says nothing, allowing more tears to fall. "I really do love him," she finally says.

Relief washes over me, and I can see the same relief on Jill and Louise's faces.

"Okay, now we can go," I announce.

"You mean that's why we came back?" Lily asks, laughing.

"That's it. Captain wanted to make sure you saw the sign."

Lily shakes her head. "How could I have doubted for a moment that this is right?"

I shrug as we gather our things and head back to the car. "Lots of women get cold feet before their wedding."

"Yeah, I guess," Lily says in such a way that makes me turn to her. Something in her eyes causes me to stumble a moment.

"Is everything okay, really, Lil?" I ask.

"Yeah, it's okay," she says, but her eyes tell me otherwise.

⑥ ❧ ⑥

"How fun is this, you guys?" I ask the Latte Girls as we settle into our seats in the auditorium, waiting for Donny Osmond to come on stage.

"This is great, Maggie," Lily says, looking all of sixteen.

Judging by the book in Louise's hand, something tells me this isn't her thing, and the look in Jill's eyes says that she is only half-interested. With all the issues she has these days, there's little wonder.

Lily and I watch the crowd and comment on the boomers coming in dressed in Donny Osmond T-shirts. Others bring in photo albums of concerts "back in the day." A few men brave the crowd and find seats next to their wives.

Suddenly, the lights dim, music begins, and Donny Osmond runs out on the stage. My adrenaline cranks up as far as it dares, and I hear somebody howling a full minute before I realize it's me.

He sings some new songs he has written, while boomers call out, "We love you, Donny." When he belts out "Sweet and Innocent," my feet start to move.

166

"Come on, I've got to get a picture!" I pull Lily out in the aisle toward the front.

"You can't do that, Maggie. Flash photos aren't allowed," Miss We-have-to-go-by-the-rules says. She tugs on my arm, but I break free.

My eyes pin her in place with one glance. "I'm going, Louise."

She drops her hold on me.

Unfortunately, other boomers get the idea and push and shove in front of us. Feeling very Inspector Clouseau-ish, I scrunch through the mix and discreetly look around for security. When a perfect view opens up, I zoom in with the camera until I can see the sparkle on Donny's teeth. I'm sure a drop of coffee has never passed through his lips. I hold my breath and lift my camera. Time seems to stand still, while my index finger hits the one button that will capture this memory forever. Click. Nothing. Another click. Nothing. Horror runs through my veins. I fumble with the camera, whack it a time or two, and finally discover my batteries are dead. Someone will pay for this.

Lily and the women around me are dancing and bumping into me. My mood threatens a nosedive, but the fast little number Donny's singing won't let me, so I decide to get into the action. I start howling and dancing—well, okay, we're actually stomping around, but it's glorious. Lily and I laugh so hard, we can hardly catch our breath.

"I haven't worked this hard since we stomped out the red ants in the kids' playhouse," I yell.

"Me, neither."

Donny kicks into "Go Away Little Girl" and invites the audience to sing along. Stagehands force us back to our seats, but we sing all the way down the aisle, collecting frowns and stares, but we don't care.

After the concert, Lily and I sneak around backstage with Louise's camera to see if we can get a picture. It boggles my mind that Lily forgot her camera tonight. She loves Donny as much as I do.

"Over here!" someone yells.

We rush over like a pack of hormone-crazed teenagers. Authorities yell at the crowd and warn us to get away. We're caught up in the frenzy and keep pushing forward. They warn us again, this time threatening to use tear gas.

Lily and I shove ourselves free just as a cloud of smoke envelopes the fans. We choke back the taste and rush out to find Louise and Jill.

"Did you see him?" Louise asks.

"No," I say, smiling.

"Aren't you disappointed?" she presses.

"Sure, but there's always tomorrow."

18

"I'll go with you to the grocery when you go, Louise," I call over my shoulder as I carry the last of my laundry to the bedroom.

"Me too," Lily adds.

"Though I appreciate it, girls, if it's all the same to you, I'd prefer to go alone. Some of my best thinking happens at the grocery." Louise adds a few more items to her list as she continues to browse through a couple of cookbooks she found in the kitchen.

Sounds good to me. Although we did spend most of yesterday resting after the church service, I don't feel all that excited about grocery shopping.

"Well, then I'd like to visit that bookstore we passed the other day," Lily says. "I want to pick up a couple of bridal magazines."

"Didn't you say you had everything set for the wedding?" I ask.

"I do, but I still enjoy browsing through the magazines."

"How about I drop you off there, go grocery shopping, and swing back by to pick you up," Louise says.

"That would be great," Lily says. "Want to go, Maggie?"

"Sure." It beats grocery shopping.

"Will you pick me up the latest Paula Deen magazine while you're there?" Louise wants to know.

"Sure." I say.

"You girls go on without me. A nap sounds pretty good to me right about now."

Jill heads for the bedroom, and the three of us finally leave for the bookstore. Louise drops Lily and me off in front of the store and heads on to the grocery.

"Oh, this is nice," I say once we step inside the store. The air smells of coffee and books. "No matter where I travel, when I step inside a bookstore—especially if there's an attached coffee shop, I feel at home."

Lily looks at me. "You should do a commercial for them," she says with a laugh.

"I mean it. This is one of my creature comforts."

"I know, I'm teasing you. I actually love it here, too. I go to the Barnes & Noble in Rosetown far too often. Do you want to snag some magazines then go over to the coffee shop to talk awhile?"

"Sure." The stress rolls off me as we head to the magazine section.

We grab a couple of readable treasures, make our way to the coffee shop, order our drinks, then find a seat.

"This is a great idea, Lily. I needed this."

"Yeah, me too. Though I have to say I'm feeling much better about things," she says.

"I'm so glad. So you think you've worked through everything?"

"I think so," she says, waving her hand and keeping her gaze fixed on her drink. "I don't want to come between Ron and Tara, but she's being selfish and needs to see it. I'm praying that eventually she'll come around."

When she averts her gaze while talking, there's something usually going on with her. I start to ask her if she's hiding something, but she cuts me off. "How's Gordon doing?"

I blink. "W—what do you mean, how's Gordon doing?"

"Well, you said he was acting sort of weird on the phone."

"Yeah, he sounded very tired. More tired than normal. You know Gordon. He's supposed to work part-time, but as soon as I'm gone, he works more hours. Then there's that whole matter of Nick being home. That boy could suck all the energy from a power plant."

Lily chuckles.

"Gordon will probably lose ten pounds before I get home. I, on the other hand, will have gained ten." With great care and expertise, I lift my straw so that I can slurp some of the whipped cream from the top of my mocha frappe.

"You know, if we drank real coffee, we might lose some weight." She stirs the whipped cream further into her latte.

"Life's too short. You said so yourself."

"True."

"Besides, I've had enough of that health talk to last me awhile, thank you very much."

Lily's brow spikes. "It's for your own good."

"Yeah, whatever."

"You still struggling with your hormones, Maggie?"

"Not as much since I started the bioidentical cream. But I have my moments."

Lily takes a drink then wipes her mouth with a napkin. "Still, you're so much better than you were six months ago. I'm proud of you."

"Couldn't you have brought out that little fact when everyone ganged up on me about the medical thing?" This mocha frappe is the best I've had in a while.

"Well, you're not quite as anal as you were. For a while there, I thought you were losing it." She laughs.

I don't.

"Oh come on, Maggie. You know it's funny. You totally obsessed about your appearance, your weight, everything."

My nose lifts. Do I want to talk about this? No.

Lily's laughing harder now. "When I think about what you put poor Gordon through with your paranoia over Celine—I always forget her last name." More laughing.

"Loveland," I say dryly. "And it's not funny, Lily. You have to admit she was beautiful, and she was working late hours with *my* husband."

"Yeah, yeah, I know. But then you thought he bought plane tickets to take her somewhere when it turned out to be a surprise anniversary trip for you to Hawaii."

I lean my chin in the palm of my hand and sigh. "Yeah, you're right. That was sheer paranoia. That trip was amazing."

"Bobby and I always talked about going, but we never made it." A weak smile tugs at the corners of Lily's mouth.

My heart squeezes. I put my hand on hers. "It's okay to move on, Lil."

"Yeah, I guess. I just feel so guilty." Tears spring to her eyes. "You know, as though my heart has betrayed Bobby."

"He would want you to be happy."

"You're right." She stirs her latte and takes another drink.

"Life changes don't come easy for either one of us, I'm afraid," I say.

She looks up. "I know you like Ron a lot."

"I do like Captain," I say with a smile. "I'm ready for you to get married so you can get back to normal."

She stirs in her seat.

"Why is it I get the feeling you're keeping something from me, Lil?"

"I have no idea," she says, squirming some more.

"Lil," I give her my stern, gaze-over-the-rim-of-my-glasses look.

Just then her cell phone rings. "Saved by the bell," she says cheerily.

"Hello? Oh hi, Ron." She smiles at me then leaves the table. She's put me off for now, but I'll pry it out of her sooner or later. I just hope I can remember.

"He says Gordon is really missing you," Lily says as she slips back into her seat and stuffs her phone into her purse.

My heart blips. "He does?"

"Well, according to Ron, he does." She finishes the last swig of her latte. "He says Gordon just drags himself around. Ron drove up there last weekend and tried to get Gordon to go play golf, but he wouldn't."

"Gordon wouldn't play golf? Wow, this is serious," I say. "Did he mention if the house was trashed?"

"Didn't mention it."

"Did he say if Nick still lived there?"

"Didn't mention Nick. Ron said they ended up eating out and going back to your house where they talked awhile. He even said Gordon looks a bit ashen."

"Probably too much pizza. We've got to get Nick back to school. Course, the fact that Gordon tries to work as hard as he did when he was twenty might have something to do with it. Well, when I get home, I'll bring the color back to Gordon's skin." I think a moment. "It's hard to realize we're all growing older."

"Hey, what are you complaining about? I'm the one who will be a grandma!" Lily says.

"Do you mind, Lil?"

"No, of course not. I'm thrilled. Though I'm a little nervous about being a stepmother."

"You'll be wonderful, Lil. The role suits you."

"Thanks, Maggie. Tara is not going to make it easy, but I'm determined."

"Just don't forget my kids or no doubt they'll feel slighted." My thoughts turn pensive. "You've always been family to us, Lily, from the time we became sisters—"

"In first grade," we say together with a laugh.

"Thanks to Ritchie Wallace," she says.

"And the yellow crayon," I say, referring to the time Ritchie smashed Lily's beloved crayon, causing me to give her my yellow one, forever sealing our friendship.

"Nothing will ever change our friendship, right, Maggie?" Her eyes search mine.

"No, why would it?"

She shrugs.

"Lily, if you think marrying Captain will change anything between us, you're wrong. We loved Bobby, and we love Captain. Besides, I'll look forward to seeing his new T-shirts." I pause a moment. "And even if you had married Dilbert—"

"Now Maggie Lynn, don't you start—"

"—I still would have loved you."

She giggles in spite of herself. "I don't know why you can't just let Dilbert alone. He was a nice man."

"With big teeth."

"Let it go, Maggie."

"Spoilsport."

We flip through our magazines.

"Hey, let's ask Louise and Jill if they want to go to Village Café for lunch. I'm getting hungry," Lily says.

"We should buy stock in that restaurant for as much as we go there." Digging my cell phone out of my purse, I punch in Louise's number and tell her Lily's idea. I turn to Lily, "She says she just talked to Jill, and Jill is feeling a little queasy, doesn't feel up to lunch. She suggested you and I take a cab, and she'll join us there in a little while or call us if she can't make it."

"Sounds good," Lily says.

While I finish talking with Louise, Lily asks the barista for a phone book and looks up the number for a cab. She calls them. By the time I get off the phone, we talk a few more minutes, throw our cups in the trash, pay for our magazines, then head out the door to watch for our cab.

Hot air hits us the moment we step outside.

"Gotta love the Florida sunshine," Lily says with a grin.

"Yeah, I'm enjoying that, but I sure could do without the combination of heat and humidity."

"I'm afraid it goes with the territory. At least your hot flashes have settled down some. As I've said, you were hard to live with during that time."

"Sometimes, Lily, your compassion brings tears to my eyes."

She shrugs. "What can I say? It's a gift."

The taxi pulls into the parking lot, and we wave furiously. Once the driver pulls up to the curb, we climb inside and are immediately assaulted by the smell of stale tobacco and sweat.

"Village Café, please," I say in a nasally voice, trying my best not to breathe.

The driver nods and without so much as a backward glance, pulls into traffic. Thankfully, it takes no time at all to get to the café. I couldn't hold my breath much longer.

The hostess is beginning to recognize us, and she seats us in our usual booth in the back corner. Beside the mirror. Soon our server delivers menus and asks for our drink orders.

"We haven't met you before," I say to the young lady standing before us, her thick blonde hair pulled into a braid midway down her back.

"No, this is my first day," she says, eyes sparkling. "I moved here from Illinois only last week."

"Oh, what brought you here?" Lily asks.

"I visited here with some friends, fell in love with the area, and decided I'd come back to live. So here I am," she says with a wide grin.

We chat with her a moment, give her our drink orders, and she leaves.

"Oh, to be young and carefree," I say.

"What? We could do the same thing," Lily says.

"Pick up and leave?"

"Sure. There's no law that says we have to stay in Charming."

"Well, that's true, but start all over in a new community, new church, new friends?"

"There's that change thing again, Maggie."

"I know. Are you telling me you could do it?"

Lily fudges here a minute. "I could if I had to," she says, glancing up at me.

"Why would anyone have to? I mean, unless their husband had a job transfer or something." My own words stop me cold. Alarm rushes through me as my gaze collides with Lily's. "Captain works from home. You said he's thinking about retiring—"

The server steps up to our table, her black heels clacking across the tiled floor. "Water with lemon for you," she says to me. "And here's your tea," she says to Lily. The ice cubes tinkle against the glass as she places it in front of Lily.

"I'll bet your mother wouldn't want to pack up and move so far from home," I say, voicing my opinion to the server before I can stop myself.

She blinks. "Actually, my dad is gone and my mom is the one who suggested we do this. She came with me."

"That's really great," Lily says, filling in the silent void, since I'm speechless. The server smiles and walks away. "See, Maggie, people do it all the time. Just because we're fifty doesn't mean we have to stop living. Don't be so set in your ways."

A squeak lodges in my throat. Am I set in my ways? "Okay, I admit I'm not big into changing things in my life, but aren't most people that way?"

"No, not *most* people, Maggie. *Old* people."

"Well, it's not as though I have to sit in the same pew every Sunday, Lily." Okay, so I only moved back one pew, I figure it still counts. "I just don't want to move halfway across the country. Who cares, anyway?"

"No one cares, Maggie. I'm just saying you need to be more flexible with the big things in life. Don't let your life grow stagnant."

There goes my blood pressure again. I can feel it. "Do you think my life is stagnant?"

"I don't know." She hesitates a moment. "Well, when is the last time you drank something other than a mocha at the coffee shop?"

I gasp. She wants me to give up my mochas? Them's fightin' words.

Lily looks at me and shrugs. "Just something to think about."

Ain't gonna happen. Okay, so I'm not flexible. Doggone it, now she's gone and put me in a bad mood.

The server comes back with our meals, places them in front of us, then turns on her heels. I swallow hard.

In a moment of inspiration I say, "Um, miss?"

She swivels around to face me. "Yes?"

"Could you bring me an iced tea, please?"

19

"I can't believe we're back on the beach," Louise says with a bit of grumble in her voice. "Our skin will be tough as beef jerky by the time we get back to Charming."

"Well, if you didn't want to come, you should have said so," Jill says. "We gave everyone an opportunity to say so."

We find a place to lay our towels, and Jill does a couple of knee bends and waist exercises before sitting down. It's beyond me how she can live like that.

"I know, but I didn't want to spoil it for everyone else." After Louise greases herself up in another bottle of lotion, she pulls a pink lightweight cover-up over her black one-piece bathing suit, perches sunglasses across the bridge of her nose, and plunks on her sombrero, leaving only her fingers showing.

"If you go home with a tan, I'll be amazed," I say with a chuckle.

"You can laugh at me if you want, but ten years from now, I'll be laughing when I look at you."

Okay, I'm not liking her attitude very much this morning. Come to think of it, they're all getting on my nerves. Louise with her whining about the sun—excuse me, we are in Florida, after all. Hello? What do people do in Florida? They go out in the sun.

And then there's Jill with her constant obsessing about this thing with Jeff and Rodney. And all that exercise drives me to chocolate. I feel badly about it, but quite frankly the Latte Girls are making me crazy.

Lily's looking all dreamy-eyed, and though I don't feel we've done much to help her romance, Captain has. But we got a trip out of the deal, so we can't complain.

And me? Well, I'm just wondering if I'll be able to wade through the pizza boxes and candy wrappers to find my living room. And if I could only get one more glimpse of Donny Osmond—if he's still around.

"Hey, Maggie, look at that," Lily says, pointing to a kid whose head is sticking up from the sand but his body is buried beneath it. "Do you remember how you always wanted to do that, but your mom wouldn't let you? For some reason the thought freaked her out."

"Yeah, I remember. Mom worried about everything." I stare at the little boy whose curly head pokes out of the sand like a period on a blank piece of paper. Suddenly, I feel the corners of my mouth lift while an idea forms in my brain. "Are you thinking what I'm thinking?" I say to Lily.

The ornery twinkle in her eyes tells me she is. "I sure am. Want to do it?"

"Yeah, let's do it." Adrenaline surges through me with the thought of being buried beneath the sand. How scary is that? Though I suspect it has more to do with rebelling against my mother. "Counseling sessions are no doubt in my future."

Lily keeps laughing. "You'll be fine."

"You can't be serious," Louise says incredulously.

"As a heart attack," I say with a laugh.

"Maggie, you're fifty years old and you want to bury your body beneath the sand—with all that icky, gritty stuff?" Louise is practically hysterical which makes me want to do it all the more. Although I have to admit that "icky, gritty stuff" comment makes me pause, but only for a moment.

"You got it."

Jill shakes her head. "Only you, Maggie."

"It will probably be the equivalent of giving myself a mud facial all over my body," I point out to Louise so she might see the cosmetic side of things.

"Or not," she returns.

Ignoring her, Lily and I search for just the right spot to do this. I don't exactly want to be on display amid the hustle and bustle of the beach. Even I have my limits.

"How about over here?" Lily says pointing to a little patch out of the way.

"Perfect."

We settle our things around the area, and Lily and I commence to digging. "Aren't you girls going to help?"

"Not me," Louise says. "I want no part of your burial."

Okay, that creeps me out a little bit. Then Lily looks at me, and we bust up laughing.

Jill gets into the spirit of things and starts scooping out sand to make way for me.

After digging for what seems days, we finally have a hole big enough for me to lie in. An uneasiness crawls over me. I'm not enjoying where my thoughts are going. Hole to *lie* in, uneasiness *crawling* over me. Do I really want to do this?

"Okay, Maggie," Lily says all bubbly, eyes shining, "Get in."

"You're enjoying this far too much, Lily. I'm not sure . . ."

"Oh yes you are. Get in," she says in her bossy voice.

"Wow, that's cool, lady. You gonna get buried?" A little boy of about six years asks me.

"Well—"

"Hey, Mom, look. She's not a 'fraidy cat," he calls out to a woman nearby resting on a towel and reading a book.

She looks up, smiles, and waves.

Okay, now my reputation is on the line. Not to mention this could be a pivotal moment in this kid's life. Backing out now could make him grow up to fear sand and deserts, thereby stripping him of all the joy of a good Indiana Jones adventure. I'd never forgive myself. *Thanks a lot, kid.*

"And she's way older than you," he shouts to his mom.

"Hey, you don't have to tell the world that I'm an old woman, okay?" The little twerp.

Lily and Jill try to stifle their giggles, but I hear them just the same. With a gulp, I ease into the hole. I can do this.

The sand feels cool and not as gritty as I thought it might. It's baby fine. Doesn't feel bad as Lily and Jill toss it on top of me. Something tells me if I hadn't read that last suspense story, this wouldn't bother me, but when they toss that sand over me, well, it just messes with my mind, that's all.

I struggle to relax while my so-called friends bury me.

"You're sure about this, right?" Jill asks with a worried expression.

"Oh yeah," I say with more confidence than I feel. "This will be fun. It really isn't all that different from pulling the lid of the tanning bed over me. It's that same weird feeling."

"If you ask me, it's about as much fun as rounding up a class full of first graders for a fire drill," she says, still piling on the sand. "You're sure braver than I am. Being trapped beneath the sand would bother me."

"Trapped?" My voice squeaks.

"Yeah, who knows what's crawling under there," Louise says.

"Crawling?" I try to swallow, but I can't.

"Maggie's up for it," Lily joins in, pretty much dumping her portion of sand on top of me. The evil spark in her eye gives me the willies. Think Jack Nicholson. *The Shining.* "She's a daredevil."

The sand suddenly feels heavier. If someone yells fire, I'll explode in a puff like a belching vacuum. I refuse to freak out. This is fun, right? What fifty-year-old would be daring enough to do what I've just done? Okay, maybe daring is not the word. Stupid? Yeah, that would be the one.

More sand piling. "Hey, Maggie, you remember that show where there was this monster on the beach that lived beneath the sand and it sucked people underground?" Lily asks, all the while still piling.

At this point, I can feel my eyes take over my face.

Louise gasps. "Well, I hope no crabs happen along."

"Cut it out, you guys, you're scaring her," Jill says.

"Isn't this the kind of thing that made Carrie snap?"

"Carrie who?" Lily wants to know.

"In that Stephen King novel?" Louise looks appropriately horrified.

"That's the one," I say trying to work up a sinister expression. I'm a little limited, what with being buried in sand and all.

They all laugh—and keep piling.

Chills crawl up my arm—at least I think it's chills. The very idea of what else it could be makes me shudder all the more. And I'm pretty sure I see the sand thumping with my heartbeat. When they finish, they brush off their hands and step back to admire their handiwork.

"That should keep you snug for a while," Lily says with a snap of her head. Just then she pulls her camera from her handbag. "Say cheese."

"Don't you dare. Lily Newgent, do you hear me? Don't you dare take that picture."

Flash.

"When I get out of here, you'd better run."

"Come on, Maggie, Gordon will pay big bucks to see this. Might even fund another trip for the Latte Girls."

She's got a point there.

"Hey, do you mind if I run up to the gift shop? The lady told me they were getting new seafood cookbooks in today, and I wanted to take a look," Louise says.

"I need to go to the restroom, maybe I'll run up there with you," Lily joins in. She turns to me. "Do you mind, Maggie?"

"Why no, I'm fine." And I am. I really am. I'm fine. Really fine. "Before you go, would you mind putting my sunglasses on me? That sun is bright."

"Sure." Lily reaches down, snatches the sunglasses from my beach bag, and plunks them on me. "There you go. Does that help?"

"Yeah, thanks." The glasses are warm against my face. I'm kind of glad I'm packed under this sand. It's cooler here.

"Well, I'll stay here with you, Maggie," Jill says, settling in for some serious sunbathing, "in case you get an itch." She laughs.

"Thanks." Lily and Louise patter off in the sand. I'm beginning to understand that whole "beached whale" thing. "You know, Jill, we never really had a chance to hear how things went with Rodney. By the way, do you think he's gone home yet?"

"I think he goes home today. I hope so anyway." She sits up and swivels around to face me. "He didn't take it so well, Maggie. I think it was a pride thing. Something tells me he hasn't been turned down very many times."

"Uh-oh."

"Yeah, he tried to tell me I flirted with him, and I assure you, Maggie, I did not. We talked together as friends. Nothing more. That's why it makes me mad."

"Yeah, some men are that way. Why is it that women have low self-esteem while men have egos the size of Texas?"

Jill laughs. "You're right. That's why Rodney made it a point to yell out to us when Jeff was here. He meant to cause a problem between Jeff and me, I'm almost sure of it."

"That's just mean. Makes me want to give him what for, but I'm not exactly in a position to do so," I say with a chuckle.

"Yeah." Jill sighs. "I guess I'll have to find another gym in Rosetown."

"Who you talking to?" the male voice calls out to Jill.

"Rodney, what are you doing here? I thought you would be gone by now," Jill says, her voice showing her irritation.

"My flight doesn't leave until this evening. I'm all packed and ready to go." He looks over at me. "You." He snorts, laughing hard. "Somehow you look good as a talking head."

I have a comeback, but I swallow it. The Lord just wouldn't be pleased.

"Thank you," I say with a slight bow of my head.

"But let me just say you'll never get *ahead* that way. You really need to put your best *foot* forward," Rodney says cracking himself up again. "Hey, you want to race? I'll even give you a *head* start."

My mouth hangs open, and I glare at him. I mean, what else am I gonna do?

He turns to Jill. "I saw the other girls leave. Where were they"— he turns and looks at me—"*headed*?" More laughing.

"My guess is they wanted to stay a step *ahead* of you," I say, *heading* him off at the pass. "By the way, don't quit your day job."

He stops and looks at me. "What?"

"Your day job? Don't leave it to go into comedy. Just thought I'd let you know in case you were *headed* in that direction."

"Okay, enough with the *head*y jokes." He blurts out another guffaw, and I'm thinking the man needs counseling—or at the very least a good joke book.

"What do you want, Rodney?" Jill says in a clearly disgusted voice.

He turns to her. "I wondered if I could talk to you before I leave."

"There is no more to say."

"Please? I'm prepared to grovel and didn't especially want to do it with an audience," he says, attempting to appeal to Jill's soft side.

"There is nothing more to say." Her words are firm, leaving no room for discussion.

Rodney shrugs. "Okay, if that's the way you want it. See ya, Jill." He tosses me a glance, then walks away.

"You okay?" I ask Jill.

She takes an audible breath. "A little shaken. I'll be fine." Seagull cries and waves lapping to shore fill the moments of silence between us. "Listen, Maggie, would it be okay if I leave for a few minutes? You know, just to take a quick walk along the beach—in the opposite direction of Rodney—time to calm down, you know?"

"Sure, go ahead," I say.

"You'll be all right?"

"I'll be fine, Jill, you go on. The girls will be back soon."

Jill saunters off and soon I'm alone. Our spot is tucked away from others, so my nearest neighbor isn't all that close. I feel a little, well, conspicuous with only my head poking through the sand. Now I realize how insignificant a dotted *i* feels. I'll never look at them the same.

It's such a lovely day, I decide to whistle. Though Gordon can whistle like Bing Crosby in *White Christmas*, my whistles don't come close. Still, the tunes are recognizable and I'm happy, so it works.

Puckering, I blow out "Whistle While You Work." People turn my way, but they don't see me. Their gazes glide right over me in search of the whistle. I'm getting a kick out of watching them so I crank it up a notch. Happy little notes swirl above my head and get carried off in the wind. Why, I haven't had this much fun in a month of Sundays. I'm feeling like Uncle Fester on *The Addams Family* when he did that talking head thing.

Just then a golden lab saunters over to me. What in the world is he doing on a public beach? He clips the distance between us, tail wagging, tongue hanging down to his paws, and stops within inches of me. His derriere plops onto the soft sand just above my belly, and he stares at me.

"Go away," I say, praying all the while he doesn't think I'm a fire hydrant. If he turns his backside to me, I'm so dead. "Go away," I say again, this time more fervently.

If dogs could smile, I'm pretty sure I'd see that here. Say what you will about these dogs, but this one sure is friendly. He inches toward me, rolls out that tongue of his like a red carpet, and in one long forward motion slurps up one side of my face, then the other. He knocks my sunglasses off one ear and now they're whopper-jawed on my face. "Get out of here, you dumb mutt." I jerk my head this way and that, scrunching my face while he covers me with dog slobber. The sunglasses finally fall off.

"Scat! Get out of here you mangy mutt!" I yell between swipes.

He thinks we've become the best of friends. Dogs are so clueless. More licking. If somebody doesn't show up soon, I'll drown.

"Sugar, get over here," some man shouts. "Sorry, um, ma'am," he says trying his hardest not to laugh.

The least he could do is wipe the slobber from my face. I'd let him have it about allowing his dog to run loose, but right now I'm just not in a position of power. I stink of dog spit.

Tail wagging, the dog trots off happily after his master, but not before turning and giving me one final glance. I'm not sure, but I think we're engaged. I've got to get out of this sand and fast before the sun dries dog slobber all over my face.

No sooner has the dog sauntered off than an egret prances over near me. This could win me a spot on *Candid Camera*.

"Go away," I say before he gets too close. They scare easily, he'll vamoose.

He doesn't. In fact, his little stick legs carry him closer until he actually hops up on top of my sand pile. "Excuse me? Go find your own pile. I was here first."

His white feathers fluff a couple of times, and he stands like a lawn ornament on the sand just over my belly. "Get out of here. Shoo," I say. Nothing. Not even a twitch.

Finally, I pull in as much air as I can and blow for all I'm worth.

His feathers lift a tad, he glances my way, then turns his gaze back toward the ocean. Finally, he takes flight, but not before depositing a little something on the sand before takeoff.

I'm barely getting over the humiliation when a Frisbee flies over me. "Hi," a man says with a smile on his way to retrieve the Frisbee.

Sweat beads on my face, but it's not from the sun. Recognition hits me like a tidal wave. Donny Osmond is standing only yards away from my buried self! Panic sears through me. My hair must look a mess. My hair! It's in cornrows. There's not a stitch of makeup on my face by now, my dog friend saw to that. I lift my head and try to look hip, but I'm pretty sure it's not happening. Especially with the little gift deposited from my bird friend mere inches from my head.

At least I don't have to worry about all the junk food I've been eating. After all, I could have a Paris Hilton body beneath this sand. He'll never know. Still, the fact that my face carries twenty-five pounds might be a clue.

My gaze darts to my camera a few feet away. Another glance toward Donny, who is so close, I can almost touch him. In desperation, I try to move my arms, but the sand is too heavy.

He sees me—well, my head anyway. "That's one way to keep cool," he says with a laugh, flashing white teeth, and then he's gone before I can blink.

They'll never believe this back in Charming.

⑥ ☙ ⑥

"Maggie, the girls aren't back yet?" Jill asks with a worried brow.

Do you see them? No, they aren't back yet. "No."

"I'm so sorry, I thought they would have been here by now. You want me to dig you out? You look really hot and sweaty."

"That would be dog spit, thank you."

She starts digging, then stops and looks at me. "What?"

"Long story, never mind."

"Ew, what's that?" she asks, pointing to the egret's gift.

"Don't ask." She makes a face and digs around it.

"You going to be okay?"

Turning a smile my way, Jill says, "Yeah, I'm going to be fine." She goes back to digging with the eagerness of a dieting woman in search of chocolate. Reminds me of someone. Oh yeah, me.

"Well, I'm glad you've got that settled, Jill," I say, meaning it.

Right then Lily and Louise show up. "Oh sure, *now* you show up," I say with disgust.

"What's wrong?" Lily wants to know.

"Nothing."

Right then Lily's eyes go to the spot of sand where the egret had been. "What's that?" she asks, pointing.

"Don't ask."

They all start laughing.

"You girls won't believe who stopped by." Before they can comment, I hurry on. "Donny Osmond!" I explain what happened.

They all look doubtful.

"I think the sun has baked your brain, Maggie," Lily says.

I try like everything to convince them, but by the time I'm finished, they've convinced me that maybe I've imagined it.

Saturday can't come soon enough for me. I'm ready to go home to Gordon and Crusher. So what if I prefer my familiar, consistent world? There's nothing wrong with that. It doesn't mean I'm inflexible as Lily wants me to believe. I'm flexible enough. I've made peace with my body, after all. That wasn't an easy thing to do, but I did it. That should count for something.

Regardless of what Lily thinks, I can embrace change as well as the next person. Though I don't appreciate it, I can do it. I've just never really had to do much of that, but I could do it.

I know I could.

20

"Whose idea was it to come to the beach this early in the morning?" Lily wants to know. She stumbles over a piece of driftwood on the sand causing coffee to spill from her cup and leave a smudge on the sand behind her.

"I thought it would be fun to see the morning sunlight on the water," Jill says all perky and pregnant. Now there's an oxymoron.

"Ever heard of the 'crack of dawn,' Lil?" The sand feels soft as a cloud beneath my feet. Maybe I'm dreaming—which would explain why I can't keep my eyes open.

She yawns then turns to me. "I've heard of it, but that doesn't mean I want to see it. Besides, I was up late talking to Ron."

"Good talk?"

She brightens here. "The best."

It's hard to tell if Lily's eyes are cloudy from love or lack of sleep. Course it could be that focus thing on my end.

An older man and woman walk near the shoreline, hand in hand, enjoying a morning stroll. He's wearing polyester shorts, a T-shirt, and long white socks with sneakers. She's dressed in a housedress complete with a tropical design and a wide straw hat with orange beads dangling from the brim. They wave and move on. That's so Gordon and me in a few years.

"I'm sorry if I've made you all come to the beach too much this trip. To me that's what Florida is all about. We can shop and do other activities back home, but we can't go to the Gulf," Jill says with a zip in her walk. She inhales a long, deep breath through her nose. "Besides, it's good for you to get up early and walk."

Let me just point out here that she hasn't had any coffee this morning, nor did she bring any with her. Still, her elbows are raised, and she's walking with purpose. The look on Lily's face when she turns to Jill reminds me Lily has a dark side.

"It may be good for me, but I'm wondering how good it will be for the rest of you with me getting up this early today," Lily quips.

Finally, someone besides me with an attitude. This is going to be a good day.

Though I'd prefer to stay in bed in the mornings, I'm always up early with Gordon, so I'm used to these hours. A slight mist dampens the air while seagulls call from the early morning sky, igniting my spirits. This is a good thing because I've only had a couple of sips of coffee. Maybe Jill's rubbing off on me.

"Truly, it does feel good out here," I say.

"In a sick sort of way, sure," Lily returns. Uh-oh, maybe *I'm* rubbing off on *Lily.*

"Actually, it might be good to come out before the sun's harmful rays are beating down," Louise says. "You know, just enjoy some relaxing time on the beach, listening to the sounds of the surf, that type of thing without all the people around and without threat of more wrinkles."

Louise looks at me here. Why is that? Just what is she implying? Okay, Lily's got an attitude, and I'm feeling paranoid. This can't be good.

"Hey, what's that?" I ask, pointing to a square section of beach that has been blocked off with rope and sticks.

"Oh, that's a nesting place for loggerhead sea turtles," Jill explains. "It's marked to keep away people and animals."

"Wow, they have smart animals in Florida," I say.

"Why do you say that?" Jill asks.

"Because they know that this marked off area means to leave the turtle's eggs alone." I chuckle and Lily does too.

"Good point," Jill says. "Okay, maybe it's just to let humans know. They're a threatened species. The turtles, not humans. The nesting begins around the first of May and lasts through October."

"That's fascinating," Louise says.

"Isn't it? The mother generally sneaks onto the beach at night to deposit her eggs. Also the babies normally hatch and make their way back to the Gulf at night. Not always, though."

"How long does it take for them to hatch?" I ask as we edge closer.

"About two months, if I remember right," Jill says.

"Oh, I don't think I'll sit and watch them, then. Once I tried to watch a baby chick hatch in a museum. For some reason I thought it would go quickly. I stood there for two hours—two hours, mind you—and he never did make it through that cracked hole he'd been working on."

Lily shakes her head. "Only you, Maggie. Knowing your patience threshold, I can't believe you lasted that long."

"I wouldn't have, only each time I started to leave, he'd make another crack in the hole. I was afraid I would miss it."

They all laugh.

"Well, this is August so if they were here in May, they could hatch anytime now. Careful, not too close," Jill whispers as I approach the nesting area.

"You afraid they'll hear us? I can't even see them." I'm thinking she's taking this a little too seriously.

"They say you need to be quiet near the area, no loud noises, bright lights, that kind of thing. Somehow those things disturb the process. You can't see them, because the mother turtle makes a sort of cavity in the sand, deposits the eggs, then covers them back with sand. That's probably it right there," Jill says, pointing to a hump in the sand.

"Boy, it's kind of hard to keep things quiet on a beach. Too bad the mother turtles don't go someplace where they have less threat of being disturbed," Lily says.

"Yeah, you're right," Jill says. "Hey, how is this spot right here?"

"Looks great," Lily says.

We place our towels on the sand a short distance from the nesting site, but not too close. Donned in warm jackets, we soon settle into comfortable conversation, enveloped by the sounds of the sea.

"It's easy to see why people come here to vacation," Lily says to me after a while.

"Yeah, this is nice." My attention turns to the few people who are now spilling onto the beach. I had no idea people liked to come so early.

"I could handle coming here every year," she says.

"Sure. Gordon and I talked about getting a time-share once, but we didn't like the idea of being locked into going to a certain vacation spot. We wanted the freedom to go where we wanted."

Lily licks her bottom lip. "Yeah, I suppose that's true."

"Here, try this on your lips," Louise says, handing her some lip balm. "This is great for when you've had too much exposure to the sun."

I'm telling you, this woman has the answer for everything. Now, if her makeup could make me resemble Jaclyn Smith, she'd have my attention.

"Thanks," Lily says. "Still, Maggie, I can think of worse places."

"Than this? Oh, you've got that right. This is wonderful." We gaze out to sea a moment. "I'm just saying I don't want to be locked into only one vacation spot. If I want to take a cruise one year or, say, go to Hawaii, I don't want to pay for that trip and a condo in Florida I never used."

"You could always rent it out," Jill says. "You know, when you don't use it."

"I suppose, but Gordon and I aren't good about those kinds of things. Most likely we'd forget, or worse yet, we would remember and just not find anyone to take it."

"Heather and Josh could always use it," Louise suggests.

"Sure, but I'd hate to charge them, and then we'd still be out the money."

"There's always Nick," Lily says with a laugh.

"Oh, yeah, now *there's* a paying customer if ever I saw one," I say, laughing with her.

Lily turns to Louise. "Maybe you aren't aware, but, well, Nick isn't exactly rolling in the dough."

"I remember my college days. Money is scarce during that time of life," Louise says.

"For the kid or the parents?" I ask dryly.

"Both?" Louise says.

"You got it. Come to think of it, I haven't had any money since Nick was born. He had intestinal issues and required special formula right off the bat. He's been costing us ever since. Still, he's worth it—most of the time."

"It doesn't help that he has those liquidy-brown eyes and a grin that could charm the last chocolate bar from a chocoholic," Lily says.

"Spoken like the godmother she is," I say.

"So how are the boys back home getting along? Are they bonding over video games, or are they ready to kill each other?" Jill asks.

"They've had moments of both, according to Gordon. He says if Nick doesn't get enrolled in college or find a job soon, we're rewriting our will."

"Oh, that can't be good," Louise says.

"That's kind of what I thought. And what with all the pain he caused me at childbirth, I kind of hate to give him up, you know? Course, I may change my mind when I get home."

Lily laughs. "He'll get a job to support his dating habit, if nothing else. It will be interesting to see who Nick ends up with."

"Won't it, though? It's kind of scary to think about—for the girl, I mean."

Jill laughs at me.

"You'll see," I say. "They grow up in the blink of an eye."

Jill absently rubs her growing belly.

"It's still hard for me to imagine that we're going to have a baby," she says. A shadow crosses her face.

"Jeff will get used to the idea," I say. "You'll see."

My gaze flits to Louise, and she doesn't look so convinced. I can't help wondering if Donald resents their son.

"We finally talked, but not for long. Someone from work called and interrupted us. He says we'll talk more when I get home."

"It takes time, Jill. He'll come around," I say, hoping I'm right.

"I'll be right back. I'm going to the car to get my book," Jill says, rising. She's most likely trying to hide her emotions and needs a minute alone.

Once she leaves I start to dig into my bag when a nearby movement catches my attention. Something small and dark is moving inside the nesting area.

"Oh my goodness, is that a baby turtle?" I stand.

Louise and Lily gasp collectively.

"I thought they only hatched at night," Louise says.

"That's what they usually do. Maybe this group is a little confused," Lily says.

"Well, hello? Anyone notice that it's still kind of dark out? The rain we had earlier has kept the sky darker than normal."

"Don't go too close, Maggie, you could get into trouble with the

Conservation Commission," Louise warns. She has no sense of adventure whatsoever.

"I won't," I say, all the while edging closer to the nest. Standing as close as I dare I see these tiny heads pushing through the sand, followed by hard shells with ridges that remind me of a shingled roof. Their speedy little legs take off lickety-split toward the sea.

We enjoy the spectacle when suddenly two hatchlings wander in the wrong direction. That would so be me if I were a turtle.

"No, no, go back this way," I say, pointing.

"Um, Maggie, I don't think they understand English," Lily points out.

By now several seagulls swoop overhead and dip toward the stray turtles.

"Oh my goodness, Lily, what are we going to do?" Instinctively, I bend over to grab them.

"Don't touch them!" Louise yells.

"Well, which is better, to touch them or let the seagulls have them for breakfast?" My gaze shoots around for something to deter the birds. I grab a couple of shells to throw at them while yelling to scare them off.

"Hey, lady, leave those birds alone." The old man's drooping jowls wobble when he shouts at me. "They're not hurting anything." His belly hangs over his Spandex like a top that lost its elasticity in 1965. There are no words to describe this visual. By the looks of things, all the hair has fallen off this man's head, sprinkled onto his heavy brows, then settled below his collarbone. Though he's bald, he has an abundance of gray hair on his sagging chest which, I might point out, is downright obscene.

"They're swooping down on these turtles," Lily says.

"It's nature's way. Leave 'em alone," the old man growls.

"That's why they're a threatened species, because predators won't leave them alone," I say, glaring at him as though he is one.

"Oh, you animal rights people are all alike," he says with a wave of his hand.

He steps closer to the straying turtles which are heading toward the parking lot. I stand in the gap overshadowing the turtles and yell at the seagulls.

The old man stares me down. "You're weird," he says to me, causing my hormonal army to rally and call in reinforcements.

"Danger, Will Robinson, warning, warning," Lily says, using our secret code that reminds us to stop and think before we do anything rash. It eases the tension for me.

The old man looks at her. "You're both weird," he says.

Love thy neighbor as thyself. Love thy neighbor as thyself.

When it looks as though he might walk away, another seagull swoops down toward the two stray turtles with whom I'm now bonding.

"Get out of here you feathered big-beaked baby killer!" I shout, arms waving with wild abandon.

"I'm gonna report you, lady!" the man says as though he owns these birds.

"I wasn't talking to you," I say dryly.

Lily blocks the turtles from going further south of the ultimate goal. Louise joins in and blocks the east side to get them turned around.

"You're messin' with nature!" he says dramatically, eyes bugging out to scary proportions.

Shoving my hands on my hips, I stare a hole through him. "You go right ahead and report me, Mr. Seagull Warden Man. I'm not letting those stupid birds hurt these turtles!"

By now some of the people on the beach want to know what all the commotion is about, so they come over to where we're standing.

"That's right. Someone has to protect these turtles!" one woman yells, fisted hand striking the air.

"We mothers stick together," another calls out, and I'm suddenly wondering if I've gotten in over my head.

Again.

"Maybe we'd better go sit down, Maggie," Lily whispers to me.

"Are you kidding? I've got an audience. I can't quit now."

"Oh, get off your high horse," the man says, his face drawn in an angry scowl as he stomps back and forth, no doubt crushing shells brought in by the tide. I'm thinking it's the most exercise he's had since high school some forty or fifty years ago.

Heat climbs my face. Either I'm working on a hot flash, or I'm a level below boiling, neither of which bodes well for the bald guy.

"You weirdos should go home and clean your kitchens!" he taunts further.

Okay, that just makes me want to pluck out his chest hairs one by one.

"Oh yeah? I'll bet you harvest alligators." Lily's nostrils flare and the veins in her neck bulge like a boa constrictor with lunch.

Go, Lily!

Lily's comment fuels me, and I try to remember the scripture I was quoting earlier, but it's just not coming to me.

"That's right, lady. Leave the birds alone," some young man shouts. It's probably the old man's grandson.

He's ugly, too.

Two more seagulls swing back into view. They don't swoop real close, though. The crowd heads off the turtles. We watch as the remaining directionally-challenged little creatures hightail it to the sea as fast as their tiny legs can carry them. They make a tiny splash and soon disappear into the deep. We all clap.

It's all I can do not to say, "So there," to the man. But that would be downright unchristian.

"What seems to be the trouble here?" a voice calls behind me. Something about the voice makes me gulp. I turn around.

"Sorry, officer," I say, quickly explaining the situation. The uniformed man appears to be with the Florida Fish and Wildlife

Conservation Commission. He calls the old man and me aside and gives us a good talking to. I try to appear appropriately ashamed, though I have to admit my adrenaline hasn't worked this hard since my teenage years. What a rush!

Jill returns with her book. "Looks like you got yourself in trouble again, Maggie."

We turn and walk away, but before I can respond to Jill, I hear the old man growl under his breath, "Go save the whales."

In a flash, Lily's hand clamps over my mouth, while Jill and Louise drag me back toward our towels, my feet carving a ditch in the sand.

"You'll thank me for it later," Lily says.

I shake my head. "Ain't gonna happen. This is the most fun I've had since we got here."

21

"Maggie Lynn, only you could cause a scene like that," Lily says as we pile inside the car.

"I sure wish I'd gotten back in time to see it," Jill pipes up with a chuckle. "I'm proud of you, though, Maggie, for sticking up for the turtles."

"Well, somebody had to or they would have been history real fast," I say.

"You should have seen her, Jill," Louise is saying, laughing all the while. "And that man! I've never seen such a sight."

"And I hope I never do again," I say, trying to blot the image from my memory.

We all laugh—well, except for Jill. She just doesn't know what she missed in the few minutes it took for her to "get her book" and collect herself.

"You know Maggie, she's out to save the world," Louise says.

I'm not sure if that's a compliment or an insult.

"Can't blame a girl for trying," I say.

"But some things can't be fixed, Maggie," Lily says. "That's when we have to accept things as they are."

"I saved two turtles from becoming breakfast for seagulls, Lily. I wasn't going for world peace. We're not getting into a deep discussion about life on an empty stomach, are we?"

Lily looks at me, lifts her lips in a smile, and shakes her head. "No depth here, Maggie. It's me, Lily, remember?"

My shoulders relax. "I remember."

"Hey, Jill, what took you so long when you went to get your book?" Lily asks when we reach the restaurant.

"Jeff called," she says.

Before we can respond, the server pads over and takes our drink orders. She's a young thing, but she's wearing comfortable shoes. Obviously, she's smarter than she looks. Once we place our orders, all eyes turn to Jill.

"He said he acted like a jerk, and he was sorry. He wants to talk more when I get home." She laces her fingers together and stares at them.

"Well, that's positive," Lily says. "At least he's not ignoring the issue."

"A baby is kind of hard to ignore," Jill says. "But you're right, it is positive. Jeff is stubborn, so for him to apologize is a big step. I just hope he means it."

"How was his tone?" Louise asks. "You can tell a lot by body language and tone of voice." No doubt Louise has taken workshops on such things, so she can tell if a person is going to buy her products or not.

"His voice was guarded, but he gave me the impression that he was trying to make things right." She bites her lip here. "I'm not sure, though."

"About what?" I ask.

"Well, he said something about changes. They were having a storm in Charming, so the wire crackled and went dead. I don't know if it was positive changes or negative changes that he was talking about."

"We'll choose to believe it's a good thing," Louise says point-blank.

"Maybe. But something in the way he said it makes me wonder."

"Don't borrow trouble, Jill. Take it one step at a time," I say.

"I suppose."

Once we finish our meal we go to a nearby shopping center. While in a dress boutique, Louise picks up a stylish black hat, tries it on, and turns to me. "What do you think?"

"It looks very nice," I say, meaning it. She looks so nice in hers, I decide to try one on. The red hat perches sort of cockeyed on my head, and the price tag dangles at the side.

"What do you think?" I ask, bracing myself as Lily strolls over to me.

"Minnie Pearl," she says with all honesty.

"Minnie Pearl," I repeat, taking it off and putting it back on the hat stand.

Lily laughs and pats my back. "You're pretty enough that you don't need a hat," she whispers into my ear.

Jill browses through a couple of dresses on the rack. "You know, this faith walk thing can be a real challenge sometimes," she says.

"How so?" I ask, wondering what brought on that comment.

"Never in a million years would I have thought that Jeff and I would be any less than ecstatic if we ever got pregnant. But that was ten years ago." Jill lifts sad eyes to us. "Now I wonder if anyone will be happy about this baby." She walks away.

I think for a moment of all that the Latte Girls are dealing with, and I can't help wondering what the Lord has in store for each of us.

"Well, hey there, gorgeous," a deep voice calls out to Lily.

We turn to see a tall, lean man with silver hair, intense blue eyes, and a smile that could charm the shell off a turtle.

Lily glances at the man, then her gaze cuts to me.

"Oh Maggie, you just have to see this dress," Louise says, practically yanking me over to a dress rack.

"Louise, that man is hitting on Lily. I don't have time for a dress."

"I'll check on her," Jill offers and in a flash, she's by Lily's side while I look at some stupid black dress that Louise is bent on showing me.

"I'm just wondering if this would work for the district Sunday School Banquet," Louise says.

It takes everything in me not to gape here. "The banquet isn't until September, Louise. Does anyone ever really worry about what they wear to that banquet?" I ask with disbelief.

Her nose shoots upward. "Well, I do."

"Who was that guy, Lil?" I ask when she and Jill reach us.

"I, uh, well, uh—"

"From the sounds of things I'd say he was self-confidence personified," Jill says.

Lily looks at me and smiles.

"You mean he really was hitting on you, Lily?" The very idea blows my mind.

Lily shoves balled fists onto her hips. Her expression turns dark. "Is that so hard to imagine, Maggie? He was a middle-aged man, and I am a middle-aged woman," she growls.

"I know, but—" I back away from her. Slowly.

"But what?" she says, stepping forward. I don't know what's come over Lily lately, but something in her manner tells me I'd better let this little matter drop, or I'll wake up one morning to a dead horse's head. Think *Godfather*.

"Nothing," I say, turning away from her. Could be that hormonal thing is finally catching up with Lily.

Jill makes a comment to Lily, and I glance around the room. The man is nowhere in sight. There was no denying that Lily looked almost pleased to see that man. I think she enjoyed him flirting with her. Didn't she learn anything from Jill's little crisis?

This whole thing is driving me to chocolate.

⑥ ❦ ⑥

"There he is again!" I say, pointing to George when we drive into the resort toward our condo.

"Who?" Jill wants to know.

"That stupid alligator. He's loose just down the road from our condo. He's near that little pond area," I say.

"He's not stupid, Maggie. If you leave him alone, he'll leave you alone," Louise says, like she's all brave or something.

"I'll bet he swallows little kids whole," I say to Louise in a spooky voice.

She stares at me.

Lily snickers beside me and I grin at her, thankful that she's not mad at me over that little incident at the store.

"I still don't like it that he's running loose and no one seems to care," I say.

"It's a fact of life down here," Jill says, getting out of the car and slamming the door behind her.

We trudge up to the condo and go inside.

"If you girls don't mind, I'm exhausted, and I think I'll take a nap," Jill says.

Louise settles in front of the TV for The Food Network while Lily and I go to the patio.

Once seated, Lily pulls today's purchase from her sack, and we admire it together. "I can't believe that little shop had the perfect bedroom suite for my dollhouse," she says. "Now I just need an armoire and lighting for the room, maybe some wallpaper."

I stare at her.

"What?"

"Your dollhouse bedroom is nicer than mine and Gordon's."

She shrugs. "I want it just right."

I'm wondering if she'll ever finish it. There's always something more she needs.

"You know, Jill's comment about wondering if anyone would be happy about the baby made me think it might be fun to go out and buy her a special baby gift while we're here."

"Lily, that's a great idea!" Leaning over, I tap lightly on the patio door to get Louise's attention. She looks up, and I motion for her to come join us.

She clearly shows the frustration on her face, and glancing at the TV I see that I'm making her miss the chef at work on some fancy chocolate dessert. Maybe we should join Louise in the living room.

"Yes?" Louise asks.

"Lily came up with a great idea," I say, and then I proceed to tell her about the gift idea. She agrees.

"How about we leave Jill a note, telling her we wanted to check out one more shop, and we can pick up the gift, then come back," Lily says.

Quickly, we gather our handbags, scribble out a note for Jill, then head out to the baby store we had seen earlier.

"Oh, let's get this," Louise says, holding up a pink ruffled dress with matching pink bonnet and booties.

"What if she has a boy?" I ask.

"I'm thinking pink," Louise insists.

"If Jill dresses her son in that, he'll have issues. I can't live with that." Lily laughs. Louise ignores me.

Though we're looking for something that will fit either gender, we break down and buy blue and pink flamingos to remind her of our trip. Hopefully, they will fit in our suitcases.

Nothing else really grabs us, so we leave that store and figure we'll check around tomorrow for something else. On the way out, Lily stops in front of the jewelry store window next to the baby store. "Maggie, look at this." She points to a gold charm shaped like a stork.

"Oh, I like it!" I say.

"Me, too," Louise says.

Lily leads the way into the store, and we stop in front of the jewelry counter. A tall leggy woman with a striking face and blonde hair rolled into a French twist steps up to greet us.

"May I help you?" she asks, brown eyes sparkling, smile perfectly in place against smooth, buttery skin.

If she uses Mary Kay, I'm buying stock.

We tell her about the charm we saw in the window, and she walks over to pull it out for us.

"A baby charm is a good idea," Louise says.

"Especially since it's a stork, it would work for baby and remind Jill of our Florida trip."

"And I've seen her wear a gold charm bracelet to church," Lily says, "so we know she has one."

The woman shows us the charm, we inspect it and decide, yes, it is worth all that money—split three ways, of course—so we buy it. When we leave the store, Lily is swinging her package holding the flamingos, and I can't help feeling a little spring in my step as well. This is going to be a fun evening. A real "girl time" of sharing in Jill's joy. At least, I hope that's what this baby brings—joy.

By the time we arrive back at the condo, we're pretty sure Jill will be up from her nap. Louise goes in first to check. We retrieve our package with the flamingos and the charm from the trunk, and Jill's neighbor, Connie Meinser, steps over to us with a five-year-old girl whom she introduces as her grandniece. I tell her about the gifts and then pull out the charm to show her.

"Oh, how lovely. Jill will be so surprised. What a thoughtful thing for you girls to do," she says.

She called us *girls*? I don't care if she is blind, I want her to be *my* neighbor. And yes, I'm ignoring completely her earlier comment about me being her age.

"Why, look how this thing sparkles," she says, raising the charm toward the sun, allowing its warm rays to dazzle and glitter against the golden nugget.

While Connie admires our little baby gift, her niece is distracted a moment by a bold squirrel. Inching his brown furry self toward us, nose sniffing the air, his movements are quick and skittish. The little girl gets nervous and in her attempt to get away from him, she gives a sharp bump into her great-aunt, whose arm jolts upward. The gold charm catapults into the air and lands just in front of the squirrel. The squirrel takes advantage of the situation, scoops the little stork up with his teeth, and runs in the opposite direction.

"He's got our charm!" Lily hollers while my legs kick into high gear, and I shoot off toward the hairy little bandit.

"Get back here, Rocky!" I shout. If I yell "squirrel," half the squirrels in the county will come after me.

I chase him around the back of the condo near the lake. He stops running a moment to turn and look at me, nugget still clutched between his teeth. With his tail whipping forward and back, he drops the charm and barks at me as though this whole thing is my fault. After speaking his mind, he scampers away. Feeling quite proud of myself for persevering and winning back our little jewel, I triumphantly step forward to claim the prize. Bending over, I clutch the nugget in my hand.

Louise's voice calls to me from the patio door. "Maggie, don't turn around. Run to the right side of the condo. Now," she says calmly, but something in her voice tells me to take off. I gulp and try my hardest to do what she says, but when I'm told not to do something? Well, I just have to, that's all.

In one swift movement, I turn to see the object of Louise's distress, and my gaze lands on Gator George who is far enough away for me to make a hasty retreat, but not to stop the pounding of my heart.

I don't care what Jill says about him being harmless. When George's eyes lock with mine, my feet barely touch the ground as I speed to the front of the condo like Superman pumped with espresso. It's only when I stumble into the front of our condo—locking the door behind me—that I dare to breathe.

22

"I'm telling you, Maggie, the look on your face when you turned to face George was the funniest thing I've ever seen," Jill says, holding a pillow to her stomach, laughing.

Maybe I won't give her that charm after all.

Louise, of all people, doubles over and belts out the most unlady-like snort I've ever heard in my life. That alone makes me hoot with the rest of them. A fresh wave of laughter erupts in the living room where we've gathered with our coffee for the evening.

"What were you doing anyway?" Jill asks.

I share a glance with the others, then lift the box with the charm. "I had to retrieve this." Reaching over I hand her the box.

Jill opens it and gasps. "What—what—is this for—"

"Baby Graham," Lily says triumphantly, as though *she* saved the charm from the rabid squirrel. Okay, maybe he wasn't rabid, but he definitely had attitude. Wait. Maybe "he" was a "she," and she was menopausal.

Tears slip down Jill's cheeks and we all hug. "Thank you so much."

She rubs her belly. "I love the charm." Her lips lift in a smile then she turns to me. "And the fact you risked life and limb to get it, well, that just goes above and beyond the call of friendship." More giggling.

We give her the flamingos and have a laugh over how cute they are, then we settle down.

"It's hard to believe our time here is almost over," Lily says, bottom lip drooped in a pout.

"Have you enjoyed yourself, Lil?" I ask, taking another drink.

"I've had a wonderful time. I'll never forget it," she says, curling her feet beneath her on the chair.

"So you've really made up your mind about the wedding? You're going through with it, right?" Louise ventures.

"Yes. I'm going through with it." A wide grin flatters Lily's face. "I don't know why I hesitated. Ron is a good man, and I love him. I was just—I don't know—scared, maybe."

"Change can be frightening," Jill says.

"It can, indeed," Louise says.

"So what made you change your mind?" Jill asks.

"Well, I was afraid I fell in love with Ron because he reminded me of Bobby. But Maggie said that's only because I'm attracted to the same qualities. I've thought about that a lot, and she's right. They're both gentle, thoughtful, nurturing type guys." She waits a moment. "Bobby would want me to be happy again. I think he would approve of Ron." She looks up and smiles. "I'd be an idiot to let him get away from me. I know there are plenty of women out there who would love to have his attention. So I'd better snag him before they do."

"Like Thelma Waters?" I ask.

"Maggie Lynn, don't you start," Lily chides.

"Shame on me, but she makes me crazy. The minute a woman in our congregation goes to her eternal reward, Thelma's on the poor husband's doorstep with a pot roast and a smile."

Louise giggles. "She means well."

"I'm sure she does," I say. "But if I kick off, you'd better keep her away from Gordon. She's just not right for him."

"Gordon would never go for her," Lily says emphatically, making me feel better. "He doesn't like pot roast."

"Oh, thanks, Lil."

Jill gawks at me. "You're serious," she says more as a statement than a question.

"Look, I just don't trust a pot roast-slinging widow."

Jill shakes her head. "I guess I need to keep my eyes open more. Devious women lurk everywhere," she says with a laugh.

"Make fun all you want, but you mark my words, if a man can be bought with a pot roast, Thelma will have him at the altar before he can scoop on the gravy." I turn to Lily. "How about things with you and Tara, Lil? You think you can work it out?"

"I'm willing to try. It occurred to me that anyone in her situation would surely struggle. Hopefully, with a lot of patience, I'll win her over. I have to. I want to be a grandma. How about you, Maggie, have you talked to Gordon lately?"

"We talk every day, but not long. He's either too busy, too tired, or stumbling over something Nick has left in his path."

Jill laughs. "This has been a great trip. I really needed it. Not knowing what the future holds, our talks will help me get through the unknown."

"I'm really glad we did this, too," Lily says. "I don't know if I would have found peace with my decision without it."

"You know, we should do something fun for our last fling in Florida." I sit straight up in my chair.

"Uh-oh, I've seen that look in her eyes before. It can't be good, girls," Lily says.

Louise and Jill groan. "Yeah, we've seen it too," Jill says.

"Oh come on." Adrenaline shoots through my veins. "There must be something we can do." I think a moment. "Hey, how about we get a tattoo?"

"Tattoo?" Louise shrieks. "There is no way I'm going to abuse my body that way."

"Oh, I don't mean that kind. What are you thinking? You know my aversion to pain," I say. "There was enough pain in getting these cornrows, believe me."

Jill smiles and nods.

"That day we rode around in the surrey I saw a place that advertised henna-painted tattoos."

"Yeah, those are fun—and painless," Jill says.

"Well, I don't know," Louise, ever-the-Doubting-Thomas, says.

"Oh, come on, Louise. It's no big deal. They fade off in a couple of weeks," Lily says.

All three of us stare at Louise, waiting for her to go along with the fun.

"Oh, all right," she finally says. "I don't have any Mary Kay parties scheduled for a few weeks after I get back."

I clap my hands. "It's all set then. First thing tomorrow morning the Latte Girls are getting tattooed!"

⑥ ∾ ⑥

When we walk into the tattoo parlor, I snap a picture. For some reason it puts me to mind of that *I Love Lucy* episode where she's dressed up in gypsy clothes and stomping grapes. The room openings are draped with dangling beads from top to bottom that tinkle lightly when separated. Wild colorful artistry decorates the walls while the smell of acrylics circles the room.

The artist and I exchange pleasantries and settle down to business.

She tells me that their henna is selected from the best plants grown in India, and the henna paste is handmade to get the perfect blend of color. She further explains there are no chemicals or dye added, and it's completely safe.

"Sounds good to me," I say, sitting down in my seat. Louise, Jill, and Lily are beside me. The chairs are all in a row much the same as in a beauty salon.

Jill doesn't look so good. I don't know if she's having second thoughts about the tattoo or if the poor thing is suffering from morning sickness.

Some of the pictures I had seen advertised in other henna parlors were kind of creepy, but this place is more down-to-earth. Here they paint flowers and vines, not quite as elaborate as having murals painted on your back. This makes me feel a little better.

"So what would you like me to paint for you, and where do you want it, Maggie?" she asks.

"Well, I was thinking I want my husband's name put on my arm. Maybe paint a pretty heart or something at either end of it."

"Okay." She thinks a moment. "How about I put his name in black letters, then I can outline a heart with stain and fill it in with face paint crayon. I'll top it off with winding green vines over the top of his name. How does that sound?"

"Oh, I like that idea."

The henna artist sets to work, explaining as she goes along how she's making the paste and how she has to strain it so no lumps can get through the Mylar cone she will use to spell Gordon's name. She also explains that she's dyslexic and prefers to spell the name going from back to front. Okay, whatever.

Lily is getting a sprig of daisies along the side of her right foot so it won't show during the wedding. Louise is going for a simple rose on her shoulder. Jill is the bravest of all. She has opted for a baby design on her tummy.

"Won't the guys be surprised when we come back with tattoos?" Lily says.

"Yeah, I'm feeling pretty hip for an old lady."

"You're not old," my artist says, and I'm thinking she'll get a hefty tip for that comment. "By the way, these designs can last anywhere from one to four weeks, depending on the thickness of your skin. Everyone's different."

"I have elephant skin. Just as tough, too. This tattoo should be good for about a year."

The artist laughs. "Well, I doubt that, but it would be great for business if they lasted that long."

Serene music lilts around the room while the artists work their magic. My gal is partway through Gordon's name when she gets a phone call.

"Ebony, it's for you," the receptionist says.

Ebony sighs, puts her Mylar cone aside, and flips off her gloves. "I'll be right back," she says. "No peeking."

"Looks cool," Lily says, looking at my arm.

"Thanks. Yours, too," I say.

Ebony is back in a matter of minutes, her face pale, lips tight. "I'm so sorry, but I have to go. My son has been in an accident. They say he's all right, but he's in the emergency room. Come back tomorrow, and I'll fit you in to finish."

"Oh sure, you go on," I say.

Ebony talks with the other gals about taking her appointments till she gets back, then she rushes out the door. Lily turns to me. "You can't come back tomorrow. We're flying out early."

"I know. That's all right. I'll just go home with half a design."

"As soon as I'm finished with my next appointment, I can take care of you," Lily's gal says.

"It's no big deal," I say. "But thank you."

"I'll be right back. I need to seal your design with extra hold hairspray," she says to Lily. "Since I've used mine, I need to get some in the back."

As soon as she leaves, Lily turns to me and leans in so the others can't hear. "Maggie, you may want her to finish it for you. Have you seen your design?"

"Well, I wanted to wait till it was all dried and finished."

"You might want to look at it. Now."

"It's really no big deal that it's not finished. Half a design is better than no design," I say with a laugh at my clever self.

"Here, let me hold the mirror for you so you can see it better," Lily says, holding the mirror up for me.

That's when I see it. My design. My half-design. The one painted by Miss Dyslexic. The outline of a heart is on the right side. Beside that are letters spelling out Gordon's name—*half* of Gordon's name. As in, D-O-N . . .

⑥ ✺ ⑥

"Only you could end up with a design spelling out another man's name," Louise says to me as we get into the car. Is it my fault that we had to leave early because our tattooist's son had an accident? No. I'm going home with half a tattoo and a whole lot of explaining to do.

"It's not as though I had a choice, Louise," I say. "You want to switch arms? I mean, at least some people shorten Donald's name to Don. No one calls Gordon by that name."

"That's true, but I call him Donald," Louise says.

"Does this mean you won't switch arms?" I persist.

"No. Besides, your nail color is chipping. I don't do chipped nails."

"You can redo the nails, Louise," I say dryly, realizing suddenly that I'm acting way too serious over this switching arms thing.

"You going to be all right till we get home, Jill?" Lily asks.

Jill nods, but keeps her face straight ahead.

"How did your gal set your tattoo, Jill? I saw that she did something different," Louise says, in a lame attempt to get Jill's mind off her stomach.

"She used first aid paper tape bandages. She said it was good for sensitive skin and excellent for pregnant women."

"That's cool. They seemed very professional and health conscious," Louise says. "I appreciate that."

Palm trees and tourist shops line the roadway in a blur as we make our way back to the condo. The scent of hairspray fills the car. An oldies station croons out familiar songs, but I'm not in the mood to enjoy them.

"You guys probably want to eat out, but I think we need to finish off the lunch meat we have at the condo, or we'll have to toss it tomorrow when we leave," Louise, aka Paula Deen, says.

Jill groans. "Don't mention food."

"Oh, sorry," Louise says.

"It's fine with me to go back to the condo. Give Jill a chance to take a nap, too," Lily says.

"Well, so much for a wild last day in Florida," I whisper to Lily.

"It's just lunch, Maggie. We'll go back out this evening," Lily says with no sympathy whatsoever. As in, *You'll survive, so get over it.* "You know, I think a boat ride would be fun. We haven't done that yet."

I perk up here. "Now you're talking."

"Hey, that does sound fun," Louise joins in.

"I'll have to see if I'm up to it. But if I'm not, you girls can go without me. I'll be fine."

"We won't go without you, Jill. But we'll relax while you take your nap. Then if you're up to it later, we can check into charter boat services," Louise says.

We all agree.

I wonder if the salt water could take "Don's" name off my arm . . .

214

"I think I'll call Gordon and see how he's doing," I say after lunch in the condo.

"Tell *Don* we said hello," Louise says, flipping on the food channel.

"I wouldn't tell him about the tattoo until you get home. It's not that bad, Maggie, really," Lily encourages.

"Right. It's just not his name. He'll have no problem with that."

Lily tries not to smile. "Well, the good news is it's not permanent."

"Yeah, I suppose there is a silver lining." I'm still not finding this thing amusing. I step into our bedroom, and Lily is right behind me.

"Hey, Maggie?"

I turn around. "Yeah?"

"Remember when I told you about Ron retiring? Well, what I wanted to say was that he wants me to retire, too. He says we can pool our resources and make it happen. It freaks me out a little to think of sharing money with him—not because I don't trust him or that I'm selfish, but because I have this fear of losing control, you know? I've been on my own for so many years—"

It seems odd that she would bring this up right now. I hope she's not starting to waver with indecision again. "Listen, don't worry, Lil. I saw this infomercial a couple of months ago about an eight-week course on sharing your finances. We bought it for one of Gordon's colleagues for his second wedding. I forget the name of it, but I can ask Gordon to find out."

I pick up my cell phone just as the doorbell rings. Lily sighs. "I'll get it."

Curious as to who's visiting, I put my cell phone down for a moment to see who it is.

Lily opens the front door. "Hi," she says with a burst of energy. She throws her arms around the person, and I'm thinking Lily's getting just a little too friendly with the mailman. Maybe we should call Captain. "I've missed you," she says before stepping out of the way.

"Hi, Maggie." Captain pops into view.

I'm speechless. First Jeff, now Captain? What, the guys can't let us enjoy a little vacation time by ourselves? Okay, maybe I'm feeling a little left out that Gordon hasn't come.

"Afraid she wouldn't come home?" I tease, then I remember his concerns that brought us here in the first place.

"I came here to drag her back," he says with a laugh. He's dressed in jeans and a white T-shirt portraying an animated muffin with the words "Talk to the Muffin" below it. Maybe Lily should rethink this wedding idea.

"Well, Ron, good to see you," Louise says, coming into the hallway to shake his hand. "We've tried to take good care of your bride."

"I appreciate it," he says, giving Lily a sideways squeeze. Although it's been six years since Bob's death, it's weird to see Lily with another man in this way. She didn't look at her dates from the Internet with the same eyes she looked at Bobby and Captain. There's a twinkle in her eyes, a glow on her face when she looks at Captain. It's been a long time since I've seen her this happy. My heart warms with the sight.

We walk into the living room to find a seat. "Can I get you something to drink, Ron?" Lily asks.

"I'll take a glass of water with ice, if you don't mind."

"Sure," she says.

"You go sit down with him, Lily. I'll get it," Louise says.

"I'll be back in a little bit," I say. "I'm going to call Gordon."

"He'll be glad to hear from you," Ron says. "He's a mess without you."

Music to my ears. "Always good to hear that," I say with a smile.

Walking into the bedroom, I close the door behind me. Punching in the familiar numbers, I wait for the receptionist at the other end to answer.

"Yates, Comstock, and Hayden."

"Hello, Heide. This is Maggie Hayden. Is Gordon there?"

"Hi, Mrs. Hayden. Uh, Gordon went home early today," she says.

"What time is it?" I ask, feeling my wrist for my watch that I neglected to put on this morning.

"Two thirty. He just left, though. So you might want to give him a minute to get home or call his cell phone," she says.

"Thanks." I'm surprised that Gordon has already left work. Coworkers or clients must be keeping him from getting something important finished. Without me there to bother him, it's the perfect time to work at home. Maybe I'll just wait and call him later so I don't bother his concentration. Disappointed, I flip my cell phone closed.

With the schedule he's been keeping since I've been gone, I'm wondering if Gordon will have time to scribble me into his calendar when I get home.

23

"So Ron, what brings you to Florida?" I ask, taking a seat in the living room.

His gaze mingles with Lily's. They're totally lovestruck. Wonder what Gordon is doing right now.

"Yoo-hoo, over here." I wave and chuckle. He turns to me. "I asked what brought you to Florida."

"Well, uh, I told Lily I wanted to come and get her and drive her home." He looks at her again and winks.

After my mouth hangs open a full thirty seconds, I snap it shut. "Didn't you know she bought a round-trip airline ticket?" I ask, finding it hard to believe he would drive all the way here just to take her home when she already had a plane ticket.

"We thought it might be fun to see some of the sights together, Maggie." Lily gives me a look that says to back off.

"Where is your bathroom?" Ron asks abruptly. We tell him, and he takes off in a flash. Must be on water pills.

"What's the deal, Lily? You aren't married yet. No hanky-panky business, or I'll tell the preacher," I threaten.

"Maggie, stop being so overprotective. I'm over twenty-one. Besides, I'm behaving myself," Lily says, her back suddenly ramrod straight.

"You can't drive home from Florida in one day. Where you going to stay, hmm?"

"We're stopping in Kentucky to visit his brother and sister-in-law. Don't you worry about that."

"Why is he here?"

"My goodness, Maggie, you don't have to give her the third degree," Louise says.

My gaze shoots to Louise. I'm just about ready to replace her cold cream with lard.

Right then Ron clears his throat and steps back into the room. "Yeah, my cousin has a sailboat that's pretty nice. Kind of got me into sailing."

And you're telling us, why?

"He lives nearby, and I thought maybe you ladies might want to go sailing this afternoon."

Ron has a daughter, a dad, *and* a cousin in Florida?

"We had talked about checking into a boat charter. That would be great!" Louise says, clapping her hands together.

Jill steps into the room and appears a little unsure about the whole thing.

"The boat is docked over in Sarasota, so if you want to load up in your car and follow me and Lily, I'll take you there," he says, still standing.

"Right now?" I ask.

"Sure, why not?" Lily says.

Something's going on. I can feel it.

A nice breeze blows, cutting through the humidity. A jaunt on the boat might be nice, but my suspicion lingers still.

"Why do you think Captain is here?" I ask Jill and Louise.

"Who knows? Probably wanted to make sure Lily came back home," Louise says.

"Yeah, but Lily knew he was coming. I heard her talking to him on the phone last night, and she said she couldn't wait to see him. Something in the way she said it made me think something was up, but she didn't say anything to me after she hung up, so I didn't ask." Jill pushed the turn signal and angled left.

Lily used to tell me—her best friend—everything.

We finally pull up to a dock where boats bob and sway with the tide.

"That's the one we'll be taking," Captain says, pointing to a beautiful white sailboat that's glistening beneath the sun's rays.

"Boy, that sure is a nice boat," I say with admiration. "Nice of your cousin to let us use it." I'm not sure Gordon would loan out such a boat—even if he had one—which of course, he doesn't. Not much need for a boat in Charming. We haven't talked about that in a long time. He used to tell me often how much he wanted one. Funny how I'd forgotten that.

"Hey, let's get a picture," Louise says. We all line up in front of the boat, and Captain takes a picture of us.

"It's a thirty-foot Catalina," he says, returning Louise's camera to her as we climb on board. The main sail has a burgundy boot stripe and matching canvas. "She's pretty fast, too."

I'm feeling a little adventurous today, but I doubt he'll want to go very fast with Jill in the boat.

"You'll need to put these on," he says pulling life jackets from the cabin for us.

"Oh, I'm a fairly good swimmer," I say, waving him off.

"Sorry, Maggie, no one rides in the boat without them."

The reprimand makes me feel stupid, but the others put on their jackets, so I try to maneuver my right arm away from them to keep my tattoo hidden as I attempt to shrug on the life preserver.

"What's that on your arm, Maggie?" Captain asks.

"Oh, it's a little surprise for Gordon," Lily says, stepping in front of him to block his view. She gives him a quick kiss while I pull the preserver on and snap it into place.

The kiss seems to make him forget what he had been talking about. He pulls anchor and starts the motor while we settle into our seats.

"You'll have to be careful with your hat," Lily says to me, pointing to my straw hat. "It gets pretty windy out on the water."

"I'll be careful," I say, not wanting to take it off. I'm having a bad hair day. These cornrows ain't what they used to be. Little hairs are escaping the braids and sticking straight out. If I take this hat off—well, it just wouldn't be right, that's all. On the other hand, maybe I should take it off, it could scare away the sharks.

"I've packed us some snacks," Captain says, passing around diet sodas and chips. My estimation of this guy just keeps going up. His thoughtfulness reminds me of Gordon. The mug in his hand doesn't fit him. The fact that it says "Rise and Whine" clearly indicates it should be mine.

The afternoon sun is high in the sky, warming everything beneath its canopy. Water sprays up the side of the boat and cools my skin as we make our way seaward. The breeze guides us along the Gulf waves that slosh sudsy foam against the hull and rock the boat in rhythmic motion.

I think the only thing that could make this better is if Gordon were with me. A familiar squeeze tugs at my heart, and I push past the lump in my throat. I've never been away from Gordon this long. One more day . . .

"Gordon would love this," I say without thinking.

Lily looks at me. "That's right. You've had several family vacations here, haven't you?"

"Yeah, when the kids were little, we brought them to Disney World, then took a couple of days to go to the beach. I'd forgotten how restful it can be out here," I say, holding on to my hat and staring up at the floating clouds.

"There's something about the constancy of the tide," Jill says. "It's like a steady heartbeat."

I smile thinking about Jill and the unborn child she carries. Surely she and Jeff will work things out.

"It's not the same without Donald here, though," Louise says waxing melancholy.

"I know. I miss Gordon, too." My gaze darts to Captain. "But if you tell him I said so, I'll deny it." I laugh. "Can't have him thinking I can't get along without him."

He holds up his right hand as if swearing allegiance. "Mum's the word. Besides, if he had to get along without you for very long, he'd work himself to death."

Captain makes the offhanded remark with little thought, but it strikes deep inside me. I'm beginning to wonder if Gordon will know how to "play" when he finally does retire.

A stronger breeze races by, causing my spirits to soar. I've had such fun and can hardly wait to get home tomorrow. Life is good.

Lily carefully steps over to me and sits on the seat beside me. "Maggie, I have to talk to you."

"What is it?"

She licks her lips and her eyes take on a dark, serious look. Too serious. I brace myself.

"Hey, Lil, can you come here for a minute?" Captain asks.

Lily throws me a I'll-never-get-to-tell-you-this look and goes over to him. Louise and Jill are engaged in light conversation about possible names for the baby.

All at once a hot flash comes on me. It appears the doc will have to up my hormone meds again. The flashes are getting more frequent. This stupid jacket is so hot I want to rip it off. My hat is hot, but there's that whole hair thing. It's amazing how we suffer for vanity.

Spotting the railing, I figure if I climb up there, I'll feel the full breeze on my face and neck and get some relief.

Tossing a glance toward Captain and Lily, I'm relieved to see their backs are to me. If he sees me he'll tell me I can't climb up there. And they say women are fussy. Louise and Jill are still engrossed in conversation, so I doubt that they'll notice.

Slipping out of my seat, I edge up the railing behind me and heave my backside onto the bar. Not the most comfortable seat in the house, but by far the coolest. The view from that side of me isn't real great, but it's not as though I care what the fish think.

One hand holding onto my hat, the other clutching the bar, I lift my face toward the sea, feeling like Leonardo DiCaprio when he stood on the bow of the *Titanic*. There's something powerfully refreshing about it all. The damp, misty breeze lights upon my face, easing the heat radiating from my body. Let me just say if I sat on an iceberg right now, I'd sink. Hmm, I hope it's not a bad sign that I've thought of sink and *Titanic* all within two minutes.

"Have you told Maggie yet?" Captain's voice lifts on the breeze and flutters my way. My ears perk. They must be discussing whatever it is that Lily's been trying to tell me.

"Struggle—time—not yet." The thump of the water hitting the sides of the boat drowns out her words.

"Show—our place—Florida." His words zip through me. *Our* place? Florida? Lily and Captain have a place in Florida? Is that what he said? Is that what he's doing here?

Suddenly, a gust of wind whips across the boat, tossing my hat high into the air. In one swift reaction my hands flail to grasp it, causing me to lose my balance. Before I know what's hit me, my body does a backward flip that could land me a job with Barnum and Bailey. I hear screams and by the raw feel of my throat, I'm pretty sure they're coming from me. I hit the surface of the water and go under. The lifejacket toggles me upright before panic sets in, though it takes me a moment to stop coughing and heaving in gulps of air.

It freaks me out to think what might be lurking beneath my feet. If anything with gills comes toward me, I'll rip its fins off. Cold, I know, but I am bobbing with aquatic vertebrates, after all.

Through blurred vision, I see Lily's worried face peering over the rim of the boat. She's shouting something, but the noise from the water lapping against the boat and the water plugged in my ears makes it impossible for me to hear.

Captain throws a rope overboard, and I suddenly feel caught up in a drama. Now that I know safety is within reach, I'd enjoy playing this up, but there's that whole dangling feet and shark thing, so I decide to get back on the boat as soon as possible.

Kicking, I edge my way toward the rope when I spot my hat to the right of me. I start to tell them I'm going for my hat, but I get a mouth full of water, which makes me choke and cough some more. The water pushes the hat my way, and I retrieve the soggy, limp straw and plunk it on my head. Something tells me this is the last time I will wear it.

Straw hat in place, I grab the rope, knowing I at least will get back into the boat with style. It takes Captain *and* the girls to pull me up, which is a little embarrassing to say the least, but at last I crawl over the rim and slump onto the bottom of the boat in a puddle.

Lily bends over me, her eyes brimming with tears. She says something, but I'm clueless. My ears are still plugged. Everyone's lips are moving simultaneously. If I could hear them, they'd probably give me a headache. Instead I do what comes natural to me in stressful situations. When I see their talking heads, I laugh . . . and laugh . . . and laugh. In fact, I laugh so hard, I can hardly catch my breath. I roll over on my side to get a better handle on this guffaw thing, and

I don't know whether it's my position or my gut laugh that does it, but suddenly my ears pop open, and I hear Louise and Jill covering their giggles and Captain's male voice chuckling a bit, but when I turn to Lily, there's fire in her eyes.

"Maggie Lynn Hayden, what were you doing? You nearly scared the living daylights out of me," she says, face contorted, eyes flashing.

And let me just say I've seen friendlier sharks.

"Hold it right there." Louise snaps a picture, nearly blinding me.

Okay, whatever dignity I might have had before the fall—wait. Come to think of it, dignity has never been my strong suit.

"Sorry, Maggie."

"At least my hair is covered by the hat," I say, hauling my soppy self up. I cough a few more times and finally say, "It's not as though I planned this, Lil." I squeeze the water from my lifejacket.

"There are guardrails on this boat, Maggie. Does that mean nothing to you? They are meant to hold people *in* the boat. People are not supposed to climb on them. What were you doing?"

Somebody snitched. I'm thinking Louise. "I was hot, Lily."

"You risk your life for a hot flash, Maggie?" Disbelief covers her face.

"You've never had one, so don't judge me," I say, hiking my nose.

"You're right, I haven't. But I can't understand why anyone would rather be dead than hot," she grumbles.

"That's because you've never had one. Besides, being dead was not part of the plan." I haul myself up and sit on the seat. Lily sits down beside me while the others go back to whatever it was they were doing.

"You scared me, Maggie. I don't know what I would ever do if I lost you," she says, tears brimming in her eyes. She pulls me into a hard hug. "Please don't ever do that again."

Okay now tears are stinging my eyes, I think. It's hard to tell because water is dripping from me everywhere. "I'm sorry, Lil. I should have used better judgment."

"Are you okay now?" she asks.

"I'm fine," I say, throwing in one more cough for good measure. "How come you never got this upset when I fell off of the Jet Ski?"

"I don't know. It was different then. You were reachable. But just now, below the boat, you looked so—I don't know—*small*."

"Small? I looked small? And you have a problem with that?"

Lily will not be deterred. She pulls back and looks at me. "You're my best friend, Maggie. Please don't ever forget that." She gets up, walks over to her handbag, grabs a tissue, then joins Captain once again.

Something in the way she says that snags my heart, then suddenly I remember the discussion she and Captain had before I fell. I'm pretty sure I don't want to hear what she has to say.

24

"Did you check the dresser drawers?" Lily asks as we pack our suitcases.

"Yeah, they're empty. You know, in one way, it's hard to imagine our time here is already over. On the other hand, it seems forever since I've seen Gordon. Maybe I better look at his photograph once again in my purse to make sure I'll recognize him in the airport."

"You'll recognize him," Lily says with a chuckle. "It will be good to get home." She shoves the last of her clothes into her suitcase. "Gordon will be so happy to see you." She zips her case closed, heaves it from the bed to the floor, and pulls up the long handle.

"I can't wait to see him, too."

Lily smiles and goes into the living room for something while I pack the last of my things into the suitcase. Once everything is set and the case is zipped closed, I spot the stuffed flamingos that Lily and I bought for Jill's baby. Everyone else's suitcases are crammed full, so I said I would fit these into mine. I may live to regret this. Carefully, I roll up my sleeves and set to work.

First I pull out all my shirts, lay the pink bird against the bottom of the case, then pile the blouses back on top. The body of the bird is long fluffy yarn, so I'm afraid it will be smashed and distorted by the time I get home, saying nothing of what it will do to the poor thing's beak. Working up a good sweat, I pull the shirts back out, arrange, rearrange, pull out, pile on, sort, burrow, roll, stuff, and finally end up with a headache and both flamingos inside my suitcase. Hopefully, they'll bounce back to their original shape by the time the baby is born.

Lily walks back into our room. "Need any help?"

"Will you help me zip this up?" I ask Lily, flopping my derriere on top of the bag. By now, I'm wondering if those flamingos have a prayer of ever getting their shape back. I know the feeling. "Okay, ready," I say, sitting on my lumpy bag, my feet dangling over the side.

Lily yanks and tugs at the zipper, and it's anybody's guess who's going to win this one. I just hope the zipper doesn't break.

"Be afraid. Be very afraid," Lily growls to the bag, yanking and twisting the zipper every which way.

"I'm sitting on it, Lily. How much worse can it get?" Lily and I have always treated inanimate objects as real. We've never grown out of that overactive imagination thing.

I redistribute my weight and can almost hear the bag groan (the suitcase, not Lily). With one final jerk, Lily takes the zipper on home to victory. I jump off and we celebrate.

It takes so little to make us party.

"I sure hope you don't have to pay extra for that bag, Maggie," Lily says, casting a wary glance its way. "It looks like Uncle Ralph after Thanksgiving dinner."

"Lily Newgent," I say, laughing. "I'd prefer to think that it looks as though it's ready to give birth. And the overage charge is cheaper than a baby."

"Maggie, I need to talk to you now before we get another interruption," Lily says, the expression on her face suddenly serious. "Can we sit on the bed?" she asks.

"Uh-oh, this is a sit-down talk? Something tells me I don't want to hear this."

Her lips lift in a weak smile and dread crawls over me, causing goose bumps to appear on my arms.

She grabs my hand. "Listen, Maggie, you know you're my best friend in all the world—"

"You're trying to tell me you don't want me to be your matron of honor, is that it?"

She smiles. "Of course not. No one else could ever fill that place but you."

I gulp quietly.

"But there is something," she ventures.

"Captain owns a place in Florida, doesn't he?" I ask, voicing what I've dared not allow myself to even think.

She blinks. "How—how did you know?"

"I heard you talking on the boat and put two and two together," I say, studying my fingers. "Are you moving?" I whisper, fearing that if I speak the words too loudly, it will come true.

"Yeah. That's one of the reasons I struggled with the getting married thing. And I couldn't tell you because we both know how you would feel about it."

With my gaze still down, I smile and nod.

"Charming is all I've ever known, Maggie. To leave you, my friends, my business, I wasn't sure I could do it."

"And now?"

"As hard as it will be for me to leave, I know Ron is right for me." She squeezes my hand. "I have to go with him, Maggie." I feel her tear plop onto my hand, and I look up.

"I understand." My mind is swirling. I need time to think. It's probably not true, but I can't help feeling that Captain betrayed me.

He asked me to talk Lily into marrying him just so he could take my best friend away. For Lily's sake, it's best I keep quiet. For now.

"We won't be moving until I can get the house sold and all that, so I'll be around for a while," Lily says brightly, but the acid churns in my stomach just the same.

I put on a happy face for her benefit. She has enough on her mind without worrying about me. We'll get through this. But we're kidding ourselves if we think things will be the same. They won't. She'll be here, and I'll be in Charming.

"Will you be moving to Siesta Key?" I ask.

"Sarasota. He has a beautiful home there. It's small but quaint. Still, it's large enough to have you and Gordon over for extended periods of time," she says, emphasizing the extended part.

"So that's why he came to Florida? You told him the wedding was back on, so he came here to get the house ready for after the wedding?" I ask.

A look of apology covers Lily's face, and she nods. "I'm sorry I didn't tell you, Maggie. I had to get things straight in my own mind first. Then I tried to tell you, and we kept getting interrupted."

"I know. It's all right, Lil."

"You girls ready?" Jill asks.

We nod. I lower my luggage off the bed and grab the leash. A lump works its way to my throat. I just need some time to get through this.

"You're sure Ron will be here any minute?" Louise asks Lily.

"We won't leave until he gets here, so we can say our good-byes." Jill presses her hand against the wall while she lifts her legs, one, two, three.

My body feels cold, my fingers stiff. The Tin Man on *Wizard of Oz* comes to mind. Hopefully, I won't clang when I walk. A hot flash would almost be a welcome relief. It would prove I'm still living.

"He'll be here," Lily says. Then she goes into this story about how he tends to run a few minutes late everywhere he goes.

I watch her and listen. How do you say good-bye to your best friend? The person you call when you want to dance to old records? The one who giggles with you when no one else understands the joke, goes through facial masks, chocolate binges, shopping sprees, manicures, and pedicures? Guys just can't relate. They aren't women—which is a good thing—but it also means they don't always understand why we do what we do. But Lily? She understands.

"I think we've got everything," Jill says, grabbing my attention. Despite the fact we've had two weeks' vacation, dark shadows smudge beneath her eyes. There's a hard road ahead of her when she gets home.

There's a hard road ahead for all of us.

"Do you want to go out and say good-bye to Gator George, Maggie?" Jill teases.

"As fond as I am of him, I think I'll just wave from the patio, if you don't mind," I say. "Besides, if he were any kind of friend at all, he'd let me make him into a purse." Funny how I'm able to push those lighthearted words past the boulder in my throat.

"Easy for you to say, it's no skin off your back," Lily jumps in.

My laugh sounds strange and old to me, as though it's coming from someone else.

We glance around the condo one last time, checking for any stray items we might have left behind.

"Before we leave, could we pray together?" Lily asks.

"Great idea," Louise says.

Stepping around our suitcases, we cluster in the living room, grab one another's hands, and offer thanks for our friendship, our time together, the future for each of us, and our trip home. Despite our great time together, emotion escapes me. I feel like aged driftwood, left alone on a forgotten beach. Left to harden and break off, one brittle piece after another.

It seems as though I just learn one life lesson and another is waiting in line. Is there no rest after midlife?

Jill sticks the key in the door, and the bolt clicks behind us.

The noise jars me. There's something so final about it. Another passage of time, another memory shared, a new day dawning.

A day without my best friend.

⑥　☞　⑥

The three of us make our way through the airport. A familiar form walks past us, stops a moment, looks at me, and points. "I think I saw you recently," he says.

With a gulp, I look straight into the eyes of Donny Osmond. My eyes feel wide, my jaw slacks open. The sound of my pulse hammers against my ears. My arms tingle. Darkness fringes the edges of my vision, and I start to wobble. "Hey, are you all right?" he says, reaching over to grab my arm and hold me steady. My arm burns where his fingers had been.

Louise steps forward. "Are you here for that big concert in Indy?"

Flashing white teeth again. "Yeah."

"Would it be alright if we got a picture of you with Maggie? She's a great fan of yours."

"Sure."

The next minute passes in a blur. Donny's wife steps up beside him and he introduces her. She offers to take a picture of the three of us with Donny. He then sandwiches himself between us. His wife snaps the picture. Before they leave, I somehow manage a smile, but my thick tongue just lays there like a slug.

Louise and Jill laugh at me. Before I can take another breath, a wide-eyed Gordon rounds the bend.

"Hey, was that who I think it was?"

My tongue loosens like a midriff set free from a girdle. "Gordon!" I hug him fiercely. "Yes, that was Donny Osmond," I say all proud-like, as though I had something to do with bumping into the star.

"Guess I had better keep my eye on you," he says as though he's jealous. My heart skips a beat at the sight of his smile. He pulls me into another bear hug.

"There's my tropical girl. Nice hair," he says when he pulls away.

My fingers absently reach for my head. "I was going to take my hair down, but thought I'd meet you with a festive flair first," I say with a laugh. "Though it looked better when I first had it done."

"It looks great, babe." He hugs me again, and he doesn't have to tell me he missed me. It's in his hug. A warm, tingly sensation rushes through me.

After a moment or two, he starts to pull away, but I hold him tighter. "Not yet," I say, squeezing hard. When he finally pulls back, he looks me full in the face.

"You okay, Maggie girl?"

Unwanted tears spring to my eyes, and I nod. "Just missing you, that's all." Which is partially true. I have missed him more than words can say. But there's more. I just can't talk about it yet.

"I've missed you too, baby." Despite the milling crowd, Gordon bends down and tenderly caresses my lips with his own. The world goes dark around me as I surrender to the sweetness of his kiss, drink in the Tommy scent so familiar to me, and linger in his arms.

When we pull apart, I see Donald greet Louise with a hug, and she reluctantly returns it. To the right of them, Jill is scanning the crowd. Jeff is nowhere in sight. Another ache. My hormones are unrelenting today.

"Gordon, I don't see Jeff here. Could we take Jill home?"

"Sure," he says.

"I'll be right back," I call over my shoulder as I make my way to Jill. "You need a lift home?" I ask brightly.

She turns to me, struggling to appear nonchalant, but she's not fooling me. "No, thanks. I called my sister to pick me up."

"You okay?"

She pastes on a bright smile, letting me know she doesn't want to talk about it. "I'm fine."

"Okay, talk to you soon at the coffee shop." After I give her one more hug, I turn and see Jeff running with a bouquet of flowers in his hands. My heart lightens, and I walk over to Gordon to give them time alone. Jeff stops in front of Jill, and they embrace.

We all walk to baggage claim together. Gordon takes the final picture of the girls, and we say our good-byes, my worried thoughts flitting to Lily.

"Well, Maggie girl, what say we head for home," Gordon says with a wink.

I'll deal with Lily later. Right now, Gordon has my full attention . . .

⑥ ❦ ⑥

I reach for my morning coffee and settle in on the patio with Gordon. Habits, traditions, familiarity. All things I treasure and yet so often take for granted.

"Are you doing okay, Gordon?"

"Doing great," he says with a grin that can still curl my toes. "Why do you ask?"

Studying the circles under his eyes, I shrug. "You just look a little tired. If I know you, you worked too hard while I was gone."

Crusher, our Chihuahua, whines at my side. I heave his slight body onto my lap where his scrawny self falls in a heap. I scratch gently behind his ears—a tradition to which he's accustomed. He instantly closes his eyes and drifts into doggy dreamland.

"Guilty as charged. Plus the fact that I don't sleep well when you're away," he says, making me forget all about the lecture I was prepared to give him.

"Well, this is my second day home. Now what's your excuse?" I tease.

"You think in two days I can get over the trauma of you being gone for over two weeks?" he asks.

"No?"

"No."

My hand reaches across the table and claims his hand. "I missed you terribly, Gordon." Crusher's thin lip curls in a slight snarl and a low growl rumbles through his clenched teeth as his dreams no doubt take him back to the glory days when he had a full head of teeth and enough sass to chase off the boldest of mailmen.

Gordon puts his coffee cup beside the morning paper and looks me square in the eyes. "I really missed you, Maggie."

"Can't handle Nick alone, huh?"

"You got it."

We both laugh.

"Speaking of Nick, I have to admit our house was far cleaner than I had expected. You guys did a good job."

"I threatened him with death."

"Threats are good," I say, taking a drink of coffee. "I even checked our closets, figuring Nick would stuff everything there. No moldy pizza, dead bodies, nothing. Still I haven't checked his room. I don't have the courage."

"Just don't leave me alone with him that long again, okay? My nerves can't take it," Gordon says, causing me to laugh.

"I doubt there will be a next time."

He studies me. "Uh-oh. Trouble in Latte Land?"

"No, we got along fine." My emotions wavering, I pause a moment. "It's just that—that—" I feel my chin start to quiver, and I don't want to do this. "Oh, nothing."

"Maggie, what is it?" The concern in Gordon's voice causes tears to surface against my will.

"Oh, I'm sorry that I'm acting so emotional," I say, brushing off the tears with the back of my hand.

"You still using your hormone cream?" he asks in a fearful voice. Why is it he thinks everything is hormone-related? He figures Maggie minus hormones spells trouble, I'm sure of it.

"Yes, Gordon, I'm taking my hormones." Which is probably a good thing, or I'd have to hurt him for that comment.

"So what's wrong then?"

"Lily is moving with Captain to Florida." Pulling a tissue from my pants pocket, I wipe fresh tears from my face. When I finish, I realize Gordon hasn't said anything. His eyes meet mine. "You knew, didn't you?"

He nods. "I'm sorry, Maggie. Lily made me promise not to tell you. She wanted to tell you herself." He grabs my hand. "I knew this would be hard on you. I'm so sorry, babe."

"Well, obviously she's okay with it. It just makes me mad that he asked me to get the girls to help Lily not back out of the wedding, all the while knowing he was taking her from me. Why didn't he tell me that?"

Before Gordon can answer I butt in. "Because he was afraid I might not help him, that's why."

"But you would have," Gordon says sweetly, jolting me.

"What do you mean?"

"You love Lily too much to stand in the way of her happiness, that's why." Gordon glances at his watch. "I'm sorry, honey, but I have to get to work. We'll talk more tonight, okay?"

I nod, stroking Crusher more for my comfort than his. Gordon comes around the table and gives me a kiss, then walks back into the house. After a few minutes, I hear his car pull out of the drive. Though the sound of the '71 Nova's engine fades as he drives down the street, Gordon's words remain loud and clear.

"You love Lily too much to stand in the way of her happiness."

Just goes to show, Gordon doesn't know everything.

Ⓖ ⚇ Ⓖ

"Hi, Mom!" Heather's voice calls from the other end of the phone line.

"Hey, sweetie!"

"I've missed you. Did you have a great time?"

I tell her about the highlights of our trip, leaving off the personal stuff, except for Lily.

"Aunt Lily moving to Florida?" Heather asks in disbelief. "I know she's your best friend, Mom, but I'll miss her, too. She's always been there for Nick and me."

"I know." My mood plunges into further despair. "Nothing short of murder will fix it," I say.

"Got any ideas?" Heather asks with an evil laugh.

"I don't have the energy."

Our discussion turns to Captain's daughter and her baby. We then get into baby names, the current fashions for infants, and finally we say good-bye.

Walking to Nick's room, I close my eyes, take a deep breath, and shove open his door, bracing myself for the mess. Much to my surprise, his room is fairly picked up. Not overly neat, mind you, but passable. My gaze flits to his closet, but I just don't want to push my luck, so I turn away. Nick is out looking for work, whether it's just for the summer or permanently, we don't know for sure. His depression seems to have let up some, but he's still not totally back to his ornery self. I close his door.

Though I would love to call Jill and Louise and see how things are going for them, I decide to wait a couple more days and give them time at home before I bother them. Instead, I use my afternoon cleaning, doing laundry, and getting our house back in order. I also spend forever taking the cornrows from my hair, washing it, and making myself presentable again. Once in a lifetime is enough for me.

After everything is finished, I run to the store to get some things for dinner. I run into Louise over in produce so I push my cart over to her.

"Hey, Florida buddy," I say, peering beyond her shoulder at the head of lettuce she's holding.

"Maggie, hi," she says, hugging me. When we pull away I notice dark shadows beneath her eyes. Knowing her face rarely has the slightest ripple, I'm a little alarmed.

"How you doing, Louise?" I ask, trying to swallow my concern.

"We're doing okay."

One look at the way she's clutching that lettuce head like it's her lifeline tells me otherwise.

25

"Maggie, what's that on your arm?" Gordon asks as we get dressed the next morning. Up 'til now I've managed to keep the tattoo hidden by wearing my lightweight pajamas with long sleeves to bed, but as I change into my clothes for the day, it's exposed in all its glory. Without thought my hand slaps against it, and I'm sure I look as guilty as a convicted criminal—which, by the way, he can spot a mile away.

"Well, you know how easily I bruise." Quickly, I pull on my shirt.

He steps over to me, and I step away.

"Maggie, let me see that." We sidestep further around the room. If we started an old record, we could give Fred Astaire and Ginger Rogers a run for their money.

"Since when are you so interested in my bruises?" I ask, breathless from all the exertion.

We come to a standstill. His concerned eyes lock with mine. "Maggie, what's wrong?"

There he goes, appealing to my soft side again.

"Nothing. You worry too much," I say. "I'll get us some coffee."

"Maggie Lynn, would you please come back here?"

His words are nice enough, but he's not fooling me one bit. I recognize an authoritative voice when I hear one.

"Just let me see it."

My pulse beats against my ears like a congo drum in bush country. Gazing up, I bat my eyelashes a couple of times. "It's nothing, dear." My words drip with honey as I swivel to keep the offensive little painting a safe distance from Gordon.

He lowers his glasses and peers over the rim. Somebody gulps, and since his Adam's apple doesn't move, I'm thinking it's me.

"Maggie?"

As if in slow motion, I flip up my sleeve. "Now, Gordon, before you say anything—"

His eyes grow big as Florida grapefruits, and the look on his face is, well, priceless.

"Is that a tattoo?" he asks, gaping, his voice coming out in a girlish squeak.

"Not a real one. It's paint. Supposed to last just a few weeks." Suddenly, it dawns on me that his first concern is whether it's a tattoo instead of the name that's written there. Isn't he the least bit concerned that another man's name is on my arm?

"Don? You had the name *Don* tattooed on your arm?"

Okay, I feel a little better here. His gaze reluctantly pulls from my arm and lifts to my eyes. To my surprise, a smile tugs at the corners of his mouth. He covers it with his right hand, but amusement flickers in his eyes. And let me just say that makes me mad. The least he could do is be jealous.

"What?"

"I can only imagine how that happened, Maggie. How do you get yourself in these fixes? So, who's my rival, Don Knotts?"

"Oh, that's cute, Gordon. Real cute."

He shrugs and goes to his drawer to pull out a pair of black socks.

"Well, you've always been a Mayberry fan." He drops a sock, picks it up with his toes, then shrugs it onto his foot.

Yanking my shirt sleeve back down, I grunt. "Just what makes you think it's not Don Johnson of *Miami Vice* fame?" Standing sideways with my stomach pulled in and chest thrown out, I attempt to look worthy of the television star and breathe all at the same time. It's not working for me here. I gulp for air and everything sags back into place.

He stops a minute. His eyes fill with suspicion and narrow to slits. "Hey, could that be short for *Donny Osmond*?" Concern lines his face, and I'm enjoying this little moment. But I don't revel too long. It's just not healthy.

"You're the only *Don* for me, Gordon," I say, emphasizing the D-O-N part.

Relief flits in his eyes. He slips on his shoes, walks over to me, and pulls me into his arms. "I love you even if you are a little, well, different." His head tilts, and he searches my face.

I want to humph, but his arms feel too good, so I snuggle against his neck instead.

"You want to tell me what happened?"

"You don't think it's for Don Johnson, huh?"

He shakes his head. "But whatever the reason, I'm sure the story will be a good one." He laughs again.

After telling him what happened, I show him the design once more and we have a good chuckle together, making our way down the hall for coffee.

"Only you, Maggie. Only you," he says, with his arm around me.

Just why do people always say that to me?

⑥　ᘛ　⑥

"Hey, I know we've only been home a couple of days, but I wondered if you and the girls could meet for coffee?" Jill asks over the phone.

"Sure, Jill. When?"

"This afternoon, say, around two o'clock?"

"I'll be there. Have you called the others?"

"Not yet. You want to call Lily, and I can call Louise," she says.

"Yeah. I'm not sure if Lily is home yet, but I'll call her just in case."

"Great. Thanks, Maggie."

We hang up, and I call Lily's number.

"Hello?"

"You are home," I say, stating the obvious.

"Well, it's either that or I'm a very polite robber," Lily says.

"When did you get home?"

"Last night." She yawns. "I'm tired, but I don't have any appointments until Wednesday, so I have time to recuperate."

I explain to her that Jill wants to meet for coffee, and Lily says she'll make it.

In no time I arrive at The New Brew to meet the Latte Girls who are already seated, coffee in hand. The familiar smells of chocolate and coffee swirl around me, and I'm rejuvenated the moment I step inside. After waving to the girls, I walk over to place my order where Tyler waits behind the counter, smiling.

She asks me to work tomorrow, and I agree. Then she rings up my mocha—at a discount—and I pay for it.

"Have a good day, Maggie. See you tomorrow."

Nodding, I make my way to our table with my mocha—stopping long enough to pick up a wadded napkin at an empty table and tossing the napkin into the trash.

"Hey, girls," I say, pulling out the wooden chair and sitting down.

We chitchat for a few minutes, and Jill brings up the reason for us being here.

"I know we were just together, and I shouldn't have bothered you yet, but I needed to talk to someone." She twists her napkin between her fingers. "Jeff was called away on business right after we got home, and we've hardly had time to talk."

A familiar ache knots in my chest.

"Anyway, I needed to meet with you because Jeff is coming home tonight. Things seem fairly positive, especially with him showing up with the flowers and all. Still I have no idea what lies ahead, and I'm afraid." Tears fill her eyes.

Louise pulls a handkerchief from her handbag and slips it over to Jill. A wave of her sweet perfume scents the air.

"Thanks," Jill says, dabbing at the corners of her eyes.

"You and Jeff will work this out, Jill. I'm sure of it," Lily says with a smile.

We all nod.

"What time will he get home?" Louise asks, drinking the last bit of coffee from her cup.

"His flight is scheduled to arrive around seven o'clock. He told me not to pick him up at the airport. He left his car there and will drive home. So I expect him around eight o'clock."

"Any plans for the evening?" Lily asks. "You know, special dinner, anything?"

Jill's face flushes. "I'm grilling T-bones, making mashed potatoes and sautéed vegetables. I've made his favorite peanut butter pie for dessert."

"Sounds good," Louise says with smiling eyes.

"By the way, how was your trip home, Lily?" Jill asks, changing the subject.

Lily lights up. "It was wonderful."

"So what was he doing there, anyway? Just came to drive you home?" Louise asks.

Lily shoots a glance my way, clears her throat, then looks up at Louise. "Well, um, Ron was taking Tara's baby crib to her and then stopped off to get me on the way to check on his house in Sarasota."

Louise quirks an eyebrow, again barely making a crinkle on her forehead. "He has a house in Sarasota? Are you moving there?"

Lily keeps her gaze on the table. "Well, that's the plan."

Louise and Jill gasp.

"And you're okay with this?" Jill asks.

"I am now. That's partly what held me back from getting married. He wanted to live closer to his dad and Tara. I wasn't sure I was ready to give up my life in Charming."

"And now you're going to do that?" I ask.

"Ron has assured me he will bring me back to visit often." Her worried gaze flits to each of us. "I will miss you all so much, but finally I feel at peace about this. I love Ron, and I know my place is beside him."

"What made you change your mind, Lil?" I ask.

"Watching the three of you, I realized we all have our struggles. Each of us has something we're dealing with. I can face the struggles alone, or I can face them with the man I love." She shrugs.

"Whatever will we do without you?" Louise asks, then looks over at me. I wish she wouldn't do that.

Now Lily's twisting her napkin. "I won't be leaving right away. Ron's already sold his house in Indiana with possession set for the buyers after our wedding. Ron will move in with me until we sell my place, then we'll move to Sarasota." She looks up and smiles brightly. "So we'll have plenty of time together before then."

Words clog my throat, but my clenched teeth refuse to set them free.

"The Latte Girls just won't be the same without you," Louise says.

"Still, we have this time together, so let's enjoy it," Jill says.

Could we move on to another subject, please?

"So how are things going with you, Maggie?" Jill asks, obviously knowing my struggle here. "How are things with Nick at home?"

"Well, we've had to lay down some rules. We had to convince him that pizza boxes are not the proper décor for bedroom furniture, but we'll get there. It's not permanent—I mean, Nick living at home. Gordon wants him to spread his wings. The amazing thing is I feel the same way. And I don't think it's just because he's messy. It's time for Nick to start his own life. Who would have thought I'd finally feel this way? Guess I'm learning that 'letting go' thing."

Louise laughs. "Yeah, I remember that whole aging and empty nest deal you went through not all that long ago," she says, her wrinkle-free face perfectly in place. Her body resembles freshly dry-cleaned silk while mine mimics wrinkled linen. Okay, so I'm not completely over the age thing, but I've come to terms with it.

I catch a glimpse of Lily's worried expression. No doubt she blames herself for causing me more angst. It's not her fault. It's Captain's, and I can't deny that I'm mad at him. Juvenile reaction, but there it is. He's taking away my best friend, and I helped him do it.

"And what's going on with you, Louise? Anything new with Donald?" Jill asks.

"Things are pretty much the same, but hopefully we'll find a balance in it all."

"You know, you'd think we'd have everything figured out by our ages," I say, making a lousy attempt to ease the tension.

"Just when I get it figured out, things change," Louise says.

We nod in agreement.

"Who would have ever thought I'd be facing childbirth at my age?" Jill asks with a laugh.

"We give up," I say.

"Well, it may not be all that unusual for women to remarry at my age, but I never saw it happening for me. Let alone moving from Charming. I thought I would live and die here," Lily says.

"I thought you would, too," I say, keeping my eyes turned from her.

Lily's hand reaches over and grabs mine. "I promise you, Maggie, I'll keep in touch regularly."

I nod, but still can't bring myself to look at her.

"How are the wedding plans coming along, Lily?" Louise asks.

"Everything is set. I'm just waiting for the big day. Now that I've come to terms with the move and my love for Ron, I'm anxious to get through the ceremony and—"

"Get on with the honeymoon?" Jill teases.

We all laugh.

"Though I'm sure you're not nearly as anxious as Ron," Jill interjects.

"Oh, I almost forgot to tell you girls. Our son is coming home for a visit. Awhile back Chad told us he had leave time coming to him, and he wanted to come home for a visit. Turns out he's coming at a good time," Louise says.

"When is he coming?" I ask.

"Should be here on Thursday," she says.

"That's wonderful, Louise," Lily says.

"I can hardly wait to hug his neck," she says. "It's been so long since we've seen him."

"Hey, when we all going to get together as couples again? It was such fun the last time we got together at Lily's," Jill says.

"Why don't we meet at my house on Friday night?" I suggest. "Unless that's too early with your son home," I say to Louise.

"No, that's fine. He's already told me he'll be gone Friday visiting friends in Rosetown."

He's not home yet and already making plans to be gone. Poor Louise.

"Great. We've got so much going on in our lives, it will be good to get together with each other and with our hubbies," Jill says. "Speaking of which, I'd better get going. I have a meal to prepare." Her eyes light up and she grins. "Pray everything goes well tonight."

We nod.

"Check with your guys and let me know if you can make it on Friday night. We'll plan for pizza and games around, say, six thirty, if everyone is able to come," I say.

We finish off our coffee and make a commotion when we scoot our chairs from the table and throw away our cups.

"I'm praying for you, girls," Lily says, glancing at Louise and Jill, her eyes then colliding with mine.

Maybe I'm in denial about the bitterness that's taking root in me. We all have our struggles, and I just have to work through this. I'll get there—I think.

26

"I haven't seen Elvira since I've gotten home. Did she go somewhere?" I ask Gordon as we sit on our patio for morning coffee.

He thinks a moment. "Yeah, she left a note in our door that she was going to her sister's or something."

"Did she say when she was coming back?"

Gordon looks at the date on his watch. "Should be getting home sometime today, if I remember right."

"How did she get there?"

"Someone picked her up, I think."

I try not to worry, but as much as Gordon works, he wouldn't have a clue if some old man kidnapped Elvira. Her image comes to mind, the blue cotton candy hair, bright red lips that resemble *The Incredible Mr. Limpet*.

"I missed her while I was gone. Hope she likes the housedress I bought her."

"You didn't." Gordon chuckles.

"I did. Lots of bright flowers." It's good to see Gordon laugh.

Still, I can't get past the dark circles beneath his eyes. "You need to slow down, Gordon. You look tired."

"Thanks," he says, taking a drink from his mug. He stretches his legs out in front of him. "Actually, I am tired. This case will soon come to a close, and I think I'll take some time off. I've earned it."

"Okay, I've heard *that* one before," I say, eyebrow quirked.

"Yeah, yeah, I know. But this time I mean it," he says.

"So what are we going to do when you take this time off?"

"You're ready to go again when you've just gotten back?"

"I'm always ready for a trip." I grin above my cup. "If you're up for it, I mean. If you just want to stay home, I'm fine with that, too."

He drains the last of his coffee. "I'll see what I can work out as far as time off, then you can plan where you want to go."

"Sounds good to me." *Though I'll believe it when I see it.*

"Well, it's that time again. I'll see you tonight, babe," he says, planting a kiss on my lips before he leaves. "How about lasagna for dinner?" he calls over his shoulder. "We'll go to that little Italian place in Rosetown."

"You don't have to ask me twice," I call back.

"Great." The door between the kitchen and garage closes behind him.

"Well, Crusher, I suppose we should get up and do something today," I say, stroking his back. Poor thing has bulges he didn't use to have. Then again, don't we all?

After I put a load of Gordon's shirts in the wash, I clean the breakfast dishes and sweep the hardwood floor. The phone rings.

"Hello?"

"Are you still talking to me?" Lily asks.

"Of course I am. It's Captain I won't talk to," I say, adding a dab of venom to my comment.

It's a good time for a break, so I grab myself a glass of iced tea and carry it with me to the sofa.

"Maggie, you have to forgive him. The Lord commands it."

"Yeah, but it doesn't say anywhere that I have to do it right away, does it?"

"I think it's implied."

"I'm not getting it."

"I'll pray for you."

"Okay." I take a drink of tea.

"You know you can come for a visit anytime, Maggie. In fact, I want you to. Ron promised that I could come back and see you anytime I needed to."

Swirling the glass in my hand, the ice shifts in the tea and reminds me of the uncertainties of life. Always shifting, changing. "Lil, you know it's not the same. How many friendships have we seen go by the wayside when someone moves?"

"Our friendship is different, Maggie, you know that."

"That's what they all say."

"We've been best friends since first grade."

"Yeah, yeah, obviously you've forgotten the yellow crayon I gave you," I say with a bitter edge.

"I didn't forget it. I still have it," she says.

Swirling stops. "What? You still have that crayon?" Boy, that whole crayon thing really was a big deal to her.

"Yep, still have it."

"That's truly amazing."

"You're my best friend, Maggie. You always have been, always will be."

"Thanks, Lil," I say, struggling to keep the tears at bay.

"Hey, want to go to a movie?" she asks with a sudden burst of enthusiasm.

"Don't you have a wedding to plan?"

"It's a small wedding, Maggie. Not much to do. I'm ready."

"I have to work for a couple of hours at The New Brew. My cut-off is two o'clock if you want to catch a movie then. There's a chick flick playing in the theater at three o'clock," I say, getting excited about the possibility of blowing off the afternoon. The plus side of living in a small town is knowing when the movies are showing.

"Sounds great," she says. "Let's have a girlfriend day."

We hang up and there's a kick in my heels as I head for the bedroom to get ready for work.

The New Brew does a fair amount of business in the afternoon, but not enough today to make the time zip by as I had hoped. Still, I'm excited by the time I arrive at the theater. Popcorn pops in a nearby bin while people chat in line, waiting to get their tickets. Candy fills the display cases, soda pop fizzes and bubbles over ice in cups, and the aroma of butter and popcorn fills the air. Okay, I admit it, these are the true reasons I come to the movies.

"Over here," Lily calls, waving. Another advantage of small-town living. There are approximately ten people in line, if that. I say hello to everyone—there are few strangers in Charming—and catch up with Lily. We grab our popcorn, Twizzlers, and drinks.

"I really shouldn't get this since I have a honeymoon to think about, but hey, he fell in love with me this way, so I figure it will stick," Lily says.

"What will stick, the popcorn or the love?" I ask with a laugh.

Lily giggles, throws a couple of kernels in her mouth, and munches happily.

When we enter our theater, we are the only ones there. We pick the best seats in the house, center seats, up several rows, and settle in for a great afternoon.

"Don't forget to turn off your cell phone," Lily says.

"Oh yeah. Thanks. You too," I say, grabbing my phone and punching the button to turn it off.

"You know, Maggie, we'll have such fun when you come to visit us in Florida. We'll go to the beach together, go boating, more para-sailing." Lily's eyes are bright and sparkly.

My spirits suddenly take a dive. Why did things have to change? Bob wasn't supposed to die. The four of us were supposed to live out our lives in Charming and spend our last days in a nursing home, wreaking havoc on all the caregivers. Now Bobby is gone, and Lily is marrying a man with two first names who knows very little of our history together. That's why he doesn't mind plucking her up from Charming and placing her in the distant land of Sarasota. Might as well be Mars.

"You're really happy, aren't you, Lil?"

She looks at me, swallows her popcorn, nods, and smiles. "I'm so happy, Maggie. Once I came to terms with the move and my true feelings for Ron, well, everything has been different since then." She chews on more popcorn and finally says, "You're okay with this, right? I mean, I know you tease about Ron and everything, but you're really all right with this? You'll come and see me?"

Worry lines her eyes, and I know I can't take away her joy. This is her time. She's been through enough.

"Of course I'm okay with this. Well, I'm not *okay* with it yet, but I'm working on it. Let's just say I *want* to be okay with this. The spirit is willing but the flesh is weak and all that. As long as I know you're happy, Lil, I'm fine with whatever you decide."

"Thanks," she says with a grin, before digging into her popcorn bag again.

The movie soon starts, and my mind wanders back through memories of the times I've spent with Lily, the weddings, our family get-togethers, the spontaneous gatherings. Once again the familiar lump lodges in my throat.

It seems so wrong to me that Captain would ask her to do this, but Lily appears to be all right with it, so who am I to question? Besides, I have my Gordon. Jill and Louise are good friends. But Lily? She's the best.

I'll get through this, right, Lord? I mean, after all, things could be worse.

◎ ✑ ◎

"It's been a great afternoon, Lil. Thanks for taking the time to get together. Despite what you tell me, I'm sure you have plenty to keep you busy, what with planning to move and all." The movie is over and the last morsel of popcorn is long since gone. We've slurped the last bit of pop from our cups and finally head to our cars.

Lily shrugs. "I'll get it done. Besides, I want to pack in all the time I can with my best buddy," she says.

Tears sting my eyes, but I blink them back.

"Ron and I are looking forward to pizza and games at your house on Friday, by the way," she says.

"Hey, isn't that Captain?" I ask, pointing to the tan Camry coming our way.

Lily frowns. "How odd. He wasn't supposed to be in town today."

Pulling his car up beside us, he rolls down his window. His face is pinched, his eyes shadowed. "I've been looking all over town for you two. Maggie, is your cell phone off?"

"Yeah, why?" I ask, a shred of fear taking root.

"You and Lily get in the car, and I'll take you to Gordon."

"Gordon? Is something wrong?"

"They rushed him to Rosetown General over an hour ago."

◎ ✑ ◎

A wave of nausea washes over me, and I try to steady myself against the information counter as I wait for the receptionist to tell me what's going on with my husband. The smell of antiseptic and cleaning products, the constant motion and patter of cushioned soles on the wax floors add to my frazzled nerves. I tell myself everything will be all right, but what do I know? My blood pressure, no doubt, is at an all-time high. A hot flash hits me, but that's the least of my worries. Grabbing a pamphlet, I fan my face.

The receptionist talks on a phone away from me. I have no idea if it's about Gordon or if she is dealing with another matter. Heart palpitations take my breath away. I blot my face and neck with a handkerchief.

"You okay?" Lily asks, her comforting hand on my shoulder.

I nod but say nothing. One word and I'm sure I'll fold.

"Mrs. Hayden," the receptionist says with a kind smile, "the doctor will come out and talk to you shortly if you'll just take a seat."

"Could I see my husband, please? I want to see my husband." I try to keep the growl from my voice as panic slices through me, but I have to say if this woman doesn't take me to see Gordon, things could turn ugly.

Compassion covers her face. "The doctor will be out shortly, ma'am," she says, excusing me.

Tears surface. "Lily, what will I do if—" My hands clutch hers so she can hold me up. My weak legs threaten to fold.

"Don't even think about it, Maggie. Everything will be fine," she says as we take our seat in the lobby. "Don't borrow trouble. We'll figure out what to do once we know what's wrong."

Just the way she says "we'll figure out" makes me feel better, knowing I don't have to do this alone.

"Hey, Mom."

When I look up, I see Nick coming toward me. "Is he all right, Nick?"

"He'll be fine, Mom." Nick pulls me into his arms, and I struggle not to fall apart.

"Mrs. Hayden?"

I turn to the woman who is dressed in a white coat with a stethoscope dangling from her neck. "Yes?"

"Hello. I'm Dr. Winters. Your husband is fine at present," she says in a professional tone. "He came into the hospital complaining of a tightness in his chest, and we're trying to get to the root of the problem," she says, repeating what Captain had told me. "His EKG came out fine, but his blood work showed we might have a blockage problem. Your husband has given his consent for a heart catheterization so we could evaluate his condition, see if there is a blockage of some kind. They're prepping him for the procedure now."

I gulp hard, trying to comprehend all that the doctor is telling me. "Has he had a"—I swallow hard just to brace myself for the words—"heart attack?"

Nick grabs my hand and holds it tightly.

"We don't know yet. Once we run some tests and perform the heart cath, we'll have more to tell you. He's not in any major pain, just a tightness in his chest that needs to be checked out."

"Can we see him?"

"They'll be taking him in for the procedure as soon as possible, but you can see him for a moment," she says, telling me where to find him.

"Thank you, Doctor," I say, standing.

"You go ahead, Mom. I'll wait with Lily and Ron. I've already seen Dad."

"All right." I walk over to Lily. "I'll meet you guys in the waiting area after I see Gordon."

"Okay," Lily says, grabbing Captain's hand. Her eyes are shadowed with fear. No doubt all this is bringing back the pain of her past with Bobby's illness.

Quickly, I make my way to Gordon and find him lying on a gurney in the hallway, white sheets draped over him. He lies perfectly still, reminding me of a mannequin—or worse. But I refuse to go there.

Gathering my courage, I take a deep breath and step over to his bedside. "Hi," I say, grabbing his free hand.

He turns his head to me. "Hi, yourself."

"Some people will do anything to get out of work," I say, chiding myself for always throwing around a joke when I'm nervous.

Gordon knowingly squeezes my hand. "I'll be fine, Maggie girl," he says, causing a tear to slip down my cheek.

"You'd better be. You forgot to take out the garbage this morning."

"I was hoping you wouldn't notice." His words are slow. Deliberate.

"I noticed." Nurses and doctors pad around the area, holding charts, talking about patients. Don't they realize that something is wrong with my husband? Why doesn't somebody fix him? I want to take him home. To our safe place. "I suppose this puts a nix on our plans to go to Rosetown for dinner tonight?"

His chest rises slowly, then falls with every breath, and I grasp his hand tighter.

"You realize this means I'll have to eat pizza with the kid?"

"I'll make it up to you."

"Are you in pain?"

"Not pain exactly. It just feels weird."

"Mr. Hayden, they're ready for you now," the nurse says, causing a fresh wave of panic to shoot through me. She tells me where to wait for him, offers the usual pleasantries of coffee and magazines as though I'm in a nice dress shop waiting on a friend.

The wheels on the bed start to move. I squeeze Gordon's hand hard. Everything in me screams to hang on to him. Though I try to shove back my fear, the truth is I'm afraid if I let them take him, he may not come back.

"I'll be fine, Maggie," he says.

"You'd better. The garbage, you know." I squeeze the tension inside me, causing my internal furnace to blaze. I'm sure I'll burst into flames like a sparkler and fizzle right on the spot.

"I know."

"I love you, Gordon."

"I love you, babe."

Fear twists around my heart and squeezes so hard I can't breathe. I bend over to kiss him. His mouth is dry and cold but not as cold as the chill that runs through me when they wheel my husband away from me.

Nick walks up to the gurney, says something to Gordon, then kisses his dad on the forehead. He walks over to me and grabs my hand again. "He'll be fine, Mom. You'll see."

Together we watch them take Gordon through a double door. *You see this, right, God? You haven't forgotten we're here?* That thought strikes fear in me. I can't bear this. I can't. Panic roars through me, and I gasp for breath.

Yet I will not forget you. See, I have inscribed you on the palms of my hands.

"It's all right, Mom. We'll get through this." Nick puts his arm around me. "You'll see."

27

After I call Heather to let her know what's going on, I rejoin Lily, Ron, and Nick in the waiting room. They are sitting on mauve-cushioned chairs, a stark contrast to the white hallways, white sheets, and starched white uniforms.

I stop at the refreshment table that holds a pitcher of iced water and a pot of coffee, along with cups, sugar, cream, and stirrers, then I run through the motions of pouring myself some ice water. Cup in hand, I turn to find my seat.

The room contains a smattering of chairs that hug the bare, light gray-colored walls. A lone phone crouches in the corner of the receptionist's desk with an empty chair hiding behind the desk. Outdated magazines are scattered on a nearby stand. Nothing in this room invites visitors to linger. It's a room for passing through, biding time, waiting, wondering, praying . . .

Before I take a drink of my cold water, another chill runs through me chasing completely away my former hot flash.

"So did Gordon tell you if this happened while he was at work?" Lily asks Ron.

"Yeah. He had been in a meeting with a client when it started. By the time the meeting ended, he decided he'd better have it checked out. He tried to call Maggie, but couldn't reach her. He got a hold of Nick, and Nick called me."

Gordon needed me, and I was at a movie.

"Now, Maggie, don't go there," Lily says, picking up on my self-loathing. "You couldn't have known there would be trouble, and we have to turn off our cell phones during the movie."

More tears.

She pats my hand. "You got to see him before he went into the procedure, and he's going to be fine. He's not in pain. That's a good thing," she encourages, but her words bounce off me.

"I've had a heart attack and survived," Captain says. My head jerks to him.

"You have?"

He nods. "A couple of years ago. It got my attention. I lost fifty pounds, started eating right, closed my business with all the stress and employees, and started working as a financial consultant out of my home. Doc says I've never been better."

A smidgen of hope trickles through me. So that's why he started working out of his home.

"The main thing is catching the problem in time before there's heart damage," Captain says. "By the way, I've made reservations at the Home Town Bed and Breakfast so I can be around while Gordon's out of commission."

His concern touches me in a deep way. Almost makes me want to forgive him for taking my best friend from me. Still, what would I have done if Lily hadn't been here for me?

"Thank you, Captain." I glance over at Nick who is staring blankly at the television screen. He's trying to be strong for me. With all the complaining I've done about him being back home, I'm wondering how I would have handled this without him beside me.

"Hi, Maggie," Louise and Jill say as they step into the room, compassion as evident on their faces as cold cream at bedtime. Pastor Morrow walks in behind them.

My heart is warmed at the sight of them. New tears slip down my cheeks before I can stop them. When my friends reach me, I stand, and we collapse into a group hug.

"We prayed for you as soon as we heard," Louise says.

"How did you hear?"

"The church prayer chain," Louise says, pointing to the pastor.

"Thank you for coming, Pastor," I say, squeezing his hand.

"Of course I would be here for you and Gordon, Maggie. We love you both." He drops into his seat as though his bony legs have given out on him and wipes his brow. No doubt his arthritis is bothering him today, though he would never complain. No one would ever know about his illness had his sweet little wife not whispered it into the prayer chain.

Pastor Morrow looks a bit crumpled and tattered, which is not all that unusual for him. Most folks say he's crumply in body because he stays up half the night praying for his congregation. I believe it's true. Kinder blue eyes, you'll never see. Some folks say he has a heart of gold, and that may be true because pure gold is all squishy and pliable, welcoming and making room for more.

"The hospital called me, and then I notified the prayer chain, Maggie," Pastor says with the kind of smile that brings tears to my eyes.

Is there anything more wonderful than family and friends? What would I do without my church family?

We talk awhile about what's happened, then Dr. Winters enters the room. My heart slams against my chest when I hear her call my name. Nick grips my arm with his hand as we rise to meet her. The hint of a smile lights her face, calming me a little.

"Your husband is going to be just fine. He did not have a heart attack, but the tightness was a warning sign that certainly would have led to an attack had he ignored the symptoms. He suffered no heart damage, so that's great news."

"Thank you," I whisper.

"He did have some blockage. One artery had seventy percent blockage, another eighty percent. We put stents in to keep the arteries open." She explains the procedure and how these medicated coil stents are great for keeping plaque buildup at bay. "They're taking him to a room where we'll observe him for a couple of days."

I nod. She gives me the room number and a few more instructions. When she walks away, I look up to Nick whose eyes are brimming with tears. We embrace then join the others, explaining everything to them.

Lily hugs me again. "You okay now?"

"I'm so relieved, Lily. I feel like celebrating."

She gives me a sideways squeeze as we walk toward the door. "Me, too."

"You guys are welcome to come see him," I say.

"We'll give you time alone together first," Captain says. "I'll take Lily to dinner, then we'll come back."

"We'll come back later tonight, too," Louise says, with Jill nodding beside her.

"Thanks, you guys. We could never have made it without you."

"We'll always be here for your family, Maggie. The distance won't stop that," Captain says, his hand squeezing my shoulder. I swallow hard.

"Thanks." Walking out with my friends, I watch them walk to the elevator, wave good-bye, then Pastor, Nick, and I make our way to Gordon's new room. He greets us with a smile when we enter.

Pastor talks to him a few minutes about all that's happened, has prayer with us, then leaves. Once he's gone, Gordon turns to me.

"They're keeping me a few days, so I guess that means you or Nick will have to take out the garbage," Gordon says, eyes twinkling.

Nick groans.

"Nothing doing," I say, leaning over his bed, mere inches from his face. "We're saving every scrap for you." I turn to our son. "Isn't that right, Nick?"

His mouth splits into a wide grin. "That's right."

"It's a conspiracy," Gordon says. "Guess I got a couple of wires holding me together." He points to his chest and pushes his lower lip out in a feel-sorry-for-me look.

"Imagine being held together by a Slinky," I say, matter-of-factly.

"Kind of puts things into perspective. I just hope I don't do that coil thing going down the stairs," he says, making me laugh.

"How about if I call you my bionic man from now on," I say.

"Would that be synonymous with The Six Million Dollar Man?" Gordon asks, trying to look taller in bed but not being able to move all that much since he's hooked up to a monitor.

"One and the same," I say.

"I'm good with that." He waits a minute. "Doc says I'll be up and running in no time."

We talk about it a little while longer then Gordon gives me a list of things to pick up for him at home. So with the list in my hand, Nick and I prepare to go home and take care of Crusher, gather Gordon's things, and grab a bite to eat before returning to the hospital. Just after we kiss Gordon good-bye, his phone rings.

"Hi, Heather. I'm doing fine, honey." He looks at us, smiles, and waves.

We wave and walk out the door. The words "I'm doing fine" soak over my spirit and chase my fears away.

Nick grabs my hand. "How 'bout pizza for dinner?"

When I pull into the driveway, I see Elvira outside getting her mail. Rolling down my window, I call out to her, "You just getting back?"

"Well, hi there, dearie," she says, gathering her mail and hobbling over our way. Her orange and yellow flowered housedress blows with the slight breeze. She bends down and looks into the car. "Hi, Nick."

I explain what happened with Gordon but quickly let her know he is doing fine. She doesn't look surprised at all.

"You knew, didn't you?" It always amazes me how fast news travels in Charming.

She shrugs. "During my prayer time, I felt impressed to pray for Gordon. God is faithful."

Her comments cause my heart to pause and tears to fill my eyes. "Thank you." Another knot in my throat.

Elvira reaches her hand through the open window and squeezes my shoulder. "I'm thankful, too," she says, tears filling her own eyes.

We talk for a moment. I let her know I brought her something back from Florida, then I hurry on so we can get back to the hospital. Once inside the house, Nick lets Crusher out to take care of business while I gather Gordon's things and stuff them into a suitcase. My gaze flits to Gordon's side of the bed, all neat and in order, not a ripple anywhere showing he had slept there. For once I wish I had left it unmade this morning.

My footsteps echo down the hallway as I carry the suitcase toward the garage. The hall clock bongs.

Nick warms the leftover pizza in the microwave, and we sit down to eat. I can only eat a couple of bites. This day has taken its toll on my stomach. Walking over to the sink, I stuff the remaining pizza into the garbage disposal, turn on the water, and click on the disposal. Suddenly, bits of crust and pepperoni spit back through the tunnel, and water collects in the sink.

"Great. Just great. You would go out while Gordon's gone." I wipe the splattered pieces from my blouse and make a mental note to buy some Drano on the way home.

"I told you all that pizza is bad for your health. Even the disposal won't eat it."

"Good one, Mom. I'd fix it for you, but well, disposals aren't my forte."

"I'll get some Drano on the way home. Listen, Nick, since Dad is out of danger, you go ahead and meet with your friends tonight."

"Are you sure?"

"I'm sure. We'll be fine."

He reluctantly agrees. I tell him good-bye, grab my car keys, and head back to the hospital. My cell phone rings.

"Hello?"

"Have I told you how much I love you?"

Gordon's voice makes my lip quiver, and I try to stay strong. It wouldn't do for me to show my fears to him. He needs to concentrate on getting well, not worrying about me worrying about him.

"Maybe once or twice," I say. "But you still have to take out the garbage," I tease.

"You're just not going to cut me any slack on that one, are you?"

"Not a chance."

"Oh, okay." Pause. "Boy, I could sure go for some pizza," he says.

The thought of regurgitated pepperoni makes me a little queasy. "You must be feeling better. But you'll have to ask the doctor about that one."

"Well, it's not as though I've been eating a lot of fats or anything. You know I lost all that weight on the low-carb diet."

"I know. Doctor says that really helped you, too. That you're doing everything right."

"Exactly," he says. "So how about some pizza?"

"Now I see where Nick gets it."

"Gets what?"

"Gordon, you've been in the hospital less than six hours and you're already trying to get out of hospital food?"

"And your point is?"

"We have to ask the doctor first. You can abuse your body after you get home," I say.

"Spoilsport." Another pause. "Can't wait till you get here."

"Why, you need your book?" I ask, referring to the science fiction novel he's reading.

"No. I need you."

Why does he say those things? Doesn't he realize I'm emotional right now?

"Gotta go, babe," he says. "The nurse needs me for something."

On the way to the hospital, I stop at the store to pick up some Drano and a plunger. Gordon normally takes care of these kinds of things, and I suppose I could leave it for him when he gets home, but I want to use the disposal before then. For a moment I wonder what I would do if I had to take care of such things myself, and I marvel that Lily has managed to survive the upkeep of a home without Bob.

"There she is," Gordon says when I enter his room. A sparkle touches his eyes, and I'm amazed that out of all the women he could have picked for a wife, he chose me.

We talk awhile, then soon Lily and Ron join us.

"So Maggie tells me she has a bionic man these days," Lily says when she and Captain walk into the room with a basket of goodies and colorful balloons. Lily hands it to Gordon.

"I've tried to convince her for years I was worth millions," Gordon says with a grin, and I almost expect to see a sparkling gold tooth.

"You're worth millions, but the garbage is still waiting on you," I say.

Lily and Captain exchange a baffled glance.

"Private joke," I say and wink at Gordon.

"Not a very good one at that," Gordon shoots back. He rummages through his basket filled with a book of crossword puzzles, an issue of *Time* magazine, candy, and a card. "I love crossword puzzles," he says, pulling out the book.

"You know, I think I've heard that," Lily says with a laugh. "I got you some red licorice, too, since it's a low-fat food."

"Don't remind me that I have to watch that now," Gordon says. "It was hard enough watching the carbs."

"What's on your blouse?" Lily says, pointing to a spot on my top.

"Oh, dear, I didn't see that. The garbage disposal acted up and evidently flipped food on me," I say. Concern shadows Gordon's face, and I wish I hadn't mentioned it.

"I'm pretty good at fixing things," Captain jumps in. "Is the disposal clogged?"

My glance goes from him to Gordon, back to him. "Well, um, yes."

"We can come over after we leave here, and I'll fix it up for you," he says.

"Oh, that's all right, I stopped at the store and bought some Drano and a plunger. I should be able to fix it myself."

"He won't take no for an answer, Maggie, so you might as well let him take care of it. He's staying in town for that very reason, to help you," Lily says.

I glance at Gordon, and he looks relieved.

"Thanks, Ron," Gordon says. "I owe you."

"What you owe me is a day of fishing, buddy," Captain says.

"You're on."

We visit a little while then Jill and Jeff come into the room.

"Hey, there's the man," Jeff says. "If you didn't want to meet this week, you should have told me," he says.

Gordon turns to me. "I forgot to tell you that Jeff's decided to join Donald and me for our accountability meetings."

"Yeah, only the first meeting I'm to attend, they call it off," Jeff says.

Jill throws me a smile. The shadow in her eyes tells me all is not well between her and Jeff, but at least it's a start.

Louise and Donald Montgomery show up right on the heels of the Grahams.

While I was off vacationing, Gordon was reaching out to his friends. How I love this man.

"Trust me, Jeff, I'd rather do the accountability thing any day. Besides, Louise promised to make brownies, so I wouldn't have missed that," Gordon says with a grin.

Feeling slightly put out by that comment, I try not to stiffen. After all, I make brownies, too. So what if they're boxed? If they're good enough for Betty Crocker, they should be good enough for Gordon.

Louise beams, doggone her.

"And of course, my Maggie makes great brownies, too," Gordon adds, reaching for my hand.

Smart man.

"Louise does make great desserts." Donald tosses a smile at his wife.

"Say, Gordon, did Maggie tell you about the unusual resident that lived near the condo where we stayed in Siesta Key?" Louise asks.

"No," Gordon says, looking at me.

"Gator George." My nose wrinkles here.

"Uh-oh," Gordon says.

The girls laugh, and we entertain the guys for the next half hour or so with our Florida stories. At the end of our last story, I see Gordon's eyelids droop.

"Well, it's time to let you get some rest," I say, and the others agree. We gather around Gordon's bed, and Captain leads us in a beautiful prayer of thankfulness for God's healing touch upon Gordon. Everyone tells Gordon good-bye.

"We'll wait for you out here, Maggie," Lily says, "then we'll follow you home to fix the garbage disposal."

"Thanks." I turn back to Gordon.

"Sorry, Maggie," Gordon says.

"About the disposal or the garbage?" I just can't seem to let it go.

He grabs my hand. "The disposal."

"Why? Did you put something down there you shouldn't have?"

"No. I'm just sorry that I'm not there to fix it. That's all." He kisses my hand.

"Gordon, don't do that." More tears.

He looks up at me. "I'm okay, Maggie girl."

Not able to speak, I nod.

"I've been doing some thinking, Maggie, and well, things are going to change," he says with conviction.

"You don't need to say that, Gordon. It's enough for me that you're all right."

His hand tugs on mine, and I lean down to him. He kisses me full on the lips as though we've been separated for months. "I wish I could go home tonight," he says, eyes twinkling.

"You get well. There will be time for you to come home soon enough," I say, chuckling.

I squeeze his hand once more, wave, and head out the door, thanking God for Gordon.

28

A warm breeze brushes past Gordon and me as we take a twilight walk around the neighborhood—a habit we formed after Gordon got home from the hospital over a week ago. The scent from a nearby honeysuckle vine reaches me, and I drink it in deeply.

"I can't believe it took heart problems for me to stop and enjoy something like this," Gordon says, squeezing my hand.

"I know. It was a wake-up call for both of us," I say, thankful I remembered to call and get an appointment set with my gynecologist.

Gordon turns to me. "I know this has been scary for you, Maggie. I'm sorry."

"Oh honey, it's not your fault." I tighten my grip on his hand, never wanting to let go. We step over a few broken twigs. Persistent weeds poke through the sidewalk cracks in a quaint, nostalgic sort of way. "Every day is a gift, Gordon."

"Yeah, it is." Another squeeze.

"It sure upset Nick," Gordon says.

"He loves you. He was afraid his presence has caused too much stress."

"Poor kid."

"His room is so clean now, it's making your piles look bad," I tease. Gordon laughs.

We walk a little further in silence, listening to birdsong, watching a butterfly flutter past.

"I sure appreciated Ron fixing the garbage disposal," Gordon says.

"Yeah, me too." I think back to how Captain helped me with the disposal and mowed the yard while Gordon was in the hospital. I had intended to give him a piece of my mind for tricking me into helping him with Lily only to move her far away, but after all his kindness, and my preoccupation with Gordon, it didn't happen.

A couple of young boys rip past us on their bicycles. Oh, to have that kind of energy and carefree days of youth.

"Say, how did your accountability meeting go today?"

"Oh boy, I haven't told you about that yet, have I?"

I shake my head.

"Well, let me just say you might want to call Louise."

"That bad?"

"I'm pretty sure she could use a friend right about now."

My heart zips to my throat. "Is everything okay, Gordon?"

"They're okay, but call her. One thing I can tell you is that their news may make things harder on Chad and Donald's relationship."

"What do you think the problem is between those two?"

Gordon shrugs. "Donald thinks he worked too hard, was gone from home too much when Chad was little."

A sparrow swoops overhead and lands on a nearby tree limb. He looks down on us as though eavesdropping.

"I was the same way, Maggie, when Heather and Nick were young."

"Oh, I don't know, Gordon. You tried to spend quality time with them."

"Yeah, I tried, but I could have done better."

"We all have things we wish we could have done differently. We just have to go from here," I say, marveling at my Obi Wan Kenobi moment of wisdom. "I'm having lunch with the girls tomorrow. Maybe Louise will tell us then."

A piece of cracked sidewalk pokes upward, and I step over it. "Did Jeff say how he and Jill were doing—anything that you can share without breaking confidence?"

"He's nervous about the baby, but he's more at odds about the man showing up on the beach. Jeff tends to be a jealous guy. Being in sales, he sees a lot of flirting going on between married men and women, and it bothers him a great deal. He's afraid Jill has given that guy the wrong vibes, whether she meant to or not. Plus, I think he's struggling with the guilt of being gone from home so much. To be honest, I think they have some issues they're going to have to work through."

"I suspected as much," I say, thinking back to comments Jill has made along the way, letting us know there were issues, but not really going into great detail about them.

"Going to a counselor will be a great thing for them."

"Yeah," I say. "Still, I don't believe Jill would have intentionally given Rodney the wrong impression. I believe it was done more out of naivete."

"Right. Jeff knows that, I think, deep down. But right now his ego is in the way."

"My goodness, I didn't know the Whites were moving, did you?" I ask, pointing to the *For Sale* sign in the yard of the home behind our home.

"Yeah. He told me yesterday he was retiring, and they are headed to"—he hesitates here—"Florida."

"Great. Everybody's moving to Florida."

"You still struggling with that?"

"A little," I say. "Okay, a lot."

"You have to let it go, Maggie."

"I know."

"Besides, you have a little time before you have to say good-bye to Lily. She has to sell her house and all. Most likely with that beauty salon in her basement, it will hurt chances of resale a little bit."

"You haven't heard?"

"Heard what?"

"Lori Bell's looking for a place. You know, that gal who came to our home that one day with Lily. She's the one who graduated beauty school not all that long ago. Remember, I told you that in order to cut back on her hours, Lily even passed some clients to Lori."

"That middle-aged gal?"

"Yep. She'd always wanted to fix hair, so after her husband left her, she went to school. She made some money on their settlement, and now she's looking for a place of her own. Says she's too old to work for someone else at this point."

"That would be perfect for her then," Gordon says, making me feel worse.

"Yeah, I guess. She's one of Lily's customers, so she's very familiar with Lily's house. She loves it."

"Things will work out all right, Maggie, you'll see."

We walk up to the house and Gordon unlocks the door, stepping aside so I can go in.

"You know, Maggie, we need to talk about something—" Gordon's words are cut short by the ringing phone when we enter the house.

Rushing over to the phone, Gordon answers it. "Hello? Heather, hey kiddo!"

It seems every time someone needs to tell me something, there are always interruptions.

Just like life.

⑥ ✐ ⑥

"So you ready for your big day this Saturday?" I ask Lily as we work out on treadmills at the new gym in town. Thankfully, Rodney is not around. Curves was great when I went there, but the fact it was located so close to a bakery was just more than I could handle.

"I'm ready."

"How are Tara and the baby doing?"

"They're getting along fine," Lily says between breaths. "I told you she called me after the baby was born and apologized. She said she realized how wrong she had been, and she needed to let her dad live his own life. She also said she wanted me to be a part of her life."

"I'm so thankful she's had a change of heart. And how nice of her to have the baby before the wedding."

"Wasn't it, though?"

"So did she end up naming the baby after her mother?" My fingers reach for my neck to feel my pulse. It's still there, so I figure that's a good sign.

"Yep, Brenda," Lily says.

My heart squeezes for Lily, and I'm hoping she'll have a great life with Ron and his family. "I'm so glad you're feeling better about things with Tara."

"Yeah, me too. We still have a ways to go, but hopefully, she'll get used to me being around."

"It's sure nice you'll only have an hour between you and the grandbaby," I say, hoping Heather and I will live closer when they decide to have children.

"If I know you, Maggie, you won't let distance keep you from enjoying your future grandchildren," Lily says, once again knowing my thoughts.

I smile. "Yeah, you're right. I'll get there somehow—and send lots of packages in between." The treadmill squawks beneath my feet making me a tad self-conscious. "You know, Captain was a great help to me when Gordon was in the hospital, Lily. I really appreciated that."

"Yeah, he's a good guy," she says, lifting her elbows in the air as she walks with gusto. I admire her enthusiasm, but I'm just not ready to break into a sweat.

"How's Gordon feeling?"

"He's doing great."

"I'm so glad. That was too scary."

"Tell me about it. While he was in the hospital, it really opened my eyes to what you must have gone through when Bobby died. I mean, I was with you through that, but I didn't think about all the stuff."

"What do you mean?"

"The broken down garbage disposals. How to put oil in the car. Adding salt to the water softener."

"Oh." Lily slows her pace. "That was the hardest part."

"Why didn't you talk to me about it?"

"I didn't want Gordon to run over every time I needed something. I knew I had to learn how to do things myself. Who knew if I would ever marry again? At that point, I sure didn't see it happening."

"Yeah. I can't even think about life without Gordon. I want to go first."

"Won't happen."

"Why?" I ask.

"Only the good die young."

"Ha, ha." I pause a moment. "I'll sure miss you when you're gone, Lil."

"I'm going to Florida, not heaven, Maggie—at least not yet anyway. I'll be a phone call away. Don't you ever forget that."

"I'm sure Gordon won't let me forget that once he looks at the phone bills."

Lily laughs. This simple bantering back and forth puts me in a better mood. We don't know what tomorrow holds, but right now, I'm going to seize the day.

"Hey, it's almost time to meet Louise and Jill for lunch." Lily says, wiping sweat from her forehead.

"Oh, okay. I've beat my body enough for today," I say, though we both know I work off more calories than this going from the living room to the refrigerator—well, if I swing my arms as I go.

She shuts off her machine, and I do the same.

"You know, Lily, I have to wonder how good it is to behave like hamsters on a wheel. I mean, something about that just bothers me, you know?"

Lily chuckles.

"Not only that, but have you ever noticed that hamsters tend to get a little, well, fat? I'm thinking the walking thing doesn't help all that much."

"Only you, Maggie. Only you," Lily says, heading toward the dressing room. "Let's go eat."

"You don't have to ask me twice."

⑥ ❧ ⑥

The smell of sautéed meats and vegetables hovers in the air as we step into Prince Charming Restaurant. The hostess seats us at a table for four, and we have a good view of the entrance so we can see when Louise and Jill come inside. I'm hoping Louise will share with us what's going on in her life. We order our drinks but tell the server we'll wait on our meals till Louise and Jill join us.

"You know, I'm surprised this whole wedding thing has come off without a hitch," Lily says, taking a sip from her glass of water.

"Without a hitch? You're kidding, right?"

"What?"

"If memory serves me—and it does—you almost backed out."

275

"Well, okay, aside from that."

"Excuse me, Lily, but that was a pretty big hitch. Goes to show we all have our moments of cold feet. And let's face it, at our age, our feet take time to warm up."

Lily laughs.

"Oh hey, there they are," I say, waving at Louise and Jill when they enter. "I'm glad they're here. After that workout, I'm starving."

Lily stares at me. "Maggie, you're famished after walking to the mailbox."

I shrug. "I have a healthy appetite, is that so wrong?"

"Not if you work out," Lily chides, as though she's a nutrition guru.

"Okay, I get enough of this from Jill, must you start, too?" I grouse.

"Enough of what from Jill?" Jill asks, performing a couple of waist twists before settling into her seat. Louise pulls out a chair and sits down.

"Oh nothing," I say with a wave of my hand.

"I was telling Maggie she needs to work out if she's not going to watch her diet."

"Excuse me, but this little conversation is irritating my happy self and besides, we've been all over that."

"It's still true, Maggie," Jill says with her authoritative voice in place. "But you're right, we've been all over that."

"Exactly." *And I don't care to hear it again, thank you very much.*

"Did you see your gynecologist yet, by the way?" Louise pushes.

"What is this, pick on Maggie day?"

"We care about you, Maggie," Louise says in the most serious voice.

"Yeah, I know." I stare at my menu. "Does this mean I can't order the chocolate torte?"

"If you plan to work out, sure," Jill says.

"I worked out already today," I say, sitting up taller in my seat.

"Tell 'em how many miles you walked, Maggie," Lily says. Maybe her going to Florida isn't such a bad thing after all. Okay, I didn't mean that.

"I didn't really pay attention."

"I did. You walked one mile."

"I did? That's great," I say, feeling quite proud.

"In an hour. Charming's oldest resident can beat that, Maggie. She's one hundred and five," Lily says.

"She has no life. I do."

"Excuse me? Why do you think she's lived so long?"

"What kind of quality life is that, Lil? Hmm? I'd rather die at eighty with a bar of chocolate in hand and a smile on my lips."

"You're pathetic," Lily says, giving up.

"I know." My eyebrows wiggle over another victory won. "And just so you know, I have an appointment set up with my gynecologist. The thing with Gordon got my attention."

"Yay," they say in unison.

"So, Jill, with all that happened with Gordon, we never got to hear how your dinner went with Jeff."

The server takes our orders before Jill can answer. I end up ordering a grilled chicken salad, but I wanted the chicken pot pie with gravy, doggone it.

We give the gal our menus, and Jill turns to us with a sigh. "Well, the dinner went all right. We had a great evening, but he just can't seem to get past Rodney showing up at Siesta Key." She fidgets with her napkin. "I quit the gym, by the way. As much as I love working out, it's not worth hurting my marriage."

"Hey, you know, you should start an exercise class for the pregnant women in our church," Lily pipes up. "I've heard several of them say they want to work out, but they have no idea what they can and can't do as an expectant mother."

"That's a great idea," Louise jumps in. "You would do a terrific job leading them, you could still keep in shape yourself, and Jeff wouldn't have to worry."

I nod in agreement.

Jill bites her lower lip. "It might work," she says, her eyes sparking to life. "Jeff would no doubt feel better about it. We're starting counseling in a week, too."

"How's Jeff doing with the baby idea?"

"Since going to the doctor together last week, we're getting more excited about it."

"That's great," Louise says.

"We even looked at baby furniture yesterday."

"That's awesome," Lily says.

"We've got a ways to go, but things are looking up," Jill says.

"Hey, I have pictures from the trip to show you girls," Louise says, reaching into her bag. "I hope to make an entire book of our trip, but this is all I have so far." Louise hands us the stack of pictures, a few of which are on scrapbook pages. We laugh and talk over each one, reliving the moments.

"It really was a great trip," I say. "I still need to get my pictures developed, but when I do, I'll give you all copies."

"Yeah, you'll have to tell me which copies you guys want of these," Louise says. "And now, Maggie, I have a surprise for you." She reaches back into her bag, pulls out one more photograph, and hands it to me.

My heart somersaults. There in my hand is a picture of Donny Osmond talking to my head on the beach. We all start laughing and passing the picture around.

"Thank you, Louise!" I say when I calm down.

"You know, when I saw him talking to you, I couldn't tell it was him, but I thought it was funny to see a man talking to a head. So I snapped it. When I got to you, Lily told me it was Donny, and I decided to keep the picture a secret until I could show you. That way I wouldn't get your hopes up if the picture didn't turn out."

"What a great memory," I say, while we admire the pictures with Donny.

"We never would have experienced the trip if you hadn't gotten cold feet, Lily. Thanks," Jill says, leaning back in her chair.

"Glad I could help."

A comfortable silence falls around us.

"So, Louise, how are things on the home front?" I ask.

She hesitates a moment and shakes her head. "You girls won't believe this. Donald has now decided that he wants to serve on a mission field."

I'm pretty sure we all suck in air here.

"Wow, when did this happen?"

"He told me the night I got back from Florida. In fact, we've been counseling with Pastor. I just couldn't bring myself to talk about it with you until I sorted through it all myself."

"How do you feel about it?" I ask.

"Well, you know my concerns about everything else. He's just moving too fast for me. I need time to know this isn't a passing thing, but that he's going to stick with it, you know?"

"Yeah, I see what you mean," Lily says. "That's a pretty big step."

"No kidding," Jill says before taking a drink of water.

"Does Chad know?" I ask.

"Yeah. Donald told him. Chad didn't take it well, which is no surprise. They had words. Chad accused Donald of caring about everyone else but his own family. It was awful."

"I'm sorry, Louise," I say.

"We'll get through it. But I'm not sure what the outcome will be." Obviously wanting to change the subject, she turns to Lily. "So, how are the wedding plans coming along?"

"I'm supposed to pick up my dress today," Lily says. "The gal who does alterations for the boutique called and said she's finished."

"Oh, how fun. Want me to go with you to pick it up?" I ask.

"Sure. I can hardly wait to try it on," she says. "This wedding sure has been a lot easier to plan than my first one," Lily says with a smile.

"You're older and wiser," I say.

"Yeah, I guess. Anyway, everything is in place, and I'm thankful."

Just then Lily's phone rings. She talks a few minutes, and when she hangs up, she looks troubled.

"What was that I said about no hitches to the wedding?" Lily asks. We look at her.

"What's wrong, Lil?" I ask.

"That was Mrs. Morrow. They are taking Pastor Morrow to the hospital for stitches. It seems he tripped over something in their living room and fell against the corner of their coffee table, making a huge gash across his forehead and slicing it pretty good."

Louise gasps. "Is he all right?"

Lily nods. "Mrs. Morrow thinks everything will be fine. He'll probably look a little beat-up for the wedding, but should be all right. She wanted me to know rather than hear it from someone else."

"Poor Pastor," Louise says.

"Is something else bothering you, Lily?" Jill asks.

"I don't know. I just hope he's all right."

We have less conversation than usual through the meal as we give Lily time to sort through the news of Pastor's fall. Soon afterwards, Louise and Jill leave while Lily and I go to pick up her dress.

When the seamstress opens the door to greet us, the look on her face makes a chill run through me.

We barely step inside, and she is practically in tears. "I'm so sorry. I draped your dress over the back of the sofa for mere minutes—long enough to get a cup of tea. When I came back, our cocker spaniel, Sparky, ran after our cat. Trixie dashed across the carpet, up the sofa, and"—she wrings her hands here and steps slowly away from the sofa —"um, over your dress."

Shredded strips of dark yellow chiffon lay draped across the sofa.

"My dress," Lily says in a whisper. She turns to me with tear-filled eyes. "That's what I get for saying everything came off without a hitch. I loved that dress."

"I'm so sorry," the woman says. "I'll pay you for the dress." She shakes her head. "I have never had such a thing happen before."

"I know this is bad, and I don't mean to minimize it, but things could be worse, Lil," I say.

"Yeah, you're right. I could pop a seam during the ceremony." She sucks in a long breath. "This too shall pass. I just need a moment to calm down."

I hug her. "Go ahead with your moment. I could call the Latte Girls over, and we could do that biblical thing like the women in the olden days and wail for you," I offer.

She laughs in spite of herself. "You're a true friend, Maggie."

"Though I could never in a million years imagine Louise wailing. Her mascara would smear, and then where would she be? Plus, wailing requires a certain amount of facial expression, and, well, we both know her face doesn't move."

Lily wipes her tears and laughs again. "Guess I'd better go shopping for another dress, though I can't imagine what I can find at this late date."

"We'll call Louise and Jill to join us tomorrow. Surely four women on a mission can find you a dress," I say.

"By tomorrow? I have my doubts."

Though I'm inclined to agree with her, I decide to keep that little matter to myself.

29

"What am I going to do, girls?" Lily punches a migraine pill through the foil and downs it with water when we stop at a fast-food restaurant. "We've been to every store in Charming and Rosetown, and there is absolutely nothing that works for me. I suppose I'll have to go back to the last store and get that tan dress that makes me resemble a sack of potatoes." She rubs her temples. "Isn't there a pretty yellow dress anywhere in this town?"

Her comment shoots a spark through me. "Lily!" I smack my forehead for not thinking of this before.

Everyone's attention turns to me.

"What?" she asks.

"You said you loved the dress I wore to my thirtieth anniversary vow-renewal ceremony."

"Yeah?"

"We're pretty much the same size, and the dress would look beautiful with the yellow roses you've chosen."

"What will you wear?" Lily asks.

"I'm not as important as the bride. I have a pastel pink suit I can wear to stand beside you, if you think that will work."

"That would be great," Lily says, eyes sparkling. "We'll look very summery. Wait. You're smaller than I am." Her comment causes me to battle with my ego for a moment. "Though I have lost some weight in preparing for the wedding."

"That dress is so elegant," Louise chimes in.

Jill nods. "It looked great on Maggie, and you would look very nice in it too, Lily."

"You'd let me wear something so special, Maggie?"

"Well, of course I would, Lil. There is nothing I wouldn't do for you—you know that. Besides, this is a special day for you, too! We could cover that 'something borrowed' thing in the process. I would be honored if you wore my dress."

The four of us talk excitedly about the dress, then Louise and Jill go on home while Lily comes to my house to try it on.

Once she slips it over her head and it slides over her hips, we're convinced it's the perfect wedding dress for her. In fact, it looks better than the original dress she had picked out.

One look at her, and I struggle to keep the tears back—again. I don't know if it's because I'm so happy for Lily or if it's because it brings back memories of all that Gordon did for me on our thirtieth anniversary.

"You're sure about this, Maggie?" Lily holds her breath as she waits for my response. She loves the dress, I can tell.

"I'm positively sure, Lil."

After we hug, Lily turns to the mirror. "This dress is perfect in every way. I can't get over it." She tugs at the chiffon wrap that goes over the dress and smoothes the front of it with her hands. "And I'm so thankful we both have big feet," she says, pointing to my matching shoes that are on her feet.

"That's just the way best friends are," I tease. "Seriously, you look wonderful, Lil."

"Thanks."

"You said Lori Bell is coming over to fix your hair, right?"

"Right."

"Aren't you nervous about that since she hasn't been doing hair all that long?"

Lily waves her hand. "Oh, no. I trust Lori completely. Remember, she's been doing my hair for the past few months. If I don't like what she does, I'll make her do it over. That's the benefit of being her mentor."

I chuckle. "Oh, that's true. Have you decided how you're going to do your hair for the wedding?"

"I'm thinking an updo with some flowers tucked in."

"That sounds really nice, Lil."

"Remember, Lori will be fixing your hair, too."

It's a struggle for me not to groan here. Lily has taken care of my hair since we were sixteen. Still, I'm not going for cornrows.

"Now don't worry. She'll do fine. If she doesn't, I'll redo it for you." She winks. "It's the least I can do for the dress and all," she says, smoothing over it once again.

Once Lily changes back into her clothes, we finalize details on the rehearsal dinner.

"Well, I'll see you tonight, Maggie. I can hardly wait!"

Walking Lily to the door, I hug her once more and wave good-bye as she steps down our walk and out to her car. Though I couldn't be happier for her, raw pain tugs at my heart with the thought that she'll be moving so far away.

The ticking of the hall clock grows louder, snagging my attention.

Gordon will be working, Lily will be gone. Most likely, Nick will be at school. I'll have to up my hours at the coffee shop or find another job. There's no way I will pine my hours away in this house. Alone.

"Well, our rehearsal was a breeze, let's just hope we do as well tomorrow at the wedding," Captain says with a chuckle at our linen-clad table in the private room reserved for the future bride and groom, Louise, Jill, myself, and our husbands. I'll be matron of honor, Gordon, best man, and Louise and Jill will be helping with the reception. Captain lifts his water glass to Lily and winks.

"It will be just fine—now that I have my dress," Lily says with a smile my way. She turns back to her soon-to-be groom, and he kisses her on the cheek. He stops and whispers something into her ear, and my cheeks grow warm. I turn to Gordon who smiles and reaches for my hand beneath the table.

"I'm proud of you, babe," he whispers to me.

My hormones must be working overtime, because tears keep springing to my eyes. For crying out loud, how much water can one person hold?

Captain stands up and clinks his spoon against his glass to get everyone's attention. He gives the appropriate accolades, sharing a few anecdotes along the way, and just when I think he's finished, he clears his throat. "There is one more thing I wish to address tonight."

Something in the way he says that brings the room to silence.

"As you know, I have a home in Sarasota, and Lily and I were planning to move there after Lily's house sold."

Dread of my own making drowns out his words. So Lori has bought Lily's house. It's not surprising that the deal went through, although I had hoped it would take a little time so they would stay here awhile. Captain keeps talking, but I can't hear him. I'm too self-absorbed with thoughts of life in Charming without my best friend. By the time I finish my little daydream, I realize everyone is looking at me.

"Did you hear that, Maggie?" Gordon asks.

"What?" I look around, wondering what I missed.

"Guess my speaking abilities are lost on Maggie," Captain says good-naturedly while others chuckle around me.

Lily stands up beside him. "I think it's best if she hears it from me," she says, and I'm hoping whatever it is, I won't cry a river in front of everyone.

Gordon squeezes my fingers, and I can't help thinking he's bracing me for something.

"What Ron was trying to tell you, Maggie, is that we are not moving to Florida permanently. We've decided to live eight months out of the year in Charming and spend the winter months in Sarasota. So I guess you're stuck with us for a while," she says with a full-blown grin.

I smile and blink back the tears. Lily walks around the table to me. I stand and we hug each other in front of everyone while they clap.

"Though I haven't been able to prove it, I'm sure those two are blood-related," Captain says.

I wipe away my tears, look over at him, and mouth the words "thank you."

The dinner soon comes to an end. By the time everyone says good-bye, the only people left are Gordon, Captain, Lily, and me.

While the guys talk about business matters, Lily pulls me aside to a nearby table. "I have something for you, Maggie," she says, pulling a gift box from beneath the table.

"What's this about? You already gave us nice gift certificates. Besides, you're the one who should be receiving gifts, not me," I say.

"You never were good at receiving things," Lily says impatiently. "Open it."

I rip through the wrapping paper and pull open a Pottery Barn shadow box. Inside the box is a scrapbook-type page on best friends, complete with a couple of pictures of Lily and me. Centered and underlined are the words "It All Began with This" and attached beneath those words is a tattered yellow crayon.

I stare at it, not trusting myself to speak just yet.

"Do you like it?"

"I love it, Lil. Who would have thought a yellow crayon would lead to a lifelong friendship?"

The guys join us.

"What's that?" Gordon asks. I show him, he smiles, and I know he understands.

"Have you told her yet?" Lily asks Gordon.

"Told me what?" I ask.

Captain and Gordon sit down at the table with us, making me a little nervous. If we have to be seated, it must be serious.

"I don't know how you'll feel about this, Maggie, but I wanted to run this by you."

"With reinforcements?" I ask, looking around the table. They smile.

"Something like that," Gordon says. He reaches for my hand. "You know we've been saving our money for some time and have a pretty good nest egg."

And he's talking about this in front of Lily and Captain, why? I nod.

"Well, Ron tells me his neighbor in Sarasota is going to put his home up for sale in a couple of weeks. I have no idea if we'll be able to afford it, but we could at least check it out. By the time Lily and Ron return from their honeymoon, the house will be listed, so we could go down and look at it, see what we think."

I'm stunned to silence.

"I know it's a lot to throw at you since we've always lived in Charming, but we could use the Florida home as a winter home and stay in Charming the rest of the time," Gordon says.

Adrenaline jolts through me, my mind swirling in a million different directions.

"The kids love the idea because they would get to come to Florida to visit. Cuts down on their vacation expenses," Gordon says.

"I'll bet Nick was the first one to think of that," I say dryly.

Gordon laughs and scratches his jaw. "Come to think of it, it was Nick."

Lily giggles and explains to Captain about Nick's gift for saving money.

"But what about work, Gordon?" This is too much for my mind to comprehend. "It was hard for you to go part-time, but to give it up completely? It's hard for me to imagine you being happy without your work."

"I'm burned out and tired. I was working to keep our finances up, but after the deal with my heart, I've decided life is too short. I mean, yes, we want to save for a comfortable retirement, but how much is enough? While I was in the hospital, I had time to think about what's really important. And well"—he looks me full in the face here—"you are what's important to me, Maggie girl."

More tears. Me—not Gordon. "Are you guys bent on ruining my makeup tonight?" I pull a handkerchief from my handbag and blot my face.

We discuss the pros and cons of the house in Florida and finally decide we'll call the owner to see where it leads us. When the four of us leave the restaurant and walk beneath the stars of a midnight sky, my heart is filled to the brim.

I don't know what tomorrow holds, but I know who holds tomorrow, and that's enough for me.

30

Sunlight splays through the stained glass windows, causing colorful shapes to shimmer across the pews and sturdy carpet. The organ music plays "Household of Faith," and Gordon walks Lily down the aisle to meet her groom. Once Gordon gives her away, he walks over to the other side of Captain, while I stand by Lily as they repeat their vows before a small gathering of friends.

Candles flicker, and the sweet scent of roses filter through the sanctuary flavoring the pastor's words with sweetness. With stitches across his forehead, Pastor looks a little beat-up from the fall, but he does a good job with the ceremony.

The congregation practically holds a collective breath when Lily and Captain face the crowd and Pastor says, "Ladies and Gentlemen, I'd like to present to you Ron and Lily Albert."

Uproarious applause then breaks out, followed by joyous organ music. If I had confetti, I'd throw some.

Heels clack against the foyer tile, and our little group forms a greeting line to talk with friends and family as they leave the sanctuary.

We greet one after another, and suddenly my heart stops cold when I look upon the face of the man who flirted with Lily in Florida.

Captain is talking with someone, and I nudge Lily in the side. "Lily, there's that man from Florida," I say, my throat so tight the words can barely slip through my lips.

"Oh, uh, Maggie, I've been meaning to talk to you about that." She shifts her bridal bouquet to her other hand and turns to me. "That's Ron's cousin. The guy with the boat in Florida."

I gasp. "What—why—when—"

9"So instead you let me worry about you getting caught up with another mass murderer?"

Lily glares at me.

For a moment, I pout. She owes me that much. "Well, I guess there's no harm done. Still, you could have told me."

"Oh yeah, that would have gone over well, 'Oh by the way, Maggie, Ron owns a home here. This is his cousin. And we'll be moving to Florida.'"

"I see your point."

"Exactly," Lily says. Just then Tara steps into view, carrying a sleeping baby wrapped in soft blankets.

"Hi," she says.

Lily gasps. "You came!" she says, pulling Tara into a sideways hug in an effort not to bother the baby.

Both women wipe tears from their eyes while Captain looks on, smiling from ear to ear. When everyone calms down, Lily makes the introductions to those who don't know Tara, and we enjoy meeting baby Brenda for the first time.

"I'm sorry Matt couldn't come, Daddy. He had to work," Tara says, referring to her husband.

"No problem, honey. It's enough that you came." Lily agrees. The proud groom looks with pride from his daughter to Lily.

"Brenda is absolutely beautiful," Lily says with wide-eyed wonder, brushing her fingers against Brenda's baby-soft skin.

"Oh, I almost forgot." Tara digs into her bag and pulls out a tiny sack. "This is for you." She hands the bag to Lily.

Lily opens it and lifts out a tiny crib.

"For your dollhouse. I figured *Grandma* would need one for baby Brenda." Tara's smiling.

Lily's voice catches in her throat. "Grandma?"

Tara nods and flashes a smile that lights up the room. More sniffles. This time Lily and Captain—okay, and me.

Lily turns to her husband. "Did you know Tara was coming?"

He shakes his head.

"No, I wanted to surprise you both. I'm sorry, Lily, about everything. I couldn't be happier for you and Dad."

Lily and Tara embrace, while Gordon and I step away. This is a moment to be shared by their family.

Family. Lily has a family now. My heart could burst with happiness for her.

While Lily's new family talks in whispers, Louise walks over to me in her stylish cream-colored dress that hugs all the right places—in a tasteful way, of course—and a wide-brimmed hat that reminds me of Audrey Hepburn.

"We've made our decision, Maggie." My breath stays in my throat. "Donald says he now realizes he's wanted to 'take on the world' to satisfy the guilt of his lost relationship with Chad. He's decided to work on things with Chad first, then we'll reconsider the mission field. He told me he can't save the world and lose his family." She blinks back tears.

Hugging her, I say, "I'm so happy for you, Louise. If those things get worked out, how do you think you'll feel about missions?"

"I'm open to what the Lord has for us. My desire is to be obedient to the Lord and support Donald. Right now I'm praying for healing in our family."

I nod.

"Once that's accomplished, the sky is the limit," she says, beaming so bright, I want to put on my sunglasses.

Leaning over, I give her another hug and get a whiff of Chanel No. 5. "I'm so happy for you. You'll have to keep us posted when the Latte Girls meet."

She smiles and turns. "Hey, look at that. Could there be a little romance in bloom?"

My gaze follows Louise's. There stands Nick and Jade Black engrossed in conversation, laughing together. My eyebrows lift. "Now that's something I hadn't thought of."

Louise smiles. "It has possibilities."

I grin. "It certainly does." Then I have a scary thought.

"What's wrong?"

"If they start dating, that means Nick will stick around the house."

"Isn't she going back to school in Rosetown in the fall?"

Hope settles over me. "You're right. Oh my goodness, I might have to work at a little matchmaking," I say, suddenly feeling all excited.

"Maybe you'd better just let nature take its course," Louise warns with a laugh. "So good to see that Tara made it to the wedding." Jill joins us, and I explain to both of them that Tara called Lily Grandma. They get misty-eyed—hopefully, I'm dried out—and we talk about God's grace and goodness.

Soon we all gather at a fine restaurant in Rosetown for the reception to wish the new couple a happy life together.

"It's good to see Aunt Lily happy again," Nick says, walking up to Gordon and me as we stand watching the bride and groom.

"Yeah, it is." I hesitate a moment thinking of what I want to say next. "So Nick, I saw you and Jade talking at the church."

"Yeah."

"What do you think of her?" I try to act all innocent in my questioning, but one look at his face tells me he's onto me.

"Listen, let me save us both a lot of time here. I've already asked her out for pizza next week."

"Pizza? Now there's a novel idea."

He shrugs. "It's a start."

I chuckle. "Yeah, you're right. You just be good to her."

"Hey, what about me? I'm your son, remember?"

"Exactly. Be good to her."

"Yeah, whatever. So you're good with the idea of moving to Florida, Mom?" Nick wants to know, eyes sparkling with the prospect of summer vacations on the beach, no doubt.

"We're looking at the house, Nick. That doesn't mean we're moving there. We're just checking it out. And we'd stay down there in the winter only. I'm not ready to give up my Charming home."

"Well, let me know when I can order my surfboard."

Fears of him living with us in Florida and becoming a beach bum niggle at my peace of mind. "And when would you be joining us, Nick?" I ask, holding my breath.

"I figured I'd come during Christmas break—I mean, we have to be together over Christmas, right?"

I sigh a happy sigh, akin to a kitten's purr. "Does this mean what I think it means?"

"Yeah. I'm going back to school." He runs his hand through his hair. "It bummed me out that I failed. Thought I might flunk out again, you know?" He shrugs. "But it was my own stupid fault for being a jerk. I'm saving money to pay you and Dad back."

Gordon and I lock eyes. A grin lifts at the corners of his mouth and he winks. Our boy is growing up.

Before I can work up more tears, Nick adds, "How does five dollars a week for the rest of my life sound to you?"

"Painful," I say.

Heather and Josh walk over to us while we're laughing. They want to know what's going on and we tell them.

"Mom and Dad, if you have a second, Josh and I have something we want to tell you," Heather says.

The look on her face tells me this is serious, but the glow on her face also says it's good news. Hopefully, they're not moving again—especially if it means more distance between us. "Okay, you have our rapt attention," I say with a grin, leaning in toward her.

She glances at Josh, they share a smile, and she turns back to us. "We're going to have a baby!"

Before anyone can say another word, I scream and practically knock Gordon out with my elbow as I push him out of the way to get to Heather so I can hug the dickens out of her. Until her announcement, I hadn't realized how much I wanted a grandbaby. Visions of soft baby skin covered in pink ruffles and a matching pink bonnet capping a full head of dark curls dance across my mind. Baby lotions, yellow rubber ducky squeak toys, angora blankets.

Tears start again, and I'm thinking I'll lose a good five pounds of water before this day is over.

Pretty soon everyone around us is huddled in a group hug and the others have to see what the commotion is about. The whole room sparks to life as we share in the good news.

"Wait. We can't move to Florida—even for the winters," I say.

Heather smiles. "Don't you worry, Mom. We'd come see you plenty if you move to Florida."

"Yeah," Nick inserts. "You'll probably see Heather more once you move."

"I've no doubt that we'll see *you* more," I say dryly.

"The question is, can we afford the groceries?" Gordon asks.

"I'll get a temp job at a surf shop or something," Nick offers.

"That's good to know, Nick. That will go a long way in helping with the college debt, too," I say.

He shrugs. "I do what I can."

"We could probably fund your entire college experience by selling off your video games," Gordon says.

"That's a low blow, Dad."

"Just an idea," Gordon counters.

"What good is a job if I have nothing to do when I get home at the end of a long day?"

"Now there's something we hadn't thought of, Gordon," I say.

"See, you have to go to college to learn this stuff," Nick says with an ornery grin that makes us all laugh.

Nick turns to Heather. "Besides, I'll be passing these games on to my nephew one day."

"Oh, I can hardly wait." Heather rolls her eyes then lifts a sisterly grin.

Lily gives me a hard squeeze. "Looks as though we'll be doing this grandma thing together."

"We'll have a ball. Diapers, baby dribble, and all," I say.

We wave at Jill and Jeff across the room.

"They look good together."

"Yeah, they do," Lily agrees. "I hope they make it."

"Me, too. You heard Louise and Donald's news?" I ask.

Gordon, Captain, and Lily turn to me while I tell them what Louise told me.

"Oh my goodness, I almost forgot!" Lily says, whispering something to Captain. He leaves the room, and we continue on in our celebration. When he returns, he has little packages in his hands.

Lily motions for Louise, Jill, and me to come over to her. "Our trip to Florida was a turning point for me, as you know. So many fears. I probably wouldn't be here today had it not been for your support and encouragement. I had cold feet big time."

We chuckle together.

"That's why when I saw these it seemed so appropriate to get them," she says handing out the packages. "Life is full of challenges that give us pause—or cold feet." She squeezes in and we form a tighter circle. "And happy as you are at this moment, Maggie, knowing you as I do, I know you'll have days of 'cold feet' on that becoming a grandma thing."

Her words surprise me and the truth behind them hits me. Grandma? Oh my goodness, I'll be a grandma!

Lily sees the dawning light in my eyes and she laughs. She hands a package to each of us.

Louise's white socks are dotted with pictures of various beach chairs. "Oh, these are great!" she says, hugging Lily.

Jill opens her package next. Her blue and white socks have pictures of two dolphins poking their heads through the water, staring up at a dazzling sun.

"And just in case I got cold feet during the wedding—" Lily's words trail off and she lifts the hemline of her dress. What we see shocks me to the core. Hugging her ankles is a warm pair of tropical socks, complete with a small picture of the ocean, palm trees, and brilliant sun overhead.

"Oh my goodness, that's hilarious!" Louise says, her hand covering her guffaw that follows.

We all join in, and it takes a few minutes for us to calm down. "Hey, you haven't opened yours yet," Louise says to me.

"Guess I got caught up in all the fun of watching you guys," I say, rifling through my package. I pull out my socks, and the girls erupt into laughter. "Ha, ha," I say, staring at the white socks, decorated with pictures of green alligators.

Lily hoots. "I'm sorry, Maggie, but it just seemed the perfect pair for you."

We enjoy a good laugh together.

"So let's make a pact. Anytime life throws us a curve, we'll put on our socks and remember a time when God used special friends to get us through the cold feet moments of life," Lily says.

"Who knew socks could provide such a bonding moment?" I say with a laugh. "Hey, Sisterhood of the Traveling Socks!"

"Yeah, but wouldn't we have to share the same socks?" Louise, ever the wise one, asks.

"That's the idea. You should share my pain with these alligators." My eyebrows wiggle.

Louise's nose scrunches up—as in, wrinkles! My joy knows no bounds. "I'm hanging on to these," she says, waving her socks. "Sharing socks is kind of like sharing toothbrushes."

Bonding moment over. "Whatever."

Louise steps forward to give Lily a hug.

"I'll probably wear a hole in mine over the next six months," Jill says. "Still, if God can get us through one challenge, He can certainly get us through another." She gives Lily a grateful hug.

"Hey, I just had an idea!"

The girls look to me.

"Well, if we're going to wear socks when we have cold feet, why not throw in Florida, too? I mean, we did it once, why not plan another trip?"

Excitement works its way around our group in such a tangible way I can almost see when it hits each one.

Jill's eyes grow wide. "Yeah, we'll need another trip come next year. Might have to bring the baby, though."

"Oh, we'll be experienced with taking care of babies by then," Lily says with a chuckle.

"Hey, this could be an annual thing," Jill says.

Louise jumps in. "Yeah, we could call it our Hot Tropics and Cold Feet trip!"

We laugh together again and soon step beneath an evening sky bright with moonlight, each prepared to go our separate ways.

"In all the busyness of the wedding, I didn't tell you that I found the perfect armoire and lighting for my dollhouse bedroom," Lily says.

"That's awesome, Lil. Guess that makes your home complete," I say. Her eyes twinkle in the moonlight. "It really does, Maggie."

"I couldn't be happier for my best friend," I say, giving her one last hug while struggling with my emotions.

"I'll call you when we get home from Bermuda," Lily says, edging toward Captain and waving at me.

I nod, wave, and watch as Lily and her husband head for their honeymoon and a bright new future together. To my right, Louise and Donald part for home and a new mission that will no doubt take a lot of elbow grease, determination, and prayer to get through. On my left, Jill and Jeff step into another chapter of their lives that will take many twists and turns but will hopefully rest with a happy ending. I'm certain the baby will make their journey all the sweeter.

Gordon and I make our way toward home with Heather, Josh, and Nick driving behind us.

Gordon slips his arm around me and pulls me closer to him at the wheel. Thankfully, the seats in the Nova make it possible. He throws me a quick smile, then turns his attention back toward the road.

My thoughts flit to my Bible reading this morning in Proverbs 16:9. "In his heart a man plans his course, but the Lord determines his steps." So there it is. Whether our steps are cold or hot, the Lord guides every one.

I snuggle closer to Gordon. Life is an ever-changing adventure. And every step I get to take with the people I love most in the world? Well, it just doesn't get any better than that.

Acknowledgments

Behind every great book (hey, I can dream, can't I?), there are . . . chocolate binges. Okay, that and some pretty wonderful people.

Thank you to my amazing husband, Jim, for enduring air-conditioning in the winter, loving me even when I'm hard to understand (I'm complicated, okay?) and happily sharing this life journey with me. You are happy, right, honey? HONEY?

To Christy Clark, reader, friend, and knitter extraordinaire. Thank you for your input on Siesta Key, your encouragement, and the "Hot Tropics" socks!!

To the fine folks at Siesta Key Chamber of Commerce for the brochures and helpful advice.

My sisters-in-law, Julie Hunt, Patti Hunt, and Beth Wallace for the trip to Florida. Thanks for the memories! I love you!

To my brainstorming buddies: Kristin Billerbeck, Colleen Coble, and Denise Hunter, who share my passion for writing, DeBrand truffles, mochas, and e-mail. Don't deny it, you know you do.

My incredible agent, Karen Solem, who knows the publishing world as well as I know great chocolate.

My fabulous editors, Ami McConnell (aka Solomon of the Editing World), and Natalie Gillespie, who breathe life into my novels.

To the creative WestBow team who makes dreams come true:

Allen Arnold, Lisa Young, Jennifer Deshler, Heather Adams, Mark Ross, Natalie Hanemann, the copy editors, and the sales reps. I'm so grateful for each of you!

And finally, to you, my wonderful readers, who are kind enough to invest your valuable time in reading my books. Thank you! We'll get through this boomer thing together, girlfriends!

Until next time, God bless you all!

Reading Group Guide

1. Maggie got through one life lesson and she immediately had to learn another one. Do you ever feel that way? What gets you through those lessons besides chocolate?

2. Lily experienced "cold feet" over getting married to Ron Albert. Did you ever have second thoughts about something you were planning? Do you feel you handled it the right way, or do you wish you had handled it differently? If so, how would you have handled it?

3. Louise's husband was making positive changes, but it was happening so fast, Louise wasn't sure how to react. Do you react quickly to situations—strike out on impulse—or do you think your response through, weighing things carefully? Is there a right and wrong way to react?

4. Jill had befriended someone at the gym and her friendship was misconstrued. Have you ever tried to reach out to someone and they, in turn, misinterpreted your actions? How did you handle it?

5. Maggie, Lily, Louise, and Jill had each other to get through the difficult times. Sometimes God uses our friends to help us through the hard knocks in life. Do you have a community of friends or a best friend to lean on when life gets challenging?

6. Maggie, Jill, and Louise encourage and support Lily by spending time and praying together. Do your friends know they can count on you when they are in need? What do you do to help them?

7. When Gordon had his heart episode, Ron stays in town and helps Maggie by mowing her lawn and fixing her garbage disposal. Lily offered friendship, support, and prayers. Can you think of someone who needs a friend right now? What are some things you can do for them to let them know they are not alone?

8. The Bible says Jesus is a friend who sticks closer than a brother. Are you that kind of friend to anyone? If not, why not? Is it hard for you to make friends? Why? If you knew that your friendship could make all the difference in the life of someone else, what would you do?

9. Sometimes the best way to make friends is to be a friend. Why not make one of your goals to reach out to someone each day through a phone call, a note, a visit, or an e-mail? You don't have to do things in big chunks, sometimes a smile is enough. People are lonely, but it's hard to hear their cries through the noise of our busy world. There may be a neighbor or a friend a phone call away, waiting to hear from someone. Is that someone you?

rv there yet?

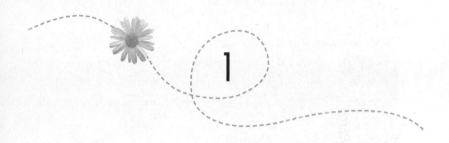

1

Remind me again. I left a shop full of chocolates behind, why?

Okay, that's lame. I mean, as a chocolatier I'm surrounded by chocolates every day. Truffles, caramel pecan patties, cherry cordials, chocolate-covered pretzels, mints. A myriad of textures and tastes. One would think I'd be sick of the rich, decadent scent that greets me every morning and causes me to drool like an old lady after a George Clooney sighting. Truth be told, I could use a break. Besides, friends mean more than chocolate.

And why is that again?

When I see Lydia Brady running out of her house dressed in jean shorts and a plain pink pullover, the breeze blowing her wavy, shoulder-length hair away from her green eyes and flour-speckled face, I remember.

Chocolate comforts me for a moment, but friends encourage me for a lifetime. Close friends. Friends like Lydia Brady and Millie Carter.

We've stayed in touch since our camp days over thirty-some years ago. It's true that at one point we dwindled down to a Christmas card, but we reconnected at the camp reunion six years ago and have stayed in touch through phone calls and e-mail ever since.

Since Lydia's husband, Greg, died last November, our bond has been even tighter. We're determined to see one another through the worst and the best of life. In the last six years, our friendship has seen us through divorce, job changes, kids, and now death. Nothing can separate us.

Well, except maybe this RV thing.

After paying the cabdriver, I push open the taxi door, causing it to squawk in protest. Lydia rushes to my side and hugs me fiercely.

"Oh, sorry," she says with a laugh, "I got flour on your pretty silk blouse."

"No problem," I say, brushing it off.

"Silver looks great on you, DeDe, makes your dark eyes stand out. Looks nice with those black pants too." Lydia looks down at her own top, then touches her hair. "I should have dressed better to meet you girls."

"You look wonderful," I say, giving her one more hug.

She brightens.

In spite of all she's been through, Lydia does look good. She's put on a little weight since the last time we were together, but then, haven't we all? It surprises me to see that she's let her hair go gray, but she still looks pretty. Older, but pretty.

'Course, who am I to talk? I have a few more wrinkles—er, uh, laugh lines—than I did in November. But, hey, I laugh a lot.

My luggage rollers squeak as I pull them over a sidewalk bumpy with age and littered with stubborn weeds that have pushed through the cracks.

"Millie should be here shortly," Lydia says, her words coming out in short bursts of air. "I can hardly believe it's been a month already since we talked about this, and here we are."

"Speaking of which, are we sure we want to do this? Could I entice you with a little gourmet chocolate, perhaps, to give up the idea?" Our gazes collide. "I'm teasing here, but then again, maybe not. You, me, Millie, packed in an RV. For endless days?"

Picture sardines in a can. Speaking of which, I've never appreciated sardines. Yet here I am feeling sorry for them. All crammed together in those little metal cans.

"You don't mind, do you, DeDe? I mean, you want to do this, right?" We step inside Lydia's home, and I set the luggage aside. The wrinkles between her eyebrows deepen at the question.

My heart constricts. Lydia, ever the peacemaker. "Of course I want to do this. Would I miss the chance to get together with my best friends?" Well, maybe I considered it, but she doesn't need to know that. And just for the record, David, Tony, Ralph, and George had nothing to do with it. Well, okay, maybe Tony, but only a little.

Her face softens. "I was afraid, you know, because of the RV and all."

"What? Just because my idea of roughing it consists of a hotel room without a view?"

Lydia laughs and leads the way toward the kitchen. "That would be it."

When we step close to the room, we are greeted by a glorious aroma. "Something smells delicious and vaguely familiar."

"I'm not surprised. There's chocolate in the air," Lydia says with a chuckle. "Cappuccino cheesecake with fudge sauce. We'll have some after dinner."

My mouth waters. Closing my eyes, I lift my nose in the air, take a deep breath, then practically start to purr. It's my natural Pavlovian response to chocolate. "I owe you my firstborn," I say.

"You don't have a firstborn," she says with a laugh.

"Well, if I ever get one, you're down for first dibs."

Another grin.

"No, wait. At my age if I ever get one, medical science will want first dibs."

"Oh, you!" Lydia playfully hits my arm. "That's why you're so good at running your business, you know. You're passionate about chocolate."

"How pathetic is that, Lydia? I mean, some people are passionate about world peace, some want to rid the world of poverty, others strive to wipe out disease. Me? My life is devoted to chocolate."

Lydia grabs some glasses from the cupboard, fills them with ice cubes and tea. "There's a place in this world for chocolate connoisseurs."

"Yeah, it's called a kitchen." The wooden chair at the table scrapes against the ceramic-tiled floor as I pull it out and sit down.

Lydia laughs and shakes her head.

"All kidding aside, chocolate is a serious business," I say in defense of my profession. "Why, did you know that the Aztecs and Mayans were the first to discover the value of the cocoa plant? That's only because *I* wasn't born yet, mind you, but still."

Lydia chuckles, and I hurry on.

"It was brought into the United States in the 1700s. So it's been around for a while. Lucky for me, or I'd be out of a job." I'm totally enjoying my little wealth of knowledge until I notice that Lydia isn't really paying attention to me. With a glance out her kitchen window, she points.

"You can see Waldo from here," she says.

I walk over to the window to see my new home for the next few weeks. One glance and I suddenly understand that "bucket of bolts" concept. Her RV looks tired. It could spring a leak. It needs assisted living. The tan-colored motor home has taupe and blue horizontal stripes around its midsection. Can we say stretch marks?

Maybe I'll just visit a day or two and go home.

"I know he doesn't look like much," Lydia says, seeming to read my mind. "He is, after all, fifteen years old, but, hey, I'm no spring chicken and I do okay," she says with a laugh. We both look out the window once more.

It surprises me to see Lydia's RV sitting in a pile of weeds. Her lawn would normally qualify for a magazine photo shoot.

"I need to work on the lawn," she says. "Just haven't had the time."

I'm wondering what she does with all her time now that the boys are out of the house and her husband is gone.

Lydia picks up a glass and hands it to me. Then she grabs one for herself. "Let's sit down at the table."

The wooden chairs creak as we settle into them at the bare oak dining room table that used to be laden with tablecloths and candles.

"You doing okay, Lydia?"

Her eyes lock with mine. "I'm fine, really. Greg has provided well for me. My church activities and friends keep me busy. Oh, and did I tell you I joined the Red Hat Society?"

"Is that one of those groups where the ladies are fifty and up and they wear red hats?" I ask.

"That's the one." Lydia laughs. "I'm telling you, those girls know how to party! They even go on cruises together."

"Sounds enticing, but since I'm only forty-nine, I'm not eligible," I say with a wink.

Lydia's left eyebrow arches. "Not a problem. They accept women younger than fifty, but instead of red hats, they wear pink ones."

"Well, there you are," I say, thumping back against my seat. "Won't happen. Pink washes me out."

"You don't know what you're missing." Lydia says the words like a jingle for a commercial.

"Actually, there is a group near my area that I've been thinking of joining. They buy a lot of chocolate from my store. That tells me they're a fun group with good taste. By the time I get back, I'll be fifty, and I can wear a red hat."

"That's right. You were always the birthday girl at camp."

I nod, and we grow quiet, each sipping our iced tea, remembering. The ticking clock on the wall echoes through the room. Lydia studies the cuticle on her index finger. "I still miss him, you know." She lifts a hesitant smile. "Things are so different now."

"I'm sure that's something one never gets over. I mean, losing the one you love."

She waits a moment, as though she's had to mentally pull herself up by the bootstraps. "Well, one thing I know for sure—Greg would want me to do this trip. He always wanted me to go out with my girlfriends." Her eyes take on a faraway look. "Sometimes I wonder if he knew I would have to go on without him one day." She glances toward me, eyes shining again. "You remember Greg. He continually fussed over me. Like he thought I was too fragile or something." She goes to the refrigerator for the pitcher and adds more tea to her almost-full glass.

My heart aches for Lydia. She and Greg had a wonderful marriage, a model family. Now she's alone. True, I live alone, but then, that's all I've ever known. You don't miss what you've never had. Oh, there was the dream of that once . . .

The doorbell rings.

"It's Millie!" Lydia says, barely sitting down before she hops up again. We both rush for the front door. Once it opens, a bright flash greets us.

We're stunned with blindness for a moment.

"Sorry, but I wanted to get your expressions on our first meeting of this trip," Millie says, clicking off the camera that's dangling from her neck.

The door frame helps me maintain my balance. Lydia steps aside and lets Millie stagger through the door with her luggage.

"Wow, you look great!" Lydia says, hugging her sideways to steer clear of the camera.

"How can you tell? All I can see is a blaze of light." My fingers continue to grip the door frame for support.

"Same old DeDe," Millie says, laughing and pulling me into a hug.

The light dissipates, and I see that Millie does look great. In fact, there's something different about her. I know what it is. She's not dressed in her usual beige polyester. Woo-hoo, the old Millie is back! She's smiling. Millie hasn't smiled since—well, for a very long time, that I can remember.

"Oh my goodness, it's true! You really do have teeth!" I say.

She laughs in spite of herself. "Well, don't get used to seeing them. I show them sparingly."

She chuckles again and reaches up to touch the blonde fringe at the base of her neck, running her fingers through the hair at the side of her face. Wispy bangs fall just above shapely eyebrows that top wide blue eyes. With a handkerchief, she blots her forehead, revealing faint lines where smooth skin used to be. Dark-framed eyeglasses are perched upon her head the way some people wear sunglasses.

Millie sees us looking at them, and her fingers reach up to pull them off her head. "I always forget I have these things up there. But it sure comes in handy to have them when I need to read something." She pulls an eyeglass case from her handbag and stuffs the spectacles inside. "Plus, you know how I'm always losing them. If I stick them on my head, I can usually find them."

Though Millie is one of the most organized people I know, she has a flaw that just doesn't match up. She has a problem with losing glasses the way most people misplace pens. When nonprescription glasses appeared on the scene, she thought she'd died and gone to heaven. Cheap glasses have relieved her of the heavy guilt she once carried for losing prescription glasses. Now if she forgets where she put her glasses, she can afford to go out and buy a new pair—especially if she finds a sale where they go for a dollar a pair. She says she keeps a pair in every room of her house.

"So good to see you, Millie. You've lost weight," I say, stepping back to look at her.

She takes a minute to catch her breath. "It's easy to drop forty pounds after a divorce." She shrugs.

"I'm glad we have God to help us through these things," Lydia says, placing her arm around Millie and ushering her into the next room.

I haven't talked to God in years. Wouldn't know His voice if I heard it—though I'm pretty sure I would suspect something was amiss if He sounded like George Burns.

"Oh my, that smells good, Lydia," Millie says once we arrive in the warm and delicious-smelling kitchen.

"It is good, if I do say so myself. But you have to eat your dinner first," she admonishes like the mother she is.

"No problem there. I'm starved," says Millie. "Those peanuts on the airplane just don't cut it for me anymore."

Lydia says a prayer for our food, then Millie gets up and snaps a picture. "Just wanted to record our first meal together."

We laugh and settle into light conversation over a dinner of grilled chicken, potatoes, broccoli sautéed in butter and spices, homemade dinner rolls, and crisp salad heavy with tomatoes, cheese, and all the fixings.

"Have you girls entered the hot flashes and cold-cream phase yet?" Millie asks, wiping her face again with the handkerchief.

"I've got the cold cream down but haven't had the hot flashes. What are they exactly?" I ask, buttering another roll.

"It's where your head heats up pretty much the same as a block of charcoal in a grill," Millie says, continuing to pat her face. "What about you, Lydia—do you get them?" she asks.

"Yes, I get them. My internal temperature seems to always be running several degrees hotter than everyone else's."

"That would explain why I've been freezing since I arrived. Of course, being from Florida, I just figured it was a climate adjustment—that whole going from south to north thing."

"I also struggle with sleeping at night and sometimes concentrating on things. I'm so forgetful," Lydia adds.

No doubt losing Greg has something to do with the sleeping and concentration problems. "Maybe you should try some chocolate. Chocolate can get you through anything, you know. Especially the smooth, rich Belgian chocolate we buy." I've never been one to linger on heavy issues.

"You always did think chocolate was a cure-all." Millie digs through her handbag, pulls out her glasses, and places them on the bridge of her nose to look at the recipe card for Lydia's dessert. She stops a moment and looks at me. "You don't make the chocolate at your place, do you?"

"See, the thing is, we don't have cacao trees where I live. You know, those tall plants out in the yard that produce cocoa beans? Those would be the ones. Don't have any. Zero. Zip. Nada. The best my tree can do is produce leaves."

Millie stares at me. "That's a shame. You'd have been so good at it, sorting the beans and all," she says with eyes twinkling.

"Could you, by any chance, be referring to my punishment at the camp where Tony and I had to sort through the mounds of green beans simply because Tony put a pine beetle in the green bean tray and I laughed?"

"That would be the one." Millie winks at Lydia.

"To this day I hate green beans."

We all laugh. Only they laugh harder than I do.

"Hey, I brought you both a box of my signature truffles."

"Oh, you're a doll," Lydia says. "Mocha?"

"Of course. Would I bring you anything else?"

Lydia grins. "My emotions thank you. I won't tell you what my hips say."

"It's better that way." I stop and enjoy another bite of Lydia's homemade dinner rolls. "These are absolutely fabulous, Lydia."

"Don't forget to save room for dessert."

"You're kidding, right?" Millie says. "Like she would ever pass up chocolate?" She puts the card aside, shoves her glasses back into the case, and drops it into her handbag.

With a shrug I say, "It's good for the hormones."

"But of course, since you're younger than us, you wouldn't really have a problem with that, right?" Millie teases.

"Right."

"Hey, won't you celebrate a birthday while we're at camp?" Millie asks.

"I'm not doing birthdays this year."

"Can't say that I blame you. Fifty isn't fun."

"Thanks for the encouragement, Millie."

"Fifty is great!" Lydia says. "We should have a party!"

"No party," I say emphatically, cutting off Martha Stewart before the invitations can be addressed and sent.

"Why not?"

"My party self will be bingeing that day. If anything, it should be declared a day of mourning." Millie nods her head in agreement—which I'm not sure I like—while Lydia gapes at me.

"You're no fun."

"Sorry to burst your bubble, Lydia. I'm just not into the attention this year, okay?"

She struggles to agree. It goes against everything in her nature to ignore a birthday event, but her aversion to arguments wins out. She finally nods.